The Equal Sky

Stephen Reardon

The Equal Sky

Steve Reardon

TheEqualSky@aol.com

First published in 2007 by Lulu.com
ISBN 978-1-84753-146-9

Cover picture: The Valley of the Little Big Horn seen from Custer's Last Stand
Artwork: Constantine Lourdas.
www.lourdas.co.uk

Lo, the poor Indian! whose untutored mind
Sees God in clouds, or hears him in the wind;
His soul, proud Science never taught to stray
Far as the solar walk, or milky way;
Yet simple Nature to his hope has giv'n'
Behind the cloud-topt hill, an humbler heav'n;
Some happier island in the wat'ry waste,
Where slaves once more their native land behold,
No fiends torment, no Christians thirst for gold.
To Be, contents his natural desire,
He asks no Angel's wing, no Seraph's fire;
But thinks, admitted to that equal sky,
His faithful dog shall bear him company.

Alexander Pope
An Essay on Man

The Equal Sky is a work of fiction. Although it has an actual historical setting and some of the historical figures existed and some of the historical events described occurred, the central characters and plot are entirely fictitious and any resemblance to persons living or dead, is coincidental and unintended.

1

Henry Turner could not remember such foul weather. Perhaps it was no surprise that it laid bare a skull. The year 1886 was one everyone in Icingbury was to remember as the year without a spring, when the winter seemed to have set in before the previous autumn was done. Snow and then rain had fallen in turn since before Christmas and the New Year brought in a deep and abiding chill.

A few nights before the skull's discovery the River Icing had risen in a matter of hours well above the highest flood mark on St Mary's churchyard wall put there a century before. So as they splashed across the water meadows together to take a look at the curiosity, Henry and his companions knew that there would be no work for them that week or many more to come. The old local saying, 'when the Icing's in spate, it'll show your fate' seemed for once a bit too close to home for any of them to repeat it even in jest.

'I reckon it's murder,' said Simon Lilley, a slightly distant cousin of Henry's by marriage, 'His head's been hacked off and thrown in the river so no-one would know him.'

'Or her maybe, Sim,' chimed in another, 'Taken against her will and then silenced.'

'She won't be local then,' said Josh Makepeace, like Sim, a day man taken on by farmers as and when extra hands were needed, 'They all do it willing round here and then blab all the way to the altar. Anyhow, who's gone missing? None that I know of.'

It was true, no-one ever went missing in Icingbury without it being remarked. The dead went to the graveyard and the few living who left would either be taking service in another village or in the army. Either way they never went missing.

'You're very quiet as usual Henry Turner. What does Mr Know-it-all have to say?' said Sim, his tone reminding them all that Henry was someone set apart from the group by being judged superior in the matter of learning. This had been a new and unsettling experience for these young men, one of the first generations to have been compelled to compete in the school room, competition that frequently spilled over into the school yard and into the lanes home, to be challenged with fists but never settled by them.

'I don't know,' said Henry, unwilling to be drawn into an exchange which would only confirm this view of him, 'Has the policeman been called?'

'The Vicar said he should be and everything left in place,' said Josh.

'So it could be murder still,' said Sim.

The Reverend Robert Earl, the Vicar of Icingbury, and the policeman, who had bicycled over from Great Duster, the next village, rather reluctantly by the look of him, were already standing at the spot on the bank of the Icing where it was just about beginning to redefine itself after the worst of the flood. As if a large bite had been taken out of the usual bank of the river, a semicircular section had been washed away. Here the skull had been exposed, held in place by matted grass roots and gravel. It was as if its eyeless sockets were staring across the flooded expanse on the other side of the Icing where the water meadows were truly living up to their name.

The little group of sightseers found themselves looking down on the domed cranium, mostly scrubbed clean by the action of the water and the grit in the bank where it had rested. It was gleaming, Henry noticed rather surprised, an orangey yellow colour

'It's murder then is it?' Sim Lilley said hopefully.

The Vicar looked up rather irritated, but his face relaxed slightly on seeing Henry Turner among what he clearly regarded as an otherwise unwelcome intrusion of local roughs. He addressed his reply to Henry, further fuelling the feeling of vague animosity between him and his companions.

'Well it might have been murder, but by the look of it, not one committed very recently.'

As he spoke he stooped down and with the crook of his umbrella hooked the skull up onto the sodden grass in front of them. No-one commented on the fact that the umbrella's handle had wedged itself in the left eye socket. The Vicar had to shake it several times to release it, and Henry could not get the thought out of his head that the skull had done it deliberately to embarrass him.

'When then?' he said quickly to cover the moment.

'Difficult to say, but probably so many years ago that we should send for an historian rather than the constable here.' Mr Earl laughed in a slightly conspiratorial way that suggested that Henry alone would understand what he was talking about.

'What are you going to do with it then?' Sim Lilley interrupted.

'I suppose I shall have to take it to the vestry for the time being. Church would seem to be a proper place for a skull, no matter how old it may turn out to be.' But Mr Earl's tone suggested that he found himself unreasonably imposed on by his position, not that he was willingly offering an appropriate solution. Sim Lilley looked thwarted and went to turn the skull over with a stick, but on an impulse Henry quickly stooped down, gathered it up and stowed it under the flap of his Melton coat.

'I'll carry it back for you then,'

'Yes,' jeered Sim Lilley, 'More like you'll take it round to cousin Annie's to give her a fright,' revealing what he himself had had in mind for the grisly trophy. But no-one feeling in a position to take issue with the Vicar, the small congregation began to disperse in different directions. The policeman, who had said nothing the entire time, swished aside his dripping cape and pushing his bicycle in the direction of the lane, indicated that he considered himself absolved by the church of further action.

Henry and Mr Earl squelched off in the direction of St Mary's.

'So how are things between you and Mrs Westwood?' the Vicar asked continuing the thought recently planted by Sim Lilley. Henry felt himself losing sympathy with Mr Earl and half began to regret his offer to act as his porter.

Barbara Ann Lilley, Henry's third cousin and Sim's too, had been Mrs Westwood very briefly until she was widowed by a combination of a harvest scythe and gangrene. Mr Earl's mention of her now reminded Henry uncomfortably that the Vicar was at least aware of the general village opinion that he and Mrs Westwood were now destined for one another. However his use of her married name showed that Mr Earl evidently did not share rest of the village's acceptance that she had already reverted to her former status as Annie Lilley.

The Lilleys always married the Turners and the Turners had always married the Lilleys in Icingbury, with insufficient accidents of birth to suggest that this was not the entirely natural order of things. The practice was so accustomed that it had come as a great surprise to one and all when Annie Lilley had announced in her quiet firm way that she would have a Westwood from Great Duster. Henry remembered the curious mixture of annoyance and relief he had felt at the news. Not that he and Annie were actually courting, but as the eligible Turner he thought that he might have been given first refusal. But the relief he felt was at the knowledge that a refusal would not have been permitted by their families and that with Annie married there were no more Lilley girls to worry about for the time being anyway.

'Nothing's decided,' he muttered, and then quickly reverting to the object under his Melton he said, 'So what are you going to do about this then?'

'Well,' said the Vicar, 'I really don't think that we have anything more here than an historical curiosity. But I do know someone who has an interest in such curiosities. Archaeology mean anything to you, Henry?'

'No,' said Henry truthfully.

'Well it's quite a new thing I suppose. But men are beginning to reconstruct our past by referring to the physical remains that are hidden just below the surface. I expect you turn up all sorts of things without really looking at them when you are ploughing.

'I'm too busy trying to keep a true line in the stetch,' said Henry. He was still struggling with his ploughing skills as his father was pushing him hard to take his place as a second or third horseman rather than taking his chances as a day man, like Sim, Josh and the others.

'No I forgot,' said Mr Earl, 'You aren't just a day man like the others are you?'

'Horseman,' said Henry, 'And a bit of shoeing and gentling.'

'You have a special gift with horses, don't you? Don't they say you could be one of the youngest in the horsemen's brotherhood?'

'People say a lot of things,' said Henry, avoiding the issue as he usually did at mention of the brotherhood. It was not something you were ever formally admitted into. If a man had the right gifts it would gradually be acknowledged amongst the others who would quietly begin to share their craft with him. Henry knew it would never do for it to be thought he was claiming a status that was not yet fully his. Sim Lilley, who would never achieve it himself, would be only too ready to exploit such a breach of etiquette to discomfort him.

Henry worked at the Veil House farm where his father was the bailiff, a post that was virtually hereditary within that branch of the Turner family and accounted for the fact that he was known to all as Bailey Turner.

Although the Veil House acreage was one of the largest in the area, it was only a few patches in the quilt of the gentry who owned it along with other large swathes of Eastern England and who were generally absent from it, much to Bailey Turner's satisfaction.

Henry's dismissal of his prowess in the furrow and his aspiration to the brotherhood had been deliberately intended to obscure the fact that he was already noted in other respects as a gifted handler of horses despite being still just turned twenty. He was trusted to buy and sell for the owners of The Veil House, where dealing and breeding heavy work horses and occasional cavalry mounts was part of the general mixed business of the estate.

The two men turned up through St.Mary's churchyard.

'As a matter of fact,' said Henry feeling that perhaps he had done himself down after all to the Vicar, 'As a matter of fact I'm going into

Cambridge on Friday to look at a chesnut[*] for my Pa.' The Suffolk chesnut was the preferred work horse in the neighbourhood.

'Ploughing,' said Henry helpfully, 'You mentioned ploughing.

The Vicar laughed. 'And archaeology,' he said and then added,

"Tis some poor fellow's skull said he,
Who died in that great victory.
There's many hereabout
And sometimes when we go to plough,
The ploughshare turns them out."

'This fellow's skull wasn't turned out by the plough, it was turned out by the flood,' said Henry.

'It's a poem,' Mr Earl said lamely.

'Well,' retorted Henry, 'I can recognise a rhyme. So did he die in a great battle then?'

'I doubt it very much,' said the Vicar, 'I have never heard of a battle of Icingbury have you?'

'So what are you going to do then, just leave him here in the vestry, vicar?'

'Bless us, you're as bad as the others,' the Vicar replied tetchily. 'No I'm not "just going to leave him," as you seem determined to put it, in the vestry a moment longer than I have to. In point of fact since you seem to be as much involved as I, you can help me by dropping a note to a friend of mine when you go over to Cambridge. An archaeologist,' he added.

As he spoke Henry unwrapped his burden and placed it on the vestment box. The acid smell of the mud still clinging to the bone in places where it had not been further rubbed clean by the folds of his coat came sharply to his nostrils and printed itself in his memory, giving the skull something more to the look and feel of it.

A voice in Henry's head seemed to say, 'This is the last smell then.'

The smell of ebbing life.

Henry wandered back through the churchyard towards the lane and past the tilting and ragged ranks of the graves his ancestors, Turners and Lilleys all. Normally he did not give them a second glance, but the revelation of the skull, and the way it had seemed to have been animated by the Vicar's awkwardness when he had retrieved it from its resting place was lodged in his mind. It was like a remembered fragment of dream that must have had a point which in isolation could not be recalled. He felt suddenly sharply aware of the skulls of his forebears in their

---

[*] *sic*

resting places on either side of him out of sight but indisputably there. Just like his own skull, thought Henry, stifling an involuntary movement to lift his sodden cap to check that it too had not been revealed by the action of the rain.

He reached the lych-gate just as a tall young woman in a woollen cape with a covered basket on her arm was passing it on the lane side. Slightly startled by Henry's sudden emergence into her immediate path she spoke first, setting him back in the physical world.

'Why cousin Henry Turner, what takes you to Church on a wet Wednesday morning?'

It was mocking, but only just. A familiarity of the kind that reinforces a bond between friends rather than distancing them.

'Good day Annie,' said Henry, touching his cap as he did so and then remembering instantly about nearly having checked under it for his skull half a minute earlier. Momentarily searching for a way into explaining the morning's activities, he began to say, ' I've been with the Vicar…'

Immediately they both blushed and looked away from each other's eyes as those few words silently spilt a milk jug of shared confusion which they both stared at mentally wondering how to mop it up and whether to cry over it or not.

The moment passed and Henry corrected himself. 'The Vicar wanted this skull from the river brought up to the church.'

'Skull?' said Annie, and as if to provide an appropriate backdrop to Henry's account of the morning's events, the baleful skies once again opened up with a sudden chilling squall. Annie gathering her cloak around her set off in the direction her errand had been taking her and Henry hunching against the sudden downpour fell into a half jog beside her.

'Where are we going?' he asked.

'Well I don't know about "we" Henry Turner,' said Annie, 'but I'm taking some things to our Aunt Elizabeth. Haven't you got any work to do today? You seem to have wasted a good deal of it so far.'

Henry gestured at the sky. 'We are mostly stood off because of this,' he said, 'As we have been too often for my liking since I don't know when. Well before Michaelmas I reckon.'

'Well I don't suppose your horses have been stood off have they?'

'They still need seeing to, if that's what you mean, but they do no work on days like this either. They're not casting shoes and there's only so much saddle soap the harness can take when all it's doing is hanging by the wall.'

'Well you can catch up on their news then, can't you,' said Annie, shooting Henry a mischievous glance.

‘I talk to them, but they don’t say much back,’ said Henry not allowing himself to rise to an obvious bit of bait.

‘Oh that’s not what I hear told,’ said Annie, ‘You tell them your troubles as if they were bees in a hive.’

‘Troubles?’ said Henry. ‘And what then do you think might be troubling me that the Suffolks could do anything about?’ It was a calculated bit of wickedness on Henry’s part and they both knew it. Annie fell silent and stared pointedly ahead into the rain.

Henry touched her through her cloak on the elbow. ‘Just a manner of speaking.’

Annie would have none of it. She quickened her pace to demonstrate that a touch on her elbow was not now going to put the universe back the way it had been two seconds earlier.

‘Annie...’ Henry began again, but with no real idea where the sentence was going. She saved him the trouble.

‘I am truly sorry if I am a trouble to you Henry Turner,’ she said, in a tone that had rather more steadiness in it than would suggest sorrow. ‘You are under no obligation to me that I know of, and I’m sure I am under none to you.’

‘No I don’t suppose so,’ said Henry wondering whether that was the right thing to say, or indeed if there was a right thing to say at all. They fell silent again. Henry wished the silence had not been prefaced by his last remark. Annie Lilley stopped in her tracks and turned half round to look Henry in the eye, ‘You’re a poor man sometimes you know, cousin. I could look for better in you and you should seek it in yourself.’

It was as if he had been run through with a cold blade. Henry knew that she had just opened him up and looked inside. He felt angry and violated. As the skull seemed to have done already that morning, she too had managed to lay a burden on him without giving him a clue as to how to shed it. Why had she chosen today to do this, he thought, when before they were both content to walk around their dilemma?

The silence between them now was deafening as one behind the other and bitterly out of step they arrived at Annie’s destination, their Great Aunt Elizabeth’s tiny cottage on the green. A keen watcher through windows of the world outside, the old lady in question had the front door open before Annie’s hand had reached for the latch.

‘I knowed it was you,’ she said in a matter of fact voice, as if to explain her haste, ‘And that Henry too,’ she added as if she had only just caught sight of him. ‘Stood off I’ll be bound,’ she said meaning Henry but addressing herself still to Annie as she led the way inside. ‘Still, stood off means he don’t have to wait until Sunday to come calling and courting.’

Henry held his breath, realising that if he took too deep a one he would undoubtedly blow himself out of the frying pan and into the fire.

But Annie was a widow, not a village maid. However much she may have wished to continue laying bare Henry's intentions or lack of them, to his relief it was clear that she was not going to enlist the aid of Aunt Elizabeth's straightforward view of courtship and marriage.

'He didn't come calling, we met by chance.'

'Then you should have,' persisted the old lady, addressing herself for the first time directly to Henry and stabbing the air in front of his chest with her forefinger. 'Wed her and give her babes. The Lord knows it was always meant. He took care of that when He took young Westwood.'

Then turning and seizing the basket Annie had brought, she bustled away into the back of the cottage.

Annie stared at her retreating back in disbelief and then turned and looked silently into Henry's face for the first time since their exchanges in the lane. The anger had gone, but so had the first soft ease of that encounter. In its place Henry could see unspoken questions and an equally unspoken determination not to articulate them. But there was something else in the look he had not seen before. It was as if Annie had reached inside for reinforcements that were now lined up behind her gaze; essences of herself brought as nearly into the light as might be, to be shown without them being destroyed, but, Henry knew, of a strength and depth that made them unassailable. They were infinitely desirable, but not for the taking. He saw then that only by becoming a part of them himself could any man possess Annie Lilley.

Aunt Elizabeth reappeared. 'Well now,' she said, inviting nothing in particular by way of response from the other two, merely setting about establishing the next path through her life's thicket.

'I'd best be off,' said Henry, 'Horses to see to.'

Annie looked away and said nothing. The old lady tried to look knowingly at them both, but failed, vaguely understanding that something had happened that no amount of cajoling would make them reveal.

Closing the cottage door gently behind him as if too loud an exit would instantly reawaken the confusion of thoughts his departure had for the time being laid to rest, Henry set off in the direction of the Veil House farm. Rounding a corner he came face to face with his cousin Sim Lilley, and Josh Makepeace.

'What you have to go and do that for then?' said Sim accusingly, clearly referring to the removal of the skull to the church. 'We could have had some fun with that tonight. We were just thinking we could have put a wick in it and made a few folks...'

'Made a few folks what then?' Henry fired at him, piqued not by their desire to play a cruel joke on the living, but, unaccountably at that moment, stirred to champion this remnant of the dead.

Sim took a step forward and for the second time that hour Henry felt himself at the receiving end of a comfortless gaze.

'You're a sight too big for your boots Henry Turner, always was. You and your learning,' Sim spat out as if hawking up the bitter lump of envy and incomprehension that was really sticking in his gullet: 'I've a mind to cut you down to size, once and for all, family or not.'

Henry held his gaze without speaking and found himself despite the very immediate threat, curious to see if anything deep was manifesting itself in this cousin's eyes that he could detect, in the way he had discovered he had with Annie just now. This insolent lack of respectful attention in Henry was too much for Sim. He butted Henry in the face and sent him staggering into Josh Makepeace's arms.

'Come off it Sim,' said Josh at once beginning to live up to his surname and rolling the dazed Henry round behind him while still keeping him upright. Sim knew what Josh was doing.

'Let him drop, Josh, I'll give him a good shoeing.'

'Shoeing? I didn't take you for a farrier cousin Sim, more of a dairy man I should say.' The level voice of Annie Lilley, who had rounded the corner at that moment, coupled with another sudden burst of icy rain, served sufficiently to dampen down the proceedings.

All three men, including it has to be said, the victim, were suitably chastened by her presence. Brawling was not something done in front of the women. Indeed it was not something that farming men normally had much energy for, once they had finished their battles with the land.

The two day men did not hang around to receive any more of Annie Lilley's verbal cuffing but made as dignified a withdrawal from the field as the circumstances would allow. Henry leaned against the wall attempting staunch his bleeding nose with the sodden cuff of his Melton. The blood mingled with the smell of the clay adhering to his dripping sleeve. A sour, dark smell. It matched the day.

'What was that all about then?' asked Annie handing him the cheesecloth out of the now empty basket she had taken to their Aunt.

'That wretched skull,' Henry said thickly through the cloth, with his head back staring up into the clouded heavens. 'I think my nose is broken' he added, moving the exchange on, not wishing to get too deeply involved in explanations that would make him appear in a chivalrous light as the champion of those unsuspecting village folk of timid dispositions who had been spared Sim's macabre pranks. In any case he had a nagging doubt that such a superficial explanation would be sufficient to explain the outburst that had led to his bloody defeat. The skull had taken up residence in his imagination from the moment the Vicar had gaffed it clumsily with the umbrella. It was a mystery demanding explanation, but seemingly demanding it of him. The skull possessed ideas, ideas that would give it a meaning or a purpose: Henry could only faintly clutch at that in his mind. He felt he had been chosen to discover what it was. He had a barely formed feeling too that it would be important to him to do so and no-one else, that perhaps from today his life would take a new turn.

'It's mine now,' he said half out loud, as the clouds around these notions in his mind began to part.

'Well now let me have a look,' said Annie, focused naturally enough on thoughts of his nose, 'It's not a new one just because its a little bit broken, it'll just be a bit out of shape. You should put a poultice on it and set it a bit if you can. Give your phiz a bit of extra character I should think,' she giggled, taking hold of the loose end of the cheesecloth he was clutching and helping to mop his bloody face with it. Henry grimaced thankfully. He assumed she had at least for the time being released him from the snare that had so recently held him so painfully fast.

'I shall still love you anyway, Henry Turner,' she added lightly, concentrating on removing the caking gore and not meeting his eyes. He wondered if he felt the snare tightening again and opened his mouth to say something or nothing. Annie pushed her end of the cheesecloth into it sparing him the decision.

'There,' she said, 'poultice now and you'll be fine.' Then she met his eyes. 'You take care mind,' she said and picking up her empty basket she was gone, leaving him sucking cheesecloth and bloody tears of rain trickling down his cheeks.

Henry watched the tall cloaked woman moving gracefully up the lane as if oblivious of the downpour. He felt dismissed but no longer admonished. This time he did not step after her even though their way was the same. He waited motionless until her figure had become indefinable through the rain and the vast and lowering sky.

When he arrived at the Veil House farm Henry took himself straight off to the stables, suddenly conscious of how long he had been away: painfully aware too of his nose and rapidly closing eyes. He anticipated a difficult conversation with his father, to say nothing of Frank, the head horseman, better known as the head baiter, about his prolonged absence, nor did he relish having to compound it with explanations about the state of his face. Because the day men were stood off did not mean that the horsemen had nothing to do at all. They were after all paid a weekly wage whatever the weather. Henry was in the difficult position as the son of the bailiff of being rather more "all found" than paid regularly, but even this, he accepted, did not absolve him entirely of his responsibilities as a horseman in the making.

Closing the stable door behind him, Henry moved unconsciously down the line heavy horses installed there until he reached the last standing at the far end. It was evidently not a random choice. The Suffolk mare he stopped by shook her head in welcome, sensing his noiseless presence behind her. Henry took off his Melton, picked up the dandy brush and began the familiar grooming ritual that bound them, burying his broken face for comfort in her warm neck.

After a while, addressing the horse by her name, he said, 'Oh Honeycomb what am I to do? You don't know no more than I, I suppose. Something's got to happen now; else I shall just be swept on forever like that Icing river moving on in spite of itself.

As he thought of the river in flood the skull it had revealed came into his mind again. 'And what's that doing in my head? Why can't it be in bloody Sim's head, or better still the Vicar's?' he complained into the mare's coat. She stamped slightly, shifting her weight from one leg to another as if to recall him from a pointless wandering. 'Well,' he said rousing himself, 'I could bloody weep, I bloody could,' and the wave of bitter sweetness that cursing by himself gave him instantly lifted his spirit and eased his pain.

His share of the day's second grooming completed, Henry repaired to the farm kitchen after judiciously dowsing his head at the yard pump. His father had apparently been closeted most of the afternoon with the seed merchant's agent, so Henry's lack of presence had not made such an impact as he had feared. As he took his place at the table, his mother caught her breath at the sight of his face.

'What have you done?' she sighed.

'Honeycomb tossed her head and caught me against the standing when I was moving her to the side to change the bedding.'

Henry felt a wave of pure hot guilt surge through him at the lie and at his implication of the mare. It was an act of betrayal. His father did not look up.

'Surprised at you of all people, getting on the wrong side of a horse,' he said, 'Thought you had left all that behind you. Hopes you can be trusted to go to Cambridge after that yearling, that's all I can say.'

The matter was now closed, Henry knew, but as he sat at the kitchen table and stared down at the food his mother had put in front of him without seeing it, he again had that feeling that a season of his life was drawing to an end; that today his horseman's gift had waxed within him making room for his future.

2

Henry's father had no intention of not letting him go into Cambridge after the chesnut yearling. Whatever shortcomings the young man still had to get to grips with when it came to ploughing a straight furrow, there was no doubting his skill at handling young unbroken horses and calming difficult ones. Henry had "the know". To the uninitiated this appeared to be a mixture of ritual ceremony and downright magic. Some of the former skill Henry had simply been quick to acquire by watching intelligently as the more senior horsemen went about the repetitive business of managing their charges. He had a naturally enquiring mind, which had been given the additional edge of ordered analysis offered to that first generation of compulsory scholars.

Henry had taken to schooling like a child given the run of the sweet jars in the village shop, no sooner trying one delight, than desperate to take the lid off another and another, each a little bit further to reach. Miss Covington, the school teacher, had only occasionally tired of his demand for knowledge, when long after the bell had been rung Henry still had his nose in another volume from her own modest library and she began anxiously to anticipate another gruff exchange with his father after church on Sunday about 'I needs his hands on the harness, not holding a book'. Bailey Turner, while more than content that his only child should be able to reckon the veterinary's bills and keep the daybook as well as he could himself, drew the line at learning for learning's sake when it ate into precious hours of daylight.

The downright magic element of Henry's horse skills was another matter. That came from within. However, it had nothing to do with incantation or white witchcraft and everything to do with an overpowering desire to sympathise with living things on their inside. He found it relatively easy to seek permission to enter into a horse's consciousness in a way that made it consent to the intrusion. People, he realised, were much more difficult.

Getting a young horse back to the farm from Cambridge would demand patience and care. It would not yet be shod and Henry was the best man, his father knew, to persuade it into the livestock cart alone and keep it calm without assistance.

'I'm loathe to pay a day man to go with you just for a yearling,' he grumbled. 'They can't pass a pub on a carrying job and you'd end up bringing them both home in the back of the cart.'

Henry knew that his father was just going through a ritual catechism by way of absolving himself of meanness towards his son whose wages were a bit erratic to say the least. Anyway he had no need or desire for any assistance. It might turn out to be cousin Sim.

'That's all right,' he had said, 'I have an errand to run for Mr Earl as well, so I'm best on my own.'

'What does the Reverend want doing then?' his father asked. 'Perhaps he should pay you a day rate.'

'It's a letter I think,' Henry had said briefly.

But in the end when he tethered the gelding in the livestock cart's shafts outside the Vicarage on the appointed day, the not inconsiderable sum of money he had about him for the purchase of the yearling should it meet with his approval, craftily included best part of what his father reckoned Henry was owed.

'You keep that safe mind,' he had said and Henry had stowed it in the hare pocket in his horseman's waistcoat before buttoning up his prized Melton over it, against the still falling rain.

'You must ask at the porter's lodge if Dr Birchall is in College, Dr Roger Birchall,' the Vicar emphasised fussily, ignoring, to Henry's relief, his mending but still bruised face. 'If not you must go round to his lodgings here,' and he pointed to a second address on the back of the letter. 'And here, you'd better take him this of course, he'll want to see it and it certainly can't stay here indefinitely.'

Henry felt an icy hand reach down into the pit of his stomach. Despite the fact that it was wrapped in a white flour sack, he did not need to ask what it was. Suddenly the nature of his journey had changed. He felt not exactly afraid, but opened up, as if his raw pluck was being displayed for the world to view. Once again the burden was about to be placed not just in his hands but inside his head. It was as if by picking it up unbidden that very first time at the Icing's edge, he could not put it down again. Almost in a trance he automatically received what the Vicar proffered over his garden wall as if he were stood at the communion rail at St Mary's on Sunday.

Taking a good deep breath, Henry placed the sack under the driver's seat of the cart and wedged it against his foot with the gelding's nose bag.

'Walk on, Duke,' he commanded. 'Gee up, boy.'

The horse laid his ears back and remained rooted to the spot. Henry got down and walked round to his head.

'What ails thee then, gaffer?' he said half to the animal and half to himself. He examined the ground in front of the horse for any foreign object that might be intimidating him and he took another deep breath, this time to see if he could detect any odour on the air. Then he ran his hands down the horse's legs to check for any signs of lameness. There were none.

'Everything all right?' called Mr Earl over the wall.

'Something's bothering him.'

'It's probably your friend in the sack,' joked the Vicar.

Henry said nothing. He knew almost before the cleric's nervous laugh had evaporated that he had hit the nail on the head without realising it. He reached up under the seat, lifted down the sack and walked with it round to the tailboard of the cart, well out of the gelding's vision. Mr Earl watched him curiously.

'Have you got any vinegar handy, Vicar?' Henry asked him.

'I'll go and see.How much do you need?'

'Just a dab on a cloth would do.'

Instead of going into the house the vicar went through the little gate in the low wall that divided the garden from the churchyard itself and disappeared into the vestry. In a little while he re-emerged clutching an enamel dish.

'This isn't vinegar,' said Henry sniffing it.

'No, I don't have any to hand, will this do?'

'It's communion wine,' said Henry sniffing it again. 'That might not be right but I suppose you should know your business better than I.'

'Vinegar or wine,' said Mr Earl somewhat loftily, clearly irritated at Henry's observation, 'Both have equally holy connotations and I suspect you are about to do something spiritual with it are you not? Anyway,' he added, 'It's not been blessed.'

'I don't have a cloth,' said Henry.

Mr Earl somewhat reluctantly began to tug a handkerchief out of his cassock. Henry waved it aside.

'No this old hyssop will do as a brush and add to the smell,' he said stooping down and tearing at a clump of the herb growing at the foot of the wall. He dipped a handful in the bowl of wine and reaching inside the flour sack he applied it liberally to the contents.

'Oh no matter,' he said, thrusting all the wine-soaked herb into the sack and pouring the small remaining amount of liquid from the bowl in after it.

'Just don't say "it is finished",' said the Vicar quickly.

‘Well it is,’ said Henry blithely oblivious of his scripture. ‘I think that ought to do the trick though. Still I think I’ll have him out of harm’s way all he same,’ and he let down the tailboard and nestled the bag in the straw.

‘Duke, gee up, then,’ he said when he had remounted the box himself and the gelding pricking his ears forward settled into a trot.

Successfully applying “the know” on this occasion, especially without entirely giving away one of the secrets of his calling to his audience, had allowed Henry for the short while it had taken, a respite from the disquiet instilled deep inside him by the object now in the cart behind him. Now, however, as they headed up the road to Cambridge, it returned with a vengeance as Henry imagined his passenger’s empty eyes boring through the white sack, a sack that looked like nothing other than the hangman’s bag.

They passed the journey in silent company. But silence to outward appearances belied the new tumult that had been growing in Henry’s head ever since the encounter on the banks of the river Icing. Noise and light were fighting for occupancy. The noise was an unintelligible roar of voices containing instructions and the light flashed randomly in the darkness seeking shapes to illuminate. If he paid enough attention to what was going on his future would become something he had the power to change as opposed to being simply something that Icingbury would decree. It was a disturbing emotion and one which frightened him. He could not put it out of his mind by thinking of ordinary things. It would not let him put off the need to decide, the need to choose.

So he said out loud, ‘I am not feared of you. So what then? What will settle you?’ And as if a golden sunbeam had suddenly shone through the unrelenting grey expanse of eastern sky all around them and lifted the rain, it came to him. ‘You want me to know, to know what you were. You want me to know what you died for. You don’t want it forgetting.’

The Waggon and Horses Inn on the outskirts of the city was reached before noon and not a moment too soon for Henry’s preoccupations. The large pull-in in front of the pub was already fairly full of horse vehicles, carts and an assortment of carriages as country horsemen, town drivers and grooms mingled, unusually, for the occasional sale “as advertised”.

Henry sought out the prospective seller of the yearling he had come to view. He was a coal merchant and undertaker from Cambridge who had as was not uncommon, bought a mare in foal two years earlier without realising her condition and was anxious to dispose of the unwanted arrival as soon as it was practicable. It was not a hard bargain for Henry to strike, therefore, although both men were anxious not to appear too eager, the seller to be rid of a problem that was eating too much, and the buyer because however keen he was to be about his other business, a horseman, particularly one as young for a Melton as Henry looked, could not afford to let his professional guard slip.

Not until their business was concluded in the appropriate way that satisfied honour on both sides did Henry allow Mr Earl's affair to regain the upper hand in his head, causing him to behave with less respect for the newly acquired yearling than he would at any other time have felt was responsible.

'Give us a lift into Cambridge if you're going that way?' he said to the rather surprised coal man, who assented while at the same time wondering if he had let this boy beat him down a bit too much after all. Henry then called up one of the ostlers from the inn and negotiated to leave the yearling, the livestock cart and the gelding in his charge for the afternoon. The ostler, pleading the abnormally busy day because of the sale was able to take rather more of Henry's long awaited back pay than was called for, confirming the coal man's view that he really should have stuck out for more himself for the yearling.

'You got a young lady to see then?'

'Maybe,' said Henry climbing up on the seat beside him clutching the heavy white flour sack he had retrieved from the back of the box.

'Got something for her there, have you then?'

'Maybe,' said Henry, feeling that he had squandered enough of his reputation on this man for one day.

'What is it?' said the coal merchant, and his undertaker's side added, 'It looks a bit familiar but I'm 'mazed if I can put a name to it.'

They were proceeding at a brisk trot by now and already within sight of the college roofs and spires. Henry felt it was time that this fruitless line of enquiry was dropped.

'Not much troubled by smell then, your horse,' he commented.

The driver glanced at him, slightly nonplussed by what appeared to be a little bit of horseman's second sight coming from a youngster whose measure he thought he had just got.

'No,' he said. 'It's the coal probably. Very pungent I find even now, even though I've been in the business all my life.'

'Do you use him on the hearse too?' Henry asked. His driver assented.

'So he's used to pulling the dead then,' said Henry. But he already knew the answer. He had it in the sack at his feet.

Doctor Birchall was not in college, fortunately, as Henry could see he would have had some difficulty persuading the porter at the gate that he should deliver the letter and the sack personally, rather than hand them over with sixpence for onward dispatch as the porter loftily expected.

'It's all right. I'll take them round to his lodgings,' he said.

'What have you got there? I'm not sure I can let you...' the porter's pompous remonstrance was lost on Henry's fast retreating back, the unaccustomed bustle of the university streets where he rarely had cause to venture and the sudden incongruity of his country garb making him acutely aware of how implausible his mission might seem if he were questioned in any detail.

To his immense relief, therefore, he found Dr Birchall not only at home, but also instantly enthused even when Henry could think of little else to say by way of explanation except, 'The Reverend Earl sent you this.'

'Oh I say,' Dr Birchall chirruped gleefully as he peered into the sack first before opening the letter. 'Oh I say. What's all this doing with it? Is that part of it?'

'That's hyssop and commun...vinegar,' said Henry hastily. 'For calming the horse,' he added.

'Oh excellent,' said the Doctor. 'Come in then, come in. Excellent. Calming the horse. Excellent.' He turned abruptly and led the way down the hall as he opened Mr Earl's letter.

'I mustn't be long,' said Henry, 'I've a yearling waiting at the Waggon and Horses.'

'Oh I say,' said Dr Birchall, 'Of course you have. A yearling. Excellent. Calm one I hope.' He shot Henry a shaft of laughter containing both light and sound. Henry felt himself melting under its warmth. He had been given permission to enter this man's consciousness.

'So,' continued Dr Birchall, now in the process of perusing the letter from the Reverend Earl, 'My old friend thinks he's stumbled on an ancient remain of some kind. He's clearly anxious to be shot of it too. Let's see what we've got here then shall we? Shall we go through to the scullery? Oh I say, *skullery*, what am I thinking of?' And he chirruped again at his unintended black humour. Henry followed him through to the back of the house, warming more and more to this man's... what was it..? This man's ability to impart something of his being in a way that made him feel that they were sharing their basic humanity, without any impediment from the relative difference of their standing, or the ten years' or so difference in their ages, or their education or indeed anything that might normally have come between them.

'He's like a horse,' he thought. 'He's like Honeycomb. Although not quite Honeycomb.' Honeycomb was such an equal that their relationship was now based on close friendship. 'But he has nobility like a lead horse.

When he lets you into his head, it's because he wants to share it with you. It's that way of talking to one another without words, just with feelings.'

By now the object of Henry's new found admiration had carefully deposited the skull in the large sink and was gently divesting it of the sticky hyssop concoction adhering to it, with a soft paintbrush he just seemed to have in his waistcoat pocket.

'Always carry one,' he explained, anticipating Henry's unspoken observation, 'And a small masonry trowel. Not in my waistcoat pocket though. Good grief no.'

After a moment he said, 'Well our friend here is a man. Man about your age I should say. How old are you? Oh I say, manners, manners Birchall. Rather younger than me any rate. Early twenties, I should say.'

'How can you tell all that from ... from just that then?' asked Henry.

'Well it's the teeth that tend to give it away,' Birchall replied. 'Let's just say he has a man's teeth not a woman's teeth.'

Henry felt surprised. Somehow he had assumed all along that he was dealing with a man. It had never entered his head that he might have been carrying a woman's skull around with him.

'Well how did he die then? When did he die?' Henry was now prepared to accept that Dr Birchall clearly had 'the know' when it came to bones.

'When is a bit difficult. Robert says that you found him by the river. What's the soil like there?'

Henry was on home territory now. 'Well it's a lot of middling clay and strong-loam all about there. Of course there's gravel by the river too.'

'So it's a heavy soil then is it?'

'Middling heavy,' said Henry. 'We sometimes have to make extra water-cuts down there when we are ploughing. My Pa complains that we have to do too many eight-furrow stetches because of the need for water-cuts.'

'Eight-furrow stetches? I say excellent. Well, clearly not so excellent in your case,' Dr Birchall put in hastily, clearly not having the faintest notion of what Henry was talking about but acknowledging that he too was in the presence of an expert.

'No,' said Henry cheerfully, 'He'd prefer all twelve-furrow work if he could have it'.

'Well we all would, wouldn't we? Perhaps not. You tell me.' Again the Doctor threw Henry a twinkling lifeline they could both grab hold of to make each of them easy with the other's superior knowledge.

'So what does that tell you, anything helpful?' Henry's own taste for exploring a problem step by step warming him to the task of unravelling the mystery. Unravel it they surely would, he was convinced now. Putting flesh on these bones, he could tell, was as much about constructing his own future and he was determined to wring every last drop of knowledge from his mentor in the quest.

'Well,' said Dr Birchall cautiously, 'The skull has...'

'Do we have to keep calling him that?' said Henry on a sudden impulse.

'I should say not,' agreed Dr Birchall without so much as a falter at the interruption. 'Certainly not. Fellow's got to have a name. Every mother's son should have a name. Quite agree. What shall it be? What about Reuben?'

'Why Reuben?' said Henry, intrigued.

'Well it's Hebrew. It means Behold your son. Mother's son, you see.'

'Excellent,' said Henry. It was infectious. 'Reuben it shall be.'

'So then,' continued Dr Birchall, 'Reuben has taken on this interesting yellowish colour. That comes from having been, as it were, pickled in the clay and peat mixture at the river margin. To get this particular shade at a reasonable guess I would say he's been there for about two thousand years.'

'Not murder then,' said Henry. 'My cousin Sim hoped it would be murder'

'Well, hold on a moment,' said the archaeologist. 'Murder has been in fashion since time began. Just because Reuben is a couple of millennia old does not mean that he died of natural causes. In fact judging by his age and where he was found, I think it highly likely that he did not.'

Henry looked at him admiringly.

'Just a guess mind,' said Dr Birchall quickly. 'I'd have to have a look at the site to be more certain, but assuming you have not stumbled across a settlement we know nothing about and given that it does not look like a proper burial place, I would say that violent death or an accident or both are highly likely. Highly likely. I must have a look at the site. Was this all there was? No other bones?'

'Not that I could see,' said Henry, 'But we didn't really have a dig about.'

'Good job too' said Dr. Birchall.

'No,' Henry continued, 'Mr Earl just lifted him up with his umbrella.'

'Did he? With his umbrella? Excellent. With his umbrella.' The Doctor sighed. He resumed gently cleaning away the remaining detritus still adhering to Reuben in places.

'Oh hello,' he uttered after a moment or two, 'This is excellent, excellent.'

‘What is?’ said Henry peering over his shoulder into the sink. He noticed that his anxiety and discomfort at Reuben’s presence had dissipated altogether since the naming.

‘This little hole here. Have you noticed it yourself?’ The Doctor pointed with his brush to the back of the cranium. Henry wanted to tell him that his close relationship with Reuben went far too deep for him to have done what Birchall was now doing with him.

‘No,’ he said slowly. ‘I didn’t think it would be quite right somehow to...’ He trailed off a bit helplessly. The archaeologist looked at him with understanding.

‘Do you feel “chosen”?’ he ventured.

Henry could have wept with relief that explanation was unnecessary. ‘Yes I do,’ he said. ‘Does that sound mad?’

‘Unluckily or luckily: I don’t know which,’ Birchall replied, ‘It’s something I have not myself experienced. But colleagues have told me it can occur when human remains are involved. It’s as if they are being given permission to do something we should all normally find abhorrent, I assume. I’m just a nosy old grave robber I suppose, so I cannot say it bothers me. But I envy you in a way, knowing what it feels like. Excellent.’

‘Why didn’t he choose Mr Earl then?’ said Henry. ‘He is the Vicar.’

‘Who can say? Perhaps he tried to and Robert resisted it. Perhaps that’s why he’s so keen to get rid of it, if I read his letter aright. Just the same, I might conjecture that it has more to do with your choosing to be chosen, if you see what I mean.’

Henry did know what he meant, only too well. ‘So the hole means what exactly?’

‘Well unless I’m very much mistaken, it’s what we call a roundel cut. It’s been made by a sword.’

Henry felt the icy hand once again reach down through his insides. But this time it was almost welcome. He knew Dr. Birchall’s words had hit upon the truth, a cold clean truth.

‘Yes,’ he said, ‘Made by a sword.’

‘If it had been an axe, now, the impression on the back of the skull would have been much larger. If only we had a few more bones to go on I could be more precise. But from the position here at the base and being at the back and the absence of any other cut marks…’ The lecturer was in full flight…‘one might reasonably presume a glancing blow on the way down to here...’ He put up his arm and with the side of his outstretched hand delivered a gentle chop to the nape of Henry’s neck. The hair on it stood up. Another cold, clean truth had been delivered.

‘A fight then,’ said Henry. But he felt that wasn’t it.

'No,' said Dr Birchall, 'Not a fight. A single blow to the back of the neck. I should say an execution. Yes an execution, excellent. Well not entirely excellent of course,' he added, catching sight of Henry's face from which all colour had drained, leaving only the fading blue black of his injury on a mask of ghostly pale.

'I'm dreadfully sorry old fellow,' he said. 'I hadn't noticed you've been hurt. I shouldn't have touched you. Really am most dreadfully sorry.'

'No, no,' said Henry recovering himself, 'It wasn't you. It was just for a moment...for a moment I... I don't know.'

'I really need some more to go on,' said the Doctor. 'I shall have to come down to Icingbury and have a poke round. It will soon be Easter. Perhaps I'll bring a few of my students who aren't going down.'

It was late and darkening when Henry eventually arrived back at the Veil House. He was bitterly angry with himself. Despite the exorbitant gratuity he had paid to the ostler at the Waggon and Horses, the yearling had been neglected as the day wore on and was in a pretty nervous state when Henry had arrived on foot and hot and bothered. He took no satisfaction in justly chastising the ostler. He rebuked himself. It was he who was to blame. His distemper radiated itself to the yearling making it even more distressed. It would not let itself be approached by Henry, who had to summon up deep reserves of calmness from within himself first before he could engage with the horse. Eventually he had been able to get close enough to breathe into its nostrils without it tossing its head up and back and something of a relationship had begun to be established.

At least he had not added to either horse's anxiety by transporting back Reuben, as Henry now constantly thought of his protege. Dr. Birchall had made it quite clear that he would now take custody of the skull. Henry had at first been half inclined to object. The bond that held them fast together was becoming so palpable that Henry's first instinct was to declare an almost brotherly protectiveness towards what had until now been a reluctantly accepted charge.

But Dr Roger Birchall had begun a process of putting layers of familiarity over this bare bone, this hard remain that time and the ancient elements had reduced to a bleak interrogative. For Henry, to make flesh out of Birchall's guesses and extrapolations was to tear his feet thankfully free of the foreboding silence of the cold clay and to change it into a warm idea, maybe an answer to everything he needed to know. Even as he was tempted to continue to claim proprietorship of the physical object in the scullery sink, he and it both accepted that it had already served its purpose, for now at any rate. He could safely leave the skull behind and in its place take away Reuben, the beginning of an idea of a man, whom it had entrusted to him.

Dr Birchall seemed to share all this with Henry without a word being spoken. 'It will be safe with me and I shall bring it…him…to Icingbury when I come at Easter,' he had said, acknowledging Henry's claim and pledging his fealty.

'Understands like a horse,' Henry had thought as he fled out of the city. He could not have paid a greater tribute.

Bailey Turner came to find Henry in the stables. 'Took your time,' he said briefly, with an eloquence that had it been put into words would have lasted into the middle of the next week. Henry busied himself with the grooming with even more than his customary preoccupation, partly to make amends to the other horsemen who had already taken much of his share that evening but mainly to avoid his father's eye. He muttered something about "the Vicar's errand" in between his rubbing down and hissing to Honeycomb.

'That old lady should give you another black eye, or I should,' said his father. 'It's not the Vicar pays your wages. You want to buck up my lad. I expect better of my horsemen. I'd expect better of a day man.

Henry blushed to the roots of his soul with mortification. His fellow horsemen at the other standings further back towards the door fell silent and then began self-consciously to chatter quietly amongst themselves. It was one thing to be spoken to by the head baiter, but it was quite another to be publicly reproved by the Bailiff.

He stayed in the stables long after they had all left. Despite the fact she had done no work that day because of the weather, Henry continued to groom Honeycomb until she had a bloom on her coat that would have earned her a prize at the county show. He confessed his shame to her silently and under his touch he felt her listening to him silently with every muscle of her heavy frame. After a while he felt sufficiently forgiven by the chesnut for his failures as a horseman to start to rehearse to her the turbulent preoccupations that had led him to fall so short in the first place. But far from making excuses of them, he found himself becoming more and more enthralled and anticipatory at what had begun to be revealed to him at Dr Birchall's. He even half began to believe that it was important enough to put the Bailiff in the wrong of it.

3

Great Aunt Elizabeth Lilley made it quite evident that she expected Henry to fall into step with his cousin Annie as they came out of church the following Sunday. Interposing herself between Henry and his mother and father, she successfully cut them out, dividing the flock into two with the experience of an old sheep dog, hardly raising the suspicions of either group in the process. Bailey Turner was not one for dawdling after church at the best of times. He regarded an hour and a half with his God as an indulgence neither of them could afford, since they clearly shared responsibility for the well-being of the land they had in their charge. Elizabeth Lilley knew his impatience to be off only too well and used it skilfully to her advantage, bustling him down through the lych-gate and up the lane, by engaging Mrs Turner, her niece, in rapid but inconsequential conversation behind the Bailiff's back, so that he strained to be gone like a coursing greyhound on the leash.

By the time Henry reached the lych-gate with Annie, Aunt Elizabeth's group was virtually out of sight, and he out of his father's mind. Mr Earl's voice recalling him to the church door, where he had been busy in conversation with others of the congregation, served to slow their progress further.

'How did you find my good friend Birchall,' inquired the Vicar, 'Have you brought it back?'

'No,' replied Henry, 'He decided to keep him there to have a closer look. He wants to look for more bones in the water meadows, I think. At Easter time.'

'Oh,' said the Vicar, 'Did he reply to my letter then?'

It occurred to Henry that in normal circumstances he should have been expected to be the bearer of a reply as well as the messenger. 'Well, he didn't have time I think,' he said lamely, 'I had to leave in rather a hurry.'

'So why did you have to leave in such a hurry, then?' asked Annie as they walked slowly up the lane in the direction of Aunt Elizabeth's cottage. 'And who's his good friend Birchall? Tell me all.'

Henry gave her as much detail of the physical events of his day at the horse sale and his subsequent meeting with Dr Birchall in Cambridge as accounted sufficiently for the passing of the hours. As for the new feelings that had entered his life that day and, he realised as Annie listened, had been invading his head since the day they had last met, he hesitated to recount. Of all the people in the world, something inside him said, Annie was the only one for whom he could think of putting it all into words. Dr Birchall had seemed to divine something of what had been going on in his head, without words. Henry wanted desperately to say something to Annie so that she would let him into her head without words too. He pictured his hands kneading her body and speaking to her fibre, in the way that they had with Honeycomb.

'So is this Dr. Birchall like our Doctor Norman?' said Annie, adding with a smile, 'He'd have a job making the skull better now wouldn't he? And who's to pay him his five shillings for it if he did?'

'No,' said Henry, 'He's not a sawbones, he's an arky something, Mr Earl said. He teaches students at the university. He's very good at it, I should think.'

'Well you've taken a liking to him, I can tell,' said Annie, 'Well so shall I when he comes at Easter.'

Henry felt emboldened to open his self ajar, to see how she would react to a glimpse of the world he was wrestling with there. 'Dr. Birchall has given him a name. They do that, this kind of doctor, give anything they find like that a name.'

'Why?' said Annie, 'What sort of a name?'

'Well it helps us to have a picture of him as a person when he was alive.'

'Us?'

'Yes,' said Henry quickly, 'He needs me to help him.'

'Help him do what? Dig?'

Henry thought for a minute. Something told him that what he was saying was not exactly an untruth. Dr.Birchall he knew instinctively did need him even though nothing had been said. He needs me because I have "the know". Henry eased open his self a fraction more.

Annie stopped and turned her head to look at him. 'You don't mean because you're good with horses, do you?' she said, 'You mean something else don't you?'

Henry met her inquiring eyes and took a breath. He wanted to tell her about being "chosen" but he still hesitated. As for the rest, he could not even begin to think of putting into words the feeling that had gripped him when Dr Birchall had touched the back of his neck. It still gave him goose flesh when he brought it to mind himself. 'It's because, we can deal with

things that come out of the land, like remains and such, better than these town people, he told me,' said Henry, 'We have a better feeling about it than they do.'
But even as he said it, he felt how shallow an explanation that was and how mistaken.

Annie nodded, however. 'It's because you horsemen have a feeling for the earth too. I've seen you. It's as if you talk to it through the horses when you are in the fields. You all go forward together, horses in front, you behind and the plough, as it might be, in between you all. And you talk to the horses, like you might say "harve" or "gee-back" and "gee-up" as I've heard you call. And like it's answering back, the earth turns and turns all along the furrow. Like a live thing.'

Henry took another breath. 'He's called Reuben. They killed him. They cut his head off with a sword down by the Icing. It was so wrong. So wrong.' Henry looked at her helplessly. She touched is arm.

'What had he done?'

'We don't know but Dr Birchall means to find out and put it right.'

'I'm sure you will,' said Annie, 'I'm sure you will.'

They walked on in silence, Henry digesting what he had just heard himself say. What had made him so sure that some wrong had been done to this man so long ago? Because sure of it he was. What had Annie said, 'What had he done'? It came to him. Perhaps it was not so much what he had done as something he was. 'I don't want him to have been a thief or a murderer,' he thought, 'No, I know he wasn't that.' He felt sure that was right.

'Well you two slow coaches,' said Aunt Elizabeth as they reached her cottage door, from which she had quite accidentally been peering. 'And what may you have been talking of all this time from church I might wonder?'

'Raising the dead at Easter time,' said Annie wickedly and Henry guffawed, momentarily lightened.

Dr. Birchall was as good as his word, duly setting up camp in Icingbury a few days before Good Friday. Naturally enough he stayed with his friend at the Vicarage, but the handful of young men he had brought with him from his College erected two large army tents down in the water meadows, much to the locals' slightly disdainful amusement.

'It's still like a bog down there,' Sim Lilley remarked frequently to anyone who happened to be in range, 'I reckon they'll sink out of sight. They might just as well pitch up in a ploughed field. That's what I reckon.'

Henry Turner's face had mended by now and the minor displacement of his nose was not noticeable. So on the basis that holding grudges, particularly in the family however many times removed, was not his style, he was prepared to accept loud inclusive opinions when they came in his general direction as a sign that Sim too had put the matter behind him. He was aware, too, that Sim's desire, at first anyway, to see Dr. Birchall's dig come a cropper probably arose from a feeling that Henry had somehow engineered the whole enterprise to get back at him.

Indeed it stood every chance of coming a cropper. The weather had barely improved and neither had the day men's tempers. There was very little work that could usefully be done outside and the indoor threshing was long since completed. So local tunes changed somewhat when Dr. Birchall suggested to Bailey Turner that their mutual interests might be served by laying some drainage in the meadows running into the River Icing. The prolonged rain with its serious threat of another poor harvest they could ill afford had already convinced the Bailiff that improved drainage might be a sensible investment, but as ever he his natural canniness with money, whether his or the owners' had caused him hesitate and rather hang out for a change in the weather. He had no difficulty therefore in accommodating Dr. Birchall's proposal despite all the outward appearance he gave to the contrary when it was first mooted, since the archaeologist was prepared to pay the men.

The men in question including, as they did, Sim Lilley and Josh Makepeace, enabled them now to lay considerable claim to the entire project's provenance, seeing 'as how we discovered the whole thing in the first place'. Henry held his tongue as usual, while their self-professed roles became more and more fundamental to the past, present and future of the dig. He frequently had cause to think back to that day at the river's flooded margin and to wonder who indeed had first stumbled upon Reuben. He asked the Vicar, who, together with the policeman had already been at the scene when Henry and the others had arrived, a fact long-since abandoned in Sim Lilley's history of events.

'Someone came and told me in the vestry I think,' said Mr Earl vaguely, 'But I don't think they were the ones who had actually made the discovery. They'd just heard. You know what the village is like. Does it matter?'

Although he said he supposed it did not, the fact was that it was becoming increasingly part of Henry's silent preoccupation with the idea of having been 'chosen'. The more he thought about it, the more it seemed to him that the incongruous group by the Icing had been summoned collectively by the event itself. It was as if an accident had happened which they had had been called upon to witness afterwards.

Henry began to struggle with an idea that this accident, if that was what it was, might still be happening.

Dr. Birchall's drainage scheme provided an unexpected opportunity for Henry to become more closely involved with what was happening in the meadows than his father would otherwise have countenanced. Relations between them had not improved significantly since the episode with the yearling, although Henry could see that the Bailiff's surliness arose not least from the persistently wet, grey days, presaging as they did the growing prospect of financial disaster. Henry's enforced idleness simply provided his father with a physical shape to the malaise and the helplessness they were all feeling but for which the Bailiff felt most responsible.

'I suppose you'd better keep an eye on this Birchall and make sure those good-for-nothings he's got laying my drains do a good job,' he had said grudgingly to his son. 'You seem to be hand in glove with him and I haven't the time to spare like you.'

Henry's joy at being given this leave of absence, quite eclipsed the prospect of having to act as foreman to the likes of Sim and Josh, but he made a mental note to cross that bridge as and when he came to it. He only knew that the nearer he was drawn now to the meadows by the Icing the more alive he felt.

'So you've been given furlough have you?' said Dr Birchall, when Henry presented himself for duty, 'Excellent, excellent. Good idea to have a chosen man alongside if we have to lift any bones. Let's me off the hook with the spirits of the ancestors.'

To Henry's relief the drain-laying was proceeding apace, Dr Birchall's inviting charm having managed to communicate itself to the normally recalcitrant workforce.

'He's not a bad gaffer that one,' remarked Josh Makepeace to Henry at one point in a conciliatory way, which Henry took to be another bit of extended olive branch. He also recognised that Josh and the others too felt inevitably drawn to Dr. Roger Birchall's self and he felt a sharp stab of jealousy at the realisation of their small intrusion into that mystery he regarded as his own. 'Still,' he thought, 'At least I don't have to boss them about.'

Although it was a grinding task against the persistence of the rain and the ever present threat that the Icing would again break its banks undoing at a stroke what little by little they were able to accomplish, the day men's efforts were gradually bearing fruit. The surface water reduced perceptibly although everyone prayed that the Icing would stay at level that would continue to take it away.

Dr. Birchall was undaunted. 'Oh hello,' he continually repeated to Henry, 'More dry land. We can get to work in earnest soon.'

Henry felt lesser men would have called it a day. But as the archaeologist chirruped on more than one occasion, 'Time and tide wait for no man. What the river has given up once it can easily take away. Easily.'

So within a matter of a few days Dr. Birchall and his undergraduates were ready to get down to the serious business. They had already been pegging out the ground.

'It looks as though you were getting ready to plough a few stetches,' Henry commented to him. The pegs were reminiscent of the wands the horsemen would set to mark their field headings.

'I really must get you to explain all that to me one day soon,' smiled the Doctor, 'I really must.'

'So this is the line you're planning to take then is it?' said Henry, making the assumption that indeed these were akin to heading markers. 'You're quite a long way back from the river bank aren't you though, if that's your main line.' He and Dr Birchall had already rediscovered the spot where the original find had been made at the flooded margin of the river from which point the Icing had already fallen back as it sought to resume its normal course.

'Well,' Dr. Birchall said thoughtfully as they stood over the indentation that by now was all that was left of the original gash in the bank that had brought Reuben to light, 'I have been giving this some consideration. I can only guess mind, but I think that the absence of any other remains at this point could suggest that if they exist, they became separated. So I have made an estimate of where the course of the river may well have been two thousand years ago. There are clues from the tree lines, and this recent flooding helps to show the river's memory of its past, if you see what I mean. The head being lighter than the rest of the body may have been carried away by the action of the River. It may even have been thrown into the river and been carried some way downstream. Yes,' he mused, as if increasingly absorbed by the plausibility of his own stream of thought, 'Thrown into the river, excellent. Well of course, not at all excellent,' he added once again addressing himself apologetically to Henry.

Henry was now coming to terms with the emotion that Dr Birchall's sudden shafts of theory always managed to thrust into him. He was beginning to realise too that the archaeologist, while he knew a great deal, still more, wishfully hoped for more than he could know. 'But he's letting himself feel the right of it, even if he can't be sure,' Henry argued to himself. He has the know when it comes to this.' The horseman stared into the rain-soaked distance across the fields beyond the Icing, as if to draw some tangible truth from the misted outlines of the landscape from which reality had all but been washed away.

'Is it all going to be true?' Henry dragged his gaze back from that focal point that is so far beyond the visible world that it vanishes infinitely into one's own mind.

'Oh hello,' Dr Birchall responded seamlessly, not questioning the question.

'I mean…' said Henry.

'I know what you mean,' said his companion.

Henry blushed unseen at the inappropriateness of his interruption.

'Look Henry…' It was the first time that Dr Birchall had called him by his given name and it was uttered not from the lofty remove of unequal status but with the sudden confidence of friendship. 'The thing is we are all rather new to this and I have to be very careful not to make a fool of myself to my few colleagues who profess to be better acquainted than I with it all. Good grief, I don't even teach this stuff, I'm an historian. What I've learned, I've learned doing what those fellows over there are doing in their spare time.' He gestured towards the students who were beginning to remove the turf along lines strung between two of the sets of pegs in the meadow behind them. 'So I can only make an educated guess, we all can, you can. We can only use our eyes and apply what we see to what we know. Then perhaps we will end up knowing a bit more or we will end up knowing nothing more. As to knowing the truth; truth is something we feel, not something we know and I think you are already far ahead of me in understanding that as we stand here, Henry my friend.'

'So what do you know already, that isn't just a guess then?' Henry spoke with a new voice that recognised the admission of frailty Roger Birchall had just made to him and accepted its implicit declaration of brotherhood.

'Well, I should have said so before, but there were some remains of a settlement uncovered close by here briefly about forty years ago. The theory is that this was a Roman Way Station on the road from Colchester to the Wall some time between the first and second centuries. That's what we know and that's what we think we have seen.'

'Where's that all now, then?' Henry asked.

'The pottery and coins and so on they found has been kept, much of it over at Saffron Walden, and I guess the site has been given up to the plough again. It often is.'

Henry looked perplexed. This was not part of the Icingbury folklore handed down to him. He put the thought to one side for the time being as his analytical inclination spurred him to pursue his examination. 'So what's your guess about Reuben, do you think he was a Roman from that time?' he asked.

'My guess? Not so much a guess, more a theory we may never be able to prove even if we turn over the whole of Icingbury. I think he was older than those finds. I think he was from the beginning of the first century. I want him to be something to do with the rebellion.'

'What rebellion?' asked Henry.

'Boadicea's, Roger Birchall replied, or Boudicca as I prefer.'

'Was he a Roman then? Henry felt they were getting somewhere at last. To him it was as if he had the archaeologist on a leading rein, just like a colt being broken to harness. Faster and faster he wanted to trot him, faster and faster. He felt his questions produce a mounting excitement in the doctor, as like horse and horseman they sought to achieve the same goal by mutual consent and understanding.

'Not a Roman Henry, nor a man either, a woman, a queen. Queen of the Iceni people.'

'Like Icingbury – Iceni? Henry leapt on the word and the idea.

Roger Birchall nodded, but Henry did not need the acknowledgement, he wanted his head to be fuller, he wanted to know the next thing and the next. Something said to him that he was on the brink, that the mystery would suddenly begin to unravel, that when it did it would sweep him along with such a speed, like a twig cast into the Icing and borne away faster than the eye could follow.

'Did they live here, these Iceni?' he asked.

'In most of Norfolk and Suffolk. Icingbury would have been on the edge of their country.'

'And then it was Roman beyond, was it?'

'Well,' said Dr Birchall, 'It was beginning to be. Down to Colchester and over into Hertfordshire it was pretty much Roman through and through. But here in the east at the time of the rebellion it was like a separate kingdom that the Romans tolerated, let the Iceni run things provided they paid their dues and didn't cause trouble.'

'But this queen wanted to cause trouble, did she?' said Henry, 'Why did she want to do that if the Romans were prepared to leave them alone? And anyway, why did we have to have the Romans?'

Dr Birchall laughed, 'What's all this "we"? There might be Roman in you and in me. Whose side do you think you are on? It was no different being a Roman then to being British now. They had their empire as we have ours and they were a great civilising force in their world as we are in ours. They brought order, trade, great buildings, roads, you name it. Most of the time the tribal people must have welcomed the Romans, they must have seen the boundaries of the empire creeping towards them up through

France and it must have been a wonder and an opportunity. These people were not savages, as many were in our empire, before we arrived. They were knowledgeable people, they would already have been trading at the fringes of the Roman world. They must have realised that it was inevitable that they themselves would become part of it. Boudicca's husband, Prasutagus, must have done at any rate, because when he died he left his kingdom to the Roman emperor in his will.'

'So what went wrong?' insisted Henry, 'Why did this queen rebel against them if her husband had already given his kingdom away to them?'

'Well Prasutagus was quite a shrewd old bird. He thought that if he left his land to the emperor in Rome as a personal gift, the local bigwigs in Colchester wouldn't dare march in and take it for themselves when he died. So everything might remain as it had been. Boudicca could rule, continue to pay her dues and be left more or less alone.'

'But it didn't work did it?' cried Henry triumphantly.

'No it did not. The local Romans from Colchester moved in as soon as the old king was dead and took what they wanted, including Boudicca's two daughters. They took the view that Rome was a very long way away and that the emperor would eventually order them to turn the Iceni lands into a proper Roman province under the Roman governor.

Henry was still digesting the story. 'Her daughters,' he said, 'You mean they...they took them in that way or do you mean they just took them away?'

'Yes, I do mean "took them in that way". They violated them in front of Boudicca herself and then they flogged her in front of her servants.'

Henry felt unaccountably angry at the thought, as if the historian were talking about someone close to Henry, talking about private, shameful things.

He looked to where Sim, Josh and the others were still digging the drains. 'Don't tell them that,' he said.

'All right,' agreed Birchall. 'Why not?' he added. 'Just out of interest?'

'Well they all like to hear that sort of thing. First they said Reuben might have been a woman taken against her will and then done away with. They like to talk to the drovers when they come through about people in Norwich gaol who have done things like that.'

'And you do not?' It was not really a question from the archaeologist.

Henry shrugged. 'I always think of how it might have happened to someone I know, like Annie Lilley or anybody and it makes me feel cold.'

'But this was all a very long time ago,' Birchall smiled, 'It is the stuff of history, as they say.'

'Well I do know,' Henry agreed, 'And I know some history. Old Canute and the waves, battle of Hastings, Lord Nelson. I do know about the Romans too, Julius Caesar.' Henry knew that his after school forays into Miss Covington's bookshelves would some day bear him fruit. 'But I didn't know about this queen in our village.'

'Well not precisely here in Icingbury. No, not precisely here,' Birchall interposed hastily. But the rebellion was all around here and further south too. She burned Colchester, and London and as far over there as St Albans. All Roman towns.'

Henry's anger burned brighter inside him with a kind of intensity that allowed him almost to stand back from it and look at it. It was as if it had been put there to be considered, to be used or to be deliberately ignored. 'But why did they do those things to her? We don't do things like that in our empire, do we?'

'Times change,' said Dr Birchall, 'And don't forget, the Romans were not Christian. They may have been civilised but they too were pagans. Cruelty was often their way.'

They both fell silent for a while.

Then Henry said, 'So what was all that you were saying earlier about it being no different being Roman to being British now?'

'Perhaps I shouldn't have said that,' agreed Dr Birchall, 'It doesn't do to see too much of the past in the present, or the present in the past. Speaking as an historian I should know that. We talk about the lessons of history, but I often think that the only lesson to be learned from history is that times change. Times change. Indeed they do. He paused in thought. If there are other lessons, real lessons from the past, then it is quite remarkable how we fail to pay any heed to them. So perhaps there aren't really lessons to be had at all. Perhaps nothing is ever quite the same the next time around. If you always look for the similarities, you will overlook the differences and so you will always be wrong. Yes, always be wrong however hard you try to be right, excellent, excellent.' His voice trailed away doubtfully.

Henry recognised again that the Doctor had reached a moment of uncertainty, had revealed something of his frailty to Henry. He was sensible enough to see as well that his own interrogations had somehow triggered these doubts. 'I'm sorry,' he said, 'We seem to have wandered off the furrow a bit,' and he put his hand on Dr Birchall's coat sleeve.

'No, no, don't be. These are thoughts one has all the time, all the time. It's the kind of thing one should wrestle with as an historian. No, don't be sorry. Excellent.'

'The thing is,' said Henry, hoping to be helpful, but still needing to bring the entity that was Reuben out of the shadows where he still hovered tantalisingly unseen, 'The thing is, I don't feel this is all about the past. It's not about ghosts or anything like that either. It's as if there is something here that I need to know so that, so that, I don't know, so that things can happen properly afterwards, I suppose. Does that make any sense?'

Dr. Birchall took a breath to reply but was forestalled by a shout from one of his young men, 'I think we've got something here.'

To Henry's ear the shout was like a bugle call to action. His heart took an almighty leap and began to race. Anticipation careered around his stomach like something alive and trapped seeking a way out. While he urged his legs to carry him skimming across the meadow like a moorhen scuttling over lilly pads, the sodden surface held him like the rear suffolk taking the full weight of the harness at the turn of the furrow.

He was desperate to reach the trench before the drain diggers, who had stopped their delving to a man at the cry and were blundering towards it at an angle to Henry from the river's edge, kicking up a great curtain of mud and spray in their efforts.

Henry, Sim and Josh all arrived on the scene at the same time, panting with exertion and excitement. Roger Birchall was still some way behind, not having been quite so galvanised as the others. Henry knew that he had barely seconds to declare his right of precedence in relation to whatever it was the cold, stripped earth had disgorged or risk losing whatever the future held for him at this precise moment.

'Gee back! Hold hard!' he roared at the astounded day men, as if he were bringing his team to an instant halt as the ploughshare bit into some unseen, unmoving obstacle, 'This is no business of yours, 'less I say it be.'

They stopped at the edge of the trench, stunned by the ferocity with which Henry had addressed them. There was a silence even Dr Birchall felt obliged to observe as he now arrived on the scene over which Henry had taken command.

'You've lost your boot,' remarked Josh Makepeace after a moment. Sim Lilley started to snigger. Henry glanced down at his feet and began to laugh himself. But the moment of challenge had passed, the territory was his and they acknowledged it. 'I say you'll all have to take your boots off if you want to get down there, this is no piece of drain-laying, this is soft work like gentling a colt to the bit,' he threw in, reinforcing his precarious supremacy as the youngest of horsemen.

'Quite right, quite right. Gently does it. Excellent.' Dr Birchall stepped carefully into the trench, which was already beginning to show signs of filling with water. The young man already standing there up to his knees between the marker lines and rather dwarfed by the commotion that had taken place slightly over his head, indicated where he should direct his close attention. The archaeologist fiddled under his manteau and produced a small trowel. 'Steady Birchall,' he said, 'Eyes first, eyes second and then trowel.'

Sim Lilley began to look as though he would press forward. Henry again took command of the watchers. 'Is it our man...Roger?' He stared down fixedly at Birchall's bent form, silently praying that his enormous piece of social temerity would be accepted by his ally and taken to heart by his foes. There was an agonising silence as everyone waited for the Doctor's response. Then in a moment, in the twinkling of an eye, the horseman knew that he had left the companions of his boyhood, his frequent tormentors, reeling and gasping, left them far behind forever and with them any prospect of a quiet life in Icingbury, as Dr Birchall stood up, and offering him his hand to steady his ascent from the freshly dug earth said, 'I think it is Henry, my friend, I think it is. Who would have thought it? So quickly. Almost as if… '

There was little prospect however of further useful work that day, either on the find or on the drains, as the rain began again to fall pitilessly. Henry felt drained himself as he wandered away in search of his lost boot. As they gathered round the undergraduates' camp waiting for their wages, the day men ignored him now. He had finally excluded himself from what little of their association remained. They had all disappeared in the direction of the pub by the time Henry had retraced his steps to the trench.

'Best get this under cover,' said Dr Birchall to the remaining hands, 'Keep the worst of the wet out, anyhow. If we get a day or two clear, perhaps we can make some progress. Excellent. What do you think Henry?'

'Maybe,' he replied, 'I do hope so.' But in his heart he wanted to crawl into the trench now and cup the earth and water away with his bare hands. A few clear days, he knew, would mean some work at least for The Veil House farm, and the thought caused him a guilty pang of dismay.

Indeed there was a brief break in the pattern of the weather that had lain like a vast wet rick cover over the land for so long, always damp and frequently relieving itself of great swashes of rain trapped in its grey folds.

For Bailey Turner the respite was probably already too late. The green spring shoots of corn were waterlogged and in many places nowhere to be seen where they should have been. Where the men should by now have been out with the horse hoes between the rows there was little to be gained and indeed more harm than good to be achieved. However, not to be totally daunted, he set some to sowing a field of late grass in the distant hope of an Indian summer. So Henry was able to take more time up at the excavation, even though it was grudgingly spared by his father.

At the Vicar's suggestion Annie Lilley had been recruited by Dr. Birchall as the commissary for his troops encamped by the water meadows, so that she too was becoming a frequent visitor to the site bearing baskets of provisions at least once or twice a day. The day after Easter Sunday, the first day that the excavation resumed, Henry met her at the edge of the field as she was bringing the dinner to help her carry the baskets and flagon over the five-bar gate.

'I've got a bit of news for you Henry Turner,' she said.

He gave her a hand down. 'Oh yes? What's that then?'

'I'm to move in with Aunt Elizabeth Lilley and keep house.

'How's that then?' asked Henry, 'She doesn't need you.' Although their Great Aunt was certainly no spring chicken, he did not suppose that she yet needed a nursemaid, so this exigency must be born out of some other necessity.

'Farmer Black needs my man's place, now I've been alone there since he's been gone. Times are hard and like to get harder this year, he says, and the place must go to a working man who's set to be married.'

Henry grunted in understanding. 'I suppose he's been middling fair since Westwood got taken. But how will you feel about Aunt Elizabeth? Come to that how does she feel about you? She's been alone there forever.'

Annie assented. 'Since our great grandfather died, it must have been, seeing as the cottage was his, but I don't remember him at all.'

They were nearly at the tents.

'I suppose it all depends,' she said.

'On what?'

'On all sorts of things. Well, what the future has in store for me I suppose. If it's meant, it's meant.'

'Do you think the future is all laid out like a marked field then?'

'I suppose I do, if I think about it. What I mean is seeing that Westwood's dead and gone it stands to reason that I would have to quit the place sooner or later. And as my mother has her hands more than full still, there's no going back there. So Aunt Elizabeth's looks a sight better than the workhouse from where I stand. I'd say that was a future squarely marked out, wouldn't you, cousin? She'll keep me for my worth and I can go to market for the extras, since she does not. The hens and garden will yield much more than they do now when I set myself to it. Besides Mr Earl has arranged with Miss Covington that I shall help out at the school. And if it doesn't turn out then I shall just have to go into service.'

There was no note of sourness or even resignation in Annie's voice. To Henry she spoke as one who had already found an inner habitation and for whom another real life was already being lived there. He had seen it in her eyes and knew it existed. Now as she laid out this commonplace that would become her daily world, he knew it belied the reality. It was only the spoor of the creature that was her self.

He was uncomfortably conscious, too, that even though she was not seeking anything from him, nevertheless he could offer to change both their futures with a few words right there in the water meadows. He wondered though. What would she say if he offered to marry her now? The things he had seen in her eyes on that memorable day of the skull, Reuben's Day, from which everything seemed now to date, they were also part of the uncertainties with which he had been harnessed that day, where before had been unquestioned order. Not following the path that Icingbury seemed to have planned out for Annie and him had been his choice until then, or so he assumed, but now he wondered whether it had ever been a path that she would have chosen, still less choose now. As the two of them reached the camp and came into immediate view of the diggings beyond, he took another step away from his past.

'Well I don't think that life is marked out for us, not in that way,' he ventured, 'Not like a field through the seasons, where harrowing follows ploughing and sowing follows harrowing and so to the harvest and then begin again. Sometimes the seasons change their minds and so the fields give us nothing or something unlooked for. And when that happens my father, Bailey Turner, and Farmer Black and the others say times are hard and likely to get harder, but they don't seek to change themselves. I think we have many lives to choose from if only we listen to ourselves and look out for the moments when little doorways suddenly show themselves to you that you wouldn't ordinarily pay any heed to.'

They put their baskets down on the trestle table in the encampment and with an unspoken accord continued on to the diggings, where under Dr Birchall's motherly eye, his young men were slowly and laboriously removing the earth.

'This is one of those doorways for you, isn't it?' said Annie.

Henry waited.

'I've found them too, you know,' Annie went on, 'But in a different way. When I've found them they seem to open into my inside. That's where I look for...not happiness precisely, but perhaps strength. If I feel strong and in command inside then I am content. For you I think the doorways open outwards and that's the difference. You are not finding strength or contentment when they open, because they show you somewhere strange, somewhere new that wasn't always there. Not like me being deeper inside myself.'

Henry had nothing to say. It was as if they were talking in unison, reciting some piece that Miss Covington might have set them to learn by heart. No response was required, nor did Annie look for one. It was sufficient that it should have been said to the end without a mistake.

'Excellent,' said Dr Birchall, as they reached the main trench. 'Just in time for our revelations Henry. We are on the very brink. Doesn't St. John say "Of the tribe of Reuben were sealed twelve thousand"? What shall we unseal here I wonder?'

'And when he had opened the Seventh Seal, there was silence in heaven'. It was Annie who spoke. There was a momentary stunned silence in that small corner of Icingbury too.

'And I should say good day to you too, Mrs Westwood,' said Dr Birchall hastily recalling his manners. 'Silence in heaven, excellent, excellent. Well perhaps not excellent. Who can tell? Anyway, look at what we have here.'

Two of the students had been carefully easing a length of dry sacking underneath the object of their attention in the bottom of the shallow trench, which was still hidden by their crouching forms from those waiting slightly above them. But their delicate task completed they slowly stood erect holding the sacking taut between them, and which after a muttered count of three they eased onto the lip of the excavation, depositing the otherwise undisturbed contents at the feet of the breathless onlookers.

It was Annie who broke the spell. 'He has no head,' she said, as if to identify beyond doubt the original owner of the skeleton that had been laid out before them on a thin mattress of earth held underneath by the sacking.

'No, indeed,' said Dr Birchall, 'We already have that I fancy. Oh I say,' he chortled, 'I say, just where I said it would be. I feel a monograph in the offing already.' He had apparently chosen to forget his earlier astonishment at the speed of their discovery.

Henry, however, stood transfixed, staring down at the bones, his mind already feverishly cloaking them with fleshy form.

'There's something wrong isn't there? He's a peculiar shape isn't he?'

Dr Birchall stooped down for a closer look.

'Quite right,' he said after a moment or two, 'He's lying on his front and the arms are crossed behind him. Did you move anything getting him out?' He darted the question quickly to the students, who indicated that they had not. Birchall produced a magnifying glass and his ever-present paint brush. With his tongue behind his front teeth he whistled rhythmically as he concentrated. Then he said quietly, 'I'm damned certain his wrists were tied. The ulna and the radius on both arms have curious linear indentations as if a ligature has tightened and tightened even after death.' He thought for a moment. 'Leather thongs would do it perhaps. They would go on shrinking in the wet.'

'So, what then?' said Henry.

'As I hoped, an execution is indicated. Well not hoped perhaps,' Birchall put in hastily, 'But you follow my drift, don't you,'

Henry stared down again, his mental effort to see beyond the bare remains to the living being, given a sudden flood of new and terrible images with which to struggle.

Once again the sour smell of the cold marbled clay came to his senses, that final smell of life, and turning away he vomited violently.

It was so unexpected and so devoid of any readily apparent cause that the silence and embarrassment which greeted Henry's discomfiture was immense. Even the normally perspicacious Birchall was lost for words. It fell once again to Annie Lilley to reach out and reorder the chaos that Henry had invoked.

'Henry Turner, I do believe you've swallowed a yew berry unbeknownst.' She went to proffer the corner of her apron to start cleaning him up as she spoke, but retracted instantly. Henry was grateful for her sensitivity, feeling foolish enough without adding to his public humiliation by having his face wiped.

'You won't be wanting your dinner now, I don't suppose,' she said, with her little laugh, 'But I expect the others are ready enough for their snap,' and turning she led the way back to the table where the baskets has been left, physically offering an alternative to Henry's predicament, that the students readily accepted.

Birchall, however, his normal composure reasserting itself, linked arms with Henry as they followed her at a little distance. 'Yew berries be blowed,' he said. 'What was that all about my friend, as if I didn't know?'

'It just seems that every time we find out a little more about Reuben, the more I feel the truth coming through,' said Henry. 'When you said his arms had been tied behind his back, something made me feel it was so true it was more than I could handle inside.'

'But I could be so wrong,' Birchall replied quietly. 'I want it to be the truth too, so much that I might be seeing things that aren't really there at all.'

'But I know when it's true and when it isn't. It's like...it's like the old gaffer who comes to look for the water. He just knows. It's like he can smell the truth of it and feel it in his bones. Horses know things too. They feel things in the air sometimes.'

Birchall listened to him. 'Well all right then. Come back now and have another look if you can bear to.'

'I'm better now,' said Henry and he led the way back to the sacking and its contents at the edge of the digging.

'Here,' said Dr Birchall, passing him his magnifying glass, 'Look at these bones and tell me what you see.'

Henry, who had never handled a magnifying glass before, but understood the principle, crouched down and after several advances and retractions, got the glass into the correct position. 'What am I looking for?' he asked.

'Lines running round the bone,' said Birchall, 'Like...like tiny furrows,' he added, sounding quietly pleased with his simile.

Henry looked steadily. The bones were discoloured and marked it was true. 'I cannot be sure,' he said at last.

'Let me have another look,' said Birchall taking the glass from him. 'Hmm,' he said after a moment, 'You know I could have sworn...but now I'm not so sure either.'

'But I am sure that what you said was true because of what happened when you said it. It's like you said before, that I had been chosen. I have had strange feelings ever since the first day, and every time we get closer they have got stronger. And then just now, well you saw,' said Henry, 'Perhaps the marks were there for a moment, and that was all it needed.'

'Henry, I am certain that there is something here that you are sensitive to, and I will go on believing it myself. But I am afraid it will not do for the British Archaeological Society. We must have evidence, evidence. I cannot say "Oh hello, there were marks there and then they were not, but Henry Turner's breakfast came up when I saw them so that proves something all right".'

'And what about me being chosen?' said Henry, 'You said your friends knew about that happening.'

'Yes,' said Dr. Birchall sadly, 'But all the same it won't do, I'm afraid.'

Henry was not to be put off. 'What about the other things, the funny shape, the way he is lying on his front? And his arms are behind his back. You can see they are. How could that be explained away?'

'Excellent, excellent,' said Dr Birchall, standing up again, 'There am I forgetting what evidence we do have. Let's see,' he said counting off the fingers of his left hand by wrapping them round one by one with his right, 'It's certainly not a burial in the formal sense of the word. If he were a Roman he would have been cremated at this time and all we would have would be an urn if we were lucky. So he's British then. And the tribes did bury their dead, but not in that position that's for sure. What else?' He held his clasped fingers in front of him.

'His head,' said Henry. 'They cut of his head with a sword.

'Indeed they probably did, excellent, I was forgetting the roundel cut. So what about,' he crouched down on his hams again beside the sacking and produced his little trowel, 'So what about the upper thoracic vertebra?'

'The what?' said Henry crouching down beside him.

'The neck bone,' said Birchall, 'Oh hello, oh I say, now there's no doubting that. Those marks aren't going to disappear when we look away. Henry, I should go and get some dinner inside you before you see this.' He laughed. 'Look. The top of the bone here has been sliced clean through.'

Henry could see that it had.

He stood up and looked across to where the Icing now ran. 'They brought him here to the edge of the river,' he said.

'Quite possibly,' began Dr Birchall.

'No, they did. I can see them. They had done things to him. Been asking him things.' A picture came into Henry's head of a young colt he had once seen when he was just a boy, refusing to be broken. Put alongside a steady mare, harnessed by the shoulder to her, but still refusing to move when she did. In the end the men did things to him, cruel things. Things he vowed he would never do.

'Asking him things?' said Dr Birchall rather sharply.

'Yes,' said Henry. 'But he didn't tell them,' and he walked back towards the tents, feeling suddenly refreshed and very hungry.

4

Although Dr Birchall's excavations continued for several days afterwards, nothing more was discovered before it was time for him to bid farewell to the Vicarage and Mr Earl and for his students to fold their tents and steal away back to Cambridge. The archaeologist was unable to conceal his disappointment, least of all from Henry Turner, that nothing more had been discovered to give credence to Henry's inner certainty about the nature of Reuben and his death on the banks of the Icing all those centuries ago.

For the youngest horseman however, there was now a fierce satisfaction in the pit of his stomach where before there had been the burning discomfort something unconsummated. The real moment of release had come for him when Birchall had asked him privately to help with the removal of the bones to the vestry.

'I suppose it is the proper thing to do,' said Mr Earl for about the tenth time after he had agreed to provide a temporary mortuary.

'Well I don't propose to put them back in the water meadows,' said Dr Birchall flatly. 'Henry and I are convinced that this man was not properly buried, just abandoned to the kites and crows. He deserves some fitting end. We shall have to give it some thought.'

'I do hope that you are not proposing to have him interred in the graveyard,' said the Vicar, 'As it is I am already considered far too unorthodox by some of my parishioners...' he shot Henry a challenging glance which Henry felt had something to do with the incident of the communion wine '...for them to countenance me burying an unbaptised pagan in the shadow of St Mary's.'

Still uneasy, the Vicar had found a decaying wooden chest in the crypt, which he reluctantly offered as a coffin, insisting that nothing should be transacted until well after evensong.

By the light of the vestry oil lamp the three of them cautiously handled the sacking down the short spiral staircase to the sub-church, Mr Earl having taken the unshakeable position that the chest was not to be brought up and left with its contents in the vestry.

'I don't want the verger or anyone else asking why I've brought the old tithe coffer out of retirement and it has no workable lock to keep out curious eyes up here. I can put something on top of it down in the crypt, so we might just get away with it. I've a good mind to make you all swear a solemn oath to keep this strictly between us, but heaven alone knows what we might invoke if we did that.

'Here,' Dr Birchall said to Henry when they had laid the sacking and contents in their now dried out mud cradle, 'You had better finish what you started.' He produced the white flour sack in which he had continued to store the first piece of Reuben since bringing it back to Icingbury. Henry took out the skull and held it in both hands, feeling his heart pounding but with anticipation this time not with disquiet. He gently laid it down where it fitted and experienced an upwelling of peace from the very soles of his feet through to his hair and out of the top of his head.

'You've put it in upside down, Turner,' said a startled Mr Earl.

'It's a long story,' said Henry quietly as he lowered the lid.

'Well I think I had better hear it all the same,' insisted the Vicar, 'I suppose I ought to know what it is you have persuaded me to be party to here. I thought when that death's head went off to you in Cambridge, Roger, there would be its resting place. Now it seems I have become custodian of goodness knows what and I'm turning my crypt into an ossuary. I certainly don't like the idea of its being upside down.That smacks of something very unpleasant.'

Roger Birchall looked at his clerical friend thoughtfully and then glanced at Henry Turner. After a moment he addressed them both as if he lecturing his students.

'What you probably have here is an Icenian warrior from the time of Boudicca's rebellion against Suetonius. He appears to have been summarily executed although I cannot be sure of that. It would account for the position of the skeleton face down in the ground and possibly the reason why the head ended up some way away from the rest of the body. Henry's intuitive gifts, which I believe are quite formidable, leads him to believe not only that all this is true, but that the Icenian was tortured presumably by Romans who were trying to get information out of him. Icingbury would place him on the route of the rebel tribes either advancing on Colchester in the beginning or on the retreat from London at the end.

The Vicar goggled at them both.

'It all sounds rather far fetched to me. Surely you cannot choose to believe all that from so little evidence.'

'Well that's just it,' said Birchall, reverting to his confidential chirpy style, 'I can choose to believe it or not and I may end up a laughing stock. But you don't have a choice in the matter, do you Henry?'

'No,' said Henry, 'It is all true. I have only been easy in my mind since these things have slowly been put together. Until we found the line, or then when we strayed off it, I was always troubled. Now I just know I'm in the right of it.'

The Vicar still looked extremely doubtful. 'What about the torture, surely that is mere fancy?'

'A picture just came into my head,' said Henry, 'It's a bit like understanding the horses.'

Mr Earl snorted. 'A vision,' he said archly, 'Oh dear me.'

'I should have thought that would have been right up your street, old fellow,' Dr. Birchall said.

The Vicar sighed deeply in a way that indicated his recognition of a superior force that he had little time to set about vanquishing just then. So turning down the wick in the oil lamp, he picked it up and ushered his tormentors out of the vestry and into the darkening churchyard. 'I shall do nothing more,' he said resignedly, 'I leave it to you and Turner to decide. No-one is to know what we have done tonight. I wash my hands of the whole blessed thing.'

'What a very Roman attitude,' said Dr Birchall, linking arms with him as they walked through to the Vicarage. 'Good night Henry,' he called back over his shoulder. 'Come and see me when next you are buying horses in Cambridge. Excellent.'

Henry watched the lamplight disappear among the yew trees. He felt deeply content for the first time in a long while although something told him the feeling would pass and that the business was still unfinished.

He did not see Roger Birchall again before he left for Cambridge on an early morning train from Great Duster station. His students had already gone with their various traps by carrier on the day of Reuben's clandestine sepulture. Life in Icingbury returned to what passed for normal that year. The window of better weather at the back end of Easter proved short lived, as if the heavens had called a brief truce to allow for the Icenian's removal to sacred ground, only to make up for lost time when it was done.

The horsemen at the Veil House worked their teams sporadically in the mangold worzel fields, but the farming year already so far advanced, as Bailey Turner kept saying, "looks like being another '79". This was deeply dispiriting news and spirits did sink.

Henry's father had reverted to paying him less and less frequently, but in the circumstances he had little to complain of. He had two good meals a day at the farm still, which was more than could be said for Sim Lilley, Josh Makepeace and the other day men. For them the drainage work funded by Dr Birchall had provided some welcome cash although the pub had had most of the benefit and now hunger began to add to their daily preoccupations.

The elation Henry had felt when he had made the Icenian warrior whole again soon turned to gnawing impatience. He constantly felt almost driven to revisit the crypt. But for what purpose? What would he do? Open the lid of the makeshift coffin? To see what? Even Henry could see that the feeling was entirely irrational. Did he expect that there would be some change, something new to explore? He did not, but even so he felt the need to be doing something. Matters could not simply be left in the air.

On an impulse one Sunday two or three weeks later he approached the school teacher, Miss Covington, as the congregation was leaving morning service. He walked back with her towards the school house despite the black looks from his father who could not bear to see him "dawdling" yet again.

'It's a holy day, not a holiday,' Bailey Turner called after his son. Henry waved back at him as if he had heard his voice but not caught his drift as he escorted his old mentor in the opposite direction.

'Must be important, Henry Turner, for you to escort an old lady home in the teeth of such a gale,' Miss Covington commented, but making no effort to dissuade him even so. Nor was she referring to the weather. She had crossed swords in the past with Henry's father over what he saw as irrelevant time wasting by Henry, but which she saw as a rare reward for her pearl scattering in Icingbury.

'Yes it is,' said Henry, 'To me at any rate.'

'Then I suppose it may have something to do with all the recent excitement by the river that there has been so much talk of. I came down as far as the gate one day but it was too wet and muddy for me to be gathering up my skirts to come any closer. Mrs Westwood was telling me all about it however and said you were very involved with the gentleman from Cambridge.'

'Dr Roger Birchall, yes,' said Henry, 'I was. He thinks that the man whose remains we found was an Icenian. Something to do with the Queen Boudicca.' He spoke as casually as he could, not wanting to reveal the extent of his entanglement with Reuben to her.

Miss Covington's mention of Annie Lilley reminded him of his cousin's new position at the school as her helpmate and something made him hold back from giving her the opportunity even to guess the difficult inner experiences he had begun hesitantly to share with Annie.

'And you want to know all about the Iceni and Queen Boudicca, I take it,' said Miss Covington.

'That's about the size of it,' said Henry, 'How did you guess?'

'Well I wouldn't suppose you were walking me home after church for my marriage portion,' she responded tartly, 'It was always my books you were after.'

They reached the garden gate to the school house.

'I may have something,' she said, 'See me after class next week. Thank you for your company. Give my respects to your poor mother.'

Henry held out until Tuesday before presenting himself at the school at dinner time, after the village children had gone home to their chores. His team was not working that day, but even so he felt he was once again playing hookey to be there. A curious reversal, it occurred to him, as he went through his ritualistic analysis of his sensations. He pushed open the door calling a greeting as he did so.

Miss Covington was not in evidence and it was Annie Lilley's voice that responded. Henry felt slightly nonplussed; he had forgotten for the moment that she was likely to be there and he wondered how much he would have to explain his appearance at the school. It was Annie who understood about the doorways and he accepted without question that it was she from whom he would finally have to seek permission to go through to whatever lay beyond. Now was not the moment. But her unexpected presence was a salutary reminder of this uncomfortable task waiting for him.

'I was looking for Miss Covington,' he said.

'She's in the whatname,' said Annie, 'But she's looked this out for you, I know. I've been looking through it myself. It's got some lovely pictures in it.'

Henry felt slightly irritated. He wanted to take things at his own pace and if there was any galloping ahead to be done he would be the one to do it. 'I was talking to her about Queen Boudicca,' he said rather loftily.

Annie glanced down at her feet and smiled briefly. Henry realised he was being gently chided and wondered whether to climb down or carry on. He climbed down.

'Is there a picture of her, then?' he asked.

She handed him the book, an heroic work devoted to glorious episodes and valorous feats.

'There,' she said coming round and peeping over his shoulder, 'There she is.'

It was a coloured engraving of a statuesque woman in a flowing white robe gathered under her bosom with a jewelled belt. She had a jewelled tiara, too, which was almost lost in her mane of deep red hair that fell over one shoulder at the front and down to the small of her back. She was standing in a chariot pointing a spear, taller than herself, towards a dark mass of armoured soldiery in the distance. The chariot had a huge sickle jutting from its visible axletree and was surrounded by warriors with flowing moustaches and tunics that looked as though they were made out of metal fish scales. Crouching behind the Queen in the back of the chariot were two other women, also in flowing robes, one blue and the other purple, but with golden circlets round their heads rather than tiaras. The two horses pulling the chariot were plunging and rearing with wildly rolling eyes.

'What's happening?' said Annie, taking it all in.

Henry stared at the picture with a sense of mounting disappointment.

'Well those horses are never harnessed up the right way for that kind of contraption for a start, he snorted, 'And they'd have kicked over the traces good and proper if they were being handled the way they are there. Only there aren't any traces that I can see.'

'Oh you...you horseman,' retorted Annie, 'It's only make-believe . Who are those other women in with her?'

'Those will be her unfortunate daughters.' Miss Covington had appeared from the back of the building unobserved by the couple absorbed in the book, smoothing down her pinafore as she approached them.

Henry looked up at the sound of her voice and then looked back at the picture with more interest. 'They were taken by the Romans,' he said hurriedly.

'Henry means they were violated, brutally raped.' Miss Covington pronounced each word separately, rolling the arrs histrionically as if to command the attention of a class. 'Why mince words?' she said.

Henry felt himself reddening. He swallowed, noisily, he thought, but neither of the women spared him a glance.

Annie took a breath. 'She doesn't look old enough to be those girls' mother,' she said, 'She must have had them awful young.' She giggled and Miss Covington joined in. Henry knew he must wrest control back from them.

'I expect this is the battle it was all about,' he interposed, 'The Romans first raped her daughters in front of her eyes and then they flogged the Queen in front of her servants. So she rose up and went on a rebellion.'

'She doesn't look flogged here,' said Annie peering closely at the book again.

'No more than the team doesn't look properly harnessed,' Henry jumped in, with difficulty restraining himself from poking a triumphant tongue at her.

'So Dr Turner,' said Annie, 'What happened? Did she beat them? I do hope she did.'

'Well she burned Colchester to the ground, and...' he struggled to remember what it was Dr Birchall had told him '...and London and somewhere over that way...it might have been Bishops Stortford.'

'It was Verulamium, St Albans now,' Miss Covington put in.

'I haven't heard tell of either of them,' said Henry, 'But Boudicca burned them all to the ground.'

'And put them, everyone, to the sword,' put in Miss Covington again.

'Axe,' said Henry, 'The Iceni didn't use swords. Dr Birchall says,' he added quickly by way of apologising for cutting across his teacher.

'So what happened in the end,' pleaded Annie Lilley impatiently, 'Did she win?'

Henry looked at Miss Covington for help.

'The Romans lured her into a trap,' she said. 'They chose a battle ground with no way out at the sides and they forced her back and back onto her own waggons full of her warriors' wives and children and they slaughtered them all. When they had finished they went round the countryside, all round here, killing and burning. Boudicca poisoned herself rather than be captured again. She knew what to expect and more. It is said that Suetonius killed more than eighty thousand of the Iceni and their allies as a punishment afterwards.'

'Even though they were beaten and Boudicca was dead?' said Annie quietly.

'Even though they were beaten already and she was dead,' assented Miss Covington.

'How could they do it?' said Annie.

None of them spoke for a moment. Henry felt the anger that had burned inside him on the banks of the Icing at Easter time, rekindle with that sudden intensity of light. He looked deep into it once more. 'He crucified them,' he said.

'Tacitus doesn't say that,' said Miss Covington looking at him sharply.

'No?' said Henry, 'Maybe he doesn't, whoever he is. But I know it.'

5

Henry half-hoped that he would have some word from Dr. Birchall, perhaps through the agency of Mr Earl if not directly. He tried dreaming up schemes that would involve him going into Cambridge with the carrier, but Bailey Turner was impervious to any such suggestions.

An emptiness settled inside Henry. Temporarily suppressed by the daily grind of making a little fruitless work go a long way, if only to exercise the horses, it would instantly reassert itself as soon as he had done with the harness and racked up Honeycomb and the other horses for the night. On such evenings after supper he would often walk down to the water meadows in the dusk, climb the gate and trudge across to where the scars of the recent diggings were still visible. There he would stand and stare down, as if hoping that, like the children of the dragon's teeth he had once come across when foraging in Miss Covington's book shelves, Icenian warriors in their hundreds, bristling with axes, would shoulder themselves out of the ground all around, wiping the mud from their flowing moustaches and call him brother.

Drawing near to the meadows one evening, disconsolately bent on one such foray, he was suddenly catapulted out of his inner meandering by the unmistakable scream of a hare.

'Wounded or trapped,' thought Henry, responding instinctively to the piteously chilling shriek in the gloaming. 'Trapped most likely, for I heard no shot.'

The sound was guillotined as suddenly as it had arisen.

'Netted then,' he thought, the instant silence evoking in his imagination and darkness the brief arc of the despatching cudgel, as clearly as if it had been noonday.

'Now who's taking "puss" at this time of year as if I didn't know?' he mused, checking for the direction of the breeze before quickening his pace. The sound of the hare had been borne towards him so he knew it was safe to continue in the direction he had been following without alerting the dogs he knew undoubtedly would be coursing somewhere up ahead of him.

'Wouldn't do to be mistaken for the keeper,' he thought grimly.

Henry's immediate thought was that some of the local day men of his acquaintance had been forced out poaching by economic necessity and belts that had run out of eyelets to tighten. His instincts were to side with whoever it might prove to be, knowing how hard times were and not being averse to setting the odd snare himself. He was even prepared in these circumstances to be sympathetic to the taking of a bit of game so early in the season, when the brown hare was less than full fed and had not yet developed its marketable thick winter pelt.

However, as it began to be apparent that the clandestine activity was probably being staged down in their own water meadows, Henry's mood began to change from one of tolerant arms' length conspiracy to one of vaguely injured proprietorship. It altered even more dramatically when, as he came along the lane towards the five bar gate to the meadows, he saw a small covered cart with a horse in the shafts standing patiently against the hedge.

The sight of it told him at once that whoever were afoot on the other side were certainly not local. The wind was soughing through the poplars down on the far side of the Icing, sufficient to cover the sound of his boots on the grassy verge and there was just enough vesper light through the scudding broken cloud to show him the sizeable haul in the back of the cart.

'A perfect evening for it,' Henry thought grimly as he peered in cautiously, having established that the coast was clear for the time being.

The fields on the other side of the lane had already been drawn, resulting in half a dozen carcases. Henry felt his anger rising. This was hardly a case of one for the pot for famished local labourers. This was more like a wholesale order from a fat Cambridge butcher. He crept up to the gate into the water meadows. Sure enough these were to be drawn next.

A fine net had been draped down one side of the gate, held along the top and on the ground beneath by middling sized stones. Just enough weight to hold the net in place until the panicking hare, desperate to escape the dogs ranging the feeding ground, would attempt to hurl itself between the bars only to pull them down and become enmeshed.

Henry guessed that the poachers were checking further down the lane that the hares' other runs had been suitably stopped before putting in the lurchers. Whoever they were, Henry knew they were alien and had to be thwarted. They were invading Reuben's preserve, unbidden, unwelcome. Their presence defiled sacred land.

'Bloody Romans,' he hissed.

Half crouching to reduce his outline he slid back to the cart. The horse was standing so patiently and quiet in the shafts it had clearly been well trained for its work. Henry breathed through his nose and half open mouth to make a muffled sighing sound. He put his hand on its shoulder and felt their selves merge. When he was sure the horse would stay still, he set about unharnessing it from the cart.

If he was worried about making a noise, he need not have been. The buckles were bound with strips of cloth already to muffle their jingling. He began to lead the horse forward out of the shafts, making sure that they did not fall heavily to the ground as he did so.

Concentrating on the task of disabling the cart, Henry had forgotten to keep half an ear cocked and they were on him before he even knew it. There were three of them, all heavily muffled, and two lurchers. Although he could not make out their features, he could tell that they were not local men even though as they laid into him none spoke or uttered any sound other than to grunt now and again with the sheer effort of the beating they were giving him.

At first they set about him together, but when he was unable any longer to keep himself curled into a protective ball as he had instinctively done when he first hit the ground, they took it in turns, one at a time to kick him and hammer him with the cudgels that so recently had been despatching hares. Two would rest briefly from their labours, before taking over again, in strict rotation, Henry noticed, despite the pain and the blessed fog of semi-consciousness which came to his aid for a few moments at a time.

He found commonplace thoughts going through his mind. He feared for his precious Melton coat. It had been his grandfather's before him and he could hear quite clearly his father's words as he had handed it to him, 'Mind you be worthy of it and wear it with the pride of a good horseman.' He wondered if he was being so badly hurt, that someone else would have to see to Honeycomb for a while. He wondered if she would mind. He thought about the horse he had just loosed from the cart and felt a wave of pity for it having to witness the savagery that was being meted out to him, and he thought about Reuben, his Icenian. He had not cried out when the Romans set about him and nor did Henry now. But he felt bitterly that he was letting the warrior down even so.

As if at some unheard signal the beating suddenly stopped. Henry on his side, waited for the next boot to come into his ribs or his stomach, whose contents he was mostly lying in. but none did. He was vaguely aware of the horse being put back in the cart shafts and then they were gone. Still not a word had been exchanged.

Henry could not move, he did not try. He was barely conscious. The smell of the cold, trammelled earth and blood beneath his nose flooded his senses as it had before from the skull, like the sudden recollection of a moment from a forgotten dream.

'Looks like someone's been out before us. The gate's been netted. They haven't taken the weights.'

It was Josh Makepeace's voice further down the lane, blending with the singing in Henry's ears.

He felt a wave of relief. So the invading poachers had not bothered to draw the meadow after they had finished with him. Perhaps he had achieved something after all. He almost laughed.

'Bugger! Who could it be then?'

And Sim Lilley too, thought Henry. He heard them coming up the lane towards him although he would not have been able to see them no matter how bright the moon if there had been one. Now they're in for a bit of surprise, he thought.

'What's this then?' Josh had almost stumbled over Henry's prone form.

Sim held his kerosene lantern, which had the wick turned right down low naturally, close to Henry's face.

'My Christ,' he gasped, 'Who's this?'

Henry thought this rather odd, but decided to tell Sim who he was anyway. The words formed in his head but nothing came out. He tried again. A kind of bubbling noise emerged. Henry wondered what that could be.

'Horseman, by the coat.' This was Josh again.

'Good,' thought Henry, 'So the Melton is all right after all.'

'Who's done this to him, then?' said Sim, turning up the lantern now and waving it up and down the length of Henry's stretched out body.

'It's Henry Turner,' said Josh.

'It bloody is too,' said Sim, 'I said he needed a good shoeing, but this is beyond all. Someone's tried to kill him by the looks.'

He laid his hand on Henry's shoulder to turn him onto his back. A huge surge of pain racked him and he cried out for the first time. Sim and Josh leapt back as if they had been burned.

'He's in a very bad way,' said Sim. 'Christ, I hope they don't think it was me, if he dies. That's a hanging job.'

'We'd better get a hurdle for him,' said Josh, 'Where's nearest?'

'My Great Aunt Elizabeth's, I reckon,' said Sim, 'I'll go, you stay with him.'

'Don't you think you should run to The Veil House though?' Josh suggested, and then immediately added, 'No, better not.'

'Doesn't want Bailey Turner asking him how he happened across me with a couple of snares in his pocket,' thought Henry, grimacing inside himself despite the pain.

Josh Makepeace was a man of few enough words at the best of times, and this, thought Henry, was not one of them. He was thankful that neither of them felt inclined to make conversation. The pain was settling down into a continuous, sickening sensation, like a persistent howl soaking into every part of his body, filling it not with sound but with hot embers. He held himself rigid against any movement. After Sim's attempt at turning him onto his back, Josh made not further effort to do so, but he muttered, mostly to himself, 'It's going to give you gyp getting you on that hurdle when it comes.'

Henry heard him and knew it would; he almost began to dread its arrival. After what seemed the entire night he heard the sound of running feet. Not Sim's, he thought.

Making a supreme effort he managed partially to open one eye and made out the shape of Annie Lilley flying along the lane, clutching a wildly waving kerosene lamp in one hand and her skirts well up to her thighs with the other. Henry wondered why she was showing all her legs to the likes of Josh Makepeace, before falling back into a black spinning hole again.

Mercifully, Annie told him later, he was still out for the count when Sim Lilley came toiling along in her wake clutching the hurdle over his back like a sack of potatoes and the three of them managed to lift him onto the improvised stretcher. By the time the pain of this had wrenched Henry back into the world, it was over.

Nevertheless, the journey back to Great Aunt Elizabeth's cottage was a blur of tortured agony for Henry, with Sim Lilley and Josh Makepeace at either end of the hurdle, their unequal build making it rise and fall like the eccentric wheel on a steam threshing machine as they cantered along oblivious now of the distress of their burden, and, by their panted exchanges, anxious only to deliver him into someone else's custody and make themselves scarce.

From what Henry could make out when they arrived at her cottage after what seemed like a journey to the moon, Great Aunt Elizabeth was not at her best with blood and pain.

'I've had no men of my own to mend and thank the Lord, Granf'er Lilley never had need,' she called out to Annie from the back area whence she had fled to fetch hot water and cloths. 'You'll have to see to him as best you may, for I shall surely swoon away.'

Annie had cleared the kitchen table so that Josh and Sim could unload Henry before fleeing themselves.

'Doctor,' she called out to them as they made for the door, 'He must have the Doctor.'

The pair of them made non-committal noises as they made off down the garden path. As the latest pinnacle of pain from being manhandled onto the table began to subside Henry was aware of Annie at the door calling into the dark, 'At least go to the Veil House and get someone to go over to Duster for the doctor. If you won't, I don't know what I shall have to say to the policeman about you "finding" him.' She slammed the door.

Annie busied herself as best she could unwrapping Henry in the light to reveal the extent of his hurt. She removed his boots, fetching a groan out of him with every movement.

'I fear we shall have to cut you out of your coat, Henry,' she whispered as if the ordinary level of her voice would have added to his pain.

He heard her even so. He wanted to gather his dwindling strength to cry out to her, 'Not my coat, dear God, not my coat,' but he could not make his jaw work. With a huge effort he shook his head from side to side on the table and made a pleading noise as if he were speaking with a bit in his mouth. To his relief she did not at once carry through her proposal but contented herself with unbuttoning his Melton together with the waistcoat and vest beneath, beginning sponge his chest and stomach gently with the warm water that Aunt Elizabeth had left at the scullery door before scurrying back to boil some more. This action was the first not to cause Henry pain.It even brought him some comfort and no little joy that he could sense it doing so.

'What does it look like?' Aunt Elizabeth kept calling.

'I fear you're a little broken Henry Turner,' Annie said, still speaking softly so that only he could hear. 'We shall have to have the doctor set you though, for I cannot. If those loons don't make shift to have him fetched, then Aunt Elizabeth must take the lantern up to The Veil House herself since she cannot do this.'

Annie's blackmail had, however, had the desired effect. In a very short while Henry's father arrived, gruff and blustering, his deep anxiety at what he might find plain to see. So much so that Henry felt warmed by his fearful concern and at the same time embarrassed at having caused it.

'Head baiter's gone for Doctor Norman over to Duster,' he said to Annie and Aunt Elizabeth, who had emerged a foot or two into the kitchen at his arrival. He took a long look at Henry then by the lamplight. 'There'll be no moving you my son, I should say.'

'But he cannot stay on my kitchen table,' put in Great Aunt Elizabeth.

‘We shall have to put a truckle in the parlour, Aunt,’ said Annie in her ‘so that’s settled’ voice, ‘We would never get him up the stairs to my bed.’

Aunt Elizabeth began one of those ‘well I’m not so sure’ noises in her throat, but Annie went on, ‘You won’t be needing it before Christmas anyway.’

‘My goodness, you don’t think he will be here all that time do you?’ her Aunt exclaimed.

All three of them fell silent at this. Then Bailey Turner said with the flatness of doubt in his tone, ‘Well, well, perhaps he’s not so bad as he seems,’ and they all murmured their assent.

Henry was hearing their voices come and go, as if they were another ploughing team away at the top of a field, with odd words caught distinctly at the furrow’s turn and others wafted away but leaving their sense hanging in the air. He heard his father say more than once, ‘What he was doing to occasion someone doing this to him, beats me.’

There was more silence, then he heard Annie say slowly, ‘I think he was trying to protect something or someone.’

‘Well who, I should like to know?’ Bailey Turner retorted, ‘It would have to be a horse with him. Was there a horse?’

They heard the sound of wheels in the lane and moments later the doctor was filling the room with his comforting ‘What have we got here then?’ He became rather more grave when he gently lifted Henry’s unbuttoned clothing to take a first look at the body within.

‘I’d better give him something,’ he said, ‘This is going to be a longish job.’

Henry was briefly aware of the mask on his swollen face and Doctor Norman’s muttered expression of hope that, given the condition of it, he would still be able to administer the chloroform satisfactorily, before he became utterly oblivious. It was a process that had to be repeated several times during the course of a long night as the doctor and his makeshift nursing team, mainly Annie, set about putting Henry Turner together again.

6

A little sunshine crept across the threshold of Aunt Elizabeth's cottage. Despite the advancing year, it was still sufficient of a rarity to catch Henry's attention. He eased himself to the edge of the little truckle bed that has been his universe for nearly two months and tentatively swung his unbroken leg over the side. His stirring brought his aunt to the kitchen door, cocking her head round the frame like a robin emboldened by the sound of a turning spade.

'Annie,' she called over her shoulder, 'He's trying to get up.'

Annie appeared in the doorway, wiping her hands on her apron. She looked at Henry half in, half out of the bed. 'Where are you off to then?' she said, 'Do you want me to fetch you the jug or is it the bowl?'

'The sun's shining,' mumbled Henry, somewhat constricted still by the bandage wrapping his head, and holding his jaw together, 'I thought I might be able to make it myself out to the jordan .'

'Well,' said Annie, 'I suppose that would make a change for both of us.' Her tone was warm and straightforward.

As for Henry, he had long since ceased to be abashed by the intimacy of the patient and his nurse. Having now managed with her aid to seat himself on the edge of the bed with both his mending leg and his good one on the floor, he made a rueful sound that might have passed for a chuckle but for his strapping and gestured with his hands, which were likewise heavily bandaged. 'I fear you'll have to clean me up and groom me still for a while, whether I'm in here or out back.'

'Yes, well, that's as maybe,' said Annie. 'If you're feeling like being up and about I think it high time the doctor took another look under those bandages and you can start giving yourself a rub down.'

She helped him into an upright position and with him leaning heavily on her, the expedition to the privy and the return to the parlour were accomplished without mishap. Annie, having deposited him once more to a seated position on the edge of the bed, stepped back smoothing down her dress and apron, and redoing her buttons that had come undone in the course of manhandling Henry through the narrowness of the cottage and in the still more straightened confines of the earth closet.

'I'm sorry,' mumbled Henry, observing her fumbled toilet.

'Well, it's of no account. I have had my hands on you for so long now in a way that only mothers and wives generally have call to do with their babes or their men, so I don't suppose seeing me bare breasted is any different for either of them.'

'Either of what?' said Henry not quite following this.

'Babe or husband I mean. This is getting foolish,' said Annie quickly.

After this first escape from the prison of the truckle bed, Henry spent the next days' waking time moving about the parlour or in one of the chairs as well as manoeuvring to the privy. The sunshine that had first called him from his bed came intermittently knocking at the window, summoning him out into the garden in front of the cottage. Here he felt his strength begin to return slowly but surely, so that when in a short while, the doctor permitted him to discard the head bandages, he was even able to exercise his mended jaw by responding in kind to the sardonic calls of his father's horsemen as they passed with their teams to the fields.

Sitting a little too long just inside the open cottage door on a day when the sun had given up trying to break through, Henry shivered in his shirt. It was not properly fastened because one arm was still in a sling and his hands were still heavily bandaged.

Both Annie and their aunt had gone out before he had awakened and Henry had simply put his less encumbered arm in one sleeve and pulled the rest of the shirt round himself with his teeth before taking himself out to the privy. Annie returned from her errand shortly after to find him in this slight disarray and looking decidedly chilly.

'Couldn't you wait then?' she chided him gently, 'You're so keen to be up and doing these days.'

'I have to be up betimes today for the Doctor. He's going to take these off.'

Henry waved his bandaged hands in front of him as if he were patting butter. The sudden action caused the shirt to slip right off his shoulder.

'You'll die of ague before he gets here at this rate,' said Annie, pulling it round him again.

'Well,' said Henry, 'Get my Melton out then, and I'll put that round me.'

Annie stared out of the open door in silence for what seemed an age and then turned to look Henry in the eye.

'What is it?' he said, sensing that something was amiss.

'Henry...' she whispered '...I'm so sorry...' She made as if to hold him close, but could find no part of him that could be comforted by the gesture.

'It's my coat isn't it? Where's my Melton?'

'You were so poorly. Like a broken bird, and the doctor so anxious to set as much as he could before the chloroform wore off each time.'

'What happened to my coat?'

'The doctor said it saved your life, being so thick. You had broken bones but nothing inside was hurt.' There was a catch in Annie's voice too. 'We had to cut it off you.'

Henry felt something inside him drain away. He sought in vain to catch it before it went, to put his feelings back the way they had been moments before so that he could block up the exits and prevent it forsaking him. But it was too late. Another piece of his former self had disappeared. He had felt balanced in familiar surroundings, naturally responding to the lie and the texture of the earth that held his being and which he encompassed effortlessly within. Now at every turn it seemed he stumbled into an emptied place where he struggled with a long dead Icenian tribesman.

'Say something, my sweet, say you forgive me.' Annie was crouching down beside him now where he sat inside the still open door. She slipped her hand under his loose shirt and its warmth against Henry's chilled flesh recalled him.

'Did you cut it, or did the Doctor? You said "we", "we had to cut it off".'

'Well I did, really,' said Annie. There was another silence.

'It matters does it? That I did it?'

'Yes, it matters.'

They did not speak.

Then Henry said, 'Hold me all round. With your other arm too, for I cannot.' He gestured helplessly with his slung arm and his bandaged hands.

'Come and sit on the bed then,' Annie murmured, standing up and holding her hands out to him.

He followed her and sat beside her. She put her arms under his and held him gently.

'Tighter than that,' said Henry, 'For I feel as if I am soaking away like...like water on the ground.'

She tightened her clasp on him, more and more.

'I am afraid to hurt you,' she said, but he did not flinch or cry out. They sat, two as close as one, and breathed in each other's breath.

For a long time neither said a word. Then Annie whispered, 'It's comic, but I feel abashed like this, though I have done such things with you and more as my patient.'

Henry turned his head and in doing so their lips touched. Annie closed her eyes for a moment and then opened them again, her nose touching the tip of his so that their eyes stared simultaneously into each other's.

'Owls,' said Annie, giggling and breaking the spell. It was a childhood game they had played. Henry snorted with laughter and irritation.

'There,' said Annie cautiously, 'So am I forgiven then?'

'There's nothing to forgive. I have brought this all on myself. It is as if I have been led on a rein these many weeks. That man we found has been leading me and leading me, further away down a furrow of his own choosing, so that nothing I can do will straighten it up.'

He thought for a moment and gave a short laugh. 'That's what the head baiter says about most of my furrows. He says I let the horses choose the line. That's because I suppose I think the horses are like to know their own minds best. That's why this Reuben can lead me so, I reckon. Because I know him like I know horses. Knowing inside by feeling what they're feeling. That's how I know him. And so he's led me on. Every step I seem to take he opens one of those doors and beckons me through. And every time I go through, he closes them behind me so that I don't know where to find them to go back even if I wanted to.'

'Don't you want to then?'

'Every time he takes a hand it gets more serious. First he got me into a fight with Sim and where would that have gone if you hadn't happened along? Then he frightened the gelding and other things that day. And it's as if he's driven a wedge between father and me, which wouldn't take much doing anyway. Now he's led me to a real good hiding and lost me my good Melton, my horseman's coat. Another door closed.'

Annie took a deep breath, as if it were she that had made the speech.

'I won't say it's fancy,' she said, 'Because that would be insulting. I know that if things seem meant, then they are meant, whether other people think that's daft or not. And it is true about doors closing and not being able to find them to go back. I went through one when I took Tom Westwood. I was ready to love him and I started finding the doors to go through so that it would happen. I ran to find them, I so wanted it to be. And then one day I opened a door, a real door and there he was broken, just like you, on a hurdle. And the next one that closed was the one they nailed down on him. So was it meant, Henry? Was it meant? When Sim Lilley came a' knocking that night and said he needed a hurdle for you, it brought Tom straight to mind. I thought...'she paused.

'What did you think, then?' said Henry softly so that the gossamer thread of her thought would remain intact.

'I thought, I am not meant to have you either, nor you me. I thought you would die too.' Annie's voice trailed off as if she were alone in the room.

'Well I haven't died, have I?' said Henry after a moment.

'No, but something has. We have been as close as man and wife these last few weeks, well almost.' She blushed a little and then looked him defiantly in the eye. 'So close and yet getting further off the more we talk. The more we touch.'

Henry wanted to deny it. He summoned up a voice inside to say the words it would take, but it was a hollow voice, not fit to be heard and he abandoned it.

'When I look in your eyes,' he said at last, 'Really look in them, I feel as though I must wait for permission.'

'What, permission to touch me, do you mean?' Because I thought we just did.'

'You know, don't you? Permission to belong to you. Really belong. Do you know what I mean?'

'Yes, I think I do,' Annie replied, 'But that's a door I cannot open for you. You have to find it for yourself.'

The appearance of Doctor Norman at that very moment, knocking loudly on the half open cottage door with the knob of his blackthorn, made Annie spring to her feet and Henry to make a sudden awkward movement that would have amounted to springing to his feet too, had he been physically able to do so. If the doctor was aware of the *coup de théâtre* his entrance had caused he affected at least not to be so.

'Well, well young man,' he said to Henry, when Annie had taken his hat and stick and quietly answered his questions about Henry's progress and the whereabouts of their great aunt, 'So this is the day when all shall be revealed and the world shall see what kind of a bone setter I have turned out to be. Will we take a look at the leg first, do you think?'

His leg, when exposed after so long a time, was very much wasted and the setting while adequate was not first class. Henry gazed down at his misshapen and, it seemed to him slightly shortened limb, with a sense of creeping foreboding.

The doctor, too, was not entirely happy with his handiwork. 'If we had been able to get you to the infirmary, we could perhaps have made a better job of this,' he offered doubtfully.

‘If cousin Sim had run to the veterinary that night I might have been shot,’ Henry put in, feeling a jest might encourage him to be more supporting, but to little avail.

‘There’s likely to be a permanent weakness here and you will almost certainly limp. A stick might be the answer.’

‘I cannot drive a team to plough with a stick in my hand,’ said Henry, as if a hasty denial would remove the prospect. From behind him he felt Annie’s hand rest in the hollow of his shoulder and her finger trace a soft ring around the rim of his ear.

‘I fear your ploughing days may be over, young man,’ said the doctor. He was seemingly unaware of the chill that settled in the parlour as he pronounced this brief capital sentence.

Then as the sling and bandages were removed from his arm and each hand separately, in what felt like an eternity to Henry as they were meticulously rolled by Annie in the process, it became even more certain that Doctor Norman’s prediction would come to pass. Although the left was a reasonable shape, several fingers of his right hand were badly crooked and the knuckles stiff and swollen despite the splints that had been applied.

‘These should improve with exercise and time,’ said the Doctor, ‘If not you could have them broken again and reset, although I personally would not care to. The hand is a complex and delicate mechanism. Gently clench and unclench them, I suggest, and for the leg and arm, swim in the river, if you can swim, otherwise just walk about. Nothing strenuous. Get a stick. Well, well, it could have been worse. I’ll bid you good day.’

And retrieving his hat without waiting for Annie to see him out, he left abruptly.

She stepped forward to close the door fully behind him and, holding it just ajar, watched him climb into his gig.

‘He’s forgotten his own stick, she said. ‘Perhaps he means you to have it,’ and putting her apron to her face with both hands she wept sudden, silent tears.

‘Well I will not use his nor any other and that’s a fact,’ said Henry, hobbling round the parlour with his newly acquired freedom. ‘Have I got any corduroys or did they get cut off me too? I’ve spent long enough in just my smalls and a rug.’

He affected a grumpy busyness in the narrow confines of the parlour, mostly filled as it was with the truckle bed and the chairs, now with the addition of two upright people. Ashamed, he ignored Annie’s back and heaving shoulders, knowing that simply to touch her now would scatter his mind into the vast emptiness that now waited for him beyond the reality of the parlour.

'Well my Icenian friend, you've finally got your way, haven't you,' he said as Annie set aside her angry grief to help him dress. 'Coat's gone. Hands gone, twisted leg. Not fit to be a farm horseman. What do you expect me to do now, I wonder?'

'Whatever is meant, I should think,' said Annie quietly.

In a while Henry was fit enough to remove himself back home to The Veil House Farm. His mother received him lovingly with little comment, letting the waters close over the past few months as if they had never existed. Henry's father soon managed to make it sound as though he had overcome those involuntary feelings of pity and affection that had welled up in him when he had first seen his son, after being roused by Sim Lilley on the night of the beating.

He gave Henry an appraising look as soon as he limped into the farmhouse kitchen.

'So you're back then,' he said. 'You had better get yourself over to the stable and make yourself as useful as you are able, although by the look of it you're not fit for much. Perhaps one day you'll find it in yourself to tell me what occasioned all this,' he added to Henry's retreating back as he did as he was bade. It had been a cause of aggravation between them ever since the beating that Henry had steadfastly refused to be drawn on what had really happened. Indeed, with the merciful interruption of memory brought about by the initial shock and the subsequent passage of time, much of the detail of that evening's walk to the water meadows was in any case an imprecise blur to him. He was content to rely on that when anyone asked him for the factual details. None but Annie was fit to be taxed with the idea that he had received his hurts as a result of his fealty to a dead Icenian warrior.

It was difficult to tell whether Honeycomb accepted Henry's return with the quiet thankfulness of his mother or the baffled annoyance of his father. As he put his bent hands on her and began to rub her down, he could sense that she was not letting herself communicate with him. There was a reproach in her muscles that only gradually left her as he carried out the familiar ritual with his unfamiliar hands.

Henry fully expected that this work would cause him pain and difficulty. So he experienced a feeling of elation when he found his hands seemingly gaining strength from their flowing contact with the horse's warm body.

He became aware of a presence although there had been no sound of the other men and horses returning for the day. It was his father who was silently watching him.

'How long have you been there, then, Pa?' Henry said.

'Long enough to see that you have not lost your touch with that horse. At least you haven't had that knocked out of you. She would hardly let anyone near her while you've been down the road at our Aunt's. Always having to be coaxed.'

'Well I'm back now.'

'Yes, and I've been speaking to that Doctor Norman. He came round to settle the bill.'

'Oh and what's he been saying then?' said Henry, knowing full well what was coming, but trying to make his voice sound light.

'I asked him straight out,' said the Bailey, 'Will the boy handle a heavy team again? He says you won't if you've any sense.'

'Doctor Norman,' said Henry scornfully, 'What does he know about ploughing.'

'A damn sight more than you know about bones,' retorted his father.

'Oh really,' said Henry holding up his hands, 'Well he didn't seem to know very much about these when it came to it.'

'You cannot go blaming the Doctor for that. You brought those on yourself, somehow. I don't know how and you won't say. But I'm sure he did the best he could in the circumstances.'

'Well I hope for your sake that's all you paid him for then,' Henry said bitterly, 'The best in the circumstances.'

For once Bailey Turner looked taken aback. 'You angry, boy?' he asked in the surprised tone of one who, living himself perpetually on the edge of irascibility which others mainly ignored, found its discovery startling in one so generally placid as Henry.

'Of course I'm angry, Pa. I know I'm never going to turn a furrow again, and I'm angry at letting you and the farm down when times are bad enough, I know. But it's more than that. I'm not blaming the doctor.' He contemplated for one wild moment trying to explain about Reuben to the Bailey.

'Something just seems set on driving me off the land,' he said, deciding to leave it at that.

Bailey Turner recovered his normal lack of composure, 'We'll all be driven off the land at this rate. Summer's come too late after a bad winter. Perhaps it's for the best, eh?'

'What? What's for the best?'

'Why, if you decide to leave the land, seeing as you've a mind.'

Henry was stunned. 'That's not what I was meaning…'

But his father carried on, paying him no heed. 'Perhaps not for good, but for a while until you get better and things pick up again. You can still get work with horses. Perhaps in Cambridge. You've a gift boy. Think about it.'

Then he was gone. The stable door closed behind him. Bailey Turner had delivered himself of what he had been determined to say.

'Since before I got home even,' thought Henry, sorrowfully, his anger all but spent now. He resumed his grooming of Honeycomb. 'Come on then my friend, where to now?' he said aloud, but he was not addressing the horse this time. 'You've even managed to get father to throw me out. Is it to be Cambridge? Perhaps the undertaker would hire me, he said he was busy.' He laughed at the thought and then again at the laugh. 'Perhaps I'm free, Honeycomb, what do you think? Has he set me free, that Reuben?'

Henry went to church the following Sunday, not having attended for the months he had been laid up. Mr Earl waylaid him as he was leaving with Annie and Great Aunt Elizabeth, and called him to one side. The women paused too, but the Vicar dismissed them with reasonable grace.

'I won't detain him long, he'll catch you up. How are you Turner?' he said when they had moved on. 'On the mend I hear. I should have come to see you more often at Mrs. Lilley's, but I gather you were in good hands and you were in our prayers.'

He glanced round rather furtively at the last of the departing congregation. 'Have you heard from Dr Birchall?'

'No. Should I have heard from him?'

'Well I have not either and there was talk of his going overseas.'

'Well perhaps he has then,' said Henry, deliberately playing daft as he began to sense what lay behind the Vicar's secretive demeanour. 'I may be going away myself soon,' he added mischievously.

Mr Earl ignored the full import of such a statement from a born and bred Icingbury man. 'But you cannot' he gasped, 'You cannot leave me with that…that thing in the church. I thought you and Birchall would have arranged for its disposal long before now. I realise you have been hors de combat so to speak. But really what is to be done?'

'I should leave well alone, vicar, if I were you,' Henry twinkled, 'He doesn't take to being moved. I should know, look at me.'

'Oh this is preposterous,' said the Vicar, 'I should never have let it get this far. I should never have presumed to take charge during the flooding.'

'Well,' said Henry, 'When the Icing's in spate, it'll show your fate. It certainly showed me mine. Perhaps now this is yours, Vicar.'

'Oh, don't be ridiculous. Just do something.'

'I already am,' said Henry, and touching his cap turned away down the church path leaving the flustered cleric's responses behind him. A sudden chill breeze disturbed the yews at the lychgate and there was a brief scattering of raindrops in the air.

Henry caught Annie up in the lane, Aunt Elizabeth having scuttled on ahead at the threat of a shower.

'What secrets did Mr Earl want to talk about without us being there, then?' she asked half playfully, but serious too, he could see. He almost caught himself revealing to her the cause of the Vicar's nervous anxiety reposing in the sub-church, but recalled, just in time to bite his tongue, his pact with his two co-conspirators. Although he told himself he had nothing more to hide from Annie after being her patient for so long, the warrior's whereabouts were a confidence entrusted to him by others.

'Mr Earl thinks I should go and see Roger Birchall before he goes overseas.' 'What about?' inquired Annie.

'Well Pa wants me off the Veil House.'

'He what?' exclaimed Annie, 'No don't tell me. He thinks a farm's no place for a cripple. Well you're not, not by a long chalk you're not. Anyhow, what has it got to do with Dr. Birchall?'

Henry could feel the snare he had innocently set for himself beginning to tighten. Too late to backtrack, even the secret of the crypt would be no use to him now.

He took a breath, 'Pa's right, I shall be no good behind a plough with these hands and the leg...'

'The leg is all right. You said you wouldn't need a stick and you don't...'

'...And Dr Birchall might be able to help me to some position,' Henry finished.

Despite the fact that Mr Earl had intimated nothing of the kind, as he heard himself saying it, it dawned on Henry that this was indeed the next door waiting to be opened.

'Well I shall have a great deal to say to my cousin, Bailey Turner,' said Annie grimly.

'And I wish you would not. It's my mind that is made up as much as his.'

Henry could hardly believe his own ears. This was twice he had spoken of going away since leaving the church door and each time with a growing certainty that it would be so. They were in sight of Aunt Elizabeth's cottage gate now, where she was chatting to a neighbour, the rain having come to naught.

Annie took a fierce hold of Henry's hand briefly. 'Meet me alone tomorrow after supper,' she said, 'We must talk.'

As he came down the lane the following evening, Henry could see Annie seated before the cottage door. She had her bonnet in her lap.

Observing Henry's approach she stood up and called into the house, 'I'm just going for a little walk Auntie, before it gets properly dark.' Then she hurried to meet Henry at the gate.

Without a word they automatically found themselves walking towards the water meadows and the scene of Henry's beating. It was for once a still, late summer's evening with the sun sinking a quiet yellow in an almost cloudless sky, the whispered sounds in the fading light, infused with the dry scents of the fields, providing a barely registered awareness of the common moment of the land and the day.

Half over the gate Henry stood up tall and gazed about. Then as he stepped down and turned to help Annie over, he said, 'These fields should be alive with men and horses now, and women and children all gathering in. But there's hardly anything to be harvested yet and the summer all but done.'

'If folk think they're hungry now,' said Annie, 'There's surely worse to come by Christmas.'

'Which makes it right that I should go, doesn't it?' said Henry.

'There'll be no men left except the olduns at this rate,' said Annie noncommittally. 'Several of the day men are thinking of enlisting. At least they would be sure of a square meal. Cousin Sim was talking about it to Aunt Elizabeth. Said he might go to Cambridge or Bury and join the Suffolks.'

'Well Sim might at that,' said Henry, 'But they'd have little use for me.'

'I wasn't suggesting you should go anywhere, Henry Turner, least of all into the army,' said Annie.

They had reached the bank of the Icing and stood awhile just looking at its flow. A kingfisher suddenly darted away downstream, its azure back flashing in the last of the sun.

'Halcyon days,' said Henry, pointing at the momentary streak of blue.

Annie looked puzzled.

'It's something Miss Covington says,' he said. 'When I asked her once, she said a kingfisher was a halcyon. It means everything is going to be calm and peaceful.

'Like a sign of good luck?' said Annie.

'I suppose,' said Henry, 'Nothing bad, anyhow.'

'Funny that,' said Annie, 'I've never heard it, a kingfisher day.'

'It seems so strange here now,' said Henry after a moment, 'All full of signs and omens for me this year, and yet I've been coming here all my life before and nothing ever happened. Now it seems every time I come here something happens to me. I've got so that even that old kingfisher must have a meaning because he's here.'

'You will go, won't you,' said Annie, half to herself, 'Nothing I can say will change you. Because you are so changed anyway.'

'Not changed, not changed. More, brought out. He's brought out something that was always going to be there, worrying away at me all my life maybe, and I would have been none the wiser and still no happier.'

Henry did not say who 'he' was and Annie did not need to ask.

'I was going to ask you to stay and be with me,' she said, her voice still faraway as she gazed down the river at the path of the long-gone kingfisher.

Henry's eyes followed hers without looking. 'And would you want me for your husband?' he said.

'And would you want me for your wife?' said Annie.

There was a long silence that said they both knew the answer but neither knew why. Henry felt a huge surge of yearning for Annie then. He wanted to say, let's go back awhile and say it all again and make things different. But he knew they would not be, and he could not.

Annie put her chin on his shoulder, smiling despite the unshed tears in her eyes. 'Something's meant by it. You had better bring me a warrior, now you've yours. Perhaps I can have both of you.'

She had again calmed the storm with a gentle touch.

Later that same week Henry had taken the carrier's cart into Cambridge, where he had not ventured since the day of the yearling. He had contemplated writing to Dr Birchall first, but concerned that he might miss him anyway decided to go on the off-chance. He had asked his father if he had any commissions for him as a pretext for going, but there were none and his request for leave of absence had been met with only the barest grunt of reproof. Henry searched inside himself for some anger at his father's growing lack of interest in him, but could find none. All he could find was sorrow that neither of them could be bothered to feel strongly about the other any more.

As he had crossed the yard, however, to go and meet the carrier his mother had called to him from the farmhouse doorway.

'I have a few commissions for you in Cambridge, if you are not too proud to do some womanly things for your mother.'

He had gone back in with her to write down a list of the few things she wanted.

'Will you be gone long?' she said, when they had done.

'No, I shall be back well in time for supper I expect,' he had replied.

But then she had taken both his hands in hers. 'Look at your poor hands,' she had said absently. 'No, I wasn't meaning today.'

Henry had looked at her, ashamed and helpless at this brief glimpse of her self, the hidden depth of which he could only guess at.

'No mother, not long I don't suppose. Pa will soon find he cannot do without me, I'll be bound, and no-one else will be able to get a day's work out of Honeycomb. And in any case it all depends.'

On what, neither of them knew nor asked.

'Read me that list over,' his mother had said, and when he had done, she had sighed a little sigh, 'I shall miss your learning.'

And Henry had run for the carrier.

Dr Birchall had met him at the top of the front steps to his lodgings in his waistcoat and shirtsleeves.

'Henry, my dear fellow, excellent, excellent,' he greeted him, 'You find me in mid-flight into Egypt. I am awaiting the imminent arrival of the brake from the station to take my advance luggage and then it's London and Dover for me the day after tomorrow.'

Henry's head had been in a whirl at the total energy of Dr. Birchall's reception as he had followed him around picking up this and putting down that, only to repeat the frenzied process all over again.

'Mr Earl said you were going away. Where is it to?'

'Egypt, my dear Henry, Egypt. I said. I have been invited to join Mr Flinders Petrie's excavations of Daphnae at the mouth of the Nile. He's part of the Egypt Exploration Fund you know. I go by degrees. Across the Channel, then train to Paris. Then on to Rome and Brindisi and so by sea to Alexandria.'

Henry had followed him in a daze as he recited his itinerary from room to room as if each one were a port of call. 'I've never been even to London,' he had ventured, when there came a pause. 'Come to that I've never been on the train. Never had cause.'

'Excellent, excellent,' said Dr Birchall, seizing a pile of books, glancing at their spines and then rejecting them. He glanced up at Henry, 'Well perhaps not entirely excellent, in your case. Are you buying a horse today?'

Henry had not known where to begin. 'I have had an accident with my leg and my hands.'

'My dear fellow,' said Dr Birchall, 'Forgive me, you had better sit down. Tea, yes of course, tea. No housekeeper this morning, as usual. You had better come through to the kitchen and I will make what shift I can.'

When he had eventually located the wherewithal and produced a pot of tea and two cups and saucers, he said, 'Well now, how has this all come about?'

Henry looked at him thoughtfully, 'Would you believe that Reuben had a hand in it?'

'Our Icenian warrior, how come?'

'I was protecting the water meadow, his water meadow and I was set upon.'

'As was he.'

'As was he,' agreed Henry, 'I think it was meant.'

'Meant?' Birchall had mused on the word, 'Meant. Excellent, excellent.'

He had looked up, aghast. 'Well clearly not excellent at all. My dear fellow!'

Henry had felt that surge of relief he had so often experienced in Roger Birchall's company, knowing he need not put into words everything he needed to say. Things he could not, would not, begin to know how to explain to others were instinctively comprehended, assimilated and taken on to the next level of understanding.

'Just like a horse,' Henry thought to himself, not for the first time.

However, Roger Birchall's enthusiasm for Henry's mental adventures had become coupled with a growing concern for the practical consequences of his predicament as he began to understand them.

'In a way I feel very much responsible for this.'

Henry understood and did not entirely disagree. 'But not for the beating,' he laughed.

'Not directly I grant you, but indirectly...indirectly. So what is to be done? Something with horses, because that is your strength. I have an idea, a very good idea as it happens, but so little time to arrange things now. I know a man, in fact I'm staying with him in London before taking train for Dover. I know you are just what he's looking for. But so little time.'

Birchall hopped from foot to foot as if his own desire to be gone, and now Henry's need for him to stay and resolve his future, were biting each of them in turn. Finally, in exasperation at his own indecision he had said, 'Look, come to London with me the day after tomorrow and we shall see. I can wire ahead. You can always return by the milk train if it doesn't work out. That's settled then, excellent.'

All the reasons for not acceding to Roger Birchall's breakneck proposal, whatever it might turn out to be, rushed into Henry's head. But when he examined them they were already concerns of the past and had no place in his future.

'I shall have to pack some things and say my goodbyes.'

'Excellent. I am on the ten o'clock from Cambridge to Liverpool Street. Join me on it at Great Duster.'

Then the railway brake had arrived and Dr Birchall had become even more frenzied. Henry took his hurried leave.

'Until Friday then,' Roger Birchall had called.

'Friday,' Henry had replied, still not having taken it all in.

He turned at the foot of the steps, 'Oh yes, and Mr Earl is worried about Reuben in the church. He wants him out.'

'Tell him it's all in hand.'

'Is it then?'

'Everything is always in hand, my dear Henry. Excellent, excellent.'

Henry forgot his mother's commissions. She never mentioned them.

7

'I'm going to London with Roger Birchall,' he told Annie.
'When?' she asked in a flat tone.

'Friday. On the train. I've never been on the train.'

'Neither have I,' said Annie. 'That's tomorrow.'

'When are you coming back, then?' said Great Aunt Elizabeth, who had come through from the kitchen at the sound of the doorstep conversation.

'Oh I don't know,' said Henry, trying to make it sound as offhand as he could. 'If Dr. Birchall's plan doesn't come to anything I suppose I will be back by nightfall.' Aunt Elizabeth seemed satisfied at this and disappeared back into the kitchen.

'And if it does come to something?' said Annie.

They looked at one another silently and unwaveringly, Henry feeling more and more uncomfortable as her eyes held his.

'What are you looking for, Henry Turner, she said after a moment, 'Permission?'

'Will you come to the station with me?' he asked.

'No, I'll see you when you get back.'

'But I don't know when that might be really.'

'Whenever,' she said and pushed him gently away from her. 'Go on, go then. I give you permission.'

But Henry was not sure whether in herself she had or whether she was the one who had to give it. He knew he had no choice but to go and he no longer had any wish to stay, but he did not feel permitted to go in himself. To have felt that would have been to have felt free and he did not, only temporarily released.

If he felt uncertain about whether Annie had the ability to grant him permission to leave, how much less certain did Henry feel about Honeycomb. She had been out with the head baiter's team that day, but Henry rubbed her down with a straw pad and the brush that evening and washed her legs and hooves carefully, wondering to himself when, if ever, he would do this again. The doubts and misgivings he had in his own self formed an uncomfortable barricade between them and she tensed to the point of indifference. He spent a long time tending to her, time that should have been a comfort to them both, worthy of a long goodbye, but in the end he felt no more freed by this parting from the mare than he had been from Annie.

His mother would have walked with him to the station at Great Duster the next morning, but Henry dissuaded her. 'I shall probably be home again before you can blink,' he said, 'And I should feel foolish at the thought of you having waved me off so recently.'

Bailey Turner made no shift to go with him, but to Henry's surprise and gratification he put down a dozen or more sovereigns on the kitchen table, carefully stacked into a neat column between his thumb and forefinger. 'Put that in your hare pocket and don't let anyone see where you keep it,' he said gruffly, 'That's all there is.'

Henry stood awkwardly and half offered his father his hand. Bailey Turner went to take it, but then hesitated at the sight of the crooked fingers and Henry changed the direction of the gesture and swept up the tidy pile of money with it.

'You'd best be off then, boy,' his father said as Henry's mother stood on tiptoe to kiss his cheek instead and Henry wished at that moment that she were Annie Lilley.

He walked the two or three miles to Great Duster station without seeing the way, his brain churning over the mass of event and emotion that had brought him to this point, in the same shapeless way it did if ever he was denied sleep in the small hours.

So far from being exercised by the adventure of purchasing his first railway ticket and determining where and how to stand on the platform, his first awareness of his real surroundings was when he heard his name being called loudly above the steamy expirations of the engine and he saw with a start Dr Birchall waving vigorously from the carriage door he had opened.

'Where's your gear?' he asked Henry as he went to climb up into the carriage.

Henry gestured at the small carpet bag his mother had found for him.

'I haven't much,' he said again feeling dwarfed by the enormity of what he was doing.

'Up in the rack with it then,' said Dr Birchall, doing it himself as the first motion of the departing train plumped Henry into his seat.

Dr Birchall was clearly used to travelling on trains and was forgetfully unaware of how momentous an occasion this was for Henry. He prattled away enthusiastically about his own forthcoming Odyssey so that Henry felt happily obliged to assist his anticipation by nodding and exclaiming at suitable intervals, putting off the inevitable moment when he could allow himself a childlike interest in his new found surroundings.

'What did you say to the learned Mr Earl in the end about our Reuben?' Birchall asked eventually.

'I haven't seen him. It's all been so quick.'

'Oh dear,' laughed Birchall, 'What do we suppose he will do? Confess to the Bishop that he has added a dead pagan to St Mary's congregation?'

Henry, who was wondering whether he should call him Roger again, while at the same time trying to gaze out of the carriage window unnoticed, was unable to respond suitably to Dr. Birchall's joshing. He also felt a little uncomfortable about joking about his vicar, even though he had himself taken unmerciful advantage of his discomfiture on their last encounter.

'It's so fast,' he said finally, looking out of the window.

If Dr. Birchall should have been pulled up short by the innocence of his companion's remark, he gave no indication of it.

'Some people maintain,' he said without a perceptible pause, 'That this is too fast for the human frame to absorb for very long. What do you think Henry?'

'Well, if the human frame means my bones it can take a great deal and recover still,' he said. 'I wasn't thinking about my bones, and such anyway, more about my brain. It's taking it all in at such a speed. I fear I shall not get used to it.'

'Wait till you see London then,' laughed Birchall.

It occurred to Henry then that he had no idea what London held in store for him at all.

'What am I going to do in London?'

'Ah,' said Birchall, 'I have good news, haven't I said? I wired my good friend from the British Archaeological Society, Major Grayston Fitzgerald. He has been retired from his regiment a while now, part of Cardwell's reforms, you know.'

Henry did not, but made no comment.

'He is a bachelor settled in Bayswater with a smallish establishment and is need of a good groom,' Birchall continued.

'I'm a horseman,' said Henry just beginning to bridle slightly, but then looking down at his hands he cut his sentence short.

'No matter, said Dr Birchall, affecting at any rate not to appreciate the distinction. 'You are just the man. He doesn't need anything ploughing in Bayswater.'

Henry felt alone and rather frightened. He took a breath and calmed himself.

'This is an enormous step for you I know old fellow,' said Dr Birchall, 'And I know it's all been very sudden, but it will be capital mark my words. You will be there for the Jubilee too.'

As the journey progressed Henry began to get used to the novelty of the train's speed, and even to enjoy it. But he still had to stifle his wonder as, oblivious of how awesome his protégé's voyage into the unknown was, Roger Birchall prattled away happily in anticipation of his own that was to come.

So finally Henry took the bull by the horns, 'Tell me about this Major Fitzgerald.'

Birchall dragged himself back from his travels. 'Well he's Anglo-Irish. His money and land are in Ireland. He was in the Hussars until the reforms threw him onto his own resources like so many others. I came across him through the Archaeological Society. He had always dabbled and has taken more and more of an interest the more time he had on his hands. There, Henry, potted history for you.'

'And why me in particular? Why will I suit? Presumably grooms are easily come by in London.'

'Well, he's a cavalry officer, Henry. He's very particular about his horses and...well, to be honest, from what he tells me he is constantly having to let his grooms go. They don't come up to muster he says. I wired him to say I had someone very special for him to look at...well not look at precisely...makes you sound like a blessed horse yourself. Anyway I thought you and he might suit one another very well, with your interest in the diggings and so forth. Excellent, excellent,' he murmured to himself slightly wistfully. 'I say old fellow, I have rather rushed you along, haven't I.'

Henry made a conciliatory gesture and the two men fell silent. Then Dr Birchall reached down a book from his valise in the rack and having sought unspoken approval from Henry began to read.

Henry looked out the window once more at stations with names at first he barely new, and then as the distance from his homeland began to stretch and stretch, names he had never heard before at all. Then the countryside gave way quite suddenly it seemed to him to town, but not town like Cambridge, not defined town with a beginning a middle and an end the other side. Occasionally the train whooped into a tunnel with an instant change of sound and pressure, into total eclipse and out again. Each time they entered the blackness, Birchall like a man suddenly possessed leapt up to heave shut the carriage window with its wide leather belt, only to spring up to let it out again as daylight burst in on them anew. Every time it did so Henry looked out expecting to see that town had once more reverted to pasture and hedgerows, as if the tunnels were stygian ways to fields of Elysium.

But it went on and on, pressing ever closer to the railway line with every passing mile so that it seemed to Henry he was being admitted willy-nilly to an unwanted intimacy with houses always seen from the back, their occupants giving up their privacy without choice or so much as a second glance at the roaring procession of blurred strangers passing within feet of them. Streets, when the line ran beside them, became more and more crowded with living things and vehicles compounded into a hard, shapeless river moving at different speeds and in many directions; people in carts, in omnibuses, on foot, sometimes cattle or sheep being driven, and Henry saw, horses, horses, everywhere horses.

'I always forget how filthy London is,' said Dr Birchall, recalling Henry's gaze from this unending carousel, but by his words clearly aware of some of the impact it was having on a country horseman. 'Look at those houses there,' he gestured to the endless terrace that seemed to have been passing outside the carriage windows forever. 'Those houses are built of redbrick, red mind you, but look at them, you'd think they were painted all over with black lead. It's not just the buildings and the brick, it's the very air itself. To me it actually tastes, when I get off the train. It takes quite a little while to get used to it. I'm forever having to put on clean shirts. The ladies do little else but change their clothes it seems to me. That and shop.'

He laughed. 'You wait, Henry, until you see a "Particular".'

'Is that a cart?'

'Bless you no. It's a fog, a real London peasouper. Cannot see the feet on the end of your legs sometimes. People get lost in streets they have lived in all their lives. They fall in the river and drown, some of them. Excellent, excellent. Well no, obviously not excellent.' He trailed off with an embarrassed chortle.

He had no need to search for a more tasteful line of conversation, for as if asserting an unquestionable right of audience, the train began to slow down for its imperious triumph into the London terminus. Onward it snaked with a continuous steel-shod squeal like the shriek of a ploughshare on the whetstone. Over the track and points it processed at a funereal pace creating in Henry mounting excitement and foreboding. Now he could see nothing from the carriage window save for vast blackened retaining walls, unnaturally angled blind arches like some hellish nave supporting above an unseen vault whose presence could be guessed at by the lurid flicker of daylight, momentarily admitted to accentuate its irrelevance.

With a final cathartic sigh from the engine, they were delivered. Henry stood up carefully as if counting his component parts.

The world of men began to reassert itself with the fussy rat-a-tat-tat of slammed doors and voices began to make themselves heard again. For Henry this part of the epic was done. He had crossed over safely from the land to the city, leaving his people behind, and knew, as they all had known, he would not be going back that night.

8

They took a Hansom cab from the station to Major Fitzgerald's residence in Bayswater, Birchall chattering all the while about London and taking wild guesses, Henry could tell, about where they were at any one time or what building such-and-such was that they were just passing.

For Henry beginning his familiar inner examination in the face of the unknown, his emotions were not new. The excitement, anticipation and downright fear, dredged from deep within him, formed a great white glow of feeling he had had before. When turning his first furrow by himself, taking his first horses to the auctions on his own, knowing his father, in his mind's eye, was watching him every yard of the way. School days when his thirst to know things meant inevitably a bloody confrontation with his peers.

He drew comfort from this fire burning inside him, knowing it could be entered now as it had been all those times before. Knowing that from it he would emerge burnished and bright.

On their arrival Birchall leapt up the front steps which were covered with an imposing glass awning and rang the bell, calling on Henry to "come along now". But the country horseman hesitated a little and waited only halfway up.

A short, spruce, middle-aged man opened the door, deferentially stepping to one side to admit Birchall when he had announced himself, but coolly eyeing Henry hovering below.

'And you are?' he inquired.

'Henry Turner,' said Henry, not offering any further explanation, not being sure at that moment who he was meant to be.

'Oh I say,' said Birchall, 'He's with me, he's with me. The major's expecting him too.'

'I dare say,' said the doorkeeper, 'But not, I fancy, by way of the hall.'

Dr Birchall glanced rather helplessly at Henry and then back at the impassive spruce. 'Now really,' he began.

'It's all right,' said Henry, locking into his friend's discomfiture, 'I'll wait. Where should I wait?'

'Knock on the area door and see Mrs Bullace,' replied the spruce loftily.

'He is,' wrote Henry to his mother a little later, 'Major Fitzgerald's sergeant-major from the army. His name is Davies or as he said to me *Mister* Davies.' Henry underlined Mister. 'I think we will get on all right when he finds I'm a good horseman because he was in the cavalry. I wonder if he ever had a The Veil House mount? I would have known he was a horse soldier from the way his chest sticks out in front as far as his arse does behind.' He thought about "arse" and went to write "behind", but then thought that "behind does behind" would look odd. Anyway, he thought, Annie will probably have to read it to her, because I'm damn sure Pa won't. She'll probably change that bit for her. Henry wondered whether he should have written Annie a letter of her own, but perhaps she wouldn't need one just yet as she'd be reading his mother's.

Working out that the area door must mean the one in the well under the front steps, Henry had descended and knocked. It was opened by a very pretty woman with dark red hair, just like a Suffolk chesnut, thought Henry instantly.

'Mrs Bullace?' he asked hesitantly.

'Bless you now, have I the look of a married woman?' she laughed.

'*She is from Ireland,*' Henry wrote to his mother. '*Her name is Catherine Shaughnessy, but everyone calls her Kitty. Her hair is like Honeycomb's mane. She helps Mrs Bullace in the kitchen and upstairs. Mrs Bullace is the cook and the housekeeper. She's very short and round, rather like the meat pudding she made for our supper. I think she looks like pictures of the Queen.*'

He crossed out the bit about Honeycomb's mane. What he really wanted to say, but didn't either, was that she looked like the picture of Boudicca and her daughters in Miss Covington's book

Mrs Bullace sniffed a little as she looked Henry up and down in the kitchen, but Henry thought he detected a kindly twinkle in her robin's eye.

'Another groom then,' she said, 'It's to be hoped you last longer than the others. Do you like 'orses?'

'Why yes, of course,' said Henry.

‘No “of course” about it round ’ere,’ retorted Mrs Bullace. ‘Seems the last thing a groom does is like ’orses. Brandy and water, they like. Sleeping in, they like, blaspheming and tobacco, they like, ’angin’ round the area railings after scullery maids they like. Losing their place, they seem to like too. But ’orses? No, I never met with one yet liked ’orses.’

Henry wondered what he should say but was relieved of the need for an appropriate response by the ringing of a bell.

‘That’ll be you wanted upstairs,’ said the cook, ‘Kitty’ll show you. Wait in the ’all.’

‘Should I take my cap?’ asked Henry, who had never before had to wait in an ’all.

Kitty hooted. ‘Yes,’ she said, ‘Then you can salute Mr Davies and the Major in fine style, and it will give you something to hold onto, sure, if you feel faint.’

Henry decided she was joking about the salute, but all the same he was glad to have something to hold onto with his crooked hands.

Mr. Davies emerged after a moment or two’s waiting in the hall and beckoned Henry to follow him into what turned out to be the library.

Dr Birchall sprang to his feet. ‘Excellent, excellent Henry. May I present my good friend Grayston Fitzgerald?’

The other man in the room, who was standing in front of the fireplace glanced at Birchall a little sharply, while from behind him at the door Henry felt the air move when Mr Davies stiffened as he proffered his hand.

However, the Major grasped it without hesitating and said, ‘Thank you Troop Sergeant-Major, that will be all for the moment. I shall take Turner to the mews myself. Everybody calls me “Major”,’ he said, looking Henry straight in the eye. But Henry had the distinct feeling that this was said for Roger Birchall’s benefit and he made a mental note to refer to his archaeologist friend as “Doctor”.

Instead of releasing Henry’s hand when he had shaken it, the Major turned it over in his and examined it. ‘Horse tread on you?’ he inquired after a moment’s appraisal.

‘I’m not so careless,’ said Henry, the professional horseman in him sharpening his tongue for an instant at the implication of the question.

‘What then?’ said the Major, ‘You don’t look the build for a prize fighter, or if you are you’re evidently not a good one.’

Henry blushed awkwardly, realising that his pride had been taken for insolence.

‘Henry was set upon by a gang of poachers,’ Dr Birchall said and Henry thanked him silently inside.

‘Does it interfere with the horses?’ the Major asked.

‘No, only my father thinks I shall not plough a good furrow again, but I can drive and ride and manage my duties in the stable.’

‘Well let’s see, said the Major, ‘Why don’t we take a stroll through to the mews?’

He led the way back down through the kitchen and basement area and so out into the garden at the rear of the house. By the time he, Birchall and Henry had reached the gate that led out into the mews behind the terrace, they had collected a procession of all the occupants of the house discreetly following behind in order of precedence, first Mr Davies, then at a distance Mrs Bullace and behind her Kitty Shaughnessy.

The Major plunged through the gate without a backward glance and crossed the narrow cobbled lane of the mews to the double half-doors immediately opposite in the row of stables and lofts that crouched behind the more splendid elevations of their respective residences. Handing a large key to Henry he indicated that he should open up.

Henry fiddled with the lock a little uncertainly. It occurred to him that he had never until now encountered a locked stable door. As one door swung open, the little group of sightseers crowded forward together, making their presence known for the first time.

The Major turned at the shuffling and drew a breath, ‘What’s all this Davies?’

‘Now come along, come along,’ Davies barked to the other two, ‘This ain’t no peep show.’

Mrs Bullace sniffed and turned to go, but Kitty Shaughnessy pouted and called out, ‘We only wanted to see if he likes horses.’

Henry waited for what he assumed would be the inevitable reprimand, his insides churning slightly with a twinge of guilt that he had unwittingly ignited this bad behaviour. While city ways might seem strange in many respects, Henry knew the risks you ran in saucing the head baiter, especially in the presence of the Bailiff.

But the moment was interrupted by Dr. Birchall. ‘Oh I say. Does he like horses? I should say so. Henry has rare gifts, I believe. He is a noted horseman in Cambridgeshire despite his years. He is a Sensitive. A member of the brotherhood of horsemen, so I believe. A...a...’ he struggled for a moment... ‘A Melton man,’ he concluded with a note of triumphant satisfaction.

Henry stared at him in amazement, as did the rest of the little audience. Henry could see what Birchall was seeking to do. His sudden effort to defuse the situation put him instantly in mind of Annie Lilley. Even though he knew it was mainly gibberish, he felt a sudden surge of pride that Roger Birchall should even attempt to give him such a patchwork reference, tacked together from the half-heard and barely understood shreds of their conversations.

A loud silence greeted the Doctor's peroration. Everyone continued to stare at him. He, himself, looked startled, 'Excellent, excellent, he murmured, 'Yes indeed, a regular Melton man.'

Then they all looked at the Major. He pursed his lips and his eyes narrowed for a second. 'Extraordinary,' he said after moment, 'Quite extraordinary.'

Henry had an uncomfortable feeling that he had no idea to what element of the situation Major Fitzgerald was referring.

Mr Davies, who had become part of the audience, now recollected his position and puffing out his chest, drawing in his stomach and thrusting out his behind in a single pneumatic movement, he sent the two women about their business, while making no effort to follow their retreat himself. For an instant Roger Birchall made as if to go too.

The Major sighed, 'Not you, Birchall, not you. Quite extraordinary.'

There were two horses in the stable. Both mares.

'May I present Shannon and Liffey,' said the Major.

Henry approached the first named mare and touched her lightly on the shoulder, then running his hand down while breathing in her ear. She lowered her head slightly and breathed out audibly. Henry breathed in her nostrils. Under his hand he felt her muscles relax in that familiar way that told him he had made contact with her self.

Then Icingbury and the Veil House suddenly seemed very far away and so long ago, so long ago. That cold hand reached down inside him and for a moment he felt terrified and lost, a child at the horse fair again who had absently tugged at a stranger's coat mistaking it for his mother's.

The mare turned her head gently and lowering it slowly against Henry's face and breathed back into his nostrils as he had just done to her moments since. Then the second mare, Liffey, in the next stall put her head across the partition and breathed in Henry's ear, stamping slightly as she did so. The moment of panic passed for Henry.

'Well I'm damned,' said Davies barely audibly.

'Quite so, Troop Sergeant-Major, quite so,' said Major Fitzgerald. 'So Dr Birchall here is right then, is he?' he added after a moment. 'I'd say you know your horses, Turner, and I'd say they know you too, by the looks.'

'I've always been able to get inside their heads, somehow,' said Henry.

'And is he right too, that you are a member of the brotherhood?'

'I'm rather young,' said Henry wary of the question.

He had never mentioned the brotherhood of horsemen to Roger Birchall as far as he could recall and could only assume that he had talked about it with Mr Earl when he had stayed with him at Easter.

'Have to serve your time, do you?' the Major persisted, clearly not to be fobbed off.

'Well it's not quite like that either,' said Henry, 'The brotherhood doesn't have meetings or anything like that. You just grow into it when the others start sharing things with you.'

The Major laughed a short barking laugh like a dog fox. 'Sounds like my club. No. Only thing is we had a trooper once, didn't we Davies? Had some strange gifts. He'd been a horseman before he 'listed but his gifts weren't just confined to the horses either.'

'Said he had "the know" sir,' chimed in the Majordomo.

'Do you, Turner, do you have the know?' asked Fitzgerald.

'Some say,' said Henry warily.

'Well Birchall, said Fitzgerald, turning to him, 'What do you say? Does Turner get inside your head?'

'Yes, I believe he does, but I don't believe it's mystical so much. I think he's a particular kind of listener and I think he gives out a particular kind of sympathy that makes horses, and people too, respond to him in kind.'

'Well,' said the Major with only half a smile on his lips, 'I don't think I want you running around inside my head. Never know what you might find. Now, what about this?'

He suddenly changed his tone and his whole stance as he stood aside to reveal a vehicle that Henry had been only vaguely aware of in the shadows, caught up as he had been with introducing himself to the horses. He had not seen anything quite like it before today and even now on such a brief acquaintance with the Metropolitan traffic he could not be entirely certain. Was it a cab? It could not be surely. Instinctively he glanced towards Roger Birchall seeking support.

'Looks like a Hansom to me, Gray, but why?'

The Major barked his short, staccato laugh again. 'I know things are bad in Ireland, but I'm not yet having to ply for hire to make ends meet. No, it's a bow fronted Hansom. Proper gentleman's equipage I can tell you. Not so stuffy as a Brougham and I can drive it myself if I feel like it without looking like a jehu.'

Henry looked puzzled.

'Cabman to you,' hissed Davies.

'Think you can handle this, Turner?'

Henry gazed at it, with its single pair of enormous wheels and a deep black lustre that reflected like a shaving mirror. He had never before seen such a beautiful piece of carriage work. 'I should think I could,' he said, 'I suppose it's all a question of getting the balance right with the horse and the driver.' He had noticed straightaway that the driver's seat was perched at the rear above the roof height. 'Like a gig only higher up,' he added.

'Well done, well done,' said the Major, himself absorbed in the equipage as if seeing it for the first time. His hands played over the rim of the wheel. 'Notice anything?' Henry did but could not say what it might be.

'India rubber tyres,' said the Major, 'Latest thing. Quiet and fast. Damn fast.'

Henry touched them, so did Dr Birchall. 'Oh I say, excellent, excellent. Really bowl along I expect. Better watch out Henry.'

The Major gave him a sideways glance. 'Not quite your thing, Birchall, is it? All this.'

'Well not entirely.'

'Come on then. Let's go and talk Egypt over a glass of something before dinner. At least I shan't have to see to the horses tonight.'

The two archaeologists walked to the stable door. The Major turned. 'The position's yours by the by,' he said to Henry, 'Davies will show you your quarters.'

'What did he mean, "He won't have to see to the horses"?' asked Henry when they had gone.

'Well he's been grooming them mostly since the last man slung his hook. Him and me. The Major's a proper cavalry man see. Always takes a turn of an evening.'

'Why?' asked Henry, surprised.

'Officer's no different to a trooper in the field. Needs to know his horse like his sabre. Horse needs to know him too. "Sharpen your own blade and rub down your own jade". Best way. He's taken to you by the way. He knows his horses, but I never seen either of them do that to anyone else on first acquaintance. Do you catch the ladies so easy?'

As he spoke, Mr Davies climbed the wooden stairs at the back of the stabling up to the first floor and Henry followed him, not sure whether this last remark required an answer. Mr Davies' manner had softened somewhat, he could tell. He supposed that it had to do with his successfully passing the first test of his horse handling in front of a critical and knowledgeable audience. But even so, something told him that he still had a long way to go before he could count the Troop Sergeant-Major entirely won over.

His quarters above the stables were sparse, of course, but no more so than at the Veil House. There was a bell, Mr Davies had pointed out. If that rang Henry was to run to the kitchen through the garden and find out what was required, horse or Hansom. 'But the wire's so long from there to here it's always breaking. The Major is threatening to have the telephone. But what with everything drying up in Ireland, he has other expense'.

None of this made much sense to Henry. He had heard of the telephone and this was the second or third time that Ireland had been mentioned that day. But as to why the one should be dependant upon the other was a mystery to him. He silently determined to find out, but somehow felt that now was not the time nor Mr Davies his best informant. Roger would be better, he thought.

But in the event, after barely two days in Bayswater Dr Birchall repacked his valise and departed for Egypt, with the scarcest of backward glances. Henry helped load the growler when it came for him. He was not to be permitted yet onto the unfamiliar streets with the bow-fronted Hansom, so could not drive him to the terminus. 'What's amiss with the Major in Ireland' did not seem an appropriate question somehow.

'Come and see me in Cambridge when I get back, excellent,' called Dr Birchall as the growler set off.

'When will that be?' Henry called back, but all he got was a wave.

Unexpectedly, Henry's first insights into his new employer's pre-occupations came straight from the horse's mouth the very next day after Roger Birchall had departed. No longer saddled with a guest in the house, the Major having returned with Shannon from a trot in the Park turned up in the mews in his waistcoat and boots to share the evening grooming with Henry, as Mr Davies had predicted he would.

While Henry used the wisp and brush, Fitzgerald combed out Shannon's tail and forelock.

'What about the currycomb?' asked the Major, breaking the silence that had fallen as they both set about their business.

'Never use it much,' said Henry, 'Save to clean out the brush with.'

'Why's that then?'

'No sense in beating her clean, she's not a carpet. I'd rather go through her coat with my fingers if she's really mired.'

The Major smiled his half smile to himself and Henry sensed that he had just come through another test with flying colours.

'Tell me about your fingers. What was all that about a thrashing from poachers?'

Henry had wondered what he would say to any of them in the house when the question arose as surely it would. He had not bargained on the first one being the Major himself, nor had it really sunk in until that evening that he would be sharing this part of his labour in the stable with him. At the Veil House he had worked among his own, even if the head baiter was owed some respect for his office and his experience. Otherwise the figure of authority had been his father. Flesh and blood for all his distance. Yet here was a man of a different kind of distance, more than Roger Birchall, more than Mr Earl even. He was a man, perhaps, thought Henry, like the "owner" of the Icingbury estates, someone he had rarely seen but whom Bailey Turner would very occasionally have to see in Bury or still less frequently in the best parlour at the Veil House. Such a man now was in his waistcoat, unchanged, unbathed, and between them a horse who was simultaneously the object of their mutual attention.

Henry had glanced up at the question and their eyes met across Shannon's withers. But even from that brief encounter Henry sensed that there was nothing for him there, no imparted being. Not like Roger then, he thought, not like a horse. Nor yet like Annie. No reserves behind his eyes suddenly called forward to challenge or escort an advance into seemingly undefended positions. They were there, he felt sure, hidden, waiting, undeclared.

He did not know if he should feel glad or sorry. It crossed his mind that sharing a bond with the horses by working together could unite the two men, but that the strength of one could sap the strength of the other

The truth of his beating at the hands of the poaching gang was difficult enough for Henry to fathom. It contained so many ingredients that it came out differently every time he thought about it. Parts of it never really did come within his grasp although he could see them sliding away into the darkness when he tried to reach for them. He wondered whether this was the moment to introduce the Major to Reuben, but perhaps there had been too much talk about gifts and brotherhoods for the time being. So he settled for the straightforward protection of property aspect of the truth and told the Major about the wholesale taking of hares for market out of due season.

'And you say they didn't speak a word to one another throughout the whole thing even though they weren't local? Then it's a guinea to a penny bun they were Irish. Don't want to give themselves away by the brogue, d'you see? Damn Fenians. They roam about on both sides of the water, offering violence to Her Majesty here, rioting and burning on my property there, defying the constables, to say nothing of trying to beggar us all with their damn Plan of Campaign. I'd take the Dragoons to the whole damn pack of them and Parnell and Gladstone too. That's supposing we have any dragoons left after that one has finished with the army.'

Henry was astounded at the outburst. It hardly seemed to be addressed to him and he certainly did not feel he was being asked to comment. He was struck by the edge of steel that had touched the Major's tone and by the sudden replacement of his ironic self-discipline with an angry passion he did not control. He felt the mare's muscles tighten under his moving hands

For a while they worked on in silence although Henry feared the noise inside his head must be heard all the way down the mews. In the space of a few seconds he had been exposed to a fiery draught of images and thoughts very few of which had any familiar shape for him. His natural thirst to analyse information and to know new things wrestled with the natural reticence of social inferiority. While the Major might be a friend of Roger Birchall's as Henry was, that did not mean Fitzgerald would accept the same feeling of inner equality between them. Indeed it had been only too apparent that the Major disapproved of Birchall's familiarity, that it was tolerated as an eccentricity in a friendship he respected for other qualities.

On the other hand Henry was loathe to let the opportunity glide by with some attempt to capitalise on it.

'Pardon me, but who are the Fenians?'

'What?' said Fitzgerald, as if recalled from somewhere distant and slightly irritated to recollect Henry's presence.

'Fenians. You mentioned them just now.'

'Good God, where have you been all the day, Billy Boy? Fenians, Fenians, Irish trouble makers and worse, political brigands, no better than damn tribesmen. Want to live on my land rent free. And the damn government wants to let them. Thought we might get shot of it all when Salisbury came in this year, but he didn't last above a couple of months.'

Henry listened with a feeling he had had before, that something inside him was ebbing away. 'That's your land in Ireland is it...sir?'

'Damn right it is.'

'But if they're Irish and you are too...I don't understand.'

'Why the hell should you?' muttered the Major, 'There's Irish and Irish.'

Somewhere on the bank of the Icing river, a long time ago, another officer decided there was no more to be gained by the exchange and to end it.

9

If he was uneasy at the mixture of first impressions he had of Major Fitzgerald, Henry's natural need to know things, pushing him on to discover more, made him force himself not to make up his mind then and there.

Tempting as it was for him to put the Major in the box marked "Romans" and leave it at that, two things made him hesitate. First there was this man's own understanding of the self of horses, which Henry was always bound to respect wherever he found it and to pity or despise those who denied it. Second there was Fitzgerald's association with Birchall, a man who had absorbed Henry into his own self and allowed him to reciprocate.

Henry realised that Birchall's friendship with the Major was based on their shared archaeological interests, to which he had not been admitted. But he wondered whether Birchall had ever blown on those other coals that glowed inside Fitzgerald in the way that Henry had done. If he had, how then had the Doctor dealt with it?

He wanted to believe that Birchall would have been just as uncomfortable as he had been. He could not admit to being mistaken in Roger Birchall. He would rather be mistaken in himself.

Chasing it all round in his head for several days to no good purpose he suddenly lit upon the idea of writing to Miss Covington. She was not only knowledgeable he decided, but she would not question his wanting to know. The only other possibility had been Mr Earl, but on reflection Henry was not at all sure that he satisfied either of these requirements or that he would welcome a letter of any description. Lurking at the back of his mind, too, was the thought that a letter to Miss Covington would most likely fall into the hands of Annie Lilley.

After some bare preliminaries, Henry wrote to his teacher in the best hand he could manage,

I would like to know something about the Fenians and their plan of campaign. Major Fitzgerald gets most heated about them because he has

land in Ireland. He thinks the men who set about me at Easter time by the water meadows might have been Fenians,

He thought about this when he had written it and then added,

But I do not think so myself.

He agonised over this for a few minutes, trying to find ways of telling her about how important it was for him to understand the nature of the tyranny of the accepted order and the quiet life, but in the end just left it at that. Until now he had rarely written anything as long as a letter since he had finished with schooling. The ideas that he had in his head of late had stretched his imagining to the outer edges of comprehension and beyond. It was the 'beyond' he wanted to understand, but it was impossible to write it down in a way that would make any sense to someone else, even supposing he wanted to expose his self in that way.

Except perhaps Annie, he thought. But, then, she understood him when their eyes met. Not in a letter.

The days began to settle into some kind of order. At first they revolved around a few hundred yards in Bayswater, Mr Davies not being prepared to let Henry much further than the end of the mews.

'I've seen young recruits up from the country before,' he would say whenever Henry proposed taking whichever was the spare horse further afield for morning exercise, 'London can panic you if you don't know it. Take it steady, first the walk, then the trot, then the canter. Any man that breaks into the gallop before the officer gives the command gets a taste of the cat. Or used to anyways. Not now, not in peacetime. Soft I call it, so does the Major. London's like a full charge and if you're not ready, not disciplined, it'll break you.'

So Henry had to content himself with walking the mares around the relatively quiet squares immediately adjoining their own and looking with increasingly impatient longing up towards the busy Uxbridge, soon to become Bayswater, Road and the glimpsed park on the other side.

If he had had more time on his hands he would have felt even more imprisoned than he was, for as well as the restrictions on his movement imposed by Mr Davies he found difficulty adjusting to the narrow confines of the streets after the wide eastern skies of home.

From the back of a Suffolk chesnut looking over the hedges, he had come to view as unremarkable the countryside rolled out for miles around, and the great billowing washing line skies of blues and greys, challenging aching eyes to take in as near a perfect hemisphere as is humanly possible in one go.

In Bayswater's straightness Henry's landscape was elegantly proportioned rather than sweeping and majestic, created by man for men, with the Almighty's contribution glimpsed with difficulty by craning his neck upwards if he remembered.

But Henry had very little time on his hands, two horses and their master requiring a rigid timetable of attention from sunrise until well after sunset. He knew too, that his day would be as long as the Major chose it to be once he was out driving the bow fronted Hansom.

Fitzgerald's impatience to be out with his toy again was becoming only too evident to Henry during those evenings when they shared the mares' grooming.

'You getting to know your way around yet?' he would ask.

Henry told him of the restrictions Mr Davies was still imposing.

'That's all very well, but it's time you got to know the way to some of my main haunts, and I need you to become familiar with the Hansom. I cannot be doing with taking a cab every time I need to be out after dark. The club's beginning to think I've had to sell up. Tell you what you should do Turner. You should walk the course to the club for a start. I'll draw you a map. Can you follow a map?'

Henry felt sure he could and was not proposing to show any doubt, faced with the prospect of escape from Bayswater. But he felt bound to ask about the horses. What would happen to their needs if he was out walking the streets?

'Tell you what,' said the Major reflecting a moment, 'First time I'll take Shannon and you can take Liffey. You can bring them both back by the shoulder and I'll get a damn cab when I'm ready. You need to bring on a stable lad really I suppose, seeing as how it looks as though you're going to stay the distance. I'll think about it. More damn expense.'

Henry was put in mind of his father and he grinned to himself, but 'I am sure we'll manage Major,' was all he said.

'I'm to go with the Major to his club,' he told Kitty and Mrs Bullace when he was called in for his supper.

Kitty tossed her red head. 'Don't you go getting lost on the way back. There's all sorts of young girls out there waiting to pounce on a fine young fellow just up from the country. They'll have the breeks off you and the money out of your pockets one way or another and you'll never feel a thing.'

Henry blushed. 'I shall leave my money at home then,' he laughed.

Mrs Bullace pursed her lips and tutted.

Henry would have liked to have retorted something daring of his own to Kitty. Everything about her said “dangerous” and intrigued and fired him. She covered her own country simplicity with her infectious laughter, a beguiling turn of phrase and her confident beauty.

If she were a filly now, thought Henry she would not break easily to the bit or harness, nor would she take her schooling by example from an older steadier mare. He glanced involuntarily at Mrs Bullace who attempted to be disapproving, but was, herself, captivated. He felt that they were both waiting for him to take the initiative as the man in the room. Kitty had thrown down a feminine gauntlet and the little crowd grew silent with anticipation. He tried to think of something clever to say, something that would preserve his mystery, but all he wanted do was ask questions. Questions that would reveal him for what he felt he was, a bumpkin. Questions that would hand him over to be a witless plaything in the hands of Kitty Shaughnessy.

As so often when he struggled inside, he became outwardly still. His eyes instinctively sought out Kitty’s and held her gaze for a moment seeking permission to impose a restraint on her, searching as he always did for a way through to the inside. To his surprise, but immediate relief, she pointedly looked away.

Henry knew that for some reason she had retired from the field, but would fight another day.

‘Tell me about the Major’s club,’ he said to Mrs Bullace.

‘It’s the United Services in Pall Mall. It’s where he meets all ’is old cronies from ’is army days.’

‘And archaeologists?’

Mrs Bullace looked blank.

‘He digs up remains and things, like Dr Birchall who was here,’ he explained.

‘Oh them. No that’s ’is Society. They don’t meet at the club.’

‘So what did he do in the army?’

‘Questions, questions,’ said Mrs Bullace, ‘You’d better ask ’im when you’re both doin’ the horses. Strange I call that, for a gentleman.’

‘Ask him what?’ Mr Davies had entered the room.

‘What the Major did in the army’, said Henry.

‘We were Hussars,’ said Davies, ‘But the Major was never one for sitting around Knightsbridge for very long, so he was what we call a special service officer a lot of the time. We were with Sir Garnet Wolseley.’

‘In Hafrica,’ Mrs Bullace chimed in, clearly having heard this before from Mr Davies, ‘And my Bullace, too.’

'Yes, on what we call the Gold Coast. We were fighting the savages, the Ashantis.'

'Why?' asked Henry.

'Bringing them into the Empire, my lad.'

'Did they want to come in?'

'It's not a question of want. They were murdering the missionaries,' said Mr Davies.

'Why?' Henry asked again, interested to see if he could provoke the Troop Sergeant Major's pomposity to bursting point.

'It's all why, why, why with you tonight isn't it? I don't know why they were murdering the missionaries, they just were. It's what savages do. It had to be put a stop to. Very good at putting a stop to that sort of thing is the Major.'

Henry smiled. 'Did he take the dragoons to them, then, like he wants to do to the Fenians and Mr Gladstone?' he said.

Mr Davies looked at him narrowly. 'We didn't have no dragoons. Like I said, he was a special service officer. Scouting out the enemy's dispositions. Putting the fear of God into those we caught. Oh yes, the Major knew how to put a stop to it all right. What do you know about the Fenians?' he added, giving Henry an uncomfortable feeling that he had asked one question too many.

'Only what the Major has said,' said Henry, 'When we were doing the horses. Trouble makers and tribesmen I think he said they were,' he added, trying to make it sound matter-of-fact.

'You want to be very careful what you say in this house about Ireland. Walls have ears and no-one wants to be mistook, do they?' said Mr Davies.

What had started as a simple conversation to cover up his awkwardness with Kitty, had somehow taken a turn down a quite different path, Henry felt. Just when he was beginning to feel at ease with in the household and becoming an accepted part of it, he seemed to have lifted a lid and let out something vaguely unpleasant. His questions seemed to be invited at first but then everyone seemed abruptly to parry the one question too many with one of those infuriating half questions that invite no answer, but merely signify an end.

So no more questions, at least not tonight. Perhaps he should ask Kitty after all, he thought. He was aware that she had left the room, but could not recall her going.

The next morning Kitty brought Henry's early first breakfast over to the mews stable as usual for him to have while he got on with the first duties of the day.

'I've got something else for you today,' she said

Henry was bent over clearing out Liffey's night bedding and had his back to Kitty. He had heard her come into the stable and had called out good morning, but when she said this he straightened up and turned. She was standing so close behind him that their noses nearly touched as he did so.

He went to step back a pace, but Kitty put up her hand and took hold of his shirt front above his waistcoat, keeping them close.

'What is it, then?' he said

'You have to promise me something first.'

'Promise you what? he said warily.

She let his shirt go, but left her hand resting there, tapping her finger to each of her words. 'You – have – to – promise – me – if – ever – you – look – into – my – eyes – like – that – again – you'll – have – do – something – about – it.'

'Look into your eyes like what?' said Henry trying to regain his distance.

'You know, so you do, Mr Groom. No wonder you can get the horses to jump through blessed hoops or whatever it is they do for you.'

'What have you got for me?' he said

'Oh no, not so easy. What about that promise?'

'Well,' said Henry, 'I promise then,' wondering what would happen if he did look into her eyes again but at the same time vowing to himself that he never would.

Kitty moved her hand from his shirt front and rested it lightly on his cheek. 'That's a promise then, Mr Groom.' She reached into her apron pocket, 'Two letters, and both from ladies I'll be bound.'

Henry took them. He recognised both hands. The first was one he had not seen for a long time, but was still familiar to him; it was Miss Covington's. The other was from Annie Lilley.

'Aren't you going to open them, then?' said Kitty.

'No, not now,' said Henry.

'Oh don't worry about me peeking over your shoulder at your secrets Mr Groom, for I cannot read nor write neither.'

This information brought Henry up short. He was accustomed to women of his mother's generation being a bit slow with their letters, but people of his own age, like Kitty, usually had enough schooling to read and write a letter. Even Sim and Josh would be able to do that if you threatened to set the dogs on them. Somehow too it did not square with Kitty's fiery beauty and her ready tongue, that she could be so physically expressive and yet not to be able to share it at a distance on paper. It was as if she had smiled her normally entrancing smile and revealed a gap in her teeth. It must have shown in Henry's face.

'Don't you go rushing to judge me like that now, I'm just a wee colleen from Cork. Schooling is for the boys who want to be priests to have beaten into them where I come from. So open your old letters, why don't you?' she snapped

'Because I've got two hungry horses to see to now, that's why,' retorted Henry, 'And because the Major will be calling me in for the day's orders and you and I'll catch it if Mr Davies or the Major find us dilly dallying here.'

Kitty threw back her head and laughed. 'The Major,' she said, 'The Major is it? I don't think so. No I won't be catching it from him.'

But nevertheless she turned on her heel and skipped out of the stable door leaving her words in his mind where they kept surfacing and resurfacing for the next few days like a parlour conundrum nagging for a solution.

Having prepared both horses for whatever the day might have in store, Henry went through to the house to receive his orders. He waited in the hall until the Major appeared from his breakfast.

'I think we'll both ride down to the club this morning and you can bring both nags back the same way,' Fitzgerald said. 'I'll draw you that map anyway, just in case. I don't mind losing you, but I do want to see the mares back safe,' and he gave his short bark of a laugh.

Henry's spirits soared and as they did, his conversation with Annie Lilley in the water meadows came flooding into his head. Another doorway was about to open he felt sure. Finding the way to the Club had suddenly taken on a significance for him beyond simply extending his horizon. It was part of the reason he was here at all. 'It's meant,' he thought.

He saddled both horses for the first time since he had arrived in Bayswater and walked them down to the end of the mews. Some of the grooms and coachmen belonging to the Major's neighbours were at work and looked up as he passed.

'He's letting you out at last is he?' called one good naturedly.

'Mind you get back in one piece,' said another, 'There's women'll eat you alive on those streets.'

'I know, I know, I've heard it all already,' Henry called back, wondering what this preoccupation with predatory women was about. Why couldn't they just send him out for a bag of nail holes for the horseshoes or new feathers for the horses if they thought him such a yokel or whatever the city equivalent was of green horn initiation.

Henry was by now on nodding terms with the other stable folk in the mews, but was pretty much happy to leave it at that. He had found none that came up to his own standard of care for their charges, let alone any who possessed or even aspired to possess his innate skills as a horseman. Their conversation was concerned mostly with ways of bilking their employers and whether he had had his hands anywhere on Kitty Shaughnessy's person or she on his for that matter that he might like to divulge to them.

He wondered whether he should let himself be less critical for the sake of neighbourliness, but knew that if he got too close to them, it would not be long before there was a falling out over their failings in the stable. Not only that, when it came to their careless obscenity about Kitty, the same could be applied to any young woman indiscriminately. They would have just as readily stripped Annie Lilley naked with their laughter if she and not Kitty were in their sights. Henry did not wish to have to stand and listen to them do it to any woman he called his friend, as the price of a camaraderie he could easily do without.

'Which is the kind of being stuck up that gets my head butted I suppose,' he thought, 'But there it is.'

He ran the humorous gauntlet to the end of the mews and led the two mares round to wait in the street outside the house. When the Major emerged he took Liffey's bridle from Henry. He was holding a folded piece of paper in his other hand. 'Take hold of the other edge of this,' he said, 'I've drawn you that map I promised but I don't suppose you will make head or tail of it unless I explain it. Never met a trooper yet who could.'

They stood, each with a horse in one hand and the map held between them with the other.

The Major said, 'You just need to know that we are north and going south and you do it the other way round to get back here. The big squares with their corners touching are the two parks. You need to leave both parks behind you coming north and you will be back on the Uxbridge Road. It's more or less all downhill going there and all uphill coming back. Nothing to it. I should think Liffey and Shannon know the way home anyhow. Just pay attention to the route, look out for landmarks and keep your eyes off the gals in the park.'

'Oh no, not you too,' thought Henry.

Fitzgerald put his left foot in Liffey's stirrup and Henry made a step with his spare hand for his right, then mounting Shannon himself they set off one behind the other at a short distance.

‘Not too close and not too far,’ the Major called over his shoulder, ‘I’ll want to point out landmarks to give you your headings, but I don’t want you treading on my heels.’

Henry felt comforted at hearing a ploughing term that he could relate to.

After a short while they turned up Inverness Terrace at the end of which the teeming main road waited for Henry like a white rushing river to be navigated with wits and muscle. His excitement was made all the more intense by being pierced with fine needles of fear at the prospect. At the junction they turned to the left, joining the stream of vehicles and riders flowing east.

‘We go into the Park at Lancaster Gate,’ called the Major. ‘Make sure you mark it for when you come back. And watch it, you will have to cross the traffic then.’

Henry nodded grimly. The occasional journey into Cambridge was in no way a preparation for this first acquaintance with the Uxbridge Road. That the flow of traffic kept to the left-hand side of the road seemed about the only rule that was generally obeyed, but not invariably. Everyone seemed to be in a different kind of hurry and at one point Henry and the Major were being overtaken by an omnibus that was itself already being overtaken by a Hansom cab which had moved squarely into the path of the oncoming traffic.

The Major, who rode tall and impassive in the saddle amid the general din did react with some irritation at this passage, barking at the omnibus driver, who in turn passed on the comments rather more ripely to the cab driver on his right before easing his two horses back a little with a very bad grace. Henry soon realised that Shannon was far less concerned with the noise and crowd than he was.

At Lancaster Gate a policeman on point duty brought them to a brief halt and Henry took the opportunity to communicate with the mare. Under his hand he felt her muscles relaxed. ‘Why should I worry when I’ve got you with me then,’ he thought, as he felt he own self-control seeping up through him in a way that both allayed and rebuked his fears. It was a rare moment of reversal for him to feel the horse beneath him calmly take unassertive command, as if she were the rider and he the ridden.

Once in the Park Henry had a feeling that the worst was now over. While it was still busy, almost immediately he could sense a different kind of code of behaviour begin to apply. The omnibuses and the commercial vehicles had been left behind at the gate to continue up the Bayswater Road. Now for many of the riders and vehicles the Park itself was their destination and a more leisurely and courteous pace took the upper hand, denying those still trying to hurry through on more urgent business any rights of precedence.

This change of pace took the pressure off Henry's concentration sufficiently for him to allow himself a good look round. The Park's greenness, its woodiness and its apparent lack of ornamentation took him by surprise. Here was something akin to the country he could recognise just a stone's throw from the perpendicular chasms of masonry he had just left behind. He could see the sky again and the sun, he noticed, although it had an unhealthy tinge to it, appearing as a perfectly visible orb through a noonday haze. Was there going to be a storm? Henry sniffed, but there was nothing familiar on the brackish city air that he could relate to.

Crossing the bridge over the Serpentine printed another landmark in Henry's mind which the Major, riding beside him now, had no need to point out, although he did. Henry was simply astounded by the vista and the impression of vast space.

'It's huge,' he called back.

Fitzgerald barked his laugh. 'It's not. It's a *trompe l'oeuil* as the French have it.'

Henry looked at him.

'An illusion, a magician's trick. All done by mirrors,' and he barked again.

They came down onto a wide sandy ride.

'Rotten Row,' said the Major, 'Hyde Park Corner next and the old Duke's house. And over there the memorial to Prince Albert, so you need to turn off here when you go back. It's on the map.'

Henry gazed at the edifice sparkling, but dimly, through the trees to his right. 'I'm in London,' he thought, hugging himself inside with glee.

As they turned off Rotten Row to leave the Park through the huge wrought iron gates, Henry suddenly felt something strike his sleeve. Shannon skipped nervously and he steadied her. Glancing towards the Major who had gone slightly ahead, he saw that they had both been at the receiving end of a shower of horse dung.

Two men who had been hidden by the gatehouse stood long enough for Henry to hear one shout, 'It'll be something harder next time Fitzgerald,' before making off at a run down the main road to be lost amongst the general passers-by. The Major dismounted and so did Henry.

'Damned Fenian bog trotters,' said the Major, but not too loudly in front of the little crowd that seemed inclined to gather. 'Never a peeler around when you want one either. Still no harm done.' He brushed himself down. Henry helped him. 'I can clean up properly at the Club.'

Henry waited for him to offer some explanation for this extraordinary episode. But Fitzgerald merely muttered to himself as he remounted, 'Not a damned farthing. I'll see them in hell first.'

After this the ride down Constitution Hill and Henry's first sight of Buckingham Palace had some, but not all, of the wonder taken off it. Then they were up past the sentries at St James's Palace and into Pall Mall.

'It's all on the map,' said the Major, who had totally recovered his composure, as he pointed them all out to Henry. And so they reached the club.

'Journey's end,' said the Major as they dismounted at the corner of Waterloo Place. 'You can water the horses round the corner there in Spring Gardens. You'll see the milkmaid with her cows. Now, can you manage these two back to Bayswater?'

'It's a bit late now if I cannot,' thought Henry as he voiced his assent.

'You'd better look sharp,' said the Major, 'I think we're in for a Particular,' and he strode up the steps between the columns and disappeared through the doors of the club.

It had come upon them like an unnatural dusk as if the daylight at noon had been nothing but a room full of candles that someone had quietly gone round snuffing out while everyone chattered on not noticing until only a handful were left burning. As Henry began to retrace his journey, having watered the horses and secured them at the shoulder, the fog began to get steadily thicker. It was impossible to say where it came from or how. Henry could have persuaded himself that it was seeping out of the very buildings that hemmed the streets, or that the road and pavement stones had lost their metal letting it rise like a vapour from a subterranean swamp. It was yellow, unwholesome and harsh. It subverted normal senses, dimming the sight, dulling the hearing. It transmuted the natural feeling of time and place and substituted an eerie, flat, fragmented world which might terminate abruptly, giving way to dark, headlong chaos.

After a while Henry had made sufficient slow progress to take him some of the way in what he was still confident was the right direction. He had recognised the sentries in St James's, hearing their boots stamping in the gloom before their outlines became visible. Very shortly after that he decided to dismount and continued on foot holding Shannon, the lead horse by the head. Strangely he began to feel not lonely, but alone. It was as if the rest of the world having been made more and more insubstantial by the fog, had gradually been swallowed up altogether, leaving only a muffled trace of its presence in his ears.

Perhaps they all had a place to retreat into when the fog came down that Henry did not know about. He put his spare hand over his shoulder and stroked Shannon's muzzle for comfort. 'What had we best do, my lovelies? This is getting worse by the minute.'

He had no idea how long the fog was likely to persist or whether it would dissipate as swiftly as it had come. His experience of fog in the country told him that it could hang around all day and lift at nightfall only to return at dawn. But this Particular was like nothing he had come across in Icingbury and he did not trust his country lore to read it correctly. 'But if we stand up,' he said, still addressing the mares, 'You will get chilled in no time.'

'Say what, friend?' A man's voice came out of the yellow nothingness around them.

'I cannot see you,' said Henry.

'Are you lost?' The disembodied voice came again.

Henry did not know what he should say. He was suddenly seized of the fact that if he moved any further he probably would be lost, but at the same time he was not at all sure it would be a good idea to reveal this to an unseen stranger. The recollection of the unsettling incident at the Park gate in the morning came flooding into his head. 'I still cannot see you,' he said again.

'I'd say you were lost friend. I'd say you would be lost even if there were no fog neither, by the sound of you.'

Henry thought about the voice. It sounded friendly, almost as if it was someone known to him. 'Yes I'm afraid we are a little lost probably,' he said.

'Well I'd be happy to set you on your way, friend. Where are you headed?'

'Bayswater,' said Henry, finally deciding to trust his instinct.

The voice materialised into a figure in a cloak pulled up around the lower half of his face against the invasive fog and an indefinable wide brimmed hat. Henry wished that he too had at least a muffler, but the weather had been clement enough that morning for a mid-October day and he was clad only in his sleeved waistcoat.

'Here friend, take mine, else you'll end up spitting blood. I have my cloak anyway.' As if he had read Henry's mind the stranger took his muffler from beneath his cloak and handed it to him. Henry thanked him and wrapped it round his mouth and nose. It had a familiar comforting smell to it that reminded him of home.

'Bayswater eh? Seems a shame to walk when we could both ride,' the man observed.

'I'm not sure,' said Henry doubtfully. 'The horses are not mine, they belong to Major Fitzgerald.'

'They may not *be* yours precisely,' said the man, 'But they are evidently friends of yours. So I would think they would be friends of mine too,' and at that he loosed Liffey from Shannon's shoulder and swung himself up into the saddle.

'Oh well,' thought Henry, 'Why not?' and he swung himself up onto Shannon.

They walked on slowly into the fog keeping close beside one another.

'You're a long way from home then, friend,' said the man after a while.

'I'm from Icingbury,' Henry replied.

'Do you miss it?'

Henry was slightly taken aback at the question. It was not the one he had been expecting next. 'Well it's home, so I suppose I miss it.'

'I miss it,' said the man.

'Miss Icingbury?' said Henry feeling rather stupid.

'I miss home,' said the man.

'And where's that?'

'Do you know, I've been gone so long I can barely remember.'

Henry felt disconcerted and relapsed into silence as did his companion.

'Lancaster Gate if I am not mistaken, friend.'

Henry was amazed. In the enveloping fog he had been unaware of time passing and they seemed hardly to have come far enough. But Lancaster Gate it most certainly was.

'I'm truly grateful. I think I can do it from here.' he said.

'I'm sure you can,' said the man dismounting.

'I'm sorry, I don't have a shilling,' Henry said.

'I don't need a shilling. Pay me the favour when you can.'

'How might that be, then?' said Henry.

'Well, if it's meant, it's meant.' The man turned and walked away into the fog.

'What's your name?' Henry called after him, but the silence of the Particular all but swallowed the reply. He strained to catch it as one might hearken after fading hoof beats, thinking still to hear his words printed in the fog long after they had ceased to resonate.

He patted Shannon's neck, 'Did you hear him say it was Reuben? I'm sure I heard him say it was Reuben. Now wouldn't that be odd.'

The fog was beginning to clear as rapidly as it had appeared when Henry arrived safely back at the mews and he realised he still had the stranger's muffler.

10

It took Henry a long time to rub down both horses. He had to brush them turn and turn about, putting a blanket over one while he attended to the other. He paid particular attention to their nostrils to be on the safe side, not being sure what the after effects of the pea souper might be. He knew how he was feeling himself and he, unlike the two mares, had had some protection from the borrowed muffler. In the end he decided to make up a steam bucket for them with pressed hay and boiling water and treat them as if they had signs of a cold. It would do no harm.

He started to wonder what his neighbours in the mews would have done with two horses to care for and guessed he already knew the answer to that. Still, the Major had talked about some help which would be no bad thing, Henry thought. There would be many other days like to today when his employer could not be expected to put in a personal appearance in the stable to share the grooming. Perhaps he would seek Mr Davies' advice about keeping the subject alive.

Before supper he eventually had an opportunity to return to the letters he had received that morning. Turning them over and over he pondered which to open first. Part of him said that he should open Annie's first out of loyalty, but at the same time he felt perhaps he should save it. Keep the best till last. But a little piece of him, deeper down, feared what it might say or worse still, leave unsaid. Eventually reasoning that if he was to be admonished in some way by Annie's he would be in no mood then to absorb the contents of Miss Covington's, he opened hers first. But the little voice deeper down mocked him for his cowardly procrastination.

Miss Covington wrote,

The School House
Icingbury
10th October 1886

My dear Henry,

I was so relieved to receive your letter and to learn that all is well with you.

Your sudden departure from Icingbury, has been the subject of a great deal of chatter and, although I would not listen to any kind of idle gossip, I was myself concerned that you had not been able to look in at the School House to say goodbye.

I spoke to your mother after church, but she, poor woman, seemed as perplexed as I, although I did not have an opportunity to speak at any great length to her as your father always seems so anxious to be on his way after he has dealt with his Maker. I have, naturally, spoken several times to Annie at the School House but I have to say, Henry, I cannot believe she does not know or understand much more about the reasons for your going than she confides to me. Although, as I have said, I set no store whatsoever by ill-founded tittle-tattle. Annie did confirm what your mother at least told me, that you and your father feel there is no future for you at the Veil House after your injuries. While I can well believe that your father would take such a view, I cannot help thinking that you have other reasons of your own for falling in with his thinking. I do not seek to pry any further, but I want you to know that you have a friend and champion here in me if you ever need one. Indeed I was heartened to receive your letter, thirsting as ever after knowledge although I must say, somewhat alarmed by the subject.

You ask about the Fenians. I cannot help feeling that these days this is not a term you should be using as it will suggest that you do not have an open mind on the vexed question of Ireland. People with inquiring minds should keep them open to persuasion. I have always urged that on any inquiring minds with which I have had dealings, although I fear that in Icingbury yours was one of the very few such. There are those who seek to obscure the difficult questions of the future government of Ireland and the undoubtedly desperate plight of her poor on the land with abuse and violence. The use of the very word, Fenian, is a symptom of that. Mr Gladstone, for whom I have a great deal of respect, has attempted to bring some relief to the Irish tenants. Some men in Ireland have made what they call the Plan of Campaign, I have read in the newspaper. I suspect your Major Fitzgerald may have fallen a victim of it. As far as I can ascertain, by this so-called Plan, tenants have banded together to refuse to pay the full amount of rent they owe but only what they can afford. It is not upheld by law, however, and one can understand that landlords such as the Major feel they must resist it.

Yet I cannot but think that the conviction of the poor Irish, that they have no recourse but to act directly, is brought about by desperation and not by greed. To call them Fenians, is to heap further abuse on them by calling them murderers, for that is what is meant by it since the terrible assassinations in the Phoenix Park, and in my experience if you give a dog a bad name he will eventually live up to it. So what started as men of ideas trying to change things by the power of oratory, has now flowered into a brotherhood of hate and violence. They sow violence in this country, particularly aimed at landowners like your Major Fitzgerald, and as they sow, so they reap, since the authorities and your master exact retribution in Ireland.

My advice to you, dear Henry, is to keep your thoughts to yourself on these matters, for your Major will not thank you for having an opinion that may not accord with his own. You and I, however, should dwell on the lesson of Boudicca who died rather than submit and put thousands of her oppressors to the sword before they took a similar revenge. When a people feels oppressed, its oppressors would do well to recognise themselves for what they seem to be, not what they think they are. Harmony cannot be imposed by force and in the end destruction destroys the destroyer physically, or spiritually or both.

After that, perhaps I should say 'here endeth the lesson', which reminds me that Mr Earl was inquiring whether I had heard anything of you. I said I would be writing to you and he asked me to remind you that he still has something of yours. I hope this makes some sense to you, for I could not elicit anything further from him. I do hope you will write again soon to your good friend

Charlotte Covington

Henry read and re-read the letter. It was the first he had ever received addressed to him personally and those that he had read second hand, passed on by his father tended to be from seed merchants or veterinarians, or occasional distant family news which his mother would get him to help her with. Miss Covington's was a real letter to him with the shining tips of ideas in it like glow worms marking the churchyard path after evensong.

Although it only made him want to ask more questions rather than satisfying his curiosity, it provided enough pieces for him to begin to fill in with some colour and depth the outline of the Major that until now was all he had. Miss Covington's reference to Boudicca both pleased and intrigued him. He was pleased that she had remembered his interest. He felt like he had felt as a schoolboy when his efforts had been rewarded, even though it probably meant that he would have to keep his wits about him in the yard afterwards. But he was intrigued that she should apparently side with Boudicca, and in such a way as to suggest that despite everything that her letter urged on him, her own mind was far from open on the question of Ireland and the Major's position as a landlord. She was signalling how she wanted him to think without positively planting thoughts that would leave him with no alternative but to think the worst of the Major.

Henry wished that he could ask Roger Birchall. He was warming to the idea of writing and receiving letters and wondered whether he could ask the Major for an address that might eventually find him. The irony of using the Major as a go-between for the possible demolition of his own character was not entirely lost on Henry so he rather guiltily decided to let the idea pass, at least for the time being, especially as the Major would find it extraordinary enough that his groom should wish to write to his friend.

And so he came to Annie's letter.

Veil House Farm
Icingbury
Sunday

Dear Henry

Your mother asked me to read her your letter and I said I would reply for her. I am reading this to her as I go along. She says she is well, but tired since you have left. That's not because you have left she adds. She misses you and hopes you will write some more letters about life in the big city. Your father is also well and would send his best to you if he were here but he is over at the stable. The horses are all well, although Honeycomb played up terribly for a while and behaved badly when anyone tried to put her in harness. The little horse you brought back from Cambridge that time is also well and ready to be gentled soon. Your mother says she wishes you could have the gentling of him, as there are none so good at it as you now you are gone. Our Great Aunt Elizabeth is well too although she always complains she is not getting any younger and needs me more and more to do things. She told me to say if I was writing, that you are a cruel boy to leave us so, but I have tried to explain it to her as best I can. Miss Covington had a talk with your Mother the other day after church and said she would write to you too. The Vicar keeps asking me if I am writing to you. He was very strange to me and wanted to know if I knew what had happened to the bones we found in the meadows. I said I did not and he said to tell you he had been asking.

Although the weather is better, the land is in a poor state, for certain. Your father was very down about the harvest and says he might just as well have ploughed it in. The day men have very little work now and cousin Sim is still talking about going over to Bury and enlisting. But you know what he is like even when he cannot afford a mug of beer. In any case he would have to walk there. Josh Makepeace asked if I had heard from you and hoped your hands were better, as do your mother and I. I thought that was good of him.

I am not reading this out. You must not pay any heed to what Miss C says about me, if she does. You and I both know what the village is like about us and this is no different. Take care of yourself and write again to your mother, who sends all her love as does

Your loving cousin

Annie

Henry read this one over and over again too seeking vainly for some clue as to how Annie was really feeling about him after his abandonment of Icingbury. Her valediction in the letter meant nothing, since she had been reading it aloud to his mother. It was the kind of pretty formality that Miss Covington had insisted on when they had had to practise their correspondence in the schoolroom.

Recalling this, he snorted with laughter at the sudden recollection of one such practice letter that Sim had had to read out laboriously. He had protested that he could think of no-one he would want to write to. Miss Covington had told him to write a letter to Josh Makepeace, sitting next to him about something that had happened at home recently and to conclude it just as she would wish to see it. So Sim had written,

Our pig is dead and turned into puddings, but not so your friend,
Simon Lilley.

Even Miss Covington had roared.

Henry's involuntary laughter at this recollection and the picture it conjured up flared up and died like a damp lucifer, leaving him spent and despondent. Part of him wanted to sit down then and there and pour out his heart to Annie. But another part of him demanded to know what was in his heart to pour out. Words written on a page might not say everything that needed to be said to explain everything he had to explain. He could not reveal what mostly remained hidden from himself, and only to reveal part would be still to conceal all.

Nor could he bring himself to burden Annie with emotions born out of self-pity, however comforting it would be to find ease this way. He had started to do that in Icingbury before he left and she had stopped him then. How much more dispiriting would another letter be from her that continued to say nothing as this one did, or worse one that accepted his withdrawal from her and reciprocated it. A letter were best left unwritten, he thought, if it needed him to be there, looking in her eyes as she read it.

So he resolved to continue talking to Annie through letters to his mother. That way she would be forced to read them and to reply without having the opportunity to stop up the doorway into her own self which Henry had made her leave open as he set off through his own.

'Mrs Bullace,' said Henry one breakfast time a few days later.

'What is it my duck?'

'Do you know anybody called Reuben round here?'

'That rascally boot boy at number three that's always 'ollerin' after the deliveries, I b'lieve 'is name's Reuben. Why, what's 'e been up to?'

'No, nothing,' Henry said hastily, 'I just met someone in the fog the other day, that was all. It's quite a common name then, is it?'

'Well, it's quite poplar, I b'lieve. These old Bible names are, just now, although they're not my cup of tea, 'zactly. I prefer the proper old names like yours. 'enry, and 'orace. 'Oratio now there's a good one, after Nelson and 'is eye.'

'I knew a Reuben once,' said Mr Davies, 'He was a quartermaster sergeant out at Hounslow Barracks. That was his surname though,' and he went back to his newspaper, carefully running his finger down the columns, his mouth silently framing the words as he did so.

'Could I look at the newspaper, do you think Mr Davies?'

'Well now,' said the Majordomo, 'This is the Major's newspaper. It has to be spick-and-span when I take in his breakfast. Can't have everyone in the house poring over it before the Major.

'Well what happens to it after he's done with it?' said Henry.

Mr Davies shot him a look. 'Questions, questions, questions, you are, Turner. I've said it before. Too much backchat by half for a trooper.'

But it was not said that unkindly. Henry's supposition that he would command respectful tolerance in a cavalry household because of his own horse skills was proving correct.

Mrs Bullace cut in anxiously, 'I can't 'ave you takin' the paper. I need it for me spills.'

'Well, could I have it the next day and pass it on for spills the next?'

'What do you want to messing with the paper for anyhow?' asked Mr Davies.

'Well,' said Henry, 'There's a lot going on in the world that I don't know about. It didn't seem important in Icingbury, I suppose, but in London, people seem to expect you to know things.'

'Like what?' Mr Davies said suspiciously.

'Well, like Ireland for a start,' said Henry, and by the look Mr Davies gave him, wishing he had not.

‘What about Ireland,’ said Kitty Shaughnessy, coming into the room at that precise moment, ‘I’ll tell you all about poor Ireland, so I will.’

‘So you will not,’ said Mr Davies, ‘You’ll be about your chores my girl. Poor Ireland, indeed. Don’t let the Major catch you poor Irelanding.

‘It’s men like the Major…’ began Kitty.

Mr Davies reddened angrily, ‘Enough, out of it.’

Henry went out too, to wait in the hall for his day’s orders.

‘I mean it,’ said Kitty, ‘I can tell you things about old Ireland now that you’ll never see in any old newspaper. Anyway if you do, you can read it to me in exchange. There how would that be now? It’s settled then, I’ll bring it over to you when Mr Davies has done with it after the Major.’

Not a good idea at all, thought Henry. But he forbore to say so. After all she was extraordinarily beautiful. What man with only two horses for company would seriously refuse her a visit?

‘You’re not supposed to come over to the mews after supper,’ he said lamely, ‘Mr Davies...’

‘I go where I please in this house, Mr Groom, and maybe I’ll tell you why,’ Kitty said.

‘I am sure we would all like to be told that, if and supposing it were true.’ The Major had appeared on the stairs to deal with Henry in the hall on his way in to breakfast.

Kitty Shaughnessy tossed her red head and swirled up past him to continue her chores. Henry held his breath waiting for the icy summons he felt sure must recall her. But none came. The Major finished his languid descent without a second glance at her nor apparently a second thought.

‘We’ll take the Pride-and-Joy out today, don’t you think? A couple of turns round the Park and then you can set me down at the Club for luncheon. Wait for me in Waterloo Place and drop me back afterwards. You can exercise Liffey when we get back and clean the Hansom this evening, I shan't be needing to go out in it again.

That would be a lot of work by lamplight, thought Henry. It was barely two months to Christmas and the days were fast drawing in. Still, he was excited at the thought of taking the bow fronted Hansom out into the Park, where undoubtedly it would turn heads. Until now he had had to content himself with a few practice runs around the neighbouring streets and squares to get the feel of the vehicle and of Shannon in harness too.

The morning went like clockwork. Henry handled the carriage well and his relationship with Shannon had clearly developed into a partnership of trusted friends. This drew more than perfunctory admiration from Major Fitzgerald when Henry set him down in Pall Mall.

Because of the configuration of the Hansom's driving position high at the rear he had had a good view of how the horse was being handled from the interior.

'Very impressive, Turner, very impressive. Like to see you drive a field gun carriage over the rough. You talk to them don't you,' he said, patting the mare's neck as he spoke, 'Talk to them through your hands. Same as when you're grooming them. I could see it coming down the reins. Like this telephone they want me to put in. You must show me how it's done, Turner. Let me into your damn brotherhood. Back here at two. Listen for Big Ben over there if you haven't a watch, that's what it's for,' and with that he strode up the steps of the club and in through the front doors.

Henry stood the Hansom up with the other gentleman's vehicles that were collecting in Waterloo Place. There he spent the next couple of hours occasionally walking Shannon round the square, chatting to others of his calling and showing off Major Fitzgerald's Pride-and-Joy to them while they attempted to hide their professional awe through that mixture of ironic back chat and apparent deep knowledge of its technical specifications.

All the while, too, Henry kept more than half an eye open for his guide in the fog, anxious to spot him again. But the more he looked into the faces of the passers-by, the more he realised that even though he had felt the familiarity of a friend in his company, he would not recognise him again unless he made himself known first.

At two o' clock sharp, as Big Ben boomed across the park, Major Fitzgerald reappeared and told Henry to 'get down. I will drive back. You sit inside and pull the blinds down. Mayn't be seen driving my damn groom, may I now, but I'm damned if you're going to have all the fun.'

So Henry found himself driven home, reclining unseen in the deep-buttoned leather interior.

'Looks like rain,' said the Major when they arrived back in front of the house, 'Better put the P and J away before you take Liffey out.'

Henry did not think it looked at all like rain, but he assented although after the morning's eulogy he was somewhat put out at being instructed in this little detail. Since the vehicle would have to be cleaned later anyway, he would have just as soon left it outside in the mews to make the most of the daylight. Now he would have to ask one of the lads along the way to help him manhandle it out again, he had no intention of putting Shannon to, just to wheel the Hansom a few yards.

And that will cost me sixpence or a favour, he thought, immediately wishing he had not because it made him feel like his father.

He backed Shannon and the Hansom into the stable and took her out of the shafts. 'I'll give you a quick rub down for now, old girl, and get our friend here out for while as she's fretting for a stretch.'

What with the unnecessary instructions about the Hansom and the fact that he could not really attend to the tired, soiled horse then and there as fully as he would have wished, Henry was beginning to feel a little 'put upon' as Great Aunt Elizabeth would say. He made up his mind that he would have to raise the matter of some help in the stable as soon as the opportunity arose. Perhaps the Major would be in to take a turn with the grooming later.

But not if he hasn't been out in the saddle, he won't, he remembered.

Saddling up Liffey, Henry set off for Hyde Park. He knew by now that as an unaccompanied groom he would have to keep to the Marble Arch end of the rides, as the Knightsbridge side was the afternoon preserve of the gentry. Once again taking advantage of the policeman on point duty he entered the park at Lancaster Gate and set off up the north side of the Serpentine.

Henry did not see what it was the mare stepped on that turned her foot. Looking back on that afternoon he often wondered how things might have turned out differently if he had had his wits about him.

Liffey pulled up at once and Henry leapt off to assess the damage. He ran his hand down her foreleg, but he had known she was lame and unrideable before his own feet had touched the ground. They walked back slowly and steadily. She could not be rushed, but Henry did not want the injury to be aggravated by becoming chilled so he did not allow her to come to a full stop.

Coming quite quietly up to the side turning from the street into the mews, they startled and were startled by two men who were coming out just as Henry was turning in with the mare. Muttering what might have been an apology or just as easily an injunction to watch where he was going, the two strangers shrugged themselves into their coat collars, as if stooping into a non-existent wind and scuttled off up the street in the direction from which Henry and Liffey had just come.

If Henry had thought anything of the incident at that moment it would have been that the men had been visiting one of the other stables in the mews. Idlers from outside were always dropping in to waste time with those idlers already there. But the sudden reaction of Liffey made him think again.

The mare stood stock still, her ears laid flat. At first Henry thought that her lameness had taken a sudden turn for the worse, but he rapidly sensed that something had alarmed and frozen her. Something made him glance again at the two figures hurrying away into the distance towards the Bayswater Road. The way they moved as one jogged his memory and took him back. They were the two men who had thrown the horse dung at the Major at Hyde Park Corner. By now Henry was alarmed, but his first concern was to get Liffey to move.

'You recognised them then, didn't you old girl? But they've gone now, so what's still bothering you. Something they smell of? Well now, let's see.' He delved into his waistcoat pocket and took out a small bottle of smelling salts. Walking out in front of the horse to the full extent of the rein he waved the bottle in a circular motion at arm's length. Liffey pricked up her ears and came slowly forward to the pressure of the rein.

'Yes my lovely, whatever it was they smelled of touched a spot in your memory didn't it? Still a lady should always carry smelling salts, shouldn't she? Never know when she might feel faint.'

Then he recollected himself and fearful of what the obviously ill-disposed men might have been about at the back of the Major's house, he made as much haste as he could towards the stable.

There was no activity at any of the neighbours' stables, which was not surprising since it was time for most to be out driving their employers or exercising their horses. Anyone else not involved in either of these activities would probably therefore have taken the opportunity to make themselves scarce for half an hour. Realising this Henry became even more convinced that the two strangers had not been there by invitation.

When he reached their own stable, one of the half doors was open. Henry was certain he had left both halves shut. He peered in over the bottom half. The blinds were still down in the bow-fronted Hansom and it was swaying vigorously on its springs as if of its own accord. If he had needed to ask himself a question, it was not what was going on, but whom it was going on between. It was soon answered.

First he identified Kitty Shaughnessy's voice. Whatever it was that was happening she was protesting at it, although not very effectively, nor indeed entirely convincingly either. Her objections, such as they were, were immediately overruled. Why, Henry wondered, was he not remotely surprised to recognise Major Fitzgerald's voice?

Now he had a problem. He could not take a turn round the square until the expected time of his return because he had a lame horse to attend to. While he dithered he was not deaf to the sounds from the Hansom. He felt guilty as an eavesdropper but it was guilt blended with arousal into something cloyingly sweet and undiluted. And then there was added a sharp pang of excitement as the strains of Fitzgerald's pleasure were counterpointed with those of Kitty's pain.

Henry's dilemma was resolved by Liffey who put her own head over the stable door and made greeting noises to her stable companion inside who returned them, stamping on the stone floor. The movement of the Hansom became less frenetic and Henry heard Kitty whisper something.

Taking a swift decision he opened the half door and led Liffey in talking to her in a loud voice as he did. ‘Come on old girl, I’ll go up and get something for that lame foot.’ He went up the stairs heavily and made lengthy rummaging noises in his room. After a good five minutes he came back to the top of the stairs and called again to the horse, ‘This should see you right,’ before making his descent. The Hansom had ceased moving and there was an air of recent departure in the stable. To make doubly certain Henry clattered upstairs and down again twice before very cautiously opening the carriage door. It was empty and he breathed an audible sigh of relief, knowing that he had saved his position and for all he knew, Kitty’s too.

He had mixed feelings, however, about preserving the Major’s dignity or whatever it was he had been motivated to do by his clumsy antics on the stairs. His own sexual arousal by proxy had moved from his stomach and had become a sour aftertaste somewhere in his head. The equivocal sound of Kitty’s pain was what abided now. It was deeply disturbing to him that anyone would wish to exact it from her or that she would apparently permit it.

As he had predicted it would, it cost him sixpence and a good helping of swallowed pride to enlist the aid of the stable lad from next door-but-one to help him wheel the Hansom out of the stable and to get him to agree to wheel it back again when he had finished.

‘Your guv’nor’s a tight one ain’t he? No wonder ’e can’t keep a groom, if ’e won’t ’ire ’im no ’elp.’

Henry made no response. His mind was elsewhere and besides he was in no mood to leap to the Major’s defence. He washed down the exterior of the carriage by the fading daylight, putting off cleaning the interior for some reason until it was too dark to see what he was doing properly even by lamplight. Taking out the foot mat to brush it down he found a woman’s handkerchief.

It was stained with blood.

Later he stuck his head round the kitchen door when he had ascertained that Mrs Bullace was on her own and excused himself from supper, saying that he would have bread and cheese for himself over at the stable and some warm stout for the lame mare he had to care for.

Much later still, as he lay in bed, Mr Davies’ unembellished remarks about the Major in the Ashanti campaign kept buzzing in his head. He realised that he must have stored away what had seemed at the time no more than a manner of speaking, insignificant puff said in passing. Now they thrust themselves to the forefront demanding to be reconsidered. He thought about Reuben, his Icenian and heard himself saying to Roger Birchall on the banks of the Icing, 'I can see them. They had done things to him'.

Henry could see them now too and they were Troop Sergeant-Major Davies and Major Grayston Fitzgerald.

Perhaps he would find a way to write to Dr Birchall after all.

11

Henry made sure that he was not alone with Kitty for the next few days. He could not face her. Pleading the lame mare he contrived to eat his supper by himself in the stable and take his first breakfast generally when she was already busy upstairs.

Major Fitzgerald's own behaviour towards Henry was unchanged which both irritated and relieved him. He did not request Henry to take him out in the Hansom either in the days that followed, contenting himself with taking one or other of the mares out in the park. As it happened he was called for by a fellow member on his club days but whether by accident or design Henry could not make out. Certainly the Major did not avoid Henry in the stable, taking the master's share of the grooming on several occasions as he had done before.

On one of these evenings something prompted Henry to mention the men who had insulted them at Hyde Park Corner.

'I've seen them again, I think.'

'Where? In the park?'

'No, Major, round here…it was…a few days ago.'

The Major stopped brushing. 'When precisely? Didn't it occur to you to mention it? Good grief Turner, what were you thinking of?'

Henry flushed. 'It was the day…the day Liffey went down lame on exercise and I had to walk her home early. I'm sorry; I was concerned for the horse. It must have gone out of my head.'

Fitzgerald looked at him levelly across the mare. 'Well I expect you to be concerned for me as well. These are troubled times for those like me. You know what I mean, I think. Now consider man. What day was that precisely?'

Henry knew well enough when it was, but he made a pretence of counting back on his fingers and getting it wrong once before he settled on the day.

'And they were here? Actually in the mews?'

Henry nodded, 'They were coming round the corner as we were turning in.'

'Do you think they had been in the stable here, then?'

Henry had indeed considered that distinct probability a thousand times over, imagining the two of them listening to the sounds he too had heard coming from the Hansom.

'I couldn't say for certain.'

The Major stopped his brushing and was silent. Then he said abruptly, 'You finish up here Turner,' and strode out of the stable.

Henry wondered what had made him raise the subject when there had been no necessity. Yet again it felt as if he had found a room in the house where no-one went even though the door was unlocked and left slightly ajar. Just by opening his mouth he was being tempted to enter, but if he did he would have to take someone's side.

As he was finishing for the night and sweeping through the stable, the closed half of the stable door opened quietly and Kitty Shaughnessy slid into the lamplight. 'I've brought you the newspaper. The Major's done with it and so has Mr Davies.'

She spoke softly, unusually, Henry noticed. He thanked her and there was a catch in his voice, too, that must have betrayed his awkwardness at this deliberate and unaccompanied encounter for the first time in more than a week. He expected that Kitty would make some teasing remark at his evident discomfiture, but she did not.

'I know you've been avoiding me.'

Henry said nothing.

'Well I wish you wouldn't. I know you heard us or saw us in there. So now you know and I suppose you think the worse of me for it. And why wouldn't you?'

He began to mutter something about it being none of his business, but she cut across him.

'Of course it's your business. Sooner or later at any rate. It's everyone's almighty business in this house.' She sat down on the straw. 'I could be doing with a true friend, and you look like the only candidate for that title that I can see at the moment.'

His commonsense told him to send her packing.

Instead he sat down beside her. 'Isn't the Major a friend then?'

He listened to himself ask the question with dizzy excitement. It was a challenge to Kitty to lay her self bare, she must see that. If she gave him an answer, true or false, he was netted as surely as the hares in the water meadow had been from the moment the lurchers were put in.

She took one of his crooked hands in both hers and looked down into the palm as if she were going to read it.

'I said I'd tell you about Ireland. Something you wouldn't be reading in that old newspaper. Well now, I'll tell you. I come from a little white house in the far south of Ireland. You, Mr Groom, would hardly be dignifying it by calling it a farm. It barely feeds the family at the best of times and there are precious few of those. The Major owns it and more beside and the tenants including my father pay him rent when they can and get their heads broken by the agent's men when they can't and then still pay anyway.'

She paused and met Henry's bewildered, unspoken question.

'Somebody usually dies somewhere along the line. That's how they pay. Maybe a bairn or two, maybe an old granny. A few less mouths pay the rent. I don't suppose the Major thinks about it. He probably doesn't believe it anyway, if he knows. Why should he? He hardly sets foot there. He'll go to Egypt now, like your doctor friend, or some other old desert place, sooner.'

'But he's given you a position here, doesn't that help?' The banal dishonesty of the question sapped him. Henry felt a creeping grey helplessness start to well up inside him. He had stopped by that unlocked room and pushed half-heartedly at the door. Now he was glimpsing what it contained. Something disappointingly familiar, half guessed at so as to be a let-down. Here was no revelation that would help him to fix his wandering self, but then he had not really expected one. He had wanted to feel seduced without there being a consequence and instead he was filling a sack with rocks to carry with him through another doorway.

Kitty laughed at the question. Not her usual sparkling lift of a laugh. It was a hard, dry rattle of a laugh, a final pointless thing to be thrown in the face of adversity.

'Is that what you'd call it? A position?'

Henry was silently ashamed.

'Well I suppose it's a position of a kind,' she said, 'I'm kept here whoring for the good behaviour of my father and his neighbours. If they don't cause the Major any trouble, then I won't get into any trouble. That's the unspoken long and short of it. Only my father doesn't know the half of it.'

Henry's emptiness filled him completely.

Kitty raised his chin with her hand and looked into his eyes.

'The thing is, I don't entirely mind. I suppose that's a dreadful thing to say, isn't it? But it doesn't make him my friend. He'd never be a friend to the likes of us now would he? He's more a friend to those horses than he would be to you and me.'

Henry found himself searching her eyes in the way he had searched Annie's, looking to see if there was a way in and if so, what to.

'He hurts you though. I heard him.'

Kitty's gaze was like a looking glass.

‘I told you you’d have to do something about it if ever you looked at me like that again. Well you can be my true friend. That’s not so difficult now is it, Mr Groom?’ She put her hand on Henry’s shoulder to stand up.

‘But he does hurt you, doesn’t he?’

Brushing the straw from her dress she walked to the stable door where she turned.

‘He teaches me to play cards with him. He plays for pain and I don’t care to lose. I may not read but, Mother of God, have I’ve learned to count. Don’t forget Mrs Bullace’s spills now.’

And she was gone.

Seeing her walk through the stable door as though to put a physical barrier between him and his thronging questions, just as the Major had done only an hour or so earlier, made him go back over that uncomfortable passage he had had with Fitzgerald. Whatever had been left unsaid then, it dawned on him, the Major’s concern was not that Henry had heard him with Kitty, but that the two strangers had.

Then as he took himself off up the stairs to go to bed, he fell to wondering what had really been the purpose of Kitty’s visit to him that evening. She had certainly come straight to the point about the afternoon in the bow fronted Hansom. And that story about her family in Ireland. Was that true, he wondered? She hardly behaved like a…what was the word…? Like a hostage. In any case how would that work? If her family in Ireland were disposed to make trouble for the Major, how could he possibly use Kitty to prevent it? Perhaps it was the threat of never seeing her again or something worse. But then the Major was using her for his pleasure anyway. Perhaps it was the knowledge that he could inflict pain that was intended to keep her father quiet.

Ever since he had first seen Kitty’s hair she had been a mixture of Boudicca and her daughters going into battle in their chariot. The picture was never clear enough for him to say she was this one or she was that one. Kitty was all the noise and the colour leaping off the page.

So now Henry saw Kitty’s father as old Prasutagus, Boudicca’s husband, the father of her daughters, the Icenian king who thought he had bought peace and quiet at a price to be paid later. But when he was gone the price had changed and the currency had become pain and rape. That was what was happening here now, Henry thought, pain and rape.

Undressing for bed he emptied out his waistcoat pockets of the bits and pieces he had collected during the day as he usually did before hanging it over the back of his one chair. Amongst the otherwise unremarkable items was Kitty’s handkerchief.

He spread it out on his washstand, stretching and smoothing it with the flats of his hands as an unconscious recognition that it did not belong to him and should in truth be returned to its owner decently folded. The bloodstains had faded from vermilion to dull brown. He thought of himself giving it back to Kitty without a word. But words would be unnecessary. The handkerchief would shout at them both. The blood would speak out. She would say that her nose had bled perhaps, knowing that, true of false, it would make no difference. The blood would speak out. Pain and rape.

Henry considered the consequences of not returning it at all. She would miss it then; she was probably already missing it. If it had been lost anywhere else, dropped in the garden, in the kitchen Kitty would have it back by now. True or false, she must assume Henry had found it in the Hansom. She would be going over and over in her mind the hurried dishevelled exit. Her need to dab away her blood, even so, would be etched into her. Henry had mentioned her pain and so had she, but in an oblique non-committal way. But the handkerchief made it real. She would know that he had been a witness. The blood bound them.

In the middle of the night Henry awoke, the events of the previous evening calling in his head. A turmoil of indistinct noise. He got out of bed and lit the lamp. He picked up the handkerchief from where he had left it on the washstand. On an impulse he poured some cold water into the basin and put the handkerchief in it, squeezing it and rubbing it for a little while before leaving it there to soak.

Turning up the lamp he took out his writing things from one of the three drawers in the plain deal chest which with the washstand, the bed, and a rickety kitchen chair comprised the complete furnishing of his room. Sitting on the edge of the bed he placed the chair in front of him to use as a writing table.

Those dead hours of the night reluctantly take an unnatural and temporary shape when sleep is denied. They do not have a normal structure in which anything or anyone should expect to exist properly. Simple thoughts and actions belonging to the order of the conscious hours, themselves take on the molten substance of the dark when they are forced to be awake then.

Now Henry felt compelled then and there to make an effort to contact Roger Birchall and to seek his reassurance about his friend Major Fitzgerald, or if not, to be given some kind of absolution from his guilty knowledge. If he could not ask the Major himself how to go about this, then someone would have to approach the only other friend of Birchall's he knew, Mr Earl. But he could not be certain that the Vicar would reply helpfully if he were to write direct.

As he sat uncomfortably bent forward over his improvised desk with the blank sheet of paper in front of him, and nothing beyond the halo of the lamplight but eternal night, he wanted to write to Annie Lilley, but he could not. If it did not pour out all his doubts and uncertainties, a letter to Annie would be a betrayal. He had left it too late. Now there was too much to say, too much to leave it unsaid.

So after his crooked hand had circled and circled over the sheet of paper, as if to pick thoughts from the air and make them flow with the ink, it was to his mother that Henry wrote.

Annie would read it to her and reply for her. She might even see between the lines that other letter for her alone that would have set down all those things that would not now be written. That was a better letter perhaps than the one he wrote to his mother. Composed in those fearful hours of the night, the things his mother would really wish to know about, the daily hustle and bustle and especially the doings of the small household seemed hollow and pointless. He could barely bring himself to mention the Major or Kitty at all, knowing as he did that the picture he permitted himself to paint was a sham. He forced himself to dress up some of Mr Davies' more pithy observations together with Mrs Bullace's kitchen wisdom to provide some feeling that life in London might be broadening his mind. But for all that, it was not a good letter. At the end he added,

When you are next at church would you ask Mr Earl if he has heard from Dr Birchall, who came to do the digging in the water meadows. I need to write to him urgently about something, but I cannot ask the Major directly myself as it would not be my place. He has gone to Egypt to dig again, but I was not listening properly on the train if he told me where. It is important. Perhaps if Annie was with you she could say it was about what Dr Birchall found.

That wasn't the whole story. But Annie would know from the mention of Reuben's remains that this was deeply significant to Henry. If anything might persuade the Vicar to exert himself, it would be the prospect of getting something done about the skull and bones. And if it were not for them Henry would not be sitting here in the dark, weighted with doubt and forbidden to sleep.

When sleep did overtake him, it came so swiftly he did not put out the lamp. Because of this he chastised himself under his breath as he began to set about his first tasks of the day. It was a cardinal sin to sleep with a flame in a stable.

The mares seen to, Henry took himself back up to his loft to splash his face and hands before breakfast. The handkerchief was lying where he had left it to soak in the basin. He spread it out again and held it up to where the first morning light was showing through the gable window. It was still stained. Henry felt guilty at having tried to clean it and failed.

It was ridiculous. Just give it back to her and be done with it. There was no need for him to say anything and knowing Kitty she would probably make some flippant remark to the kitchen in such a way that none of the others would give it a moment's thought. But she would see he had tried to remove her blood and she would know why.

'Mrs Bullace,' he said, as breakfast was coming to a conclusion.

'What is it my spoonful?'

'Is there a lemon I could have?'

Mrs Bullace sucked her teeth a little, 'Lemon is it? Lemons don't grow on trees. Won't a drop of my barley water do you?'

Mr Davies looked up from his scrutiny of the newspaper, leaving his finger resting at the point in the column his eyes and lips had reached. 'I expect he wants to be making a bit of punch for one of his blessed horses, Mrs Bullace. It was warm stout the other day. Whatever will it be next? A glass of dog's nose or a bumper of the Major's port I wouldn't be surprised.'

'It's not for me and it's not to drink. There's some mildew on one of the Hansom's cushions I noticed. Lemon's just the thing my mother always says.'

'Well if your mother says you are to 'ave one, my codling, then I s'pose there's no argument, especially if it's for the Major's Pride-and-Joy. Though 'ow it should come to 'ave the mildew beats me.'

Henry could see that this seemed unlikely to Mr Davies, too, and not waiting to be interrogated further, he seized the proffered fruit from the cook's hand and fled back to the mews.

Back in his room he carefully squeezed all the juice into a beaker and then pared most of the rind into it as well. Then he stuffed Kitty's handkerchief into the compote and left it. 'Now all we need is for the sun to shine today,' he said.

When he returned from the morning exercise the sun was indeed lighting up the narrow mews and spilling into the stable through the half door. Henry retrieved the handkerchief soaked in lemon juice and hung it over a piece of twine on the largest patch of sunlit wall he could find in the stable.

By suppertime the sun's rays and the lemon's acid had done their job and the handkerchief had been bleached of its tell-tale stain. Henry folded it and put it in his pocket to take over to the kitchen. During the meal he surreptitiously took it out and let it fall under the table. Kitty or Mrs Bullace could find it later or when they swept through in the morning.

A couple of days later Kitty brought Henry the latest newspaper over to the mews before he had had time to collect it from Mr Davies himself. He was busy with one of the mares and she watched him in silence for a while as he carried on with his task in a deliberately preoccupied way, hissing through his teeth as he gave his charge an extra unnecessary rub down.

'Where did you find it?' said Kitty, at last breaking the silence without preamble, 'And don't say "find what" in that mumbly way of yours.'

'In the Pride-and-Joy,' said Henry without looking up.

'You washed it. That was good of you. Why did you do that? Why didn't you just give it back to me straight away?'

'I don't know. Is it important?'

'Seemingly so, for you to go to so much trouble. Anyone would think you were trying to hide evidence of a crime or something.'

Henry straightened up and turned to look at her. 'Pain and hurt is a crime isn't it? That's just what it was, evidence of your pain and hurt.'

'But sometimes pain can be a pleasure,' said Kitty.

'It didn't sound like it to me,' said Henry, 'Or if so, the pleasure was all on one side. What kind of pleasure is it that ends up spilling blood? And in any case, what was that you said the other day about playing cards with him? What was that all about?'

Kitty was silent for a moment and then said in a conciliatory way that suggested that she wanted to bring this exchange to a quiet close, 'Is that why you went to so much trouble to get it out? You shouldn't worry too much about it. It was only a drop or two shed in a moment. Less than nature takes every month. Mostly he gets as much pleasure and pain as he gives.'

Henry resumed rubbing down to occupy his embarrassment and confusion. With a few words she had managed to take him further through the open door of the unlocked room. Now he could see it was a room in which she herself was part of the contents, disappointing him as he had begun to recognise their familiarity.

She should be magnificently angry at her abuse like Boudicca. Her blood should cry out for justice and instead she seemed to want him to believe that it had been shed with permission as an act of complicity in her own betrayal. If he allowed himself to believe that, then he might simply find a place for his Icenian warrior in the room of disappointments and obliterate whatever was driving him to understand what the Grayston Fitzgeralds take from the earth and what they give in return.

'I've shocked you now, so I have,' said Kitty. 'I do believe you never have been with a woman have you now?' Her normal teasing laughter began to reassert itself in her tone. 'So how far have you been with the lass who writes you letters?'

Henry looked fixedly at his crooked fingers as they worked their way through the mare's coat and thought of Annie Lilley's loving months of care for his broken body. Bitter tears started in his eyes and he did not turn. '

She wrote for my mother,' he said, 'Not for herself.'

'Well, well now. And perhaps you and I should climb aboard the Major's Pride and Joy then.'

'Don't,' said Henry.

Her voice softened and the laugh went out of it again. She put a hand on his shoulder blade. 'Perhaps we should, you know, Mr Groom. Perhaps it would be good for the both of us.'

The stable bell wire tightened and snapped before it could transmit a summons and in a few moments Mrs Bullace could be heard calling for Kitty down the garden.

'I thought you wanted a true friend,' said Henry as she turned to go, 'What kind of a friend would I be if we did? How would I be any different to the Major?'

'Dream about me and ask me again. But don't be taking too long about it.'

She opened the door and was gone from sight, so that only her voice carried through. 'I might just change my mind you know.'

12

About a week later Mr Davies came into the kitchen at supper time with the post in his hand. 'One for you again, Turner,' he said, managing to convey a mixture of slight disapproval and grudging admiration.

The Troop Sergeant-Major was never known to receive a letter himself and it was clear from his attitude to Henry's deliveries he regarded them as an achievement bordering on a liberty.

'That'll be from your young lady then,' Mrs Bullace surmised expectantly.

Kitty darted up and snatched the envelope from Mr Davies' outstretched hand before Henry could take it.

'No!' she cried exultantly as she made a pretence of scrutinising the address, 'It's from his mother. His young lady, if there is a young lady, does not write for herself.'

'Whatever do you mean, Kitty, you wicked little jam pot?' asked Mrs Bullace, 'I made sure 'enry 'as mentioned a young lady. Well then, 'enry Turner, is there or isn't there?'

They all looked at him and waited. Henry visualised himself walking out of the door without a word, but knew thought of escape was hopeless. He called out silently to Annie, standing at Great Aunt Elizabeth's gate watching him approach with that calm half-smiling look at his discomfort.

'It's from my cousin Annie,' he said thankfully to his tormentors, 'She's a widow and lives with our aunt. She writes for my mother as Kitty said.'

'Oh dear!' said Mrs Bullace, suitably disappointed, 'A widder, just like yours truly.'

But Kitty gave Henry a look of immense satisfaction as she stood over him and offered him his letter. He grasped it and she held on to it, too, for a fraction. He met her eyes, searching for a mere second, but they instantly became like a looking glass again.

'We don't get many letters,' said Mr Davies. 'The Major does of course. Writes all over, does the Major, about his antiques and such and his expeditions. Bullace don't get many letters, and of course Kitty don't know a soul who can read or write anyhow, do you Kitty?'

He glossed over his own complete lack of correspondents, but his confidential manner indicated that he regarded Henry's as a windfall to be shared among them. Henry sensed he was being painted into another corner.

'Talking of expeditions, has the Major heard from Dr. Birchall since he left for Egypt?' he asked as innocently as he could manage.

'Oh that's right,' said Mr Davies, 'The gentleman who doesn't know his place.'

'Is that what the Major thinks?' asked Henry deciding to chance his arm and attempt to move the conversation further away from his letter.

'Dr Birchall is what we call a scholar,' said Mr Davies loftily, 'And as such, his mind is on other things. The Major knows him because of his Society, expeditions and such. Dr Birchall is not army, not the Club. And no, I don't believe he has heard from him, even supposing that were any of your business. But I forgot. He's a great friend of yours isn't he, now? Curious that, for a farm boy. How does that come about?'

Henry considered. There didn't seem to be any harm in revealing something of the origins of their friendship. It might serve to take Mr Davies down from his high horse a little. So he told the kitchen assembly the plain facts of the first discovery of the skull, how he had fetched Dr Birchall to the scene, the discovery of the rest of the skeleton and how Birchall had deduced they belonged to a long dead ancient British tribesman.

'Well I'm blessed,' said Mrs Bullace. ''Owever did he puzzle that out?' making no shift to disguise her interest in the unfolding tale, unlike Mr Davies whose face indicated that he realised he had been out-manoeuvred by a tactician and lost control of the kitchen.

Kitty, her elbows on the table, rested her chin in both hands and stared silent and unblinking at the storyteller.

In the face of such satisfying responses, Henry was almost tempted to throw Mrs Bullace an exotic titbit from beyond her comprehension, the merest hint of Reuben's occupation of his horseman's head. But his pride stayed him, loathe to squander his real gift in a momentary act of vanity.

Instead he said, 'It was the way the bones were found mainly. It made it look as though he had been executed at the edge of the river. I…we…that is Dr Birchall worked out that the Romans had probably been trying to get some information out of him about the rebellion.'

'Taken by a scouting party I expect he was,' interjected Mr Davies, the hurt look disappearing from his face and replaced with one of renewed interest.

‘Often a good spot to wait for a chance prisoner for interrogation, by a river. Especially if he was mounted. River slows them down you see. Might have wanted to cross it, but he’d have to pick his spot. Might have to reconnoitre up and down on foot, leading the quad. Might even have been off his guard, watering the beast, both taking a drink, horse’s head down, him flat on his stomach. If there was a track down to the edge, that is where I’d have waited. Chargers out of sight in the trees and hooded with their troopers’ tunics to keep them quiet. Three good men at the edge of the track, hunkered down. One a little ways up with his shaving mirror to flash from behind when m’laddo has passed him by. One flash, man alone. Let him come, let him come, gently, gently. Wait for him to dismount. If he goes straight in mind, wing the horse to throw him in the water. But he won’t, he won’t, he’s tired and scared, his mouth is dry. It’s late afternoon, it’s been a long day. He’ll take a mouthful, fill his bottle. Then you have him.’

He fell silent and stared into a dark corner of the room.

‘Then you have him. That’s when they talk.’

‘Then what would you do, Mister Davies?’ said Henry quietly.

‘Take him to the officer, of course.’

‘That would be the Major would it?’ said Henry

‘Well he wasn’t a Major in those days. He was a captain.’

‘And he asked the questions?’ said Henry, his voice becoming still softer.

‘You could call it that.’

‘What would you call it, Mr Davies?’ Henry almost whispered.

‘I’d call it asking questions if I was in mixed company.’

‘Ooer,’ said Mrs Bullace, breaking the spell, ‘Was this in Hafrica?’

‘Some of the time,’ Mr. Davies had regained control of his kitchen audience again but only because Henry had triggered something from inside him. He could not have done that deliberately with Mr Davies, could not have looked into his eyes and beyond the guardians of his self, still less have laid hands upon him and talked directly to it.

Davies was not a willing horse like Roger Birchall, advancing to meet him halfway, still less was he like Annie who lovingly coaxed him to be a worthy champion and dared him to succeed. Mr. Davies did not offer any doorways into his self. They had long since been stopped up, if they had ever been there in the first place. Henry had opened one unawares with a magician’s word, releasing a flood of pent up experience and memory. Things put away in boxes marked ‘best forgotten’.

The way was still open for a moment maybe. He felt a surge of wicked exultation, sensing he might kick wide the entrance, march on in and loot whatever he might find.

'I didn't suppose the tribesmen would have ridden horses in Africa.'

'No, the Ashanti and the Zulu travel on foot,' Mr. Davies agreed.

'So who were you talking about just then?'

'Your man, your skeleton man. He would have ridden a horse, I'll be bound. Probably stole it from us. Had to sleep with them we did, and our carbines,' said Mr. Davies.

Henry's point had been adroitly disabled as if an axle pin had been removed, bringing the wagon crashing to a halt leaving the freed wheel to career onwards.

He made a final attempt. 'Stole it from us? How do you mean 'us'? The man we found by the Icing lived hundreds and hundreds of years ago.'

'It never changes. Never will. It's always about order, about getting things right and proper. He was the enemy wasn't he? Whose side would you be on?'

Mr. Davies had faced the challenge and seen it off. He rose magisterially, straightened his coat and left the room.

But if he had forgotten Henry's letter, Kitty had not. As he too left to set about what remained of the evening's business she followed him into the garden.

'I suppose you're going to read your old letter now, aren't you?'

'Probably.' He continued ahead of her up the path towards the mews gate.

She quickened her pace and caught him by the arm. 'Will you read it to me in the Pride and Joy?' she said.

He wondered whether if she had been the first to get her hands on it instead of Mr. Davies, she would have cajoled Mrs Bullace into steaming it open. Presumably the cook could read, receipts at any rate. Davies had only said she didn't receive many letters, not that she wouldn't be able to comprehend them if she did.

'It's just from my mother,' he said, 'Really it is, just bits of news from home.'

'I know, I know, sure I know that. But I never get one from my home and I never can send one neither.'

He began to relent but then he recalled her look when she had snatched the envelope from Mr. Davies.

'Maybe another time,' he said, 'I have the horses to see to and the Major's still to come in from the Club.

'Soon then?'

'Yes, soon,' said Henry.

As he set about racking up for the night he thought about the picture that without doubt he had managed to conjure up in Mr. Davies' head. The Troop Sergeant-Major evidently had his own demons there too and by the sound of it not particularly benign ones.

Henry wondered whether Mr Davies was driven by his as he was by Reuben. It had not occurred to him to question whether Reuben was ill-disposed to him or not. He was demanding, even tyrannical, but Henry had not questioned whether his warrior deserved his loyalty or not.

Shannon swung her head round and nudged Henry's shoulder as if to rouse him gently from his preoccupation.

'Mister Davies saw him come on a horse,' thought Henry becoming aware of her physical presence, 'I'm sure that was the truth he was seeing then. There was a mess of people in pain so that together they seemed like one, and then there was a horse. Reuben was a horseman too then, sharing things with me, one of the brotherhood.'

Major Fitzgerald looked in at the mews having returned from the Club in a cab shared with a friend. 'Shan't be needing anything more until the morning, Turner,' he said, 'You can turn in if you like. I'll take the Pride and Joy out tomorrow by myself. By the by, have you seen any more of those two Fenian rogues?'

Henry said he had not.

'Well you be sure and mention it if you do. To me mind. Good night.'

Henry turned up the lamp and opened the door to the Hansom to check one more time that it was in good order for the morning. Then on an impulse he climbed in, settled himself down on the cushioning and opened the letter.

It was a mixture of Annie writing for herself and replying for his mother. His stratagem was working. The conversation with Annie was such as he would have if his mother were in the room with them, recognising the impossibility of committing to paper what they could only rehearse to one another alone. In the letter they were together, but chaperoned.

Henry clung to that thought as he sat by himself in the Hansom, but he could not honestly say he was comforted by it.

My dear Henry, Annie had written,

Once again your mother has asked me to write her reply. You are being kept well fed by your Mrs Bullace from what you say, so that is the main thing. Many of the day-men are on short commons here although your father, the Bailey has been doing what he can for some. He has sold some of the saved seed as well as two mounts to the army

We were all surprised to learn that cousin Sim has indeed enlisted. No-one thought he was truly minded to do it. You know what an empty chaff bin he can be. It seems he may be going overseas. He may not be the only one. Those that are not eating well will have to go before they get too famished and fail the regulation. What with you in London, too, the letter writers will be kept busy (your mother says).

Our Aunt Elizabeth is beginning to feel her bones, I fear. She has some pain now and does not go about much except to church. I am doing more and more and may have to give over my work at the school. The garden is in a fair way and keeps us, although there is little enough for market in the way of vegetables, the weather being so poor again, but we do manage to take eggs and ducks. We are fattening a pig and three turkeys. Aunt says that turkeys give more than geese for the same bait.

Your father is very despondent about the winter sowing, especially as he has had to delve into the seed to pay the men. Mr Earl told him that the bad weather was something to do with an island blowing up on the other side of the world, but the Bailey never pays him much heed even on a Sunday. Talking of which, your mother asked Mr Earl about Doctor Birchall. He seemed very anxious that you and he should write to him. He shall try to find an address from Dr Birchall's college. Your mother sends her fondest love as does your affectionate cousin

Annie Lilley

At the end she had written something more. It was evident this had not been read to his mother.

You should know that tongues have stopped wagging in the village, as by now I would be too far gone for it not to show. I am sorry to disappoint them.

A.

His discomfort at keeping Annie on an invisible leash like this had until that moment been tolerable to him. It allowed him to convince himself that there would be a time when all would be said that needed to be said, when everything meant would come to pass. He had allowed himself to be persuaded by Annie's last letter that Miss Covington's oblique remarks about village gossip all those weeks ago were wide of the mark. It was part of keeping Annie to himself without taking any responsibility for her. He could even make himself believe that Annie wanted it that way too and that she was conniving with him.

But now it was hard. His shame at what he was doing seized hold of him inside, sucking him in on himself so that he physically curled up in the corner of the Major's Pride and Joy. Even though there could never have been a possibility that Annie was carrying his child, he wished now that she had not had to bear alone the knowing looks and whispers in church which he knew always accompanied such a general expectation.

'*I am sorry to disappoint them'.* He wanted to know if that was meant just for him or for the world, but he could not tell unless he heard her say it aloud.

The door of the carriage clicked open, startling him from his miserable self-pity. Kitty Shaughnessy slipped in and curled up close against him without a word. She had her outdoor cloak on over her shift, her hair fell loose over them both.

Henry went to say something, not knowing what it might be. His right arm was trapped under her body and the left wedged against his side of the Hansom. Kitty put her hand up to his mouth to quiet him, then freed his left hand and put it under her cloak. Her breasts moved, denting softly under his touch, released, like her hair, for the night. He felt her nipples harden as he touched them through the cotton. Her lips brushed over his face and her mouth fastened to his. She raised herself to pull up her shift to her waist. Henry's hand went down between her legs. She was wet. He looked down in the lamplight and saw that her hair was red there too. She pulled her face away from his, holding his head in both her hands, her eyes moving fiercely, focusing on each of his in turn.

'Don't stop,' she whispered harshly. Then she reached down, undoing the buttons on his trousers, feeling for him.

Henry did not move. It was over for him before it had started.

A hollow sadness filled him completely. He wanted nothing more than to sweep up the last few moments as they rolled away in the dust and cram them back into the straitness from which they had burst.

'I'm sorry,' he said.

'No you're not, at all. I'm the one should be sorry. Look at me. Don't be sorry. It'll still be your first time with whoever she is. I wish it were mine, oh I do so!' and she wept silently and deeply, her barely-clad shoulders shuddering as each muted sob fought to break free.

Henry became aware of their surroundings again. Reality had until then evaporated. What had happened to them both had been set in a presence without place and in an existence without time. Physical discomfort and sudden, ordinary fears that they might at any moment be discovered, raced in to fill the shapeless emptiness in which he was suspended.

She had done this, not he and he wanted her to be gone. She had visited her self on him demanding a remedy for her pain that was not his to provide. The remedy had failed simply by being demanded and the pain had been redoubled in them both. Nothing was finished and the way ahead was now more bleak and unremitting.

'This is all so wrong,' said Henry at last.

'Don't make me feel like a whore. I came to give myself freely to you.'

'That's not what I mean. I mean this solves nothing for either of us. How can either of us look the Major in the eye now? It was bad enough before for me…knowing about you. But now. How can either of us carry on as if nothing has happened? What will you do when he…when he wants you again himself?'

'I don't know, I don't know. Perhaps I can be ill for a while, I have done before.'

'What would happen if you just left?'

'Where would I go? Back to Ireland? What would that solve? It would only make things worse for my father and besides I have no money.'

'I have money,' said Henry. 'Upstairs.'

He would have handed all his father's guineas to her then and there if she had given the slightest indication that it would serve a purpose. But he could see her lack of money was not a real obstacle, it was a just a way of saying that she was imprisoned in the wide world. However and wherever she might go now she would be lost and without purpose. Kitty could only cling to herself to avoid being swept away entirely. She surrounded the infinitesimal space she occupied with her laughter and bravado, her beauty and her sex. Outside that she was nowhere, she was nothing. She had been wrested from her earth and only there, wherever it was, would she find her true self.

They both heard it at the same time. The stable door was being tried by someone who clearly did not want to make a noise. Henry put his hand to his lips to warn Kitty to be silent, but she needed no telling. He dowsed the light.

'It's open,' said a low voice, sounding rather surprised.

'Are the nags there at all?' a second voice said.

'Be still,' whispered the first, 'You'll wake your man upstairs.'

Henry eased himself gently across Kitty and very slowly raised an inch of the Hansom's side blind and peered out through the slit. By the light of the shaded bull's-eye lamp one of them was carrying he could make out two figures by the door. He could not see their faces but their shapes were familiar: Henry had seen them twice before. Once in Hyde Park and the second time at the entrance to the mews. They moved further into the stable and crouched down beside the Hansom just below Henry's line of sight.

'Shall we fire the place then?' whispered one.

Henry's blood ran cold and he began desperately to think what he should do.

'No,' said the other voice after a pause, 'It'd look like an accident and they'd just blame the groom. I want that Fitzgerald to know.'

'What then?'

'Cut them, cut the nags.'

'Sure and they'll make a terrible blather.'

'So we'll just do the tendons on one. She'll never feel a thing and we'll be away, gone. He'll still have to shoot her. He'll know all right.'

The two men stood up and moved towards the nearest loose box. Henry felt an icy calm come over him as his first indecision gave way to pure hatred and anger. He threw open the Hansom's door violently so that the sudden unbalancing caused the vehicle to rear up on its single axle. At the same time he fetched something out of the depths of his waistcoat pocket and shouted a single word at the top of his voice.

The two mares, as if being pulled in unison by unseen strings backed heavily, kicking out with their hind legs. The man with the bull's-eye dropped it in the confusion of noise and movement. As he stooped instinctively retrieve it, Liffey backed into him snorting and whinnying, sending him sprawling backwards.

His companion shouted, 'Leave it Jimmy, leave it,' and fled to the stable door pursued by the huge writhing shadows being cast all round in the fitful light of the fallen lamp.

The first man half rose and hesitated for a moment. Henry struck him hard on the side of the head with the toe of his boot, shouting filthy things at him at the top of his voice. The man hesitated no longer, but fled headlong out into the night. Henry heard their nailed soles rasping roughly on the cobbles above the sound of his own deep gulping breaths.

As the sound of them retreating died away round the corner of the mews Henry lurched to the stable door. Lights were beginning to be lit in his neighbours' stable lofts as well as in the houses. He turned and strode back to the tilted Hansom.

'Quick Kitty,' he whispered urgently, 'The whole of Bayswater will be in here in a moment.'

But there was no sign of the maid nor of the fallen bull's-eye lamp. What little light there was came through the open stable door.

Henry's next care was for the horses. He calmed them with a murmured word or two, breathing into their nostrils in turn, then retrieved his oil lamp from the floor of the Hansom where it had fallen.

The first to arrive on the scene were a couple of his neighbours from either side. Henry reassured them that all was now well, but they hung around outside all the same until Mr Davies appeared preceded by his best barrack square voice giving intelligence to the Major close behind him as he came down the garden to the mews gate.

Henry told them the bare truth in answer to their questions. He had heard two men creeping into the stable intent on doing some damage to the horses.

'And you set about them with your boot did you?' Mr Davies said, 'Well done, well done.'

'Good job you still had them on,' said the Major thoughtfully, 'Bit late to be up still wasn't it?'

Henry felt that uncomfortable feeling again that Major Fitzgerald had an uncanny knack of inducing simply with a slight tone of voice. Henry said something about having come down to settle the horses.

'So where were you when they opened the door?'

Henry gestured vaguely in the direction of the loose boxes.

'And what happened here?' Fitzgerald was examining the Hansom tilted at its crazy angle. 'Something must have happened here, this isn't the way we stow it.'

Mr Davies who had fallen silent was now listening in a different kind of way. He moved slightly, out of Henry's line of sight. But Henry noticed it and it added guilt to his discomfiture.

Suddenly without any outward signal that he could divine, Mr Davies and the Major had adopted a pattern familiar to them both. They had become a team. He could feel himself changing the way he was standing, trying to make himself look as natural as he was trying to sound, not with any success.

'I think they were the two men we have had trouble with before,' he heard himself say.

'Of course they were,' said the Major softly, 'Of course they were. There, that didn't hurt did it Turner. Why didn't you say so at once?'

Henry could not think of a reply. His mind raced. Had he been about to give up this knowledge to Fitzgerald or had he been set on keeping it to himself? He could not now be certain either way. Nor indeed could he fathom why he would wish to keep it a secret, if that had been his intent. But now he had been drawn further into something which he would rather not have been part of. He had been burdened with knowledge but without understanding and not for the first time. Something was happening to him that was another of the meant things, not just the space in between them.

He had gone through another doorway.

Then as if a moonbeam had shone through the window pane, the atmosphere cleared. The Major relaxed perceptibly and his Troop Sergeant-Major became Mr Davies again, back in view in the lamplight.

'You've done very well Turner, saving my cattle and not getting yourself a hammering this time,' Fitzgerald gave his short, foxy bark, 'But keep the stable locked at night, eh? This isn't the country. Come on Sergeant-Major, I think we can stand down the guard now, what d'you think?'

When they had gone, Henry checked the mares one last time before climbing the stairs to his room above the stable. There he found Kitty Shaughnessy sitting hunched on the side of his bed still clutching the bull's-eye lamp.

'Why did you have to say they were those Irishmen?' she asked without looking up.

'I don't know. It was them anyway.'

'Yes, but now there'll be more trouble at home, I know it.'

'Why?' said Henry, 'They could be anyone.'

Kitty looked up at him in the lamplight.

'Why?' Henry repeated. Then he understood. 'You knew them didn't you?'

She said nothing.

'Didn't you?' he insisted.

'They'll have locked the kitchen door now,' she said, 'I'll have to stay here until it gets light and you'll have to keep Mrs Bullace occupied while I slip in. If she looks in my room first thing she'll only think I'm with him. Which will make her bad tempered until she puts it out of her mind again.'

Henry saw her again for what she had become. A secret that no-one could really be bothered to keep. He was angry with himself for the way he had been drawn into it, and ashamed at all his impotence. That anger had exploded in defence of the mares, uncomprehendingly cast as victims in a continuing trial of human strength and frailty. That Liffey and Shannon were helpless bystanders needing his championship he did not doubt for a moment. But what did Kitty deserve? Was she any less worthy of defending than they? And what of the two Irishmen? He had informed on them to the Major and Mr Davies and he could not get it out his head that it had been a betrayal.

Kitty put out her hand and touched him softly on the sleeve. It made him start, so much did the gesture call Annie to mind, that sudden gentleness to break an iron spell.

'What was that word you shouted that made those horses rear so? It sounded like a tinker's cursing word to me. And what in God's name was that smell?'

The unhappiness Henry had felt at the way his own self control had been put to flight so easily simply by Fitzgerald changing his inflexion, and Davies confusing his sense of reality, just as a conjurer distracts the eyes with nothing more than an irrelevant movement, had completely overshadowed the fact that he himself had done the same to the horses with such devastating effect.

He felt in his waistcoat pocket again and found there the slightly soft lump of candle wax he had reached for when he had leapt out of the carriage.

He squeezed it out of shape in his palm. Then he fetched his hand out empty and held it to her face.

She wrinkled her nose. 'That's it. What is it?'

'Just something the horses don't care for ground into a few old melted candle ends.'

'Why would you want to do that at all, if they don't like it?'

Henry thought of telling her about marking gates and stakes to keep a horse contained to one small area to stop it straying without being tethered. But even now, despite feeling confined with her in this deep, unlooked-for intimacy, he drew back from revealing the horseman's magic. It wasn't just about it being an ordinary trick of his trade. It was about being able to impose his will without pain when to other men nothing but inflicting pain would appear to be left. Just as the Major had done. It was about wielding power.

'That's for me to know,' he said. 'Listen.' He went to the top of the stairs and just made a pass in the air with his greased hand in the direction of the stable below. Even though the scent on his hand without the wax was far less pungent than it had been earlier when he had taken it right out of his pocket, they nevertheless both heard the horses shift their feet fretfully.

'And what was it you roared at them then? Is that for me to know or not?' said Kitty.

Henry could hear the word once more resonating in his head but he would not utter it again in cold blood. Perhaps it had added nothing. Perhaps the bitter oils had been enough in such a small space to make the mares react as violently as they had. He wondered when he might ever say it again, when the heat of the moment was supposed to give it meaning.

'It's just an old word. They seem to understand it.'

'Say it to me now, I want you to.'

'No I cannot, not just like that.'

'Well, well,' her teasing voice beginning to reappear, 'It must mean something very bad.'

'It's a bit of the word from the beginning, some say,'

'The beginning of what?'

'The beginning of everything,' said Henry. 'You stay there in my bed now. I'll go down with the horses till morning.'

Neither of them suggested any other arrangement.

13

After the night of the intruders, Major Fitzgerald began to spend more time in the stable taking the master's share of the grooming once again. Although his manner towards Henry was outwardly the same as it had been, there was an unspoken understanding that there had been a contest between them, like children trying to stare one another down and Henry had looked away first. But despite the fact that Fitzgerald had gained the upper hand and had consolidated his superiority in the natural order of things it must have been apparent he had revealed something of his self that he would have preferred to have kept hidden. As with Mr Davies, the very presence of Henry Turner among them seemed to be a lever turning over the present like a heavy stone revealing the past as part of it still on its underside.

Sensing that the Major would have to come some of the way now to meet him and address their changed relationship, Henry felt inclined to take the initiative in their conversations when it suited him.

'We found some bones by our river, Dr Birchall and I,' he ventured one evening, to see where it might lead.

'I believe so,' said the Major, 'Birchall mentioned it to me when you first came.

'We took them out of the ground and moved them.'

'Naturally. That's the whole point of a dig.'

'Yes. But is it right, moving things like that?'

'How could it be wrong?' said the Major.

Henry cogitated. He knew what he meant by 'wrong' and he was fairly sure the Major understood him too but was teasing him out to see how carefully he might express himself. If so then it was a slight, ever so slight, admission of equality, a tiny opening after the bruising of the interrogation, if only while they shared the labour of the grooming.

'I think I mean wrong in the church sense of right and wrong,' he said cautiously.

'You mean, is it morally wrong?' Fitzgerald said.

'I suppose I do, if that's the word.'

‘Why would you suppose taking things long buried and forgotten in the name of science might conceivably be morally wrong?’ The Major’s question was an admonishment too.

Henry knew he had to be very careful about what he said next. He wanted to say that things long buried and forgotten, especially when they were people, seemed, in his experience, to take on a new and disturbing lease of life when they were found again. But it would not do to rush that thought out, particularly as he was desperate to know what view Fitzgerald might have of it and did not want to allow him to slip off the hook with a wrong move.

‘Well, you wouldn’t dig up graves in a churchyard would you?’

‘That depends.’

‘On what?’

‘On what you think you might find if you did, for one thing. And whether you might be harming anyone living if you did so. And of course whether you were breaking the law or not. Suppose, for instance, you had good reason to suppose that a grave might contain something from its own time that might solve a mystery in our own time. You might be able to determine a true line of succession for instance.’ The Major punctuated his thoughts with strokes of the dandy brush.

‘Or you might find out how someone had died?’

‘Yes that might be important. But I wasn’t thinking so much about catching criminals.’

‘No neither was I. But it might be important to know how somebody died even if it was a long time ago.’

‘Historically, scientifically, yes it might.’

‘But even so, don’t people and their things laid in the ground hundreds of years ago have a right to be left in peace? Do they lose their dignity just because the flesh has withered off them? Shouldn’t their pots and pans and things that you and Dr Birchall look for be left where they put them?’

‘You might ask yourself if they weren’t hoping that they would be found,’ the Major countered, ‘Perhaps that is their immortality. No, I don’t think you should get too sentimental about it, Turner. The dead are dead, but if they have any useful secrets then they should belong to the living. You cannot have people taking knowledge and ideas, taking their thinking with them to the grave.’

‘And should they have to take their pain with them to the grave, then? If we bring them back into the light of day for the sake of what was in their heads and minds, don’t we have to accept their pain too?’

‘Well if there was pain, as you so curiously put it, then it might be important to know of it.’ The Major was beginning to sound a little irritated with his groom.

‘And to do something about it…morally?’ Henry persisted

‘Why on earth would you possibly want to do that?’

Henry took a deep breath and busied himself on the other side of the mare out of the Major’s eye line. Maybe he had managed to manoeuvre their exchange to the brink of revelation.

‘Roger…Dr Birchall that is…thought that the man we found had been tortured by the Romans before they executed him.’

Fitzgerald, if he had noticed the solecism, ignored it.

‘What made him think that?’

‘Well, his wrists had been bound tightly with leather behind his back.’

‘If they had been about to execute him,’ said Fitzgerald quickly, ‘They might well have done that anyway. It doesn’t necessarily mean he was tortured first.’

Henry remembered the pictures that had formed in his head on the banks of the Icing and the cold fire that had surged through the heart of him.

‘Then why tie him at all? Why even kill him? Why not make him a prisoner? They wanted him to tell them things and he would not. I know it for sure.’

Fitzgerald stood up straight and met Henry’s eye across the mare’s withers.

‘Just supposing you are right, and I don’t question your inner workings, Brother Horseman, but I, a mere scientist, a seeker after truth, would ask for some hard evidence. Just supposing you are right. His captors could have been in no position to release him. Too close to the enemy for comfort, probably. Too few in numbers to handle a prisoner, no-one to escort him. Scouting party perhaps...’

‘Mr Davies said that…’Henry broke in.

‘…so they were in a hurry for their information, let’s suppose.’

The Major pondered briefly and then said in matter-of-fact tones, ‘These bones you found, were they scorched at all?’

Henry did not know, nor did he need to ask why.

‘Were any of them broken…fingers…toes?…no perhaps not fingers and toes…no time …something quicker. Definitely scorch marks and signs of dislocation, thumbs probably. Shoulders?’

Henry knew these questions were no longer being addressed to him, nor was he expected to provide the answers.

But he would. One day he would.

Major Fitzgerald seemed to recollect himself. Their conversation had gone far enough. Once again Henry's persistence was beginning to find things best forgotten.

'No,' the Major said briskly, 'No, I don't have a problem with taking things out of the earth, provided I have the owner's permission, assuming there is one to give it. I do have strong feelings about that, ownership of the land. Mine by right, mine by law, to have and to hold from this day forward and all that. And I'll break any who try to alter that, by God I will. Whose land was it at home…your father's?'

'Well in a manner of speaking it was. He's the Bailiff.'

'Good enough. And what's Birchall done with the remains?'

Henry thought about his promise to Mr Earl. 'Well he hasn't put them back where we found them as far as I know.'

'And you think he should?'

'I don't know…perhaps it would be for the best.

'You're a strange one, Turner. I get the feeling you are searching for answers to questions that haven't even been posed. This skeleton is a constant preoccupation for you. I believe it has actually driven you off the land. That really why you are here, in London? You hiding from it?'

'No,' Henry replied quickly, 'I'm not. I'm here because I cannot properly earn my keep as a farm horseman.'

'Ah, yes,' said the Major slightly mockingly, 'The famous broken hands and legs. .But then, don't you blame your warrior friend for those too?

Blame was not the right word, Henry knew. But there was a connection, a cause and effect. His own injuries were part of the things that were meant. Reuben was in that sense responsible for them. But he could not be blamed any more than the Icenian could be blamed for his own injuries. They had dug up Reuben's pain and brought it back into the living world and Henry was the only one who could feel it, the only one who was meant to feel it.

'It's not a question of blaming anyone. If anyone is to blame for my hands it is my own stupid self. I should have left well alone that night and no-one need have known I was even there.'

But you didn't, did you?'

'No, because Dr Birchall said I had been chosen.'

The Major snorted. 'That old superstition. Scientists ought to know better. Lot of damn mumbo jumbo.'

Henry saw that he had lost him. There would be no more revelations that evening, nor any other perhaps.

He decided to have one last attempt. 'Well I know I am meant to do something about the pain this man had. I am meant to…to understand something important from it.'

'Pain is pain. All you do is feel it. All you want to do is make it stop. I should know. What else can there possibly be to learn from it?'

The Major straightened up again on the other side of the horse and rinsed his hands in the bucket. He slung his jacket over one shoulder and nodded good evening

Something, Henry thought, something was there to be learned from it. Something about people and the earth they go back to.

Quite near to Christmas another letter came addressed to Henry. Very much to his surprise and the slight awe of those assembled in the kitchen for the public opening, it was from the Vicar, Mr Earl himself.

'Well, well my little piping bag,' said Mrs Bullace, 'Oo'd 'ave thought you'd get a letter from a gentleman like that?'

'Now then Mrs B,' said Mr Davies, 'I expect he's discovered our Henry has run off with the church silver. Your secret's out Henry.'

Fortunately for Henry, the letter contained a reference to his Great Aunt Elizabeth's increasing age and infirmity, although not sufficient to alarm him, so he was able to fob off his audience with that while keeping to himself its main purpose.

Mr Earl's letter concluded,

As you know, I remain distinctly ill at ease with the presence in the church. Perhaps it might seem to you that I am making a fuss over nothing, but I have a constant feeling that this is a piece of unfinished business and that St Mary's should not be considered its final resting place. I am sorry to write so obliquely but something tells me that no good would come of the matter becoming public. I seriously thought about asking young Simon Lilley if he would dispose of it, as he was there on the occasion of both discoveries. I was forestalled in any case because when I approached his mother after church to ask her to send him round, she told me he had that very day gone to enlist. I am not sorry, as I fear, on reflection, I could not have relied on his discretion, as I can on yours.

So I am writing to Dr Birchall and I urge you to do the same. He must make some permanent arrangements, through his College perhaps. I am told that letters may be sent to him in Egypt and may await collection from the General Post Office in Alexandria.

Henry felt a surge of relief, not least that Sim Lilley had not been asked to take a hand. And here at last was the means of contact with

Roger Birchall. Already he felt closer simply by holding Mr Earl's letter in his hand. As for his worries about the skeleton in the under church, they did not seem quite as irrational to Henry as the Vicar seemed to assume they would. When the skull had first been revealed Mr Earl had been content to take charge of it as long as he thought it the responsibility would pass to Dr Birchall. Mr Earl's unease had begun to manifest itself truly when the entire skeleton had been unearthed and placed in the church.

'That's because it's not meant,' thought Henry, 'And the Vicar is being given the heebie-jeebies by Reuben because something else is meant to happen, 'And whatever it is only I will be permitted to do it.'

Despite Mr Earl's purpose in writing, the question of removing Reuben from St Mary's was not what Henry began to agonise over, when, a day later, he found time to write to his far-flung friend. Putting his anxieties about Major Fitzgerald into words on paper was not an easy task and he had more than a few attempts before he had something that approximated to his emotions.

I do not know what to make of the Major and I would be grateful if you could put my mind at ease about him. You will understand if I say I need to know whether he is a Roman when it comes to the way he behaves towards his people in Ireland. There are men here, in London, from Ireland who, he knows, mean him harm, but while I know that to be wrong, something in me says perhaps he deserves it. I also think Kitty Shaughnessy, the maid of all work here, is being treated like Boudicca and her daughters. She says it is not so, but I have good reason not believe her.

It was a child's picture he had painted. Maybe Birchall would make sense of it and see the greater sweep of troubled vision that he really intended. But Henry felt exorcised by the very act of distilling the clouds in his mind and giving them a humble shape on a piece of paper. To send it to his friend to share, to make a silent connection far away, even if there were no solutions in return was sufficient in itself. The response, if there was to be one was perhaps already immaterial.

As he consigned the envelope to the mystery of the continental postal systems Henry felt his heart quicken as the thought crossed his mind that he should really have sent one to Annie.

On Christmas Eve Major Fitzgerald permitted a festive supper in the kitchen and as was his custom, so Mrs Bullace informed Henry, he put in an appearance himself to drink his staff's health and to give them presents before taking himself off in a cab to dine with friends, this gesture being made to allow Henry the night off to join in the fun.

'We always gets a new set of duds and something else besides,' Mrs Bullace confided.

'Well he can hardly have us going around in rags now, can he?' said Kitty, 'And if I get the usual sovereign beside it will be less than I deserve,' she added half to herself.

'You, missy, 'ave got a mouth on you like a tuppenny mouse trap sometimes, you 'ave that,' said Mrs Bullace for whom the *sotto voce* had not been *sotto* enough. 'You can keep your goings-on out of my kitchen if you please. It's Christmas an' all.'

The drawing room bell summoning them all upstairs interrupted this pointed exchange, much to Henry's relief, and they all trooped off to find the Major with his back to the fire and a set of working clothes for each of them laid out on the ottoman.

Fitzgerald invited them to go across and single out their own, but when he did so, Henry could not immediately see anything befitting a groom.

'Not you, I'm afraid Turner,' said the Major seeing his slight perplexity. 'You had new clothes when you joined in September, so I assumed you wouldn't be needing anything so soon.'

Henry stood awkwardly, not being able to think of anything appropriate to say. The others looked up from the business of holding their new wardrobes up against themselves in the mantelpiece mirror and fell silent too.

The Major moved languidly away from the fireplace and went over to the ottoman himself, allowing the silence to persist just long enough for it to change from awkward to embarrassed.

Mr Davies cleared his throat. 'Well Major, on behalf of myself and the servants as usual I would like to thank you very much and invite you, as is the custom, to join us in the kitchen for a…'

'…But I thought you could probably do with one of these, Turner, as I believe the last one you had, had to be cut off you.' Fitzgerald reached down behind the ottoman and produced a brand new Melton.

The collective sigh of relief at the situation defused was audible.

'Here, try it for size,' said the Major offering to help Henry into it himself. 'I had my tailor run it up. Quite a new experience for him, but I'm told it's the real thing.'

'I don't know what to say, Major,' said Henry in confusion. He had supposed that he would not put on another Melton now until the Bailey's came to him in the fullness of time.

'This is by way of a thank you from me for saving my mares from an unpleasant fate and for your courage in the face of the enemy,' said Fitzgerald clapping him on the shoulder as he shrugged into the coat and giving one of his foxy barks.

Then, as if he had read Henry's mind, 'I understand from my tailor that these things are meant to be heirlooms, so I hope one day it will be handed on to your own son, but not too soon eh?' And he barked again. 'Right now Troop Sergeant-Major, what was that you were about to say? Something about a drink as I recall.'

Over Christmas Major Fitzgerald dined out at friends' houses and either required being delivered or collected in the bow fronted Hansom or would drive himself one or both ways. However, he did not go to the club which often meant that Henry could leave the Pride and Joy and the mare in the charge of the host's stable men, either spending the evenings with them himself or sometimes walking for an hour or two, gradually improving his knowledge of the capital and learning to connect up in his mind streets and neighbourhoods so that a picture of the whole began to take shape in his mind's eye.

When time permitted or the Major was dining in the vicinity Henry found his steps taking him towards Pall Mall pausing always to stare at the sentries at St James's Palace, half hoping to run across his guide from the fog.

His memory of that day was becoming as ethereal as the world of the Particular had seemed to him at the time. The gradual adulteration of reality, as the passage of time watered down the facts and topped them up with fancy, served almost to convince him that his mysterious saviour had actually revealed himself as Reuben. That if he had lowered his cloak he would have revealed his mighty walrus moustache and if he had swept off his wide-brimmed hat, his flowing red hair falling to his shoulders, he would have stood before him, a bodyguard of a queen of the Iceni.

In the stables of the Major's acquaintances where Henry would pass the evenings waiting to drive him home, generally when he had decided that the care of Fitzgerald's horses could not safely be entrusted to the host's grooms, talk turned increasingly to the preparations for the Queen's jubilee in the year to come.

It seemed that there was to be entertainment and spectacle on a lavish scale for ordinary folk such as they, not just for the nobs. It was on one such evening that Henry first heard of Buffalo Bill and his Wild West, a vast staged re-enactment of scenes and life on the frontiers of America which was to be held over in Earl's Court.

'We're involved with it,' one of Henry's hosts for the evening had said, puffing himself up by proxy for his employer. 'It's part of the American exhibition that's coming; just like the one we had at the Crystal Palace. My guv'nor knows Mr Landreth, the American gent what's organising the whole thing.

'Is he Buffalo Bill then?' asked Henry, deliberately misunderstanding so as to entice his companion into popping himself by his bragging.

'No he ain't Buffalo Bill. He's the one what's bringing Buffalo Bill. This Wild West is just part of it.'

'Buffalo Bill shoots all the Indians,' the stable lad volunteered.

'Shoots Indians in Earls Court?'

The lad looked at Henry witheringly. 'No mate. Where 'ave you been? They just pretend. They get up afterwards.'

Even his pompous superior was not about to allow this kind of lip and clipping his ear smartly sent him about some unnecessary chores.

'Still,' he observed to Henry, 'They might just as well shoot them from what I hear. They're just a bunch of savages.'

'Like the Iceni?' said Henry sweetly.

'Who are they then?'

'The Ashanti then?' Henry offered.

His host's face began to suggest that Henry was in danger of presuming on his hospitality. 'Don't know of them either,' he muttered.

'Well the Fenians, the Irish. Are they like them?' said Henry.

'You want to watch what you say, you do. Shooting Irishmen at Earl's Court, the very idea.'

At that point their exchange was brought to a close by Henry being summoned to drive the Major home. 'I know someone who wouldn't be altogether against that idea though,' Henry chuckled to himself as he held the door of his Pride and Joy for him.

Mrs Bullace was still up with Kitty in the kitchen spooning newly-made pickles into their kilner jars when they arrived back in Bayswater. Henry sat down and tried some with a piece of cheese and some cold mutton.

'I should 'ave thought you'd be wearin' your new coat this weather,' observed Mrs Bullace. Henry was still in his groom's livery clothes as he had been ever since Christmas.

'It's a horseman's coat,' he said, rather shortly, 'Not a groom's. 'It's not for the town.'

Kitty looked at him narrowly. 'So are you not going to put it on at all? That's a bit of an old slap for the Major isn't it, sure now?'

Henry reddened and stared down at his plate chewing slowly on his pickles and mutton.

'What was all that about the other one being cut off you?' Kitty carried on, the note in her voice indicating that she was in pursuit and the hunt was up.

'Now, now,' Mrs Bullace intervened, 'Who's 'ad 'er tongue in the knife box?'

'Well, there's far too much mystery about Mr Groom if you ask me,' said Kitty provokingly.

'You know I was attacked by poachers,' said Henry wearily, 'Well they had to cut my coat off to set my bones and such.'

'I'm surprised you let them do that at all, since it obviously means so much to you. Who did the cutting, that widow of yours?' It was a chance shot by Kitty, but she was not one to leave a bird winged when she might bring it tumbling to earth with the second barrel.

Henry's palpable silence even left Mrs Bullace hanging in mid-air for his response.

'I bet that wasn't all she cut off you then.' Kitty pressed on.

It was too much for the cook. 'That's enough in my own kitchen, you nasty little kettle. Come on, out,out, out!' And she swept Kitty before her to the door as if with a broom.

'I'll wager she had the shirt off your back, and the breeks off your…' her sentence was cut short by Mrs Bullace's slamming it behind her.

The new Melton had remained folded in Henry's room, unworn since Fitzgerald had helped him on with it on Christmas Eve. It lay there in the drawer, challenging him to come to a decision every time he opened it. The Melton was very special to horsemen, handed down from grandfather to grandson in the normally hoped for span of life, but where early demise intervened, then from father to son. It was deeply troubling to Henry that he should have been given one by an outsider, a coat not imbued with ancestral provenance nor shaped already in the memory of brother horsemen. This Melton in the drawer looked up at him like a cuckoo in the nest, wheedling him to call it his own, demanding to be put to work, to be given a place among the exalted.

He could not do it, should not do it, he knew. His work here was not worthy, nor was the Major of all people the right person to make the gift and create a new hereditament. That Fitzgerald, however unwittingly, should have made such a presumption only served to grind out Henry's innermost conscience and to give more and more definition to the space between them.

Smarting with impotent anger he stormed from the kitchen himself and up to his room above the stable with no word even for the two mares. He sat rigidly on the side of his bed, his head bowed, his elbows on his knees and his hands clenched together in front of him, the badly-mended knuckles showing as white as his rage, at the injustice Kitty had just done him. There was nothing he could say or do to her. It was plain enough to him that she felt compromised and perhaps even threatened by what she assumed was his rejection of her.

She also knew who the intruders were, that much was plain. Now she did not trust him with the vulnerability she had shown him and was retreating behind an even more exaggerated bravado than she normally evinced to defend herself.

Henry seethed inside. How dared she make assumptions about him, and how dared she have the temerity to reduce the passions that drove him, to the common and banal, when her own, like his, were lodged dark and deep within her self?

Eventually he rose and opened the drawer where the Melton lay. Kitty had somehow sensed that it held some knowledge of his inner self and had enlisted its aid to diminish him.

Henry stared down at it and it crossed his mind that he should take it out and burn it. He picked it up and half turned to the stairs with this purpose. But something stayed him. The coat had been brought into existence for some purpose. Something was meant by it. To destroy the coat might be to destroy something else, another doorway perhaps. A vision of Annie came into his head. What had she said about his doorways? About not finding contentment through them, but them showing him a way forward nevertheless?

Something had possessed the Major to have this coat made. Henry's entitlement to wear one had been mentioned only briefly by Roger Birchall. And the fate of his own, where had that knowledge come from?

He turned back and replaced it in the drawer. As he did so felt again that total upwelling of peace he had had when he had put Reuben's skull with his bones in the church crypt.

In the morning he parcelled the Melton up with note pinned to it that said simply, 'Please keep this safe for me. It is something meant'.

Later he took it to the post office and sent it to,

Mrs Ann Westwood, Icingbury, by Great Duster Cambridgeshire.

14

Henry thought it must have been around the anniversary of the unearthing of Reuben's skull that his long awaited letter from Roger Birchall arrived. It had clearly been on its travels and was so covered in stamps and postmarks as nearly to obscure Henry's name and the address altogether, so much so that Mr. Davies' purpose in having taken it straight to the Major might almost have been accidental.

So when he came out into the hall to give Henry his instructions for the day, it was the Major this time who quizzed him about his correspondence.

'This appears to be for you,' he said laconically, 'It's Birchall's fist.'

Henry's heart jolted, once with excitement that his pains had been rewarded and that the exercise of mystery and imagination that linked the pillar box in Porchester Gardens and a far off place that might as well have been the Hanging Gardens of Babylon for all he knew, had magically worked, but then a second time when he saw that the envelope had been opened.

'I opened it assuming it was for me,' said Fitzgerald.

Henry waited, his heart now in his mouth, wondering what Birchall had written in response to his questions about the Major, partly dreading the thought that the Major, his employer, had just read it but also sparking with excitement that Fitzgerald, the man, might have done.

'I suppose you wrote to him first,' said the Major, not meeting Henry's eye which was in any case transfixed on the letter in his hand.

Henry felt that creeping feeling of panic spreading out from somewhere in the pit of his stomach, just as he had that evening in the stable. The hair began to rise on the back of his neck and his back felt damp with perspiration. He almost looked round to see if Mr Davies had re-emerged from the kitchen and taken up station behind him. He thought frantically what he should say, whether he should tell the truth or whether he should attempt to show surprise that Dr. Birchall should be writing to him at all.

'Yes,' he said, after what seemed to him like an eternity, 'Dr Birchall said I should.'

It was not really a lie. Doubtless Roger Birchall would have suggested it had his farewells not been conducted leaning out of a fast-disappearing growler.

Fitzgerald shot him a glance. 'Yes,' he said, 'Birchall says he received it.'

'What else does he say?' said Henry as naturally as he could, realising that he had been tested.

'Oh I couldn't say. Doesn't do to read another fellow's post, you know. I just saw that at the beginning before I realised it wasn't for me. I knew I hadn't written to him.'

He handed Henry the envelope, looking steadily into his eyes. He seemed to be inviting Henry to disbelieve him or believe him, as if he had declared a hand of cards.

Henry crammed the envelope into his pocket, 'I'll look at it later.'

'Indeed you shall, because now we have business to attend to and places to be,' said the Major.

Later Henry wondered whether it was odd or not that he had shown no further curiosity in a letter from a fellow archaeologist written from Mr Flinders Petrie's expedition in the Nile Delta. But then it was another fellow's post, after all.

Thus it was with several conflicting emotions that Henry eventually settled down hours later to read Dr Roger Birchall's letter, not the least being that it had already been unsealed and removed once by someone else.

He held it to his nose, even so, half hoping that a breath, a murmur from a faraway place might still be held between its creases, but if there ever had been it had evaporated that morning in the Major's study.

And when the seventh seal was opened there was silence in heaven, Henry thought. Annie had quoted that at them, and he wondered, as he had then, what it might mean. Perhaps it was the silence left by something that should have been there but was no longer. A silence waiting to be filled

Tell Defenneh
17th February, 1887

My Dear Henry,

I should say my dear old fellow perhaps. What a strange letter you sent me. When I had managed to overcome the surprise and delight at hearing from you so unexpectedly, it still took me a moment or two to decipher your coded meaning. Then I did recall our conversations in

Icingbury, but I had not until now realised how seriously you had taken them to heart.

I said to you then, did I not, that we should none of us seek too diligently into the past for the keys to our present or our future? As one who has these last months delved physically into the remnants of history on a scale hitherto undreamed of by a humble scratcher of surfaces such as I, it has only served to make me more certain that I am right in this view. The poet Shelley summed it up when he said, 'Round the decay of that colossal wreck, boundless and bare, the lone and level sands stretch far away'. I should know, for I am in just such a godforsaken place as he must have envisaged, as I write to you now.

I will not deny the excitement I experience almost daily at what we are finding here and the feeling of immense pride and satisfaction that what we are uncovering is probably proof of the Book of Jeremiah, turning the Bible from an act of faith into an historical work. Yet as each chamber of what is undoubtedly the palace of Psamtic the First is unearthed and its gold, silver, lapis lazuli, to say nothing of armour and weapons begin to reveal themselves with almost every turn of the trowel, the more I begin to question what this really tells us about the human condition. Is it just a grim reminder that everything falls, in the end, to dust and that no matter what we seek to achieve, all in the end is so much dross? I begin to think that the only lesson of the past is that we have no future and that the sand and salt marsh which surrounds me here is our only lasting destiny.

What has this to do with your own perplexities I ask myself, other than that your seeking after some simple values by which to judge your fellow men has unlocked in me a deep feeling of helplessness? I cannot say whether my friend is a Roman in every sense of the word. I know him as an archaeologist of some repute but as to his Irish connections I know very little. I read what you said about the maid and Boudicca and if I understood you aright then I can only hope that you are mistaken.

I cannot, especially at such a distance, put your mind at rest, but perhaps you will accept some observations that may help you to come to terms with the way things seem.

In the end might may not be right but we British, of all people, have to accept it. As nations we are conquerors or we are conquered. Oh yes, we might rub along with the rest of the world for as long as it suits us and call it compromise and diplomacy, but when these have been played out what is left but the testing of might? What is true for a nation holds just as true for the individuals within it. The rule of law is the exercise of might and for the most part we acquiesce to it so that we may go about our business. The ownership of land within a nation is guaranteed by that hidden sword, the law, just as the ownership of a horse or my pocket watch. Fitzgerald will defend his land against the moonlighters in Cork, just as he would defend his pocket watch against thugs in the street. If that is to change then he has to be the one who has to decide in his heart that he no longer wishes to exercise the might that has been conferred on him. He has to agree to give it up even if it is the Government that is trying to change the order of things. We may, any of us, outwardly accept something that is forced upon us, but the sense of wrong will remain. If it is big enough it will outlive us and be passed down from generation to generation. If it is not freely accepted it will in the end destroy both the conqueror and the conquered. It may take a thousand years or more, but one day someone will sift the sand away and show that it was so. Probably someone like your good friend

Roger Birchall

He had added a postscript some days later.

The Military Hospital
Alexandria
22nd February 1887

I had hardly finished writing to you and gone back out to the excavations from my tent in the late afternoon than I had an accident involving my leg and a wheelbarrow being manhandled by one of our locals, as a result of which I am laid up here at Alexandria. The army surgeon who is looking after my case is threatening to send me home by an early steamer from Port Said as I have a rather obstinate wound as well as a bad fracture.

Apart from needing to tell you that, I have to relate a most extraordinary encounter here today. I have been put in a small room off one of the main wards here, there being no other room in the officers' wards further down. So I have been watching the comings and goings amongst the soldiery.

This is so extraordinary. I glanced up at one point and saw a familiar figure but could not instantly put a name to the face, which is hardly surprising in the circumstances. It was young Lilley who helped with the draining in Icingbury. I don't think he could believe his eyes either. Poor chap, he looked terribly washed out, and his arms protruding from his shirt like some scarecrow's broomsticks. He is recovering, if that is the right word, from some dysentery-related fever that is so prevalent here.

He is a private in a battalion of the Essex Regiment quartered here in Egypt. They may send him home, but frankly I have my doubts as to whether he would survive the journey. Still we can but hope. You may see me sooner than you think. I shall write ahead to Gray Fitzgerald and beg a bed when I arrive.

RB

Henry found the postscript difficult to take in. That a breath of Icingbury should drift in from a place so far away seemed impossible. Instead of Birchall's letter leaving a tantalising flavour of Egypt in his imagination, a place only vaguely familiar in sporadic images, images formed in church and school, the land of Moses in the bulrushes, of Pharaoh and plagues, of fat kine and lean kine coming out of the Nile, He was left with a vivid memory of the headlong rush across the water meadows of the Icing when Reuben's bones were unearthed to prevent at all costs Sim Lilley getting there ahead of him, Sim with his lack of respect for them. A memory too of a nightmare journey on a hurdle with Sim at one end and Josh Makepeace at the other.

All this managed to put to one side Roger Birchall's discussion of the nature of men's power over men and to whom the earth belongs. The Icenian warrior had once again drawn everything back to the centre.

'He put bloody old Sim in my letter to stop me wandering off the furrow,' he said to Liffey's flank as he brushed her down that evening. 'Whenever I try to find the answers by myself, all in one go, he has to put me back on his path. He'll show me a little bit more and then a little bit more. Always the same questions over and over again. I could almost think he sent Sim out to Egypt just so he could be in my letter. And anyway what's he doing in the Essex's? He should have joined the Suffolks.'

Then an even darker thought occurred to him. Sim Lilley had been sent out of the way, just as Mr Earl was about to ask him to dispose of the remains. Sim who had wanted to put a candle in the skull to fright the village folk.

'And if he did send Sim out to Egypt, then he must have bust Roger's leg so that they would have to send him home. What's that all about then? Wasn't he meant to have gone to Egypt? And what about me, then? What am I doing in London while Reuben's in Icingbury? What's he got in mind for me?'

As he lay in bed later he tried to remember everything that had happened since finding Reuben's skull a year ago. Everything which had seemed to have been meant, as Annie had put it. He tried to join them all up with a common thread of purpose, one thing leading to another. He wanted desperately to see a point, a whole thing that he could hold in his mind like a hen's egg in the palm of his hand.

But one thing led to another and another, back and forth, back and forth, like mirrors set opposite each other, into infinity and in the end, sleep.

If Major Fitzgerald had read Henry's letter, he never let anything slip to indicate it. Henry watched and listened for hidden meanings and constantly looked for ways into his self but, if anything, the Major was even less forthcoming than he had been before, which was saying something. Henry wondered if that in itself was a sign that he had indeed read the letter and could not now say anything having denied it first.

Fitzgerald did ask him once why he was not wearing the Melton, but seemed to accept in a disinterested sort of way, Henry's rehearsed explanation that he was keeping it for a special occasion and had sent it home to Icingbury.

Kitty Shaughnessy did not exactly keep out of Henry's way but something seemed to him to have changed, although he could not precisely say what. He did feel it was by design not accident. She still brought him the newspaper from time to time when the Major and Mr Davies had finished with it, but Henry sensed that she would cut short their exchanges fractionally so that they did not stray into difficult water.

So inch by inch the tie that bound them was snipped away by Kitty, allowing them imperceptibly to drift from the dark pool of their intimacy to a grey kind of amity at its outer edge.

In a perverse way Henry sometimes thought about rowing back, to take her wrist, look in her eyes, and lead her back into the bow fronted Hansom. The passage of time had left only the bare print of their encounter in his mind, the complicated intricacies of how it had really been had little by little sifted away.

Even so he was not tempted to translate his fantasy into action. The thought of doing so was always accompanied by those cold fingers reaching into the pit of his stomach and a dim premonition that, beyond his imagining of what it would be like for him, nothing but regret waited for both of them.

For the first time in his life Henry began to experience pangs of loneliness. As an only child it had never been something that had occurred to him to feel. Later as his gifts as a horseman became apparent he had experienced the companionship of the heavy horses at The Veil House with a greater intensity than most lesser mortals of his calling, while the bond between the walking man and his team in harness was one of equality and shared endeavour.

In London, while he had a relationship with Liffey and Shannon which even prompted Mr Davies to come and watch him at work in the evenings when the Major was not taking a hand himself, the role of the groom as a street carriage driver and rider demanded an assertiveness from Henry over the two mares that tended to set itself above friendship. This was the cause of a creeping sadness in him that he began to ascribe to loneliness.

After the letter from Roger Birchall with its grim news of Sim Lilley, his mind turned more and more to the Icingbury skies he had taken so much for granted. Often in the Park he would stand tall in the stirrups in an effort to push the narrow horizons further away. He would try to untie the metropolitan sky and let it billow over the perpendiculars of Kensington and wash away the turrets of Whitehall which seemed always to be stapling it up.

He thought more and more, too, about Annie. Every passing day that became the weeks since he had sent her the Melton coat he wrestled with himself about writing to her. He had not written to his mother since then either. The events that had occurred and the disturbance that they had caused in him made the kind of letter he would normally have written impossible.

He could not contemplate writing about Kitty, the Major, or even Mr Davies, feeling as he did about them. That only left Mrs Bullace and the horses but to write exclusively about them and to ignore the rest of the household would only underline those feelings.

The more he thought about the terse note he had written to Annie, the more he knew it was as if he had slapped her face. He kept picturing himself being there, looking over her shoulder as she opened the parcel and explaining everything it was meant to say. But now when he did, he always saw himself back in Icingbury. From the moment he had left, the doorways that, as Annie had said, had always opened out, had always seemed to take him further and further away from the village. Occasionally before, he had caught himself wondering if he ever would go back. Now he became certain that he would. That something would happen to bring it about, something outside his control, not a decision but an inevitability. He began to feel that soon his purpose in being in London would be achieved and the Icenian would call him home. The letter from Egypt had said a great deal more to him than Birchall had ever put in it. He was being prepared. His feeling of loneliness was part of it. Henry found himself waiting and watching.

15

'Big evening for the Major at the club tonight,' Mr Davies announced to the kitchen at breakfast one morning, 'That Buffalo Bill is being dined as a guest and the Major is one of the principal hosts.'

Buffalo Bill's Wild West Exhibition at the showground out at West Kensington had stormed into London in March for the Queen's Jubilee, quite eclipsing the rest of the American Exhibition. Henry had followed almost daily accounts of the cowboys and Indians in the heart of the capital in the Major's newspaper and wondered if he might get a chance to go himself to see the fancy riding by those legendary exponents of horsemanship. The prospect of being close to Buffalo Bill Cody in person tonight when he drove the Major to the Pall Mall club filled him with excitement and some relief, as it would give him something to write to his mother about.

He did not need telling by Fitzgerald that the horse should be turned out well. They always were, under Henry's care. But this afternoon he put a county show shine on them both and re-cleaned the harness even though there was no need for it. He felt it was only right to prepare both horses, even though only one would be needed.

'I wish we had a Brougham or something,' he confided to the mares, 'Then you could both go tonight. As it is I shall ask his nibs to decide which of you is, for I cannot.'

Major Fitzgerald grunted approvingly at Henry's handiwork. 'Got them both turned out ready I see. So am I to choose best in show?' He barked his foxy laugh. After a not-so-mock inspection he selected Shannon.

'It's a big affair tonight, Turner, and there's something on at the Athenaeum over the road too, so waiting might be a little tricky. If Waterloo Place is full you'd better set me down at the door and try your luck in Warwick Street.'

Henry frequently waited there behind the club, just off Cockspur Street where the deliveries were made.

'I'll assume you are there if you are not in the Square and I'll come and find you. I don't want to be hanging around outside the door as if I'm waiting for a growler.'

Henry went over to the kitchen for his tea before putting Shannon into the shafts. It was going to be a long night, he could tell.

'I've put you a piece of bread and cheese in a butter paper for later, my little dripping jar,' said Mrs Bullace solicitously.

'Have you not to come back while he's there, then?' said Kitty, her mouth full of bread and jam.

'No,' said Henry, 'I'm to wait. He doesn't want to have to hang around as if he's looking for a cab.'

'Do they have a livery stable at the old club then?' Kitty asked.

'No,' said Henry, 'We wait in the Square outside. Only that will likely be full tonight.'

'So what will you do?' Kitty asked him.

'I'll wait in the street behind the club, I expect,' Henry replied.

'Will you wear the coat tonight?' Kitty asked.

Henry pretended he hadn't heard her through the bread and jam.

'I'm off to the post then for his nibs, Mrs B,' said Kitty standing up and wiping her mouth, 'Is there anything else you'll be wanting while I'm out.'

'No,' said Mrs Bullace shortly, 'And you mind you're sharp about it too.

As the Major had suspected, Waterloo Place was nose to tail with carriages.

'Fallback position then, Turner,' he said as he descended from the bow fronted Hansom outside the door, 'I'll come and find you.'

When he had gone up the steps, Henry drove round the square to come back into Pall Mall in the opposite direction. As he waited to turn right he heard cheering and clapping coming down Regent Street in front of him. He waited curiously.

Two riders appeared one slightly in front of the other.

There could be no mistaking Buffalo Bill Cody. He wore a large wide brimmed felt hat with a low crown from which his long hair fell to his shoulders, a fringed leather jacket, leggings and high boots. His reins were held in one hand encased in a huge soft gauntlet with fringes too, its partner being thrust into a monstrously buckled belt. With his free hand he acknowledged the reception their appearance was causing

Henry took in every detail, mentally ticking them off the descriptions of the man he had become so familiar with from the newspaper.

Then, as the two rode at a studied walk across Pall Mall, all the traffic having come to a sudden halt to allow their passage, Henry took in the second rider.

He rode a pony but with no saddle; he too wore soft leather leggings below a woollen blanket (like a horse blanket, Henry thought) but soft leather slippers, not boots. His long black hair was braided like a woman's and in it at the back of his head he wore a single feather. His face, streaked with colour, was impassive, staring straight ahead as if deaf and blind to the applause of drivers and pedestrians alike marking their progress. Henry was looking at his first Red Indian. A warrior tribesman, he thought suddenly, like Reuben and a warm feeling spread up his back as if he were stripped to the waist and the sun was shining on his naked skin.

Cody dismounted at the entrance to the United Services Club and handed his reins to his companion.

The press of traffic queuing up behind Henry at the junction of Waterloo Place had become too impatient now for him to wait there watching any longer and he was forced to move on down Pall Mall to seek a standing place at the rear of the club.

He settled Shannon with her nosebag and went to ring at the back entrance for a bucket of water. When he returned he saw to his wonderment Buffalo Bill's Indian coming towards him on foot now, leading the two horses. There were a number of other equipages standing in the narrow street and as the man walked his charges slowly and deliberately between and around them, so he collected a small retinue of curious grooms and assorted drivers, silent for the most part, keeping a respectful distance in his wake. As he reached Henry he stopped and pointed to the bucket of water he was still holding.

'Where?' he said.

It did not cross Henry's mind at that moment that he had been addressed in English. The warm glow he had felt down his back before, returned to consume him as an almost unbearable, searing heat. As he stood there he could not believe it possible that flames were not flickering through his coat and dancing round his head, that his self was not being smelted down to gush from his body and run across the cobblestones as a pure stream of precious metal.

'Have this one,' he said, 'I'll get another.'

When he arrived back with a second bucket, the Indian had hitched his horses loosely to the offside wheel of the Hansom and had set the water in front of the one Henry recognised as Buffalo Bill's. His little audience watched him open-mouthed as if the act of watering a horse were a new and wonderful revelation to them.

Henry managed to recollect himself sufficiently then to see to Shannon's needs. When he had done so the Indian was standing impassive, his arms folded under his blanket, staring ahead just as he had done on the ride to the club door. His spectators were now recovering their powers of speech and beginning to comment on him as if he were a waxwork at Tussaud's, not a living being presumably with some feelings.

At first they pointed out the obvious to one another. 'Look 'e's got a fevver in'is 'air', and 'see all 'is paint, that's war paint that is' and 'where's 'is bow an' arrer?'

Then emboldened by the man's apparent total obliviousness to their existence, they began to speculate as to how many men he might have killed with his own hands and it was only a matter of time before the more knowledgeable among them began to describe in lurid terms to those less well up on the detail of Buffalo Bill's Wild West Exhibition, the delicate art of taking scalps.

Henry felt a sad resignation come over him. Hearing this little group, he felt he was again splashing across the water meadows by the River Icing listening to Sim and Josh and all the lads from Icingbury as they went to look at the skull.

'Your horses may take a chill if you're not going to walk them,' he said to the Indian, 'You know…cold?'

The group fell silent. Henry was the only one to have addressed the man directly and to remind them that it could be done.

'Yes, I know,' he replied, moving his head ever so slightly to look Henry directly in the eyes. It was as if a coin had been put into a fairground peep show making the figure within slowly surge into life. Henry, meeting his gaze, felt the sudden shock of a familiar but unexpected sensation. He was being searched for a way into his self.

The man unfolded his arms and removed his blanket. There was a gasp of horrified excitement from the watchers as their eyes took in his bare arms and chest hardly concealed at all beneath a loosely fitting rough shirt. He turned and threw the blanket over Cody's horse. 'Charley is old,' he said, 'I will walk the pony.'

'No need,' said Henry, 'I have a blanket in the Hansom.' He reached up to the driver's box and lifted the seat squab to get it.

'My thanks,' said the Indian, accepting it graciously, 'But I will walk him all the same.'

'We could walk them all between us,' said Henry indicating Shannon whose head was down as she stood in the shafts, 'It's going to be long night by all accounts.'

So they did. Henry took the mare out of the bow fronted Hansom and the two of them walked the three horses up and down the hundred yards or so of Warwick Street.

Henry thought about suggesting they should take a turn down Spring Gardens and into the Park, but something told him that this would not be an easy experience for either of them.

After a while the Indian resumed standing stock still, almost as if he were in a trance. Henry had said almost nothing to him as they had walked their horses. It was evident that he spoke and understood English, but Henry could not think it would be very much and besides he felt a shyness amounting to being in awe of the man. The Major's newspaper represented the Indians with Buffalo Bill's Exhibition with a mixture of condescension and humour as brave but primitive savages with a propensity for bloodthirsty acts that it was better it did not dwell on too much. They were certainly lesser beings, it implied. They would the ones to be overcome with awe at the sophisticated might of Great Britain. After his brief acquaintance so far, it was not an image that Henry could sustain in relation to this Indian even if he did share his blanket with his pony.

As the evening wore away, Warwick Street began gradually to empty as grooms collected their passengers from club or theatre and bore them away into the darkening night. In a while Henry and his silent companion were alone with their horses. There was little gaslight in the narrow street, just a single lamp at the junction with Cockspur Street at the far end. Henry lit the lamps on the Hansom, but their little pools of illumination merely served to exaggerate the darkness all around.

The Indian was so still that he seemed to have melted into the darkness and only the restless white shape of Cody's horse, Charley, indicated where he must be.

Henry must have nodded off briefly having sat himself down on the rear step of the Hansom to wait for the Major. He became aware of a man's figure approaching from the Cockspur Street end. He was swaying slightly. Then he heard the unmistakable tones of Major Fitzgerald, if a little slurred.

'Blast you Turner, is that you? I can't see my bloody hand in front of my face down here. Whose bloody idea was this, anyway? Should've come roun' to the front.'

Henry started to his feet guiltily, realising that the Major's mood was not likely to be improved by the fact that he had not yet put Shannon back in the shafts. She was happily dozing into her nose bag on the other wheel of the Hansom.

'Down here Major,' he called, 'I won't be a moment. Do you need a hand, sir?'

'Bugger needing a...' Fitzgerald's repost was suddenly cut short. He was still a good sixty yards away and had by now disappeared out of the light cast by the gas lamp at the end of the street

There was a sound of oaths and violent altercation. Then the Major's voice again and the hiss of steel on the roadway. The unmistakeable sound of one man alone, beset by several, resonated from the cobblestones and echoed off the narrow, looming walls of the buildings.

Henry sprang forward into the darkness towards the noise, struggling to accustom his eyes after sitting in the light of the Hansom's gig lamps. There were three, four, perhaps five around one. Fitzgerald was desperately trying to keep them at bay with the blade he had drawn from his cane. But in the darkness and the rush they were already at too close quarters for him to extend his arm. Then they were on him and he was down beneath their boots. There were cudgels raised. A knife. Henry flung himself among them with no plan or aim other than to surprise perhaps, add a moment of time, make a little difference.

'It's the bloody groom,' said a voice, 'Kick him out of it!' Henry was slammed hard, twice, against the wall and lay winded and stunned.

When he took stock moments later, but what seemed to him like hours, he dimly saw that another figure had come among the dark mass of men. Henry had not given a thought to the Indian, so silently part of the dark. He suddenly leapt among them, almost as if from above it seemed to Henry.

He did make a difference. He moved so fast and purposefully, with grace and ease. Fitzgerald's attackers seemed by contrast to move now like men in a quagmire, as if their boots were made of lead and their arms hung with chains.

But then the Indian slipped. He half fell over one of the bodies that he had already stretched prone upon the road, close to where Henry was half rising, half hesitating, uncertain what part he should now play. In an instant the balance had shifted. There was the hand with a knife. It went for the Indian's throat, but he turned. It must have struck him on his collarbone and the hand slid away upwards and to the right. It poised for a second thrust.

Fitzgerald's fallen stick blade lay almost touching Henry's left hand. He snatched it up and saw it, as if held by someone else, arc upwards to meet the other's knife-hand in a single, perfect, symmetrical movement. The opposing sweep of the blade in Henry's hand sliced through the tips of the other's fingers and thumb. They and the knife fell in a small, bloody mess onto the roadway.

'Shit, oh shit! Mother of God. What you do that for, you bloody eejut? Kitty said you were all right. You should've bloody minded your own business.' The wounded man struggled to unwind his neckcloth and began to wrap it round his bleeding hand.

'It's him that needs to bleed.' He waved his bloody parcel towards the crumpled figure of Fitzgerald a little distance off. 'God, and doesn't he make my sister bleed?'

All the men apart from the unconscious Major were now getting groggily to their feet. As they all listened to Kitty Shaughnessy's brother it was clear that the fight was over. No-one made a movement.

'I'm sorry,' said Henry. 'I just wanted you to drop the knife. You were going to kill him.'

'Who's he anyway,' said Shaughnessy, 'I took him for some kind of a bodyguard.'

The Indian had withdrawn a little and was standing quietly in the dark.

'I don't know,' said Henry, 'I've only just met him tonight.'

It had all taken perhaps no more than two minutes, maybe three. The back door of the Club opened and light flooded out. Figures appeared perhaps drawn by the commotion, perhaps just leaving that way. Henry could not tell. They seemed in no particular hurry. He knew he should call out, run towards them, cry murder. But he did not.

'You'd better go,' he said.

'Shunka, that you?' One of the men emerging from the back door of the club was Cody himself, looking for his horses and their minder.

Without a word the Indian loped back down the street to intercept him. The light from the doorway lit up the area just sufficiently for Henry see as far as the Hansom now, although he guessed he and the Major's motionless form on the cobbles would still be invisible to the newcomers on the scene. The Irishmen had melted silently away. The bloody fingertips and a knife beside a couple of cudgels the only testimony to what had so recently occurred.

Henry saw the Indian talking to Cody and his handful of companions from the Club, by the Hansom and their horses for what seemed an age. Then to his surprise and relief too Cody shook hands all round and he and the Indian mounted their horses and rode slowly back towards him, while the other men laughing and puffing on their glowing cigars went back inside the Club.

He waited until the two riders reached him. They both dismounted and Cody, grunting an acknowledgement to Henry, immediately went across to the Major, still lying motionless on the ground.

'He's alive anyhow,' he said, more to himself than to the Indian or Henry. 'Go and get that fancy rig of yours, we'd better get him home.

And get rid of this and whatever those are. He gestured at the assorted weapons on the ground.

Henry could not be sure whether Cody had seen the bloody morsels beside the knife or if he had, whether it had registered what they were.

He put Shannon to the shafts of the Hansom with a speed that even amazed him as he was doing it with only the light of its own lamps to aid him. Then he walked it back up to the three men. Cody and the Indian lifted Fitzgerald into his Pride and Joy.

'Now this kind of publicity I can do without,' Cody said to Henry, 'I don't know the half of what occurred here tonight. All I know is that this gentleman here had more to drink than was good for him and had to leave suddenly. Next thing he's out here like this surrounded by cold steel and blood, with one of my Sioux holding his hat and going on about a war party. Now those gentlemen in there…' he nodded in the direction of the club '…are none the wiser and I would be happy for it to stay that way. I've already gotten one of my cowboys up before the judge for fighting in a bar and frankly I don't need this. Especially not with this one,' he gestured at the Indian. 'We don't need it, do we, Shunka Wicasa?'

The Indian said nothing.

'Do we?' said Cody again, like a parent admonishing a child.

'No Colonel,' he said, 'We don't need this.'

Cody turned back to Henry. 'Now you drive. Shunka Wicasa will go inside with him and I'll take our horses back to my livery tonight. I rely on you to get him back to Earl's Court quietly tomorrow. Don't worry, he's quite house trained for a full-blooded Oglala Sioux.'

The Major stirred and groaned in the Hansom.

Henry's uncertainty must have shown in his face. 'The police…' The question in his voice was left unfinished.

Cody gave him a hard look. 'Shunka said something about somebody's sister,' he said, 'Sounds like something best kept in the family, I should say. Especially an Irish family,' he added, 'I should know, I come from one myself.'

Henry looked towards the club door through which Fitzgerald's fellow members had gone back in laughing.

'Rest easy,' said Cody, catching his anxious glance, 'He said it in Lakota.' Then he added, 'He also said something about you saving his life.'

Henry stared at him.

'That's quite a burden you may have taken on there, son,' said Cody.

Henry drove the Hansom with its two strange passengers round to the mews. Driving back to Bayswater he could see through the roof hatch that the Major was conscious, but only just. What with his hurt and the drink he was clearly unaware of the nature or identity of the human prop beside him.

'Wait here,' Henry said to the Indian, as he hurried up the garden to the kitchen. He could see Mr Davies snoozing in his chair, waiting for the Major's return. He tapped on the glass. Davies awoke with a start and unlocked the door. By the time it was open his face was already registering surprise and concern.

'What's wrong?' he said, 'Why aren't you at the front? Where's the Major?'

Henry was already heading back down the garden. 'He's in the Hansom, there's been…there's been … he's been attacked.'

'Is he alone?'

'No. One of Buffalo Bill's Indians is with him. He helped. He saved his life.'

'Christ! Did the whole world see it then?' Mr Davies gripped Henry's arm bringing him to a sudden halt.

'No, it was round the back. No-one knows. Only Buffalo Bill and he's saying nothing.'

They arrived, breathless, back at the stable. The Troop Sergeant-Major opened the door of the Hansom.

'Does he speak English?'

'Yes,' said Henry.

'Well, you stay here and keep out of sight, see,' Mr Davies barked at the Indian. 'Right Henry,' he said beginning to recover more of his composure, 'You get his legs and I'll get his arms and we'll take him in through the garden. How bad is he? Did you see it?'

'He took a good shoeing,' said Henry, 'At least one in the head.'

'His arm is broken,' said the Indian, who had not until then uttered a word.

'How do you know? Which one?' said Mr Davies?

'I felt it as we came. It is his fighting arm.

'His right? Well, he's left-handed.'

'I know this.'

'Can't be helped. We'll have to get him in anyhow,' said Mr Davies.

The Indian twitched aside his blanket. 'It is broken here.' He indicated on his own arm.

'You must tie him like this.' He held his left arm across his body, bent at the elbow, with the fingers touching his right shoulder. As he did so Henry saw that his shirt was soaked with blood.

'You're hurt too. I remember.'

'It is much blood but little hurt,' the Indian replied, 'The wound you stopped would have been worse.'

'Get some harness, Henry, something we can buckle,' said Mr Davies.

They strapped the semi-conscious and weakly protesting Major as the Indian had shown them and carried him across the garden, into the house and up to his bed. Despite their grunted exertion on the stairs, the house remained still and unawares.

'Right,' said Mr Davies when it was done, 'You sit here. I'm going for the doctor. He's only a few streets away. I'll think what to say as I go. But I don't want you telling him the truth till I've heard what you think it is and I haven't the time now, so I'll go. You stay.'

'What about the mare?' said Henry.

'What about the bloody mare?'

'She'll need taking out of the Hansom and bedding down.'

'She'll have to wait. You'd do better to think what you're going to do with the savage,' Mr Davies hissed with impatience.

It was about half an hour before Henry heard the front door open and close again followed moments later by the appearance of Mr Davies and the doctor in the bedroom. The Majordomo could not wait to hustle Henry out, leaving him wondering what tale he had spun to the doctor about Fitzgerald's condition.

He was not sorry to have been sent on his way; he was anxious to see to Shannon. But when he stepped through the gate in the garden wall, he was amazed to see the stable door setting open and the Hansom already wheeled away. Inside the Indian was hand rubbing Shannon with obvious care. Henry stared at them for a moment or two. He could read in the way she was standing and receiving his attention that the mare was being handled by someone very special. In the next stall, Liffey looked on with obvious interest too.

To Henry it felt as though he were watching himself with the horse, as if he had left his own body working there and gone to stand at a little distance to appraise his own performance.

'You know about horses then,' he said.

The Indian did not look up, but said, 'It is my name. It means Man-Who-Hears Horses. You too hear horses; I know this already. We cannot hide it from one another.'

He punctuated his words with the strokes of his hands and the stretching of his arms. 'The man who was hurt tonight, he lives with horses and the other who was here.' 'But they do not hear horses like you.'

'Cavalry men,' said Henry, 'Soldiers.'

'Yes,' said the Indian, 'Soldiers.' He stood up. The bloodstain on his shirt was showing scarlet again in the lamplight. The effort of grooming had opened his wound afresh.

'Do you need the doctor?' asked Henry, 'He may still be over at the house.'

'I have my own medicine at our *wechote*[*]. The wound looks more than it is.'

'Let me see,' said Henry, 'Come upstairs, you have done enough here for one night. I can finish racking up.' He led the way up to his room and motioned to the Indian to remove his shirt. As Henry thought he had seen, his attacker's knife had missed the neck and throat and skated along the collarbone leaving a cut that was long and thin but not very deep.

He went back down to the stable and fetched up some lint. Then he poured some water into the basin and proceeded to wipe the wound clean.

'It doesn't need stitching,' he said, 'But you will have a fine scar. It will go with all these others.' The Indian's naked torso was fairly etched with old cicatrices. 'I have some chloride of zinc for the horses, down below, that will help it mend quickly.'

He went and fetched it and some fresh lint and binding to hold it all in place.

'You too have fighting scars,' said the Indian. He had been looking at Henry's hands.

'Not a fight I looked for,' Henry said, 'Nor one I won.'

'Then there is a day still to come, when you will and I will be with you,' the Indian said without any emotion.

'What on earth do you mean?' said Henry, startled.

'We are brothers in blood,' said the other simply, 'I owe you my life. I will repay.'

'It was nothing,' said Henry almost ashamed, 'You must not think any more about it. Look, you'll be as right as rain in the morning.'

'It is meant,' said the Indian calmly.

'Oh bugger,' said Henry.

'What have you done with the savage?' said Mr Davies, sticking his head round the stable door shortly after first light.

'Nothing yet,' said Henry, 'And his name is Shunka Wicasa. Buffalo Bill said I was to see him back to Earls Court. I was thinking of putting him in the Hansom with the blinds down. He attracts a lot of attention otherwise.'

---

[*] Camp

'I was thinking you could take him on the railway from Queens Road. This Wild West show is right by the station at West Kensington, but perhaps you're right.The Major won't be needing the Pride and Joy for quite a while,' said Mr Davies.

'Is he all right?'

'Could be worse, a sight worse. Broken arm, sore head, lost some teeth. Bloody Irish savages.'

'How do you know? Did he say?' Henry felt himself becoming defensive.

'He didn't have to. Kitty's gone. Never came back from the post yesterday Mrs Bullace tells me. She thought…well I suppose we both thought she was upstairs waiting…never mind what we thought. It must have been all set up. She'd better pray we don't catch up with her and that family of hers. Cork can't hold her. Ireland's not big enough. She'd better run all the way to America and then some.'

There was nothing for Henry to say. Davies had said 'we'. He shivered inside, knowing what a fell team Fitzgerald and his Troop Sergeant-Major could be when they put their minds to it. So Kitty had done it after all, fled her narrow prison in Bayswater only to cast herself into a vaster one that was the whole wide world.

Shunka Wicasa had bedded himself down with his all-purpose blanket in the straw with the horses, but he was standing motionless in the shadows at the back of the stable when Henry turned from the door and Mr Davies had taken himself off. He smiled at the Indian shyly, not sure whether he should say good morning in the usual way.

'So he will live then?'

'Apparently,' said Henry.

'Good. He should not go into the spirit world without teeth.'

Henry decided to let this pass.

'Your English is very good,' he said. 'Do you all speak English as well as your own language? What did Colonel Cody call it?'

'Lakota. No. I am one of the older sons who were sent to the schools in East after the Custer fight. I have a speaking and hearing gift. It is easy. You also have this gift I know.'

'Well I don't know,' said Henry, 'I've only ever spoken English. I've never tried anything else. Miss Covington at school didn't try to teach us any French.'

'Then you have not tried your gift. But you speak to horses and hear them, so why not men?'

There was a calm certainty about the Indian that made Henry very comfortable, sure that whatever he might say was true, would indeed be true.

'I don't speak to horses out loud…' he began to say, but then realised that he had done so all his life and mostly had expected to be understood, that when he had his hands on them he had always been able to feel what they were saying even if they did not use a language like men.

'Would you like some food? Breakfast?'

'Some meat would be good.'

Henry was not sure whether he should take his new-found friend to Mrs Bullace's kitchen. Mr Davies had made a point of coming over to the stable himself presumably to forestall a sudden terrifying appearance below stairs. He had said nothing about feeding and watering him, only about getting shot of him. Still Henry was feeling very well disposed towards their saviour of the previous evening and decided finally that Mrs Bullace would turn out to have been very disappointed not to have had a real live Sioux Indian in her domain if he denied her this opportunity. Besides his presence would perhaps deter immediate discussion of Kitty.

He motioned Shunka Wicasa to follow him as far as the kitchen door, and then to wait a moment. Popping his head round it, he saw that the cook was on her own.

'Mrs Bullace,' he said, 'Don't be alarmed. I've got someone here who needs some breakfast before going…home.'

Mrs Bullace had a sullen, put-upon air about her.

''Ave you 'eard about that good-for-nothing little pot scourer? She's 'ooked it and left me and us all in the cart. And the poor Major upstairs in such a state. And you want breakfast for some crony. I 'ope it is a crony and not some common serving girl as should know better than be out at this hour.'

Henry nevertheless took this as acquiescence.

'He's a Red Indian,' he said, not knowing how else to explain things but feeling somewhat awkward about the sobriquet, 'He helped the Major last night and helped me bring him home.'

Mrs Bullace, whose whole demeanour said she had made up her mind the day was going from bad to worse, did not even bother to shriek as Henry ushered in their guest. She surveyed him up and down as if he were a dubious delivery from the butcher.

'Is he clean?' she said.

'Not enough for your house,' said Shunka Wicasa, 'Cleanliness is next to godliness as I have been told at the military school. There I bathed every week and had a clean shirt. In my people's village we bathed every day in the creeks. I have not bathed today or yesterday. I shall eat with the horses.'

Mrs Bullace stared at him open-mouthed. 'Wherever did 'e learn to speak like that?'

'At school,' said Henry, 'He says it's a gift.'

'It may be, but I can't 'ave 'im telling me about washing in my own kitchen.'

'He would like some meat for his breakfast, Mrs Bullace,' said Henry.

''Ot or cold? There's a leftover lamb cutlet or two in the larder and tea in the pot.'

Shunka Wicasa took the cutlets happily and a mug of tea less so, back to the stable with Henry. In the end he drank water from the mews pump.

While they were still eating, Mr Davies reappeared. 'Come along Henry. Hurry up and get that savage back where he belongs.'

'Doesn't the Major want to see him first?'

'What one earth would the Major want with him?'

'To thank him for saving his life. Saving people's lives and having your life saved is an important thing to this man.'

'What does he want? A bloody medal?' The Troop Sergeant-Major looked venomously at Henry, 'Just get him off out of it,' he said and turned sharply on his heel and departed, slamming the door into the garden behind him.

Henry and the Indian watched the space where he had been in silence.

After a moment or two Shunka Wicasa observed in a matter-of-fact voice, 'He has taken many scalps that one, but always from dead men others have killed.'

Henry did not understand the idea, but the words worked like a familiar scent on the air, painting a picture deep inside of something half remembered in time, perhaps from the past, perhaps from the future. Who could say? Perhaps not even from a time of his own at all. He felt he saw a kneeling figure, bound, by the river and a raised sword. But then too there was smoke and gunfire and the sound of frightened men he could not see, in pain and out of the smoke walked Mr Davies and Major Fitzgerald. He saw it all, simultaneously in the twinkling of an eye and then it was gone. Like a vivid dream from which one awakes and disremembers, watching it fade, unable to hold any part of it in the memory, save its emotion.

The two men glanced at one another.

'We shall be brothers and hunt together,' said Shunka Wicasa, 'For you and I have the *maka nongeya*, the earth ear.'

'I have to get you back to West Kensington first,' said Henry.

16

Henry opened the hatch in the roof of the Hansom.

'How do we get in?'

Shunka Wicasa, who was sitting stony faced wrapped in his blanket in the darkened interior, looked up.

'How do I get out? This coach is like a bad hole.'

The Indian encampment was at the eastern corner of the huge open-air arena that had been built to stage the Wild West alongside the Earl's Court exhibition hall which housed the American trade and culture fair. Henry released Shunka Wicasa who took the mare by the head and led them to a side gate.

Some men in low crowned, broad brimmed hats and leathers (cowboys, thought Henry excitedly) who were lounging and smoking just inside whistled and catcalled at the sudden apparition of the Major's Pride and Joy. Then they caught sight of the Indian, who had been hidden on the other side of Liffey, leading it.

'Hey,' called one, 'It's Man-Who-Hears-Horses.'

'Yeah,' said another, 'Man-Who-Heard-Custer's-Horses more like it. Surprised the Colonel's let him out of his sight.' The idlers sauntered towards the Hansom to intercept it as it attempted to pass them by.

'Well now soldier scalper, Man-who-puts-dead men's eyes out, where you rushing to? Why don't you stop and tell us one more time what a brave boy you were decoying the Seventh Cavalry into a duck shoot at the Big Horn? 'Cause we know what a fancy speaking American education you got, don't we boys. Maybe we should loosen that mighty fine tongue of yours and get you to tell us what some of these other friends of yourn like to do to decent white women and children, because they don't seem to speak American so good as you.'

There were five of them, standing round Liffey's head boxing Shunka Wicasa in. As they spoke they pushed him in the chest to emphasise their words. The Indian said nothing but just stood impassively looking the one in the forefront straight in the eye.

That'll get his goat for a start, thought Henry from his vantage point on the back box, painful memories of his broken nose suddenly flooding back. He reached into his waistcoat pocket and his fingers found his soft lump of wax.

‘’Ware my horse,’ he called out, ‘She’s middling nervous today.’

The little group stared up at Henry, as if noticing him for the first time.

‘You got a problem friend?’ said one, ‘’Cause I don’t recall asking you what it was.’

‘Well, don’t say I didn’t warn you,’ said Henry, squeezing the wax ball in his hand as he spoke. Liffey’s ears went back and she plunged forward in the shafts, scattering the men at her head.

As the Hansom took off briskly in the direction of the Indian encampment they could only stand back and watch. As it passed Shunka Wicasa, who appeared to have had the uncanny presence of mind to let the bridle go at precisely the right moment, he stepped smartly up onto the side step. The cowboys broke into a trot after them whooping and beating their hats on their flanks as if they were boys urging on broomstick horses.

‘C’mon boys, this here’s fancier than the Deadwood Stage,’ shouted one. But the moment of unpleasant menace had, at least for the time being, turned to one of humour as other members of the show, Indians and cowboys alike, began to emerge from the background to see what the commotion was about and so turning the private confrontation into an audience spectacle.

As the Hansom reached the first of the Indian lodges the pursuing cowboys stopped and then strolled back to the gate, laughing and muttering. Henry brought the vehicle to a stand and got down from the box, uncertain what to do next. Shunka Wicasa walked off and disappeared behind the first row of lodges, reappearing very shortly after with a bucket of water for Liffey.

‘Come,’ he said to Henry, leading the way through the encampment, stopping in a little while at the entrance to one of the hide covered structures. Motioning Henry to wait a moment, he stooped down low so that he was almost crawling on his hands and knees and disappeared through the low opening. After what seemed an age to Henry, who was soaking in the strange surroundings and already composing a letter to his mother, imagining it being read aloud by Annie to the assembled kitchen at the Veil House, Shunka Wicasa re-emerged.

‘He is ready. You must go in. I have told him we are brothers now.’

He turned and called in his own language to two Indian women seated outside a nearby lodge.

'They will see to the she-horse. Bend low to the ground inside and sit beside him.'

Henry did as he was told and as he had seen the Indian do earlier. At first he assumed that he was required to enter in this manner as some mark of respect to whomever was on the inside, but even if this was the case it also served a practical purpose. It meant he entered the lodge below the level of the smoke from the small open fire in the centre. The smoke hung in a layer at what would have been about waist and head height had he been standing upright, before it was slowly but steadily drawn upwards and out by the updraft of the tent's twisted peak. He was also still at the level of the low entrance hole which admitted the only daylight into the interior, enabling his eyes to become more readily accustomed to the semi-darkness.

He sat as he had been bidden beside the Indian already there. He was a man of about the Bailey's age or so it felt to Henry. Shunka Wicasa who had followed him in sat down on the other side. There followed a brief exchange between the two Indians in their strange tongue while Henry waited to be told what he should do next. Somehow shaking hands and commenting on the weather did not seem entirely appropriate although it did flit across his mind for a moment.

Then Shunka Wicasa said to Henry, 'He is called *Mato Ska*. It means Bear-with-white-fur. He is of my father's family. I stay with him and his woman with others like me here who do not have their own woman yet.'

Mato Ska turned slightly to Henry and addressed him at some length. When he had finished Henry looked at Shunka Wicasa questioningly.

'He says you are welcome because you are good medicine to the Bear people. I have told him about the knife in the dark and about the men at the gate. I too am Bear people. My birth name was *Mato Sapa*[*].'

'Would you say that I am very pleased to meet him too,' said Henry, 'And say that I really didn't do very much at all.' He thought for a moment and added, 'Tell him I have never had any brothers. I'm not quite sure what I shall do with one now that I seem to have been given one.'

Shunka Wicasa spoke again to the older man. Henry supposed that he had truly translated because his shoulders moved in a gentle chuckle. Then Mato Ska reached behind him and produced a roll of soft leather which he undid in front of him on the ground to reveal an elaborate smoking pipe.

'I have told him that you have horse medicine, too,' said Shunka Wicasa.

'Why, is his sick then?' said Henry.

---

[*] Bear-with-brown-fur

'No, it is not that,' said Shunka Wicasa, 'Medicine is the gift you have. Medicine sets you apart from other men. It must be tended or it will die and maybe you with it. Mato Ska wishes you to smoke a pipe with him so that some of your medicine will come to him.'

'Well I don't smoke, as a rule' said Henry, 'But I wouldn't wish to cause offence. Tell him it would be a pleasure.'

Henry was not at all certain that it was going to be a pleasure. Mato Ska lit the pipe with an ember from the fire and took several deep puffs. A strange fragrance began almost at once to compete with the smell of wood smoke and the pungent reek of the kippered hides of the construction surrounding them. As he breathed it in, Henry found his misgivings melting away and being replaced by a yearning to hold the pipe and to suck in the sensuousness of the smoke. It was as if all his life up to this point had been an unrealised preparation for this moment. An almost unbearable tension began to wind itself tighter and tighter inside him and he knew then that there was something not of himself dwelling there, being roused from slumber. Oh so slowly did the pipe seem to come to him and fuse itself into his waiting grasp, into his hand that seemed to him to melt and reshape itself, gently washed clean of its crooked hurts.

There were sounds of a slight commotion outside and even as Henry was putting the pipe stem to his lips the covering to the entrance hole blinked daylight briefly as it was pulled aside before the silhouette of a woman filled it again. She called inside in her own tongue.

'The Colonel has come. He is outside,' said Shunka Wicasa peremptorily.

The ceremonial was clearly at an end. The three men emerged singly from the lodge, Henry alone blinking in the sudden glare and his eyes smarting from the wood smoke inside.

Cody was standing with a few other white men. He was less gorgeously dressed than on the previous evening but nevertheless presented a striking figure, one that demanded instant acceptance of his authority. He glanced at Henry and nodded his head briefly acknowledging him. Then he beckoned to the two Indians and took them on one side, out of Henry's earshot and the small group that was gathered there. He was clearly laying down the law about something. The older man seemed inclined to argue, but Shunka Wicasa stood silently saying nothing. Whatever the exchange was, the Colonel would brook no denial. After a while they walked back over to Henry.

'How's Major Fitzgerald this morning?' Cody asked him.

Henry said he was in poor shape but not likely to suffer any permanent injury.

'Not as permanent as those men intended it to be, no small thanks to you and Shunka here I guess,' said Cody, 'Is he sitting up and taking notice yet?'

Henry was not sure.

'Well if you can wait a while, I'd like you to take him a note from me. I'll get someone to show you around if you would like, but I guess it had better not be Shunka here. I have to keep this one close where I can see him, more's the pity. But it's for his own good. I hear he had some more trouble at the gate this morning.'

Henry allowed himself to be led away like a dog with two tails by one of Cody's lieutenants, thankful that it was not one of the lounging cowboys that had been deputed to the task, but slightly awestruck that he was being accorded so much ungrudging attention by a gentleman. Even if he is an American, Henry thought. He was sorry though, that his friend had had to be whipped in and could not be the one to illuminate his delight.

After his tour of the show's behind-the-scenes, they fetched up at the tent that served as Buffalo Bill's offices when he was in camp and not at his hotel in Regent Street.

'Did you like what you saw? I'll bet you did,' said Cody, greeting Henry as they entered.

'Especially the horses,' said Henry.

'I'll bet you did. Now here's a letter I want you to deliver into your Major's own hand and if he ain't in a fit state to read it, I want you to read it to him yourself. I assume a smart fellow like you knows how to read, don't you? This here is between the three of us here and the Major.'

Henry pocketed the envelope curiously and feeling himself dismissed, turned to go.

'Oh, and I guess you'd like some tickets for the show wouldn't you? Do you think you'd be let out? Do you have someone you'd care to bring with you?'

Henry almost blessed the Major's incapacity. It meant that there would be very little to prevent him getting to see the spectacle the whole of London was talking about, especially if he made sure of a ticket for Mr Davies.

'Could I have two…no, three tickets, do you think?' he said tentatively.

Cody sucked his teeth in mock disapproval. 'I see you mean to take advantage of my generous nature after only a short acquaintance, but I suppose the profits can just about run to it.'

Mr Davies was not at all happy about letting Henry up on his own to see the Major, but however much he tried to conceal it his mood lightened considerably when he learned that Henry's excursion that morning had resulted in some free passes to the Wild West Exhibition.

'I shall have to go and see whether he's up to having visits at all, let alone from his groom. What's so important anyway that I can't take it up to him?'

Henry had thought about this carefully on the way home with the Pride and Joy, foreseeing just such an obstacle being thrown in the path of his undertaking to Cody.

'Well, Buffalo Bill's handwriting is a bit difficult to make out so he's read it over to me in case the Major needs some help with it.'

The Majordomo grudgingly bore himself off upstairs, his grumbling asides leaving Henry in no doubt that one of the tickets in his possession had his name firmly on it.

While he was gone, Mrs Bullace clattered about in the kitchen making it very difficult for Henry to ignore her presence.

'There's one for you too, he said, unable to maintain his teasing silence a moment longer in the face of her imperious bustling.

At once she was all smiles and unconvincing denials of any expectations on her part.

'I'm not sure we shall all be able to go, leaving the poor Major upstairs in bed.'

'No,' agreed Henry dubiously, 'Perhaps not. Oh well…'

The cook was not prepared for her unintended words to be taken so literally.

'No matter,' she said, 'Pr'aps the Major would be up to 'avin' one of 'is club cronies in for supper if 'e's on the mend and I could get Mrs Pivett in from next door to sit for the bell. I'll talk to Mr Davies.'

Mr Davies came back into the kitchen at that moment.

'Five minutes that's all Henry, five minutes and don't think you can make a habit of this. And don't talk to him about that Irish slut.'

Henry wondered what made him think he would want to anyway, but said nothing.

Major Fitzgerald was propped up in bed, his head bandaged, one arm in a sling and looking considerably bruised and swollen about the face so that his eyes were barely visible. Henry was taken aback by the extent of his attackers' handiwork and for an instant he regretted having allowed Kitty's brother the opportunity to make a run for it. He looked at the Major and saw himself not so many months previously, propped up on the truckle bed at Great Aunt Elizabeth's.

Something of the sort must have registered with the Major.

'Had to cut me out of m'dress tails too,' he mumbled, 'Thought about you Turner, after. Davies says you've got a letter from Cody.'

'Yes,' said Henry, 'I was to give it to you personally, myself.'

'Op'n it then.'

Henry did so and held it for Fitzgerald to see.

'No, can't make it out,' he said without even really making an attempt.

'He said I was to read it to you if you could not,' said Henry, 'Shall I?'

'Odd,' said the Major, 'But I s'pose you'd better. Damn'd odd,' and he winced with the effort.

So Henry read him Buffalo Bill's letter.

Earls Court Arena
West Kensington
18th August 1887

My Dear Major Fitzgerald,

I am sorry indeed this finds you in such a fix after we had spent such a convivial evening together at the United Services Club. We must be thankful that my Indian was on hand to prevent a worse outcome the like of which it is best not to dwell on. If you can recall anything of our dinner conversation and I, for one, would not be surprised if our pleasant exchanges had entirely fled your mind, you may remember that I discussed this very same Indian (Shunka Wicasa in his own tongue) who as luck fell out was happily on hand.

Not to put too fine a point on it, his usefulness to the Exhibition as a bare back rider and as one of my best interpreters is in grave danger of being set at zero since some of my men have found out about his past and how he got his name. He has, my dear sir, not made enemies so much as found them again. Indeed, he is not a man who goes about making enemies, although it has to be acknowledged that, given cause, all Indians will carry blood grudges to the death and pass them to their sons to carry on. This is natural and done with pride. Some of my men, I have to admit, are just plain quarrelsome and will pick a fight first and find the reason for it later, although in this case enough of them feel they have a just cause.

I may have mentioned to you last night, that I already have one of my cowboys in one of your jails for fighting and assaulting the police and I cannot be doing with this kind of publicity when we are in the way of entertaining Royalty. Shunka's part in last night's goings on was fortunate for you but, my dear Major, to be blunt, the episode is not something either of us would wish to become the subject of common gossip if that can possibly be avoided. I am sure we are of one mind on that, even though our reasons may differ.

You told me that you had it in mind to take on an extra hand to help with your horses, someone who might also be useful to have around the place at night. I need to get Shunka out of sight until we head back home, otherwise I fear I may have a killing or two to explain here in West Kensington.

He seems to have taken quite a liking to your groom, so my dear Major, I propose you take him for his keep alone until the end of our final run in Manchester after which I will ship him back home with us. Do this and you will ever have the true friendship of your servant

William F. Cody (Colonel, United States Army, retired)

Henry paused for breath. It had been a difficult letter to read aloud anyway, but more to the point the content had caused a mounting excitement in him as it progressed. So the Indian was to come and live with him in the mews then. Although the Major had as yet made no comment one way or the other on what, Henry later reflected, was an altogether extraordinary request, made with a slight edge of menace, Henry knew it was a foregone conclusion, as he uttered the letter's rank-pulling valediction, which would have earned Miss Covington's approval. It was meant.

His waiting and watching for the next significant piece of his life's pattern to show itself had come to pass. Shunka Wicasa had been in no doubt, but Henry had been unable to see how he could be part of its central motif, contained as he was within the confines of the Wild West Exhibition.

'But gaffer Reuben has fixed him good.' Henry made the voice in his head sound like the Head Baiter at the Veil House talking of one of Bailey Turner's horse deals. He grinned inside himself as he did, knowing that it was no accident that an Icingbury commonplace should choose to assert itself right now.

'He shall come and we shall go to Icingbury together,' and he realised he had said it out loud.

'Remains to be seen' mumbled the Major.

Henry had quite forgotten him.

'Not impossible I s'pose, not impossible. Might send you both packing sooner than Cody thinks. Both bring me nothing but trouble. Can't write. You'll have to take it down. No better still, telegram, send him a telegram to his rooms in Regent Street, s'more private. Club'll know where.'

'What should it say? Henry had never composed a telegram, but knew the more you said the more it cost.

'Just say "Yes stop send him round stop Fitzgerald".'

Henry turned to go.

'Oh and tell Davies and Bullace and Kitty. Have to know sooner or later. No, I'd better tell Davies. He can tell them. Good order 'n discipline 'n all that.'

Henry opened his mouth and heard the words come tumbling out before he could stop them.

'Kitty's gone, Major.'

Even the pallid, swollen and bruised Fitzgerald managed to look ashen.

'The devil she has,' he croaked, 'Get that damn Troop Sergeant-Major up here on the double'.

'It just came out,' said Henry, 'I thought he would have known by now.'

The sound of the Major's displeasure with Mr Davies at having been kept in the dark about Kitty's disappearance had managed to carry down two floors despite his injuries. On his return to the kitchen he gave Henry a long look that made his blood run cold, but all he said was, 'What's done is done'. Then he told Mrs Bullace about the imminent arrival of 'Turner's savage'.

Mrs Bullace took the announcement with an uncharacteristic silence that perplexed Henry. Then she said 'And when are we going to see the cowboys?'

'I'm not so sure we shall,' retorted Mr Davies spitefully, 'I'll have to see,' and he stalked off with his chest and backside out.

For a few moments Henry was fixed in self-absorption. His elation at the thought of having Shunka Wicasa under their roof was now smudged with the recrimination that two words out of place from him had caused.

When he came out of his preoccupation he saw that the cook was sitting crumpled and forlorn. It shook him. He could not believe that the prospect of perhaps not going to the Wild West Exhibition after all could have brought her so low. It was as if the normally chirpy and acerbic Mrs Bullace had stepped aside. What was now seated at the kitchen table, Henry instinctively understood, was the reality that dwelt within her self. It had been awakened, as his had begun to be in the Earls Court tepee. But hers was a sorry thing, a shadow of her, as if a consumption had instantly wasted her inside her clothes without any warning.

‘Why Mrs B. Whatever is the matter?’

‘They’ve gone for ’er; I ’eard ’im talkin’ to them in the area. ’E’s set ’is dogs to find ’er and God ’elp ’er, poor soul, when they do. Reckoned on ’avin’ ’er back ’ere before the Major knew she were gone. Present for ’im, Mister Davies said. *Mister* Davies. Mister Devils-in-hell more like.’ Her shoulders shook soundlessly as if she were suddenly cold.

Henry needed to ask very little. He took in all she was saying in the twinkling of an eye. The pictures swirled and jostled in his head, too many to be seen altogether, but glimpsed like coloured papers blown in the wind.

‘They’re men from the army days, aren’t they, these dogs of his?’

The shadow of the cook nodded hopelessly.

‘Something like this has happened before then…to Kitty?’

‘No, not Kitty. Irish boy. Family. She ’ad to watch. I try to put it out of my mind. I try and I try. I make myself bluff old Bullace an’ I made myself nasty to ’er so as they won’t twig I know. And then nothin’ ’appens for a long while, so I do begin to put it out of my mind. But now it’s all come again, an’ when they fetch ’er back ’ere, what will old Bullace do? ’Ide away as usual.’

‘And the Major…does he…did he, before?’

‘No ’e doesn’t get ’is ’ands dirty, ’e don’t ’ave to. So ’e can deny all knowledge if it comes to it.’

‘Perhaps they won’t find her,’ said Henry softly. But something told him that they would. They were meant to.

Then came the grim realisation. None of this was just about him, was it? Dr. Birchall’s letter had shown him that one thing was consequent on another and another and another. He had lain with that thought until his brain hurt and cried out for sleep. But this was altogether a more terrible idea. In digging up Reuben and listening to whatever it was he had to say he was not just opening doors for himself, he had made consequences for others too. He asked himself how would the world stand now if curiosity had not taken him to the edge of the swollen Icing more than a year ago. Would everything now be just the same except for his participation in it, the Major fit and well, Kitty not stalked like a broken bird? It was not possible to say ‘yes’ to that. The whole fabric of everyone else’s experience he shared would unravel in an instant if his piece of it were removed, so how could it ever have been there without him?

‘I might be hurting people I don’t even know about yet, may never know about,’ he whispered to Liffey’s flank as he worked his fingers through her coat that night. ‘People might be dying just because I’m here now. But everyone must be doing that too, I suppose, not just me, so perhaps what I might start, someone else might stop just by not being somewhere. And if it weren't for that Reuben, I would never have thought about it. That's the bloody difference. Now I know it's all my fault.'

The next morning breakfast was consumed in near silence. It was, thought Henry, as if someone had died in the house. After a while a subdued Mrs Bullace ventured to ask who should take the Major up something. Mr Davies nearly always did this but Henry could see that her question was a veiled invitation for them to discuss the consequences of Kitty's absence. It was not lost on Henry that she had put aside the rancorous abuse which she had poured out on the subject of the maid's sudden departure before, and he could not see how Mr Davies could not notice it either.

'I'll see to it,' said the Majordomo, adding, 'You'll have to put out some feelers for a new girl, the house is going to rack and ruin. It's a good job it's summer and the grates don't need laying.'

Henry stood up and began to move to the garden door. 'I must get on,' he said.

'I was wonderin' if Kitty mightn't turn up after all,' said Mrs Bullace, 'But I'll walk round to the agency directly.'

Henry was flabbergasted at the sheer danger of Mrs Bullace's words. He had all but closed the door behind him but he paused with it slightly ajar.

'She's got about as much intention of turning up here on her own say-so as Sergeant Bullace,' he heard Mr Davies say in a very unpleasant tone, 'And we both know what he got when he did, and why. So don't you go forgetting to mind your tongue, you old cat, or I'll whip it out.'

Henry heard the door to the stairs close sharply and he peeped back in.

Mrs Bullace was sitting stock still at the head of the kitchen table, clutching the screwed up hem of her apron to her mouth and chin with both hands. For an instant Henry thought Mr Davies had actually carried out his nasty threat. She was staring straight ahead, not seeing. Henry sat down quietly to one side of her and gently took hold of her wrist nearest to him. She turned her head towards him then and lowered her apron. There was a look of ghastly panic in her eyes and around her mouth.

'Sergeant Bullace?' Henry spoke softly to her.

'My 'usband as was.'

'And what happened to him? What did they do to him?'

'I can't say. Don't make me say. Not 'ere, not now. Just 'ope they don't catch that girl.'

17

Henry assumed that there was now no question of any of them going to see the Wild West Exhibition. The atmosphere in the house was changed and tense. Kitty's absence was not referred to. It was as if each of its occupants knew some part of what lay behind it but were avoiding laying out their separate pieces in case the whole should fire and fuse as they came together. Mr Davies was hardly likely to reveal his knowledge, Henry could see that, and he could only guess at what the sum of it was. Mrs Bullace's knowledge weighed on her like some bad thing she had eaten and wished she could vomit up but, like a child in the night, feared more the physical anguish it would entail.

The more Henry thought about it, the more he wondered what he was really sure about. That Kitty's brother had set out to wreak some desperate harm on the Major or, indeed worse, that much he knew. But had Kitty been the informant who had brought about the murderous ambush? He could not say. Perhaps she had disappeared because she knew of it, but was powerless to intervene. Had she pleaded with her brother to leave things be, not to make things worse? The woman Henry knew was more likely to seek to absorb the pain for which she had already accepted there was no quick remedy. But he wanted too, to see her as Boudicca and her daughters, taking the insults and the suffering, being treated as people with no belonging, owned and not owning, and then rising up with fire and rage, becoming terrible and just. Henry wondered what small moment in time had brought them all to this pass and how many more people in time to come might hang their own misfortunes upon it.

Within a day or two Mrs Bullace had installed a new maid-of-all-work, named Ivy, from the agency. Her presence in the house forced an air of normality to re-establish itself, so when word came that someone, preferably Henry should contrive to extricate Shunka Wicasa discreetly from the West Kensington encampment and fetch him to Bayswater, Henry managed to bring himself to exchange more than a few words punctuated by heavy silence with Mr Davies.

He told him there was little point in him taking the Pride and Joy because of the incident it had provoked when he had been seen with it before.

'You'll have to take a growler then,' said Mr Davies, 'Only that will cause a lot of talk too when you arrive at the door with a painted savage in tow.'

'I could take him some stable clothes,' said Henry, 'He'll have to wear those when he's here, anyway, I should think. If I can get him into those and do something about his hair…'

'Scalp him, I should,' said Mr Davies nastily

'…then perhaps I could even walk him here without him being noticed,' Henry concluded, not to be put off.

'Or bring him on the underground train,' suggested Mrs Bullace.

Henry was a bit dubious about that, having not yet steeled himself to take a ticket and disappear into the bowels of the Metropolitan Railway at Queens Road. He was aware of the smoke, sparks and deafening roar that emerged from the vent just off St Petersburg Place and the frisson it gave him. What effect would it have on a Sioux Indian?

Mrs Bullace must have caught something of Henry's hesitation.

'I know what,' she said, addressing herself to him and obviously intending to exclude Mr Davies, 'We could take ourselves off to see the show with your tickets and fetch the savage back with us. We could go to the matinee.'

'His name is Shunka Wicasa,' said Henry wearily.

'Chunk o' what? Some sort of cheese?' said Mr Davies. 'Anyhow,' he continued as Henry refused to be provoked, 'I'm not having you two off gallivanting on your own. One of those tickets is mine.'

Much as Henry had no desire now to spend the afternoon with the Troop Sergeant-Major, he was relieved at this further affirmation that something of the household's equilibrium was returning. He had not expected to hear the trip to the show mentioned again.

'That's settled then,' said Mrs Bullace as if it were, 'We'll all go and Hivy can listen for the Major's bell.'

Henry half expected the proprietorial Mr Davies to object to this arrangement for his master, but he did not. The suspicion began to insinuate itself into his head that maybe Mr Davies was more concerned not to let the two of them out of the house together where he could not see or hear them.

'Will you be able to find him?' asked Mr Davies.

'I think so, if I know where he's going to be waiting. I was given a good look round the ground and the Indian camp. If I go and get him just before it ends, we can all mix in with the crowds when they leave. I don't want the cowboys on the gate to see us on our own.'

'This is beginning to sound like a great deal of fuss about nothing,' said Mr Davies.

But Henry reminded him gently of the part that Shunka Wicasa had played in rescuing the Major from his attackers, 'Neither he nor Buffalo Bill want any word of it to get out, and where Colonel Cody is the newspapers are never very far away.' He emphasised 'Colonel'. It had the desired effect.

There was a three o'clock performance the following Wednesday, Henry discovered from the newspaper. Another telegram was authorised by the Major upstairs and it was proposed Shunka Wicasa should be waiting in Cody's tent on that day. The telegraph boy was instructed to wait for a reply which, when it came simply said 'Agreed'.

The prospect of at last getting some help in the stable would in itself have been enough to keep Henry in a state of high anticipation. That it was to be his very own Indian warrior meant he could barely contain himself, despite Kitty's disappearance and the changed air it had brought about in the kitchen.

Mr Davies was evidently determined to let the house find its own level again. He acted more and more as if nothing untoward had happened, which became easier to believe as the next few days passed without incident. Henry was preoccupied with planning for Shunka Wicasa's arrival and the matter of living accommodation and sleeping arrangements. Mrs Bullace, while still much subdued, returned to some of her customary terms of endearment and reproach drawn from her perception of the qualities of the kitchen utensils around her. She began referring to 'Hivy' as her 'little wooden washing dolly', sometimes shortened to just 'my little wood' both of which Henry privately thought entirely appropriate although he doubted whether Mrs Bullace had given the sobriquet more than cursory thought.

She had faded almost visibly in the days since she had learned of the hunt for Kitty and was finding it difficult to recover her flowery self again, although Henry could see she thought it would somehow help Kitty's case if she kept up her old appearances at least in front of Mr Davies.

Henry exercised both the mares early on the Wednesday morning and apologised to them for the disturbance to their routine. He packed up the set of stable clothes he had obtained for Shunka Wicasa, whom he judged to be about the same age and height as himself. 'Perhaps a little taller,' he said aloud to himself for about the tenth time that morning, 'And maybe a year or two older, maybe not.' These two thoughts had assumed an importance for Henry that he could not shake from his mind. As they kept chasing round in his head he realised that he had no impression of how old Reuben had been, but 'a young man though, surely, like us.'

When he put in his appearance for early dinner in the kitchen as arranged, he found Mrs Bullace in a state of animation the like of which he had almost forgotten.

'What is it then Mrs Bullace,' he ventured cautiously, wary of what might have brought about her high colour and dither. The fragility and anxiety that he had been putting to the back of his mind suddenly came surging forward with a vengeance at the sight of her.

'It's 'im, 'e's not comin' after all. Put 'is 'at on and left, sayin' we'd 'ave to manage without 'im.'

The cold fingers reached down into the bottom of Henry's stomach, grasping at his fear. He had almost forgotten their existence. He must have looked as solemn as he suddenly felt. Mrs Bullace stared into his face, reading it.

'Oh no,' she said, 'You don't think they've gone and found 'er?'

Ivy came into the room.

'No, I shouldn't think so,' said Henry, 'Don't fret about it.'

They relapsed into silence, but it sounded in Henry's ears like rushing water and running feet.

Mrs Bullace was an old hand at the Metropolitan Underground Railway, taking it on some of her occasional free afternoons to visit an acquaintance at the back of the Edgware Road.

'We'll get three returns,' she whispered confidently, clearly assuming the transport responsibilities for their foray were hers, 'Then we won't 'ave to 'ang about on the way back causin' a stir with 'is nibs.'

'Shunka Wicasa,' said Henry absently, too preoccupied taking in the bustle of the tiled ticket hall and elegant wood and iron stairway at the end leading down.

'Yes, we'll 'ave to do something about that name. Too much of a mouthful, by 'alf.'

When he had thought about it at all, Henry had convinced himself he knew all there was to know about railway travel after his journey from Great Duster. Yet the tunnel vent near St Petersburg Place with its infernal bursts of fire and brimstone spoke to him of a different kind of creature altogether. Not that he was merely frightened of the unknown, if he felt anything it was more the trepidation he had had when dared to take on those extra few feet of the climbing elm on the way from school, at the risk of getting stuck too high when he was already overdue at home for his chores. Something too, told him that railways and horses did not mix. Already today he found himself going somewhere without using either his feet or a horse's. Henry felt odd about that, almost guilty. It was a small betrayal.

The platform was already packed. Mrs Bullace seized Henry unceremoniously by the wrist and propelled him crabwise in front of her to part a way near to the edge. Henry thought at first that she would push him onto the track, but satisfied with their position she brought him to a standstill.

'This'll do,' she bawled at him pulling his shoulder down to reach his ear.

Henry still felt exposed and vulnerable so close to the edge and with such a press of people around them. They swayed as a single entity every few seconds like water in a basin being carried upstairs, as more and more folk descended the stairs from street level.

But the tension he had was nothing compared to what he experienced as a growing distant hiss beyond the darkness of the tunnel mouth grew and grew in intensity and then suddenly, what had started first as sheer noise, became movement and took shape. In an ethereal mix of black and gold, blurred with steam, the engine and its carriages burst into the glassy daylight of Queens Road Station, rumbling and squealing past him, filling his vision, so close he could have reached his hand out and touched the heat and the hardness of it and it would have devoured the flesh and the bone of him as he did.

Mrs Bullace gave him another shove and then they were jammed in the carriage with the rest of the world or so it seemed to Henry. From the disconnected snatches of overheard conversations around him, he gathered that such a crush at this time of the day was unnatural and due entirely to Buffalo Bill's Wild West, whither they were almost all bound.

He reflected that since leaving Icingbury the substance of his life had been periodically reinforced by significant journeys. Often his realisation that he had reached another one of Annie Lilley's doorways came after a journey. Coming to London with Roger Birchall was the biggest of course, but there had been others, leaving things behind for good and moving him on.

As he swayed mechanically to the demands of the train and caught the sulphurous bite of the tunnel's atmosphere at the back of his throat and in his eyes, he thought of that journey in the Particular and how different had been the felted silence of the fog. He thought too of taking the Major to the Buffalo Bill dinner at the club, how Warwick Street had been a sinister tunnel of darkness, unrelieved by the wispy glow of gas and gig lamps. The journey he and the cook were now embarked on was already speeding him through another doorway, he sensed, and it was barely begun.

Much, much later in the small hours, with the ferment of his most extraordinary day still bubbling round his body denying him sleep, he sat on the edge of his bed and pulled his kitchen chair writing desk quietly towards him so as not to disturb his new companion in the stable below.

He wrote,

Bayswater
Thursday 20th August, 1887

My dear Mother and everyone,

Today I went to Buffalo Bill's Wild West with Mrs Bullace by the underground railway. It goes from very near us in Bayswater. I do not know which was the more exciting, the journey there or the spectacle at the end. I am not sure about railways, they don't seem very fair on the horses somehow. I sometimes wonder what will happen to them all when everyone goes by train under the streets. The buses and trams that go down the Uxbridge Road - I should say the Bayswater Road now, because it has had its name changed for some reason this year – are always coming to a halt because there is so much traffic in the way and they carry so few people, not like the Metropolitan Railway. When Mrs Bullace and I boarded ours there must have been two hundred people or more with us by the time we arrived at West Kensington which is the station right beside the show ground. Maybe all the horses will end up just as performing beasts like those in Buffalo Bill's spectacle.

The riding was truly grand, especially by the Indian warriors. People call them savages but I cannot believe that is right as they are magnificent horsemen. I know a man cannot be just called a savage who understands his horse as they do. They ride without saddles and a simple bridle without a bit and can hang down one side of their ponies and fire rifles and arrows under their necks without breaking pace. There were some real buffalo brought from America too, which the Indians and the cowboys pretended to hunt. There are so few of them now they say that soon there may be none left. Will it be the same for horses too one day perhaps? It is hard to believe such a thing, but then there are so many machines coming on, like we have for the threshing.

At the end a coach called the Deadwood Stage Coach came on and drove round the ring. It is much bigger than a circus ring, but even so it was difficult to believe that the coach would not topple over at the turns so fast did it go. Then just when I thought that beat all for spectacle, all the Indians on their ponies came pursuing it with shouts and cries that made me wonder what it would be like if they were truly after the coach and I were in it. There was such a hush from the crowd I think the same thought had gone through all our heads. Then the cowboys dressed as cavalrymen came riding in to the rescue with Buffalo Bill himself at their head and we all let out a cheer, even Mrs Bullace. The Indians all had to play dead or ride off, but they all got up at the end.

I should tell you that I have met Buffalo Bill or Colonel Cody as he really is and I have also made friends with one of the Indians who has been to school and speaks English although this is very unusual, I believe. I met them when I was driving the Major.

I hope, Ma, that you and Pa are both well as is
Your loving son
Henry

I hope you are well, too, Annie. I will tell you that my friend the Indian is a warrior and a horseman like Reuben. He is to be my help in the stable. I have been thinking about Icingbury lately and you and the folk there. I have heard that Doctor Birchall is coming back and saw Sim. I have been puzzling over why he joined the Essex's.
Henry

He pondered over this spare postscript. It was more than he had said directly to Annie since she had declined to go to Great Duster Station with him. It had never been his intention to say more about how the Buffalo Bill day, as he was beginning to think of it, had ended. Even though time had run its course and he was writing, waiting for another day to break, he could not regard the day as done.

It had been quite extraordinary. That white hot glow had returned, that he felt when he was having to test himself, jump into the unknown, the glow he had felt on his very first arrival in Bayswater.

Hardly waiting for the first round of tumultuous applause to subside and the calls of 'encore, encore' to begin to revive it, he and Mrs Bullace had pushed their way out of the stand, much to the irritation of those inconvenienced, the cook expostulating to any who took their early departure amiss, 'When a lady's got to go, a lady's got to go'.

They had made their way round the back of the stands to the Colonel's own tent, more or less unchallenged, especially when Mrs Bullace intimated that she was 'in need of the conveniences'. Fortunately Cody's personal secretary, who was evidently in the know, was on hand as they approached. He nodded them in and raising his hat to Mrs Bullace motioned her to a chair in the outer vestibule to the lodge, which certainly had far more imposing and manageable entrance arrangements than the Indian tepees at the other end of the ground.

Henry meanwhile had gone further in to where Shunka Wicasa was waiting patiently, standing stock still with his arms folded, a stance which Henry was beginning to find familiar. To his immense surprise, however, the Indian was dressed in trousers, shirt, waistcoat and some kind of pea jacket. He had looked warm. The vermilion and ochre face paint had gone, as had his feather, but his hair was still in a long bound braid hanging over down over his shoulder at the front.

'I brought you some things, but I see you don't need them.'

'These are better, I know,' said Shunka Wicasa, 'But not these.'

He looked down and so did Henry at the laced black boots he had on.

'I was struck many times at the school for refusing such as these, but now...' he opened his arms and spread his hands in a gesture of humorous resignation.

Henry smiled too. It was the first time he had seen him capable of not being serious.

Mrs Bullace's aid had been enlisted to pin up Shunka Wicasa's braided hair. She had pins a-plenty in her bag and contrived a kind of bulging French roll with his braid so that it would more or less sit out of sight under the broad-brimmed hat provided for him. There had been no question of cutting it off.

To Henry's amusement, he saw that Mrs Bullace could not wait to get her hands on the Indian. She pushed and turned him about like a child being got ready for church, pulling his head down to her diminutive reach. Her every gesture said that she had not embarked on this adventure to remain in primitive awe of a savage. She was anointing their new ally into the divided house that awaited him.

She stepped back to appraise her tonsorial handiwork.

'You still look a bit foreign' she said, 'It's the 'at. Rather Bo'emian.'

Henry had supposed that this was a signal that Shunka Wicasa had passed muster. He grinned wryly at him.

'Come on,' he said, 'Time to get lost in the crowd.'

He had picked up his now-redundant bundle and Shunka Wicasa had shouldered his evidently more-precious one. The private secretary who had said nothing before, throughout, had said 'so long' to the departing brave, and to Henry as an afterthought, 'I guess the Colonel and Mr Fitzjohn will be in touch.'

'Fitzgerald, it's Major Fitzgerald,' Henry had said.

'No matter,' said the factotum. And they had gone.

As they joined the departing crowds slowly pressing their way towards West Kensington railway station Henry had started to explain to

Shunka Wicasa what he might expect as they approached their descent to the underworld. For him it had already been a new baptism, nor would the return journey wind the experience back. At Queens Road, Bayswater he would emerge to a new heaven and a new earth. He had struggled to compose his thoughts.

'You may find this journey underground rather disturbing the first time,' he had said.

'It is not the first time,' Shunka Wicasa had replied gravely. 'We were taken by the *London Evening News*'.

Mr Davies still had not returned when the little party had arrived flushed and triumphant at the house, via the mews and the back garden gate.

Discovering this from Ivy and the further news that the Major was asleep in his room still, Mrs Bullace had pulled off her hat and dumped herself down in the kitchen armchair with a huge gusty sigh. It was as if the sky had suddenly turned black for her and great drops of rain begun to patter down. Henry felt the sudden return of her former mood and could almost see the melancholy anxiety coming out of her like an old wet dog steaming in front of the range.

Nevertheless, he still had an overriding sense of elation. The knowledge that Shunka Wicasa was now a permanent resident in the household, at least for some time to come, made him feel in control of things there much more than he had ever done before. It was as if he had acquired a good right arm and new fists. The very mention of Mr Davies had instantly brought to mind his silent presence at the interrogation in the stable, but only because in his head Henry had put Shunka Wicasa in place of himself, standing impassive as a rock with his folded arms, looking ahead.

'What's to eat, Mrs B?' he had said, refusing to let her see that he had sensed her rediscovered morbidity. And so that had galvanised her afresh as her foreboding about what lay behind Mr Davies' continued absence gave way to almost greater fears about what to give the savage for his tea.

To her delight he had eaten everything she put in front of him in the way of cold meats, condiments and baked potatoes from the oven, these last having been a final instruction to wooden Ivy as they had departed that afternoon.

Afterwards Henry and Shunka Wicasa had gone to make their peace with the neglected mares, since Henry had merely glanced in on them when they had arrived. He offered the Indian a canvas campaign bed he had obtained from Mr Davies who, Mrs Bullace informed him, kept various relics from his and the Major's army days locked in a largish cubby hole at the far end of the cellar. Shunka Wicasa accepted it without comment, leading Henry to suppose that in all probability he would not use it especially as he insisted on making himself at home in the stable under the racking where the bow fronted Hansom stood rather than share the tiny room above.

Henry had tried to insist, but had been met with 'it is better for me on the earth', which he supposed meant that Indians did not like upstairs, save it be a platform to the stars.

The lamp had begun to burn low in Henry's room and the flame starting to flicker recalled him from his abstracted raking over the day. He re-read the postscript which Annie would not read aloud to the Veil House kitchen. To anyone else it would have seemed disjointed, deliberately provoking by suggesting a conversation was going on between them when it wasn't.

He was guiltily satisfied with it. Annie would have to have that conversation with him even though they were far apart. Perhaps it would make her understand that he would be coming home, and he was making her prepare her thoughts for their meeting.

18

Mrs Bullace was like a cat on hot bricks when Henry and Shunka Wicasa presented themselves in the kitchen for breakfast. Mr Davies had evidently only come in as dawn was breaking and had taken himself off upstairs.

''E's with the Major now,' Mrs Bullace said, 'I sent Hivy to stand in the 'all to listen where 'e went.'

The cook had lost no time in consolidating their position as dissidents. Henry could scarcely credit the change that had come over her. The chattering bluster instead of being the sole front that she presented was now only remembered as an afterthought. Whatever it was that she had banished from her memories had resurrected itself, but she had found a new poise to fill out the collapsed shell Henry had sought to comfort at the kitchen table. He was intrigued because he too had found just such a new strength with the arrival of Shunka Wicasa.

'Where's he been all night then?' he said, but he knew that neither of them had an acceptable answer to that question they were prepared to voice. He wondered why he had said it. Perhaps he wanted to tempt the new Mrs Bullace to confide what she knew and share what she guessed at. She must know who the men from the army days were and although Mr Davies never visited friends, her lack of response to the question told him that she believed he had been with them or that they had played a part in his absence. She just didn't want to give tongue to her fears for Kitty.

After breakfast Henry and Shunka Wicasa returned to the mews to complete the stable tasks they had begun at daybreak. The Indian was a ready learner and in any case had already acquired many ordinary skills from the Wild West tour to add to the intuition he had been born with.

Henry was delighted to have an assistant at last, especially one so able and who shared his own knowledge and gifts. It occurred to him how remarkable this would seem to an outsider, that two people from opposite ends of the earth should both know of things that neither had been taught. He said so to the Indian who replied simply, 'It is like breathing, or hearing. It is spirit knowledge. It is not taught. It is given.'

The stable door darkened and they both looked up to see who had entered. Henry felt a rush of mixed emotion. It was Mr Davies, and leaning on his arm Major Fitzgerald. Henry realised he had not seen him since bringing the message from Cody. This was the first time the Major had stirred out. He felt excited and apprehensive, as if they had come to look in his head and see what he knew. He straightened up and waited silently as they came, convinced nevertheless that every fibre and bone of him must be shouting out loud 'I know you're looking for Kitty Shaughnessy.'

'Thought I'd better come and greet my new stable hand,' said the Major, 'Goin' to do the honours Turner?'

Henry recollected himself. 'This is Shunka Wicasa, Major Fitzgerald.'

'And what does that mean, Shunka Wicasa?' said the Major addressing him directly now.

'It means One-who-hears-horses, Major Fitzgerald.'

The Indian's eyes did not waver from the Major's, the cool tone of his voice said that he was addressing no lesser man than himself, nor being addressed by a greater.

'Well One-who-hears-horses, I believe I owe you a debt of gratitude.'

'It is paid, by this,' replied Shunka Wicasa, indicating his new lodging and his half completed attentions to the bridles and girths. 'It was not a blood debt. You are not my brother. That is owed by us both to this one, Henry Turner, who turned the knife that would have killed us.'

'Is it though?' said the Major thoughtfully.

Mr Davies thrust himself out front and back.

'And I'm *Mister* Davies and that's enough gobbledegook talk to the Major. We may have given you a roof over your head, but you can leave your savage ways at the door, if you please. For a start, what are we to call you, Shunka or Wicasa? We can't be having that great long speech of what it means every time the bell goes. I think we should just give you a proper short Christian sounding name and be done with it. With your permission Major,' he added, drawing breath to acknowledge his place.

'At the school we were given names like yours. They called me Reuben Brown Bear. I am of the Bear people.'

Henry froze. 'That won't do Major. There's a lad in the stables at number seven called Reuben. It would just confuse things and draw attention…' He trailed off helplessly.

'Don't like it myself. Bibles and hellfire kind of a name' said the Major. 'Anyway, fellow's not going to be here that long I hope. Can't go changing his name just for a few weeks. Shall we just settle for Shunka or Wicasa.' He looked at the Indian.

'Colonel Cody calls him just Shunka,' Henry put in hastily.

'Settled then,' said the Major. 'Now I was thinking you might give me a turn round the Park in the Pride and Joy, Henry. Out front in ten minutes shall we say.'

Henry had not realised until then, how much he had become his own man and not the Major's, since Fitzgerald had been confined by his injuries. The bow fronted Hansom had had no outing since he had taken Shunka back to Earls Court the day after the attack on the Major and even then Henry had regarded himself as having been about his own business, not his master's. As for Liffey and Shannon, they had been his alone since the day he had first spoken to them. He wanted to tell this Roman invader he no longer had the time nor the wish.

'Ten minutes it is, Major,' he said.

As he tooled the Hansom around the park, Henry cogitated on Fitzgerald's reappearance with Mr. Davies. The Major had seemed relaxed enough and although he was moving slowly with difficulty and had needed a supporting arm it was probably just coincidence that he had arisen this particular morning. It was logical that he would want to cast an eye over Shunka (*not* Reuben, for God's sake not that!). Yet Henry had a distinct feeling that the Major had wanted to see how he himself would greet his presence.

He wondered what Mr Davies might have been saying to the Major. If the Major was his usual calm, controlled self, the same could not be said of Mr Davies. He was most certainly in a prolonged foul temper. Henry could almost convince himself that the pair of them had been reconnoitring, gathering intelligence. Mr Davies had offered an opinion, perhaps, and the Major had decided to test it out. Henry followed the skein of this idea. Mr Davies must have said something about Henry's trustworthiness. After all he told himself, the questions he kept asking himself about the Major and Kitty and where and what part Mr Davies was playing in it all must be written all over his face. How could the Troop Sergeant-Major not have persuaded Fitzgerald that Henry was a traitor and a spy?

However, the Major said nothing amiss to Henry when they returned to Bayswater, merely thanking him for a smooth ride in the circumstances and offering a mock apology for not being able to take part in the evening grooming for a while, although he might 'Look in and see how that Indian fellow is making out. He must have a few yarns to tell.'

Outwardly Henry agreed with him but inwardly heartily wished that the Major would not put in an appearance at all. Shunka Wicasa was to be none of his business if Henry had anything to do with it. Something told him that there would have been times when the Major would have ridden down men like Shunka Wicasa without so much as a glance over his shoulder to see what he had done, and in that moment a picture came into Henry's head of the horse being used to do it, whether it would or not.

As he walked the mare and the empty Hansom up the mews, Henry began to relax and to persuade himself that his fears were groundless, only to have them all leap back into his mouth as he led the unharnessed Liffey into the stable.

At first he saw only Shunka standing motionless with his arms folded. Henry started to greet him and then Mr Davies stepped out of the shadows. There were no courtesies from him and Henry knew at once that whatever had or had not passed between the Major and Mr Davies that morning, his intuition about Mr Davies' suspicions had been right.

'What happened to the Fenian boys then, Henry? We never did get to the bottom of that one, did we? Your friend here doesn't seem to know what I'm talking about all of a sudden, but I'm sure you catch my drift, don't you Henry.'

'What Fenian boys?' said Henry stupidly.

'Don't play daft laddie with me or you'll regret it good and proper. It seems from what I can make out that you and the savage must have had the drop on them, so how did they all get away?'

'Well I wouldn't say that exactly,' said Henry, 'There were several of them and only two of us...'

'Listen, the Major may have been given a good licking but he wasn't altogether out of it. He has it fixed in his mind's eye that men had been brought down and that there were reinforcements within shouting distance...'

'Well I don't know about...'

'The Major can't be sure but he thinks he heard you and the ringleader talking quite civilised, like two old wives over the fence and you told him to make himself scarce while the going was good. Might almost think you knew him.'

Henry felt aghast. He had not assumed that the Major had been in any condition to be aware of anything from that evening. But he remembered his own encounter with the poachers and how, while drifting in and out of consciousness some things remained etched on his mind as if the pain itself had branded the memory with a livid image. He thought rapidly.

'I think the Major must have been mistaken, Mr Davies. Perhaps he heard Shunka and me talking to Colonel Cody afterwards when we were getting him into the Hansom.'

At the sound of his name the Indian stirred himself for the first time. 'They ran away,' he said simply. 'It is true.'

'And why would a bunch of tough Fenians do that then. They'd come too far to be bested by a couple of boys in the dark,' Mr Davies sneered.

'Perhaps it was because I took this from one.' Shunka Wicasa stepped back into the shadows of the stable where his bed and bundle were and produced a small handful of something soft which he offered to Mr Davies who instinctively took it into the light to examine it.

'Christ!' he said, dropping the offering as if it had been a poisonous spider, 'Don't tell me. That's a bloody scalp isn't it, you bloody savage.'

Henry and Mr Davies stared down at the matted black hair lying like a wilting funeral posy on the floor. The horses moved nervously, rasping their hooves on the standing. For a moment or two no-one said anything. Then Mr Davies, attempting to recover the situation but with still a distinct note of uncertainty in his voice, said, 'But there was never a body. No-one said anything about a dead man. We'd have had the peelers round here by now, no matter what the club might have said.' The accusatory tone began to reassert itself in his voice.

'I told you,' said Shunka Wicasa quietly, 'They ran away. He was not dead when I took his hair.' The Indian touched the top of his head, 'He will have no skin here when he enters the spirit world, but this did not send him there.'

'You bloody savage bastard,' said Mr Davies. But there was a note of admiration in his voice, Henry thought, not disgust.

Whether or not Henry had sounded convincing to Mr Davies, the Majordomo looked as though he had to be content with Shunka Wicasa's explanation and the grisly evidence. But as Mr Davies took himself off he gave Henry a long sideways glance that said, I believe him but I still don't believe you. Henry knew that he was still under suspicion, not simply of disloyalty to the Major, but even of complicity with Kitty Shaughnessy and her brother.

'I didn't see you do that. When did you do that?' he demanded of Shunka as soon as they heard the garden gate close behind Mr Davies.

'I did not. This is one I took earlier. A long time ago. If he knew anything about men's scalps he would know an old one when he sees it. See, the skin is dry like a dog's stomach bag.' He proffered the artefact to Henry as he was in the act of putting back into his bundle.

Henry felt a revulsion, but also huge relief that Shunka's story had been a fabrication. He tentatively took the scalp by the hair and held it up at arm's length as if he had a rat by the tail but was not entirely sure whether the terriers had done their work efficiently.

'Where did you do this then?'

'At the Little Big Horn. It was my first.'

'What was that, the Little Big Horn?'

Shunka Wicasa gave him a long, long look. 'So there are men in the world who know nothing of the Greasy Grass.'

Henry was not sure whether this was a question and in any case he could make no sense of it if it were.

Not waiting for an answer however, Shunka Wicasa continued, 'It was a great fight. I was not yet a brave. But afterwards they gave me my brave name.'

'One-who-hears-horses?'

'Yes'

'Because of something that happened then?'

'Yes, because of something that happened then.'

'How old were you?' Henry asked, really needing to put an age to Shunka Wicasa now.

'I do not know. We do not count the years as you do. It was two or three summers before I went to the school. What age are you now?'

'I'm…I'm twent…no twenty-three…no I'm not… I must be twenty-four by now.' It suddenly dawned on Henry that two birthdays had passed him by uncelebrated. This year he had had no-one to remember it for him and last year, well last year he must have only just had his beating at the hands of the poachers. He had never given it a moment's thought before. What a way to spend his birthday. No wonder his mother and Annie had let it go. But he felt a pang of resentment that Annie had not remembered it this year. It crossed his mind she might have written, careless of how unreasonable a thought that was.

'See, you do not count so well either. Have you finished with my medicine?'

He meant the scalp which Henry realised he was still holding.

Taking it from him, Shunka Wicasa continued, 'So let us say we have passed the same springs you and I, I know from Colonel Cody that the Little Big Horn fight was in '76. What does that make me then?'

'Thirteen or fourteen'

'It may be. What did you do at fourteen springs?'

'I suppose I was already doing things with the horses, ploughing and suchlike.

Henry remembered his fourteenth birthday. Taking his first unsteady steps in the furrow under the stern gaze of his father and the Head Baiter, still lacking the strength in his upper body, which would come in time, to hold the plough steady, but making up for much of his slightness as his gifted hands spoke to the horses, a gift the Baiter had long before guessed at and the Bailey had come grudgingly to witness that day.

'Look at that mazy furrow,' he had grumbled. 'If you lined a stetch on that it would end clean into the next field.'

'Yes but look at the steadiness of that team. It may be mazy but he hasn't had to pull them up once. He's talking to them through his hands, Gaffer. You've got a horseman there and no mistake.'

'These were a man's things you were beginning to do?'

'Yes,' said Henry, 'A man's work I suppose you would say.'

'I too was beginning to do a man's things and to become a brave and more. I began to have *maka nongeya.*'

'What was that – a sickness?'

Shunka laughed, a brief staccato bark, not unlike the Major's. 'Some would say it is a sickness. It can be hot like a sickness when it comes in the sweat lodge. It means I have the earth ear. You have it too, I know.'

Everything the Indian said seemed only to lead Henry from one question to another. He was almost embarrassed by his lack of understanding of the ideas that were being offered to him. He had a feeling for them though. He knew a whole way of seeing the world might gradually be revealed if only he would persevere and not dismiss it out of hand as so much as so much 'gobbledegook talk' as the likes of Mr Davies would have it. It was there like the water meadows by the Icing in the early morning, waiting for a rising sun to clear the mist.

He waited to see what further clues might come, but it seemed that Shunka had said enough.

He had finished rubbing down Liffey and reached for the glycerine mixture Henry had showed him to put on the hooves.

'Not that now, not at this time of day if they're not going out again except for a walk round the squares. I don't see the need for it every day anyway, as long as you keep the hooves brushed and picked clean, not just sluiced with water.'

Henry warmed to his theme, glad to have some knowledge of his own to impart in return.

'Some folk down the mews here use tallow and I've even seen what looks mightily like lamp black and lard. They've no right to have a care of horses some of them. Well that's what I think anyhow. The hoof needs to breathe you see. You can tell it's live all right if you ever see the farrier shear a shoeing nail off if it's gone in too deep at the wrong angle.'

Shunka put the glycerine mixture back on the shelf. 'We do not shoe our ponies. A rider is burden enough.'

Henry had no answer to that. If the man himself declined to wear boots why should he impose them on his horse. 'Excepting, they wouldn't last five minutes without going lame on the roads,' he said.

'True,' said Shunka gravely.

Henry felt quite pleased with himself. He had managed to impart some knowledge and a lesson, albeit a very tiny, obvious one. But it was satisfying to know that he had picked away absent-mindedly at Shunka's smooth buttress of spiritual calm and certainty and found a small chink of ordinariness in it.

'So why did you tell Mr Davies a lie?' he asked.

'I learned to do this at the school with men like him. It is not the Sioux way. But among your people I have learned that truth and words are weapons to be used when others cannot be. This man struck you again and again with his words. Were we people of the Plains I would have fought with him and stamped his mouth into the earth where such words should lie buried. But in your city world words must be fought with words and true words are not always strong. For a time he believes he knows the truth and so does not think he has lost his fight. Perhaps we will have a different fight another day with different weapons. For today, these must do.'

'So you think Mr Davies is a bad man, do you? An enemy?'

'Yes.'

'So do I. But why do we think that?'

'He is a man who knows inside himself that he is free to choose the path of life or the path of death and knowing this he always chooses the path of death.'

'But he was a soldier. Isn't that what all soldiers do?'

'Most braves and soldiers do not see there is a choosing. Their choosing is made for them by their chief. This Davies is different. He always knows inside himself he can choose but he does not. It is what he knows inside himself that makes him what he is. He is not a man to have at your side as a friend in battle because he will take you with him down the path of death. But as an enemy…it is a simple matter between you.'

Henry wanted to say 'And what about the Major?' But he had already had his answer to that question. Major Fitzgerald had set his Troop Sergeant-Major on to trap Henry just as surely as he had lain in wait all those times before, times Mr Davies had rolled into one quilted memory of the rider by the river. What had he said then in the kitchen? "One flash, man alone. Let him come."

'Only,' whispered Henry into Liffey's flank, 'I'm not a man alone, now, am I?'

19

Two nights later just as he could sense the first inkling of dawn Henry was startled by the sound of the bell from the kitchen to the stable. He tumbled down the stairs pulling on his shirt and waistcoat and clutching his boots in his teeth by the laces as he did so. Shunka, needless to say, was already standing in his shirt and trousers with his arms folded. Even in his haste it crossed Henry's mind that he had not taken them off in the first place.

'Boots, Shunka, boots,' he said through his gritted teeth, 'We may have to put one of the mares to the p and j. Maybe it's the Major needs the doctor or something. Wait while I go and see.'

He opened the stable door and started across the mews to the garden gate. Although it was not yet fully dawn there was enough grey between the shadows for him not to need a lamp. As he reached the gate, still hobbling as he stamped his feet into his unlaced boots, it opened, first a crack and then wider. Mrs Bullace peered through.

'Is that you 'enry? Wait there I'm comin' to you.' She was whispering hoarsely and Henry sensed the need for him to remain quiet. They returned to the stable and Mrs Bullace turned swiftly and closed the door behind them when Henry failed to do so as he followed her in. She was in her substantial night things with a huge shawl wrapped round her as well for modesty or warmth or both. Henry couldn't help noticing the famous spills turned into curlers under her night cap.

'What is it Mrs B? Is it the Major? Do we need the Hansom or should I just saddle up?' The cook stepped into the lamplight and pulled both men towards her by their sleeves, launching into a half-whispered torrent of speech as she did so.

'They've brought 'er back. Someone came to the area earlier and knocked quiet. Didn't ring the bell, which I thought was odd. I 'ad me 'ands up to the elbows in pastry dough, so I says to Hivy to see 'oo it is. But then Mr Davies calls down a bit sharp, "It's all right Hivy, I'll see to it." Then there's a bit of low talkin' which I can't properly 'ear and then 'e sticks 'is 'ead round the kitchen door with 'is 'at already on and says 'e's goin' out and I'm not to wait up. Well I sat up till gone midnight anyway and then blow me down the Major comes down to the kitchen lookin' for a glass of water, 'e says, and then says "Still up Mrs B – better be off to bed now" and just stands there till I go. So I stood in the 'all for a moment and I 'eard 'im go down into the cellar. So I went back to the cellar door which was open a crack and then I 'eard 'im undo the bolts to the coal chute.'

She fell silent. The two men waited. The cook seemed to have drifted away somewhere, as if the urgent energy of her speech had burned her to a paper cinder tossed in the fire draught. She still had a tight grasp of their sleeves and Henry could feel her trembling.

'What is it? What about Kitty?' he said after a moment.

Mrs Bullace looked back up at him when he spoke, as if seeing him again after a long absence.

'It was them bolts goin' back. It was the same the night they came for Bullace.'

Henry's mind tripped and stumbled over this piece of information. He steadied himself. There would be another time.

'What about Kitty, Mrs B?' he asked again.

Mrs Bullace took a breath and gripped their sleeves ever more tightly, as if to say she would not be put off the order of her catechism, that it was important to get it right. In that moment Henry knew that there had been a time before when she wished she had said it all and had not.

'I put me night things on and did me 'air slowly, in case the Major came knockin' to see if I 'ad really gone to bed. When I was sure 'e wouldn't, I slipped down the backstairs to the kitchen to come and get you.'

'So what about Kitty?' Henry was becoming confused and anxious now.

'Well, no sooner 'ad I got into the kitchen than I 'eard them in the street above, openin' the coal 'ole. They was bein' very quiet, but I was listenin' 'ard, I was that frighted. So I opened the cellar door just a hinch. I 'eard them comin' down the chute and then the trap was shut. Someone must 'ave been in the street. On goes a lamp and I just sees Mr Davies dustin 'is 'at on 'is sleeve and this other one. They 'ad 'er in a bag.'

'Where is she now?'

'She never come up. I 'id in the larder, so still I nearly wet myself. Mr Davies and this other one, they come up and Mr Davies lets 'im out by the area door. When 'e's locked up, 'e goes upstairs and I waits for 'im to be gone up, but the next thing the Major comes down with 'im. 'e 'ad 'is stick this time and 'e goes down the cellar while Mr Davies just sits at the kitchen table and I think 'e must be starin' straight at the larder door and I think 'e's goin to come and look for a bit of cheese and if I do wet myself, it'll go under the door and give me away anyway.'

She paused again. Henry knew better than to interrupt her silence this time.

'I 'eard 'er cry. Only once, just for an instant. Mr Davies, 'e 'eard 'er too and 'e goes to the cellar door and calls down quiet like "Everythin' all right there Major?" Then it's all quiet and then the Major comes up, puts the lamp back on the shelf and says "You can lock up now, Troop Sergeant-Major."'

Henry sensed that Mrs Bullace had said everything that she had felt compelled to say. For a moment he too was a witness trapped in the larder, taking in every detail so that they might be remembered later and recounted, as if the careful recollection were intervention enough. Only as he looked and saw a figure bundled up and heard her cry in pain, Henry saw not Kitty Shaughnessy but Annie Lilley.

'Is the woman dead or hurt only?' said Shunka Wicasa, breaking the spell like a snapped bone.

His patient, emotionless question said that for him every detail of the story had been essential to understanding what must happen next. Henry felt ashamed that for him it had become an abstraction and in its conclusion he had been left only with a feeling of time wasted.

Mrs Bullace choked on a sob. 'Never say she's dead. That poor girl. When I think of 'ow I've dealt with 'er and all because of what Bullace done.'

Shunka looked at Henry. 'What must be done?'

'Something,' said Henry.

'Nothing is always possible.'

'But we do not side with people who walk the path of death, do we?'

'But we can walk away.'

'Like you did behind the club that night.'

'Then we must do something,' Shunka assented.

'Where are they now, the Major and Mr Davies?' said Henry to Mrs Bullace.

'Gone up to bed, I made sure, though 'ow they could catch a wink beggars belief.'

'We'd best get over to the house,' Henry said, making it sound more like a question and looking at Shunka for inspiration.

'We can take these off, it will be better.' Shunka cast his eyes down at their boots with an air of obvious satisfaction.

As the trio crept across the mews and through the garden gate Henry's anxiety mounted as he saw the first orange ribbons of dawn showing. It was going to be a fine day and Ivy would be stirring any minute. He could not believe Mr Davies would be having a lie in, either, all things considered.

'What about Ivy,' he hissed at Mrs Bullace as they approached the garden door to the kitchen.

Mrs Bullace paused only for a moment before showing more of the decisiveness she had exhibited abundantly already that night. 'Wait 'ere. I'll see to Hivy,' and she disappeared into the kitchen. After what seemed an age to Henry she reappeared at the door and beckoned them in. 'She was already in the scullery, which makes a change. Wouldn't you just believe it. I made out I'd just come down. I've told 'er to put 'er 'at and coat on and get some fresh strawberries from Notting 'ill and not to come back without them. That'll keep 'er busy till mid-morning if I knows Hivy.'

There was still no sign of Mr Davies to Henry's relief. But he knew it could not be long. He wondered what the Majordomo and his master had in mind for Kitty. More to the point he wondered what plan he and Shunka had in mind for her and the cold fingers reached down into his bowels as he tried not to imagine the state she might be in.

'It is like a *pinzehna*[*] hunt,' said Shunka suddenly, as if he had read Henry's thoughts, 'She-Misses-Bee must keep the dogs and ponies away and still until we have found the *pinzehna* and stopped their burrows. If she is here making a kitchen noise the Major and his soldier will not come until they have made a plan for her.'

'But she's not dressed, Shunka. Won't they smell a rat?'

Shunka looked puzzled.

'Won't look right,' Henry explained.

'I've got some clothes ironed in the laundry room that 'aven't gone up yet. I can put them on. No peekin' mind.'

The two men waited with their backs turned while Mrs Bullace made what speed she could to make herself look respectable for the day. Henry could hear the measured tick-tock of the kitchen clock. It seemed to him that it must be heard all over the house and would at any second precipitate Mr Davies into the kitchen.

'There,'said Mrs Bullace after an unbearable five minutes.

'Spills, Mrs B. You've still got your curlers in.'

'Never mind that 'enry Turner. I'll see to them. You get down to that poor girl.'

There was no gas in the cellar and Henry took the lamp that was on the shelf by the door. Shunka Wicasa stayed his arm.

'It will look wrong if they come. They will...they will sniff a rat.'

---

[*] prairie dog

'But I've never been down there.'

''Ere's a candle and lucifers,' said Mrs Bullace rummaging in a dresser drawer.

Shielding its glimmer in his cupped hand Henry followed Shunka who had already preceded him down the cellar stairs, Mrs Bullace closing the door behind him. The Indian seemed to have no need of the light although barely any was coming in from the tiny barred half-window that gave out into the well of the area.

'There is no-one here,' said Shunka after a moment. 'Dead or alive.'

'How can you tell? We haven't looked properly.'

'There is no *oh'mna* – no…scent.'

Henry was not convinced. The cellar was full of smells all competing for supremacy in one homogenous fustiness.

He cast about with the candle. There were the usual pieces of unwanted lumber, but none that could contain a person. There were chunks of stone, as well, that looked as though they might have come from old buildings. It dawned on Henry that he was looking at the rejected artefacts of Major Fitzgerald's archaeological pursuits. Gradually other objects came one-by-one into the light of the single candle. At one point the light was shed on some short throwing spears and a narrow hide shield.

'What do these mean?' said Shunka curiously.

'They mean he's a Roman and takes what is not his to take,' said Henry, 'I'll explain it one day.'

'There is no need. I think I understand,' said Shunka.

The Indian's sense had been right it seemed. There was no trace of Kitty in the cellar. Henry was beginning to think that perhaps she had been taken away while Mrs Bullace had been over at the stable. Perhaps they had taken her upstairs. But then they must have supposed that Mrs Bullace and Ivy would have heard them. He began to think that perhaps Mrs Bullace had just had a bad dream.

'Hold hard, though,' he said aloud, 'There's supposed to be another little room down here somewhere. It's where your bed came from, Shunka.'

They moved further in.

'It is here,' said Shunka, but he drew back from it, letting Henry go in front of him.

'Is there something wrong? Can you…can you smell something?'

'Maybe, maybe not. It is like the dark place where they put us in Carlisle. It is a bad place. A place to make you *chonzeh*.'*

---

* mad

Henry tried the door cautiously. It was locked. He held the candle up to see if there was a key anywhere to be seen: there was not. He went quickly back to the cellar stairs and padded up in his stockinged feet. He put his ear to the door and hearing nothing but an unusually loud rattling of pots and pans from the other side, guessed Mrs Bullace was still alone. He opened the door a crack.

''Ave you found 'er?'

'No. She might be in the cubby hole though. Is there a key?'

'Mr Davies keeps it.'

'Is there another?'

'There might be, but I don't know what it looks like because Mr Davies always keeps it.' Mrs Bullace went to a wooden board beside the house bells and fetched a large bunch of keys. She counted off a good few of them and held them firmly together in her fist, leaving the remainder dangling.

'I knows what these are, so if it's 'ere its one of these others.'

With growing anxiety at the prospect of imminent discovery Henry tried the keys that were unaccounted for one by one. It seemed like an eternity. He felt sick and badly needed to urinate. Shunka's usual equilibrium, too, seemed to have been rocked by the sight of the little locked room.

'There is no light from the sky,' he said unhappily for the third time as Henry's fumbled attempts find the right key met with no success.

'Sshh!' whispered Henry, 'What was that?'

At the other end of the cellar the door to the kitchen at the top of the steps opened a fraction. They could hear Mrs Bullace who, from the sound of her rather raised voice was standing with her back to it.

'Morning Mr Davies. Goin' out already? Don't you want no breakfast first?'

The Majordomo's reply was indistinct. Then Mrs Bullace again with a projection that would have done Ellen Terry credit, 'So you'll be a couple of hours then.' The cellar door closed again quietly.

Henry let out his breath thankfully and resumed his search. The very next key fitted and the lock clicked back. He opened the door. 'Hold the candle up, Shunka, I can't see a thing in here.

'She is in here,' said the Indian, 'I can smell her now. She is not dead.'

They stooped low and felt a large untidy bundle like a badly wound bolt of ticking. With some difficulty in the confined space of the cubby hole, cluttered as it already was with paraphernalia impossible to identify in the semi-darkness, they manoeuvred their discovery out of the door and into the main area of the cellar. Henry's expectation did not leave him in any doubt that the bundle of canvas tightly secured with two belts would contain Kitty Shaughnessy. By the flickering light of the nearly spent candle he pulled apart the wrapping.

Her red hair flowed out of the gap he had made, like blood from a deep wound. Her face showed deep bruising, her eyes were closed, and her breathing was harsh and erratic. She was alive. But only just.

Shunka Wicasa bent over her face and sniffed. 'They have given her *pezuhtah* – medicine,' he said. 'To make her bad. Not to make her well.'

The cellar door opened again, making Henry start. Mrs Bullace came a little way down the steps and called into the gloom. 'It's 'er is it? Davies 'as took 'imself off out.'

She continued to the bottom of the steps and made her way towards the light of the candle, although the daylight was now beginning to strengthen a little through the half window.

'Poor girl, poor broken little jug,' She murmured when she came close and looked down, 'Whatever, she never should 'ave come to this.'

'We must get her upstairs and over to the mews somehow without being seen,' said Henry, realising that he was completely devoid of any plan. He went to unfasten the belts around Kitty's binding.

'Better to leave her in this,' said Shunka. 'If we are seen it could be anything.'

It was the first time Shunka had referred to the possibility of discovery. It occurred to Henry then to wonder what the warrior would have done if Mr Davies had surprised them in the cellar. He would ask him maybe another time, not now. The two men bent down to lift Kitty between them.

'Oh my good God,' cried Mrs Bullace.

They both stopped. She was staring at something that had been caught underneath the cloth bundle.

'It's Bullace's 'at,' she said, 'They must 'ave 'ad 'im in there too, the so-an-so's, the villains.'

It was a flat moleskin cap, the kind with ear flaps that tied over the top with a lace when they were not needed. Covered in dust and cobwebs it must have been on the floor in the cubby hole and been dragged out when they had been removing Kitty. Henry stared at it and then back at Mrs Bullace. She did not touch it. Once again he realised this was not the time for questions.

'Bring it,' said Shunka sharply, 'It cannot be found, it will betray us.'

Henry and Shunka manhandled the unconscious woman in the bundle of canvas up to the kitchen. Mrs Bullace went ahead down the garden to the mews gate and cautiously peered out into the cobbled alleyway. She beckoned to them to come up. There were signs of activity further down the mews but no-one was actually outside. Henry signed with his head for Mrs Bullace to go across and open the stable door and they slipped across undetected.

They laid her on Shunka's campaign bed and Mrs Bullace, taking charge, undid the belts that bound Kitty with some difficulty and began to unwind the canvas ticking and pull it out from under the still unconscious girl. It did not take long to see that she was virtually naked. The remnants of her underclothing were torn and dirty and her body like her face was heavily bruised. Her drawers were torn and stained with blood.

None of them said a word. Mrs Bullace face set in a grim mask and her eyes were clearly full of tears. 'Warm water and cloths,' she said, 'And while you're doin' that you can think what must be done. She needs a doctor bad I would say.'

'I can't believe the Major would be capable of this or would allow Mr Davies to…' Henry's voice trailed off and he went to see about warm water. The stable copper had not been lit yet, of course.

'Kettle's on in the kitchen,' said Mrs Bullace, seeing his hesitation, 'Go and fetch it over. And stoke the range while you're at it, seein' as Hivy's out.'

Henry's mind tore around inside his head. Fractured images jostled with one another, anger at one turn, cold bleak emptiness at another.

It was Annie he was seeing there, not Kitty. He tried to make her into Kitty, lying there abused and bleeding and still it was Annie and his anger and his despair was not at the Major, but at himself.

When he came back with the water, Shunka was crouched beside Mrs Bullace. He had the beaded, fringed bundle that he had been so determined to bring with him to Bayswater. He had unrolled it and was sorting through its contents, extracting a number of little, tied bags.

'She has been given bad medicine to make her sleep like this. But she will not die. Her bones are not broken, but She-misses-bee will not let me look here.' He gestured at Kitty's blood stained drawers.

'You're not a proper doctor. A proper doctor should look at 'er there.'

'Among the Lakota, I am beginning to be…like a doctor. Among the Lakota, the women would see to her. They know what must be done.'

'Well,' said Henry, 'We can't very well call the Major's doctor. Have you had a look at her, Mrs B. It may just be…well you know…nothing serious.'

'I was just goin' to' said Mrs Bullace defensively, 'I was waitin' on the 'ot water.'

Henry turned away and began to measure the horses' morning feed in an absent-minded way.

'You too, Chunky. Go and see to those nags,' said Mrs Bullace.

Henry and Shunka Wicasa looked levelly at one another across Liffey's withers.

'What on earth is to be done?' said Henry.

'Do they mean to kill her?'

The same question had been haunting Henry. The Major had hardly had her brought back like this to reinstate her in the household. The stealthy comings and goings at the dead of night clearly meant that her presence was to be kept a secret and, in any case, Mr Davies had made it quite clear that Kitty's betrayal of the Major to her brother was to be punished. Punishment to Mr Davies was an exact science. Henry had learned that. It was one of the many things he had learned about people since he had encountered the presence of Reuben what seemed like a lifetime ago.

'Surely this isn't meant,' he said half to himself, half to the mare. Liffey's warm presence against his chest and chin seemed to soothe the pace of his thoughts, to put them into some kind of orderly procession, to let his logic start to reassert itself.

'But everything is meant.' Shunka responded.

He met Henry's eyes. 'The earth cannot hold together unless everything is meant. Meant for all time. Listen to the earth ear and you will know. The mountain is made of many stones and they are each one thing. But the mountain too is one thing.'

'So you're saying…what? That there's nothing we can do. What will happen will happen.'

'But you and your medicine are part of what will happen.'

'What is this medicine word you keep saying? What do you mean?'

'It is what the Great Spirit gives you for your self. It is your gift. It is your knowledge and your power that will make things happen.'

'Now, now.' It was Mrs Bullace interrupting them as she rose to her feet. 'This doesn't sound to me as if it's a plan goin' anywhere. What about this poor girl?'

'Have you…? Have you…?' Henry struggled.

'I'd say someone's done somethin' to 'er that ain't natural, if you know what I mean. But I think she'll live, nothing's broken, though what she'll 'ave to carry in 'er 'ead is another matter.'

Henry thought of Kitty's handkerchief. Perhaps he had been too ready to do his bounden duty that night behind the club.

'They want to know something. That is why she is here and still alive. Where her brother is? They have already started to ask her. They are destroying her as a *weenyon*[*]. It will be slow so that her brother will come and fight for her,' said Shunka. 'If she is to live, she must hide among her people.'

'Not very likely,' said Henry. 'Her people are too far away and in any case the Major's friends would find her and bring her back. Her people can do nothing. Kitty's like a prisoner they keep to stop them doing anything.

'I understand. We were the same at Carlisle.' Shunka looked thoughtful. 'Can she go to your people?'

'Perhaps, but not now, not today, not this morning. They are too far away, too, and who is to take her without them knowing where she was?' But Henry knew his practical excuses were an act of betrayal.

'Then she must go to my people. They are near and the women can care for her.'

'But 'ow can we get 'er over to Kensington, even supposin' it's a good idea,' said Mrs Bullace, 'Davies'll be back in a trice and I 'spect the Major is already up. What's to become of us when they find she's not in the cellar but over 'ere?'

'This would be easy on the Plains. It would be decided under an equal sky. The Davies soldier and I would settle it and she would go to my people. He would go to the *hechahpa*[**] who swim the air with their black wings like fish in the water.'

Shunka's voice took on a far away, almost wistful tone. Hearing him Henry forgot the pressing urgency of their situation for a moment. He too could see a vast Cambridgeshire sky and the hen harriers quartering the ground, relentlessly, back and forth, back and forth

'Well, it's no good gazing like a couple of junkets in a bowl.' Mrs Bullace's sharp tone recalled them to the reality of the business in hand.

'Where did Mr Davies say he was going?' said Henry.

''E just said 'e 'ad to organise somethin' for the Major urgently and 'e would be back in about two 'ours.'

'Yes, well I suppose we can guess what it is he has gone to organise. Something involving Kitty disappearing for good this time,' said Henry.

'Then we have time to take her in the *pee'n'jay* to my people's camp.' Shunka was already preparing to put to one of the mares even as he was speaking. Henry's logic began to assert itself.

'Think, Shunka, think. If she is gone from the locked cubby hole, then the Major and Mr Davies are going to know it had to be us who let her out. She could not possibly have freed herself and broken the door down

---

[*] woman
[**] vultures

and got away without our knowing about it and helping her. After that it won't be long before they work out that she's either with her brother, or with your people. I don't have anyone here and Mrs Bullace only has a friend in Paddington.'

Shunka folded his arms. 'You people are like your cities, full of turnings that you cannot see around and walls you cannot see through , but everywhere windows where you watch and are watched. It is like the game Captain Pratt played in Carlisle with squares and soldiers and a chief who must be checked.'

Henry did not know what he was talking about. He carried on with his train of thought.

'First of all they'd think the Fenians had done it. Kitty's brother, the men we fought behind the club. But the Major's still upstairs, he'd have to hear them looking for her. And they'd suspect me. Mr Davies already thinks I'm hand in glove with them, you know that. No, Kitty has to disappear for good somehow, so that they don't go looking for her again.'

'She'd 'ave to be dead before they'd believe that,' said Mrs Bullace, 'And if we don't think of something quick, she soon will be and us along with 'er more than likely.'

'I can make her seem dead,' said Shunka Wicasa.

Henry and Mrs Bullace stared at him.

'What?' said Henry, not sure he had heard him aright.

'I have something to give her.'

'Will it harm her?'

'No. It is a secret *pezuh'tah.*'

'Medicine?' said Henry. 'What's it for?'

Shunka looked Henry in the eyes. 'It is a secret, Horse Man. You have them, you know what they are for.'

Henry knew. It was the frog's bone, the vinegar and hyssop, the communion wine. It was a trade secret, to preserve the mystery of the Brotherhood from the common man. He glanced at Mrs Bullace, but she was once again tending to the still unconscious, but increasingly restless Kitty Shaughnessy.

'So you can seem to raise the dead?' he said half under his breath to the Indian.

Shunka Wicasa merely flicked his eyes towards the ministering cook and said nothing. Just the knowledge of the trick was already more than she should have learned for his comfort.

But Henry's mind was already racing on with the possibilities raised by Shunka's revelation.

‘So if she’s dead, how does that help? They’d still dispose of the body and we’d be none the wiser. We have to be the ones to be allowed to take her away, otherwise it won’t work.’

‘We could find the body and show it to them and say we will take it away so that the Major will not be blamed,’ suggested Shunka.

‘Why should they believe that? They’re already suspicious of me and why should they trust you?’

‘You don’t ’ave to do it. Me an’ Chunky can find ’er.’

‘Well I don’t know. Why would they trust Shunka any more than me?’

‘Because Soldier Davies thinks I am a scalp hunter like him.’

Henry was not convinced. It was on the tip of his tongue to say ‘Why don’t we just fetch a policeman,’ when Mrs Bullace said,

‘And they know I can’t say anything because of what ’appened to Bullace.’

Kitty Shaughnessy groaned, half turned on the campaign bed and fell out. ‘Holy Mary, Mother of God,’ she whispered, ‘I need a drink of water,’ and once again the question on Henry’s lips was gone.

He knew that time would very swiftly take the upper hand if they did not do something very soon. The only course of action they had managed to cobble together could hardly be called a plan it was so full of loose ends and question marks. All that could be said of its outcome with any certainty was that it was one that they fervently wished for.

But he had become a believer in the power of the unexpected. He had to accept that something as momentous as having a half murdered woman in the house had to be meant. It had to be taking him through a doorway. He felt sure Reuben the Icenian was moving him towards some goal. Kitty Shaughnessy was part of the pattern that was being laid down for him, just as Sim Lilley’s meeting with Roger Birchall had been in Egypt. There was no coincidence only a continual reworking of the pattern, an adjustment here, a compensation there. He was being allowed to see some more of it than was just under his nose, but as he strained to see its further edges his imagination petered out into darkness. He thought about Shunka’s words only a moment ago, *the earth cannot hold together unless everything is meant.*

‘We’ll all do it together,’ Henry said finally in a voice that brooked no argument, ‘The Major and Mr Davies cannot possibly do anything to all three of us together. I’ll just have to persuade them that we are on their side. Mr Davies is a firm believer in knowing which side you are on. But we will make them think that they’ve killed Kitty and I shall say I believe they didn’t mean to do it…or some such. We will take them by surprise anyway. Must count for something.’

He thought of the hares bolting for the stopped hedgerow as the lurchers were put in. Yes, surprise must count for something. But who were the hares and who the lurchers, he wondered?

Shunka took some dried leaves from one of his little bags. 'Tell her we are giving her something to make her sleep well and when she wakes she will be safe,' he said to Mrs Bullace. The cook did as she was bade, but it was not clear whether Kitty either heard or understood her.

'I must make this with hot water,' said Shunka.

Henry began to despair. 'We must be quick,' he said. 'How long does it take to work?'

'Only a short time.'

'Let me see,' said Henry taking the leaves in the palm of his hand and putting them to his nose. 'It's aconite,' he said after a moment's looking and sniffing, 'I'm sure it's aconite. I give it to the horses for fever and such. It's wicked stuff if you give too much. I've a bottle of the tincture upstairs, it'll be quicker than these, but I wouldn't know how much to give a human.' He sprang up the stairs to his room and was back in a trice with the bottle.

'How much for a horse?' said Shunka, removing the cork and sniffing the contents.

'About ten to twenty drops. You give it gradually until the pulse quietens.' He put two fingers to the artery in his neck.'

'We should give her the same for a small horse.'

'We might kill her.'

Shunka shrugged, 'The soldier Davies will if we do not. Soon we will have no choice. Why do you think he has gone away now, leaving her?'

Henry had been giving that some thought too and could think of no answers that were not unpleasant.

'Mrs Bullace,' he said, 'You should go back to the kitchen and do what you would normally be doing. It may give us some breathing space if he comes back too soon. In any case it should keep the Major out of the way, although if I know him he won't come anywhere near if he hears you about. He'll be leaving it all to Mr Davies. If it's all clear give a ring on the bell every couple of minutes and good long pull if it's not.' It was the best he could think of.

Mrs Bullace paused at the stable door. 'Is it goin' to be all right?'

'Bound to be, Mrs B. We've got two warriors on our side, three if you include me.'

Shunka had put Kitty back on the bed and had raised her up with his arm round her shoulders. He had the bottle of tincture in his other hand and waved it towards Henry.

'Give it to her quickly before she falls to sleep again.'

Kitty opened her eyes at the sound of his voice. 'Who the hell are you?' she mumbled, 'Some bloody tinker by the look of you.'

The mares blew softly and rasped their feet on the standing.

'Bloody tinkers, an' I'm at a horse fair wi' them.'

Henry had poured a good measure of the aconite into a beaker of water. He offered up a silent prayer. 'Take this, Kitty, and when you wake we'll have you away from all this.'

'Is it you Henry Turner? An' where's your fine coat, th'day?' She was barely conscious but drank some of the water as Henry held the beaker to her lips. The kitchen bell to the stable rang briefly and was silent.

'Tastes vile, wha'is it?'

'Just something to make you sleep, so that we can get you out of here in one piece.'

He waited a few minutes. The bell rang again. The coast was still clear. He coaxed a little more of the mixture into Kitty's mouth. She had fallen silent now and her breathing was becoming shallow. Shunka opened one of her eyelids with his thumb. Her eyes were beginning to turn up. They waited saying nothing. The bell jangled, still a short pull. Henry could see that Kitty would soon pass out altogether. He squeezed her mouth gently into an oval and dribbled the remaining liquid into it, holding her chin up, as if he were dosing a horse.

'There it's all gone,' he said. 'Now we must wait and hope no-one comes looking yet.'

The bell sounded. Still short. The only other sound was from the horses champing on their feed. It was past daybreak now. Henry could not believe that there was so little activity. But then he remembered it was Sunday.

'What tribe?' said Shunka breaking their silence and making Henry jump. 'Who is the other warrior beside us?'

Henry understood him. 'Iceni,' he said softly, and something made him add, 'We both are.'

'This other one, he is a spirit warrior?'

'You could say so.'

'Have you seen him?'

'Maybe.'

'Do you have his medicine?'

'What is that?'

'Do you have a gift from him to show he is with you?'

'He's always inside my head.'

'Then there must be something he has given you. Anything. A bird might bring it.'

Henry thought of his encounter in the fog. 'There's a muffler. That might be something.'

'What is it? Muffler?'

'You wear it to keep out the cold, here.'

As he spoke he put his two fingers to Kitty's neck. He could barely feel her pulse and as his fingers rested there it seemed as if it died away, like the sound of a bell tolling the last stroke of the hour, its fading resonance becoming an imagined print upon the ear. She was icy to his touch and her lips were turning blue.

The bell from the kitchen jangled and the wire snapped.

'Shit,' said Henry 'Now what does that mean? I'd better go across and see what's happening.'

When he reached the back of the house he sneaked up to the kitchen window and peered in. Mrs. Bullace was on her own. Catching sight of Henry she signalled to him to come in quietly.

'Davies 'as come back just about five minutes ago. I rang the bell.'

'I know. The blessed wire snapped again, so I didn't know what to think.'

''E's gone upstairs to see the Major. 'E wanted to know if I was goin' out marketing, but I said I'd already sent Hivy. 'E didn't seem too 'appy.'

'We'll have to move quickly,' said Henry, 'You'll have to keep him out of the kitchen somehow until we've brought Kitty back.'

'I'll say I've 'ad to wash the floor. Everyone always 'as to wait till it's dry. I'll put the mop and bucket in the way of the door.'

It was a slim chance, Henry knew. But they could not wait. Who could say what plan Mr Davies had hatched up for Kitty and with whom? He certainly wanted Mrs Bullace out of the way and he would probably be round at the stable next checking up on his and Shunka's whereabouts. He scurried back down the garden hoping that Mr Davies was indeed ensconced with the Major in his room at the front.

Shunka had been busy. 'I have put her back in the cloth. She is as the dead.'

'I hope we haven't given her too much aconite,' said Henry nervously as they lifted the lifeless parcel between them and set off across to the house again. The rest of the mews was still quiet and for once Henry blessed the lazy inattention of his neighbours he so often despised.

Mrs Bullace beckoned them in frantically from the kitchen door and they staggered down the cellar stairs and through to the cubby hole at the far end, just in time to hear an urgent knocking on the kitchen door and Mr Davies' voice demanding to be let in.

Henry could hear Mrs Bullace putting up a convincing defence of her wet floor and telling the Majordomo to 'give it five more minutes or better still, ten.'

As they laid Kitty back in the cubby hole Henry felt her neck. Perhaps there was a pulse, but it was probably just his wishful thinking. Even now he felt like trying to shake her awake just to satisfy himself that she was still alive. After all what could Mr Davies and the Major do against so many witnesses?

The bunch of spare house keys was still in the door. Henry went to shut it but as he did so Shunka pulled out the old moleskin cap and threw it in beside Kitty. 'Perhaps it is medicine, it may be missed,' he said.

Henry turned the key and removed the bunch. The two men went back up to the kitchen. Mrs Bullace took the keys without a word and replaced them on the board.

'Now it gets interesting,' said Henry, trying to make it sound as though he felt in control of what was going to happen next.

'What do I do now?' said Mrs Bullace.

'Call Mr Davies down and tell him you've heard a noise coming from the cubby hole and has he the key about him?'

'Where will you be?'

'We'll arrive when he opens the door.'

'Suppose 'e doesn't open it.'

Henry had not thought of that possibility, but it was already too late, Mr Davies was once again hammering on the kitchen door demanding to know if the damn floor was dry yet. Henry and Shunka slipped out into the area leaving the door ajar.

Mrs Bullace let him in and at once started what sounded to Henry a very convincing account of how she had just been down to the cellar to fetch up a bucket of coal for the range, 'what with Hivy bein' out, as should 'ave been back this last 'alf 'our.'

Their two voices came and went as Mrs. Bullace's account of what she had heard in the cellar clearly had the desired effect of hurrying Mr Davies down there presumably to see how the land lay. Henry waited an agonising moment or two longer and then motioned to Shunka to follow him back into the kitchen and over to the open cellar door. He was about to go straight down, but Shunka held him back.

'Let the fish swallow the *wah'ton** deep inside and we may pull him better.'

They listened.

---

* bait

Mr Davies was berating Mrs Bullace. 'What do you have to go hearing noises for? I can't hear any noises.'

Mrs Bullace was not to be faced down and was insisting on having the cubby hole opened up.

'No I won't, I don't have the key.'

Mrs Bullace's insisting began to sound desperate and got louder. She was clearly wishing that her reinforcements would appear.

Still Shunka held Henry back. He had a look of concentrated interest on his face. 'Wait, wait,' he whispered.

'Well, if you 'aven't a key about you, I'll run and fetch the spare, I will,' Mrs Bullace positively screeched. She was at the foot of the cellar stairs now.

The hair on the back of Henry's neck stood up as he heard this slip of the tongue. Mr Davies took it in too.

'What spare, what spare, you meddling old sow? Have you been in there? You have, haven't you. Haven't you?'

Mrs Bullace cried out. It was obvious Mr Davies had seized hold of her.

Henry shook Shunka's restraining hand off his sleeve and threw back the cellar door.

'Why Mrs B,' he called out, 'Whatever is the matter?'

'Down 'ere 'enry, down 'ere.' The cook was on the brink of tears and was rearranging her bodice.

'Yes down 'ere, Henry, down 'ere,' Mr Davies mimicked her mockingly, 'Oh and the savage too, quite a little party. Almost by invitation one might say.'

Henry did not know whether to continue with their pretence or simply call it off and face Mr Davies with what they knew.

'Open this.' Shunka Wicasa had moved swiftly and silently to the back of the cellar and was standing in front of the locked door, 'There is someone dying in here.'

The other three stared at him and then at one another.

'Don't be ridiculous,' said Mr Davies hoarsely, but Henry for one could tell that at that moment the Troop Sergeant-Major believed the Indian could see through the door. He almost believed it himself.

Henry often relived that moment.

It was as if they were all standing at a place where many roads joined and no-one could be certain which to take next. He used to ask Shunka what he would have done if Mr Davies had defied him, but the Indian's calm recollection of the authority he had felt over the situation then, only became simpler and smoother with the passage of time.

After what seemed like an eternity of silence, Mr Davies stepped forward and producing his key from his waistcoat pocket unlocked the door. He stepped back and waited. Then it dawned on Henry that Mr Davies didn't have a plan either or if he did it had now gone so badly awry that he really did not know what to do next.

Shunka stepped into the cubby hole and pulled Kitty half out of the door. The cotton ticking had fallen away from her face. Mr Davies raised the lamp a little and Mrs Bullace gasped. Kitty's deathly pallor seemed intensified by the red frame of her hair; her lips were blue and her head lolled this way and that as Shunka slid her gently into the cellar, unresisting, lifeless.

The Indian put his ear to her mouth. 'There is nothing,' he said, 'She has gone.'

'You move aside,' said Mr Davies grimly. 'She's not dead till I say so.'

He took Shunka's place beside Kitty, felt for her breath too and finding none pressed his fingers hard into her neck for her pulse. Henry held his own breath.

Mr Davies cursed long and low. He had detected nothing.

'A little premature perhaps. That's a pity. Still, she should have died hereafter'

The group in the cellar turned at the sound of Major Fitzgerald's voice. He was standing halfway down the cellar steps. Henry had no idea how long he had been there.

'The wench is dead, then, Troop Sergeant-Major?'

'Seems that way, Sir.'

'In front of rather a lot of witnesses, by the looks. Now I wonder how that came about, young Turner?'

Henry looked back at him, singled out, the Major's soft, steely tones once again seeming to say to him as they had done before, 'I already know what you have done, so confess your sins now and I will give you absolution.' Henry's mind began to melt, as if there was no-one save him and the Major there, nothing but the two of them in a circle of light and an infinity of outer darkness.

'You villains,' cried Mrs Bullace, breaking into Henry's drifting consciousness like a brick through glass. 'What 'ave you done, what 'ave you done? To think I've "poor Majored" you day in and day out.'

Even in spite of the chilling unreality that the world had taken on for him, Henry was himself taken aback by Mrs Bullace's passion. He could not tell whether she was acting the plot they had begun to put together in the stable or whether she had finally broken under the weight of their predicament.

Then he saw she was shaking something in her clenched fists at the Major and Mr Davies. It was the moleskin cap. She must have picked it up as it had been rolled out with their body.

Mr Davies had seen it too. He could hardly avoid it from where he stood as she thrust it under his nose.

'That looks like Bullace's hat,' he said, looking at her with surprise. 'Where did you get that?'

Shunka managed to nudge Henry gently as he folded his arms. 'Medicine,' he whispered.

'In there, it was in there all the time. What did you do with 'im, you wretch? What did you do with 'im?'

The Major cut in, still from his elevated position on the cellar steps.

'I rather recall it's what you did *to* him that was the point at issue at the time, Mrs B.' His voice had taken on that lazy drawl that told Henry, the Major was beginning to recover and relish his natural superiority over them.

Mrs Bullace crumpled and sat down heavily on an ancient stone trough that had found its way to the cellar in Bayswater from a long forgotten city in Asia Minor.

'Oh come along, Mrs Bullace, I'm sure we'd all like to be reminded. You're rather used to finding bodies in the house, aren't you? Is Kitty another one of yours too?'

'Bullace wasn't dead. You know 'e wasn't dead. Mr Davies said 'e'd get 'elp for 'im.'

'I think your accomplices here should know the whole story, don't you?' drawled the Major. 'The fact is, Turner, Mrs Bullace found Sergeant Bullace, who was one of your predecessors in the stable, not a very satisfactory groom, I have to say, but he had had other uses to me in the army. I thought I might need again from time to time. Anyway, she found him *in flagrante*, enjoying himself with Miss Shaughnessy there, although whether she was enjoying it we were never certain. Never were sure who had started it, who was the more willing, he or she, were you Mrs B? So what did you do then?'

Mrs Bullace gave a muffled sob.

'No? Bit of a teaser after all this time? Well I recall it very well. You pushed a boning knife into his leg. Nearly up to the hilt, wasn't it Troop Sergeant Major?'

Mr Davies laughed. 'He had rather a lot of leg showing at the time, Major.'

'E wasn't dead. 'E didn't 'ave to die. Mr Davies said 'e'd 'elp 'im.'

‘There was no helping him,’ said Mr Davies. A cocksure tone had returned to his voice now, too. Henry saw their slender advantage was slipping away but he could not tell where it would end up.

‘I put him in there in a hip bath and he bled to death.’ Mr Davies gestured at towards the cubby hole. ‘Saved us the trouble of doing it for him really. He had started getting a really loose mouth when he had drink taken. Getting a bit too free with the Major’s business.’

‘Yes, well that’s enough said on that score, I think Troop Sergeant Major. I think we can all appreciate that it will be very difficult to keep our cook from an appointment with the hangman now that she seems to finished what she started with Kitty Shaughnessy. You were never really convinced your husband had to force her were you Mrs B?’ The Major gave his short foxy laugh.

Mrs Bullace was looking up at them all now, a look of sheer disbelief on her face. ‘But she’s not…it wasn’t me…that Chunky said he could bring ’er back; I ’eard ’im.’ Her voice tailed off and she looked wretchedly at Henry.

‘This gets more and more fascinating by the minute,’ said the Major, ‘It sounds as though a red Indian, whom I have brought under my roof out of Christian benevolence and through a belief in the innate goodness and simplicity lurking in his savage breast, has been your deadly accomplice in all this, Mrs Bullace.’

‘He took a Fenian’s scalp. I’ve seen it. Turner knows.’ Mr Davies sounded as though he was beginning to believe the Major’s contortion himself.

Fitzgerald was impressed. ‘Did you though? Pity, I could have used a man like you once. So, Henry Turner, we must, I suppose, find a part for you in this unfolding comic opera. Nanky Poo, I fancy.’

Henry thought hard. He could not for the life of him see where this was leading the Major. If he really meant to hand them all over to the police, his incriminating invention would only hold water for as long as Kitty remained dead. Henry prayed inwardly that they had not overdone the aconite. But then he did not want her suddenly to start coming round in the next few minutes either. It was particularly important that he kept Mrs Bullace from blurting out any more details of their leaky plan too. As he struggled inside his head he saw a tiny doorway opening an inch and, with his heart leaping into his mouth, knew he was meant to race for it.

‘If we were to get rid of the body for you, then we’d all be up to our necks in it, wouldn’t we? And nothing would have to be said in court or anything. Mud sticks my mother says. And who knows who would start coming forward if it all got out. What about the Irishmen who saw what you were doing to Kitty in the pee and jay?’

The Major eyed him steadily and Henry realised that with that little morsel of information he had just fired his last barrel. He waited to see if Fitzgerald would blast him out of the sky with his.

'But if I am not mistaken, the Troop Sergeant-Major here has already taken care of that, although perhaps not for a day or two yet.'

But the Major was winged. Henry began to breathe more easily and his thoughts began to assemble themselves in some proper order again. Mr Davies said nothing. He looked as though he was having difficulty keeping up with the turn of events and Henry felt vaguely jubilant that he had stolen the dialogue with the Major from him.

'Nothing that can't be undone, I don't suppose,' Fitzgerald mused. 'What would you do with her?'

'Best you don't know,' said Henry quickly. 'I know a place she won't be found.'

'Don't want her turning up in three days' time in the river.'

'She won't, trust me.'

'Funny thing is Turner, I don't entirely. Never have done. Too close to the horses. Couldn't put my finger on it till now, but you draw a strength from them that other men have to take from the proper order of things, master and servant, officers and other ranks, friends and neighbours even. We all have to accept it or else, chaos, revolution. You don't need it. I want my horses to do as they are told, not to have a discussion with them. No I don't trust you, Turner, because the only thing you trust is something I can't begin to understand.'

'We will go now. It is best.' Shunka Wicasa had picked up Kitty Shaughnessy in his arms.

He must have been removing her bindings while the Major had been speaking. Now she was a woman again, bruised, and seemingly lifeless. Some of the self-assurance deserted Fitzgerald at the sight. He and Mr Davies moved aside automatically to let Shunka through. It was that or physically restrain him. It was a moment of acquiescence. They bowed to his might.Henry knew they must not hesitate now, must not give the Major time to reflect on what he supposed was happening.

'What about me? What's going to 'appen to me now? I don't understand anythink any more,' Mrs Bullace whispered.

'You go and prepare the luncheon, Mrs B. It'll be all right,' said Henry.

'What have you ordered, Mrs Bullace?' asked the Major, as if nothing whatever untoward had transpired.

'Beef, Major, it's Sunday, and strawberries from the Sunday market if and when that Hivy puts in an appearance.'

The cook had quietly put back the lid on her past until the next time.

20

Henry now had to worry about Shunka's reappearance at the Wild West Exhibition from which he had only recently quietly departed. As he hurriedly put Shannon into the shafts of the Hansom, the difficulty of smuggling both the Indian and the still lifeless Irish girl into the Sioux encampment at Earls Court unobserved by the cowboys, began to press on him. The very appearance of the fancy carriage even at the back gate would be very likely to provoke the kind of attention it had on its previous outing there and this time there could be no connivance by the management either.

'How are we going to get her in to your people, Shunka?' he asked anxiously, 'Do we have a plan?'

'We must wake her first, but not here. Then it will be easier. Bring some clothes for her.'

'But I don't have any women's clothes, only men's clothes.'

'All the better. Put them in the carriage.'

So with Henry seated up behind the Hansom and with Shunka and Kitty inside with the blinds down, they set off down the mews. As they passed the front of the house, Mr Davies emerged from the area door and skipped up the steps holding out a restraining hand. Henry brought the equipage reluctantly to a halt. Mr Davies opened the door a fraction and looked in; he seemed satisfied, but for one numbing moment Henry thought he was going to get in with the two passengers.

However, he closed the door quickly and glowering up at Henry said, 'You have thought about the Hansom being seen, haven't you?'

'Don't worry,' said Henry, 'Everything is in hand,' trying to make it sound as though it were. Not wishing for any further discussion he whipped up the mare and set off down the street at a brisk trot, trying not to imagine the Majordomo's hard, narrowed eyes boring into his back as they left him at the kerbside. When they were out of sight he slowed down to a walk and opened the roof trap.

'What shall we do? Drive straight to Earls Court, do you think?'

'No,' said Shunka. 'Now I have a plan. We will drive until she recovers and then you will take her back to the stable. It is like walking back on our snow tracks. They will think she is gone and we can take our time. I shall prepare my people and return later. Meantime you shall prepare her. This is a good plan.' Shunka sounded well pleased with himself.

'How long before she recovers then?' Henry could see that it might just possibly work provided Mr Davies was not too quick off the mark when he returned with the Hansom minus Shunka Wicasa.

'I think not long now. I have given her *ahbahyehna* root. I have chewed it and spat it in her mouth.'

Henry drew the Hansom to an abrupt halt. 'What is it this time? That girl has taken so much poison this morning, we'll really have a corpse to get rid of as like as not.'

'It is good medicine, *ahbahneya*. It means Be Still. It is Be Still tree. It will make her heart beat strong. See, she is already warm.'

Henry drove into the park and joined the procession of vehicles taking the late summer air. Those that were not open at least had their blinds up and their windows down, making the Hansom seem rather incongruous, but Henry decided he could not worry about that.

'They will just have to assume we're empty if they recognise the pee and jay, that's all,' he muttered to himself, rehearsing what he would call out to any grooms who knew him by sight if he were accosted.

At the third circuit Shunka knocked on the roof trap. 'She is with us. I will wake her gently as we go. Take me near to my people. I shall walk the last part so as not to be seen.'

They caught one another's eyes. Henry laughed out of sheer nervous relief and Shunka permitted himself a wry smile.

'You weren't so sure, were you?' Henry said. 'This isn't a plan at all. It's a whole dung heap of luck we've trodden in, that's all.'

'Great victories are made with less,' said Shunka, 'Soon I will tell you of the Custer fight.'

Henry dropped the roof trap with a thud, wheeling off towards the Knightsbridge gates and on towards South Kensington.

Their luck held out. 'Perhaps,' he thought as he helped a very groggy, but definitely alive Kitty Shaughnessy out of the Hansom and up the stairs to his room in the loft, 'We should see our luck for what it really is and stop trying to think we can do anything that isn't going to happen anyway.'

A sudden heavy shower flecked with summer hail had emptied the mews of any life, human or equine, moments before the Hansom had turned into it and the striking bell on Holy Trinity in the middle distance was enough to tell Henry that Mr. Davies and Mrs Bullace were at that very moment sitting down to an uncomfortably silent helping of roast beef. The coast was well and truly clear.

Kitty Shaughnessy had no very real recollection of what had happened to her which, judging by the state of her injuries, was nature's kindness. She felt very nauseous after the doses of some of the unkinder things nature had to offer and had no appetite for anything other than quantities of water. Gradually, though, Henry began to refill the emptinesses of her recent past with what he knew. He tried not to watch her in the confines of his room as she surreptitiously examined what had been done to her body.

He felt ashamed to be there and to be a man and even after all that had been said and done, found it easier not to connect it personally to Major Fitzgerald and Mr Davies. It was easier to deal with the business of persuading Kitty of the need for her to lose herself for a while in the Indian encampment if he did not at the same time have to handle such things as anger, justice and revenge, feelings that would only cloud his judgement.

The most pressing thing was for them not to be immediately discovered. The stable was somewhere that the Major and Mr Davies might descend upon at any time unannounced, especially now. Making a virtue out of necessity Henry went down to see to the horses and tested how softly he could speak to Kitty in the room above without being inaudible. He found that they could converse quite well and for it to sound to anyone coming in from outside as though he were talking into the mares' coats as he constantly did. He and Kitty would have to rely on the fact that no-one would go up to Henry's room above unless they were searching for someone, which it was to be hoped they were not.

Kitty was at first unconvinced of the plan for her to disappear amongst the Indians.

'Why don't I just wait here a while and then take myself off,' she kept repeating at intervals, not with any particular determination, more in the manner of an incantation that would eventually make this the better of two bad ideas.

As for Henry, he had never questioned the wisdom of Shunka's proposal, uttered as it had been with the unadorned certainty of a man for whom survival was largely a process of eliminating the weakness of complication and leaving in its place only the strength of simplicity.

There was a rightness about it too for Henry which he would have loved to have been able to explain to Kitty. He wanted to tell her about Boudicca's betrayal, about the public violation of her daughters, about her taking poison.

'And you are all of them Kitty,' he wanted to say, 'But you didn't die. You came through a death and should be with these people, tribal people who own the earth and from whom it has been stolen, people like us.' If she had been a horse he could have put his hands on her and she would have understood.

In the end it was something rather more practical that persuaded her that she should be among women for while. She used the chamber pot and the pain made her catch her breath audibly even to Henry in the stable below.

'Are you all right?' he asked urgently.

'There's a deal of blood in my water,' she said with an edge of panic in her voice.

'Shall I get something…what do you need?' Henry struggled in unfamiliar ground, 'I don't want to go over to Mrs Bullace until Shunka gets back, really.'

'It's not the curse, you eejut! I'm carrying Fitzgerald's child and I think they might have done for it, so I do.'

Henry summoned all the control he could find within himself not to rush up the stairs, snatch up his father's guineas and disappear into the gathering dusk.

'Does he know?'

'I shouldn't think so,' said Kitty, appearing dangerously at the top of the stairs and wrapped in a blanket, 'And if he does, he'd care less. I'm dead aren't I? All the more reason.'

Henry felt a chill of utter despair around them as if a door had blasted open somewhere out in the wide world, letting in an icy howl.

'That's Shunka's blanket.' he said, 'You should go to them. They will know what to do.'

Shunka Wicasa slipped back into the stable after dark. He had walked all the way back. Henry was impressed. In a day of oppressive unreality he had given no thought to the actual fact of a Sioux Indian abroad in the great metropolis on his own.

'You found your way all right, then'

'As you see.'

'You didn't need to ask?'

'Where we have been once we can find again. My people are used to wander. The world is a place, a tepee is a place, there is nothing to forget. One day soon we shall return to the land of your people and you will know the ways.'

'I expect we will take the train,' said Henry briefly. But all the same the words made a sudden gust of pictures in his head, of countryside seen unfurling through grimy windows, of the lane from the station at Duster to Icingbury with children sitting on a gate watching for the trains they had no call to take, of Annie Lilley tending to his hurts, of Kitty Shaughnessy's blood and pain upstairs.

'It is agreed,' said Shunka, 'Our women will hide her until she is well. They will change her hair.'

'And then what?' said Henry

'And then at least I won't be dead. Nor I won't be hunted down.' Kitty had reappeared at the top of the stairs at the sound of the men's voices below.

'You will if you keep hollering like that,' Henry said, motioning to her furiously to retreat. Then he said to Shunka, 'We must go over to Mrs Bullace and get some food and things for Kitty.'

Mrs Bullace was sitting silently at one end of the kitchen table with Mr Davies facing her similarly at the other. It looked as though he was watching a condemned prisoner and she waiting for her reprieve.

'Taken your time,' he said.

'We had a long way to go,' said Henry insolently. As he saw Mr Davies sitting there and thought of what had been done to Kitty, the connections he had up till then resisted in his mind began to flow together into a growing, angry globule.

Mr Davies may have sensed the tone. He began to assert himself. 'Things have to start looking normal around here. There's been a sight too much to-ing and fro-ing. This is the Major's house still and you are just a groom, worth a sight less than the damn horses you care for and don't you forget it. And as for you,' he turned his attention to Shunka Wicasa, who unperturbed was eating cold beef and strawberries with his knife, 'You are a stinking savage and you belong nowhere the Major doesn't say you belong.'

The Indian finished his mouthful slowly, balanced a final strawberry on the end of his knife, flipped it into the air, caught it in his mouth, swallowed it and said, 'Are you brave, Soldier Davies? You will need to be brave. A time will come when you must have none of the fear you feel now.'

He sprang out of his seat, leapt behind Mr Davies and putting his head down to the Majordomo's ear made a sound that reminded Henry of the triumphant crowing of the victorious cockerel at a bloody cockfight once where he, Sim Lilley, Josh Makepeace and others should not have been.

The blood drained from Mr Davies' face. He, too, leapt to his feet, scraping back the chair and knocking it over. He would have had to have been warped through with steel hawser to have remained calm and still.

Henry felt as if the wind had been blown out of him, but he was extraordinarily elated and at that instant something blindingly obvious burst upon him.

They were free of it.

He had to stop himself shouting down the table at the wavering figure of Mr Davies, 'Where's the body? She's gone. You cannot hold onto us.'

Mrs Bullace who had all but fainted away, had her hands over her ears like a child shutting out something fearsome and unseen. Ivy whose existence had been overlooked, appeared at the door from the scullery looking alarmed and apprehensive. Despite having been shaken to the core herself, Mrs Bullace recovered her position in a trice.

'Just Chunky 'avin a laugh with Mister Davies, Hivy. No call for you to take your 'ands out of that sink.'

The Majordomo took his cue from this and visibly shrugging himself back into shape, chest and backside out, said, 'Quite so, Mrs B, quite so,' as he marched out of the kitchen with what dignity he could muster.

Henry hooted with laughter as the door closed behind him. 'That saw him off, Shunka.'

'Yes, but he will return. It was a little fight. He will not give up the ground for so little a fight. Something must happen.'

The sound of slipping saucepans on the scullery draining board reminded them of Ivy's presence again. Henry signalled with his head and eyes to Mrs Bullace who nodded silently.

'Hivy, you can finish that off now. Put your' at on and take yourself off to chapel with that one next door. I doesn't feel like it tonight some'ow. And no 'angin' around after with them boys from the mews either, like the flighty duster you are, just because I'm not there.'

They waited as patiently as they could until the maid had gone out through the area and then, with the kitchen door open ajar so that he could see up into the hall in case Mr Davies should reappear, Henry explained what they had done about Kitty.

'When will she go?'

'As soon as possible, Mrs B. Tomorrow if we can manage it between us. Shunka says she should dress as a man so it will be easier for him to take her into the camp without either being noticed. Will you see to her hair? It'll need pinning up or something.'

'There's a hawful lot of it. I'll still 'ave to cover it up some'ow and you two'll need your 'ats yourselves.'

The three of them looked at one another as a single thought occurred to them simultaneously.

Mrs Bullace voiced it first, although not without a tremor. 'She can 'ave Bullace's 'at. It 'as flaps what come down over the ears. They'll 'elp.'

'It is good medicine,' said Shunka.

Once again their plan could barely be dignified with the title. Henry was, however, growing more and more confident. He was now convinced that this was something that was meant and was as a result beginning to feel invincible. Belief was enough now, belief that something would happen. Belief too that, while his efforts alone would be part of its pattern, they would not shape its end. The straightness of the furrow was conditioned by more than the hand upon the plough and its yield at harvest time by still more.

As for Shunka Wicasa, there was a limit to his ingenuity as Henry had already discovered. He planned for fighting with subtlety. He could use the power of his inferred strength to stun and surprise. But he did not plan well for evasion. Between them they combined to produce a strategem that left much to the imagination.

Henry and Shunka would take both mares loose for exercise. Mrs Bullace would set off on her marketing as usual but instead would take Kitty to West Kensington on the Metropolitan Railway because she knew the way without asking. They would wait outside the station for Henry, Shunka and the horses to arrive. Leaving Henry, Shunka and Kitty would walk the horses into the show ground through the side gates closest to the encampment. This subterfuge was Shunka's.

'There are many horses to be exercised. Things are brought every day, food for animals as well as people. Horses make a hiding place while they walk.'

Henry knew that was true. He had seen the Indians make themselves almost invisible on their horses with great skill. The principle was the same although Shunka and Kitty would simply walk the horses. Once safely delivered to her new lodging. Shunka would re-emerge with the horses and rendezvous with Henry outside the show ground. Mrs Bullace would already have gone about her marketing and would be back in Bayswater.

'What if the Major needs the 'ansom tomorrow?' said Mrs Bullace. 'And what if…'

'And what if those cowboys spot Shunka?' thought Henry.

'It will be all right Mrs B. Just you see.'

Henry and Shunka saw to the horses early the next morning and presented themselves for breakfast in the kitchen. Mr. Davies, however, had nearly finished his and was clearly anxious to have as little contact with Shunka as possible.

The atmosphere of oppression felt after Kitty had first disappeared had returned. Henry could almost touch it. It was as if the house in Bayswater had become a house of cards and all inside were holding their breath to see how long it would be before it collapsed.

Henry had already stopped living there in his own mind. He had entered a state of limbo, certain that he would be moving on very soon, but without any idea of when or where. Something would open a doorway and he would see the next move.

He tried to convince himself that Kitty's removal to safety was part of it, and that everything would flow from that. It was such an enormous displacement in his life, it surely had to be.

Now that Henry had divined for himself the influence of Reuben as his pathfinder, he wanted to see more and more of him, to be able to refer to him and to receive his sanction. In short, he wished Reuben would keep pace with him now that he had put aside his last doubts about his existence. Now that he needed him so much.

The front door bell rang with a peremptoriness at once uniting the attention of all the protagonists in the kitchen.

'I'll see to that,' said Mr Davies in a tone that betrayed his relief at being able legitimately to assert his authority. He wiped his mouth deliberately, stood up, straightened his waistcoat and stalked upstairs to the hall.

'Pop your little mop 'ead up the area steps and see 'oo it can be, Hivy,' said Mrs Bullace.

When Ivy came back she announced that it was the 'telegram boy'. For some reason, Henry's heart sank. Perhaps it was nothing much. But here, all the same, was an intrusion, something unexpected to be taken into account in an already precariously balanced day.

They heard the front door close and when Mr Davies did not immediately reappear, Mrs Bullace said rather unnecessarily, ''E's gone upstairs to the Major with it.'

They waited in silence and the tension for Henry became almost unbearable. Shunka meanwhile was quietly making a collection of comestibles from the table and wrapping them in his large linen napkin for which he had had no other use so far. Henry knew he was putting them together for Kitty.

'He gets very hungry during the morning,' he said for Ivy's benefit, 'He's naturally a hunter,' he added with what he hoped was the kind of conviction that begged no further questions. Shunka went back to the mews by way of the garden.

Mr Davies re-entered the kitchen looking even more authoritative.

'Where's that savage gone? Job for you two this morning, which is better than sitting around on your arses like you have been used to lately.'

Henry could have wept. His scheme for Kitty depended on the extraordinary reversal of roles and ranks he had engineered, continuing for a while longer. Yet here was something or other that was conspiring to put all the round pegs back into the proper holes.

'What is it, then?'

'What is it then *Mister Davies*? I think you mean to say, my lad.' The Majordomo had also sensed the chance to consolidate his brief advantage. 'What it is, is that friend of the Major's what brought you here in the first place is arriving at Charing Cross this morning after ten and you are to bring him here in the Hansom. You'll need to take your savage with you, there'll be baggage. He might need a handcart. I hope he does. He needs to run off some of that steam of his.' The Troop Sergeant-Major swept out.

Henry did not know whether to laugh or cry. Roger Birchall was back. This must mean Reuben again and a doorway for certain.

'That's torn it,' said Mrs Bullace.

Henry was thinking furiously. If this was meant and it surely was, then Dr Birchall was intended to play some part. The fact that he was arriving on this day of all days simply confirmed it, as far as Henry was concerned.

'At least, this means we get to use the pee and jay all morning with permission for the pair of us.'

He looked at Mrs Bullace. It sounded right. He had been meant to say that.

'We'll just have to take Kitty with us, that's all there is to it. You stay here, Mrs B. and keep your eyes and ears open.' It still sounded right.

'Shall I come over and do 'er 'air, then?'

Henry thought about this. 'No. She will manage. Shunka will braid it for her. He does his every day, anyway.'

Dr Birchall's unexpected reappearance had suddenly changed the pictures of the coming day in Henry's head. An unseen hand had smoothed over the furrows he had already made in the earth, demanding a new pattern be drawn. Yet the earth was the same, nothing had been added nor taken away. He felt now the spring of optimism that had already begun to water his caution, truly welling up at the thought of enlisting Dr. Birchall to their cause. The pace was quickening. He was seeing the three of them as a unity, as an image of horsemen flowing into one another and apart again momentarily, as a team moving through heat haze on the far side of a wide, wide field.

Line abreast, first the walk, now the trot, soon the canter. Three coming, let them come, let them come.

21

As the moment for departure had been announced Kitty had fallen silent. She had stopped bleeding at any rate and Shunka's Be Still Tree had begun to restore her abused heart. While Henry and the Indian went to put Shannon into the shafts and to prepare Liffey to be led, Kitty began to prepare herself carefully and quietly. When she appeared at the top of the stairs, she paused as the two men below looked up at her.

She was dressed in Henry's Sunday clothes, brushed and tightly buttoned coat and trousers, a clean, white shirt with no collar. The waves of her red hair fell over the black like the last rays of the sun defying the gathering night. Henry felt it was as if she were a widow finally putting aside her man whose body would now never come home, paying her final respects in his absence by donning his funeral clothes.

As she came slowly down the stairs, she started to gather her hair over her shoulder to braid it. Still dividing the tresses she stepped up into the bow fronted Hansom as Shunka held the door open and then followed her. Without a word he took the three hanks of her hair she had already separated and began deftly to plait them. Henry wondered whether he would ever see it again.

'Never thought I'd be in this old trap again,' Kitty said, half to herself, as Henry closed the door and mounted up. It had been a long few moments. Anyone might have walked in and come upon the preparations for their departure.

But they had not. It was meant.

At Charing Cross station Shunka stood at Shannon's head while Henry went to wait at the end of the platform for the arrival of the train from Gravesend where Dr Birchall had been disembarked, rather than waiting for the tide into the Pool of London. As he waited Henry rehearsed over and over what he might say to his friend that would instantly apprise him of their predicament as well as make him embrace its resolution with enthusiasm.

He had still not come up with anything to convince himself when the train drew in, enveloped in a miasma of sulphurous smoke and steam, temporarily obscuring the alighting passengers whose presence could only be determined by the slamming of unseen carriage doors.

It was a sound that immediately cast Henry back to the day of his arrival in London, unlocking a total impression of his time since, like a great mess of food that has been swirled all together on a plate destroying each original taste and colour. At this moment he could pick out nothing that distinguished one emotion from another. The optimism he had felt earlier was submerged. He felt only that the past year led him from one great railway terminus to another, waiting passively for his future to be fulfilled.

'Oh I say, old fellow, you look a bit far away,' said Dr. Birchall, coming upon him suddenly out of the smoke, 'I thought it was I who had been on a journey.'

Henry smiled at him joyfully and then they both laughed, holding one another at arms' length. Everything that Henry had thought about saying first went flying.

'I have only this for now,' said Birchall as a porter with a barrow with a single valise fetched up beside them. This train of thought reminded Henry sharply of what awaited in the bow fronted Hansom.

'You have to trust me, now,' he said.

'My dear chap. Trust you? Of course I trust you. Whatever is it?'

Henry looked at him. 'It's about Romans and reprisals and it's about rescuing a hostage. It's about Reuben.'

Dr Birchall reached in his pocket for sixpence for the porter and finding only a shilling gave him that anyway.

'This will be about Gray Fitzgerald then, I presume.'

'Yes and Kitty Shaughnessy.'

'The maid?'

'She's turned out like Boudicca and her daughters all rolled into one.'

'Can you tell me about it when we get back? I take it you've brought the whatsitsname, his equipage.'

'We're not going straight back.'

'Then you had better tell me now. Let's go and sit over there.' Dr. Birchall pointed at a bench on the platform with a walking stick that Henry only then noticed.

'You've a stick.'

'Yes old fellow, and a limp to go with it. Lucky to have a limp. Nearly didn't have a leg to limp with. Excellent.'

It was, therefore, some little time before the two of them emerged onto the station forecourt. Shunka Wicasa was, needless to say, standing patiently at Shannon's head staring impassively in front of him, heedless of the curious stares of the passers-by. However, his orthodox stable clothes and his hat pulled well down had at least prevented a crowd from forming around him as it would have done a few weeks earlier.

'I am pleased to know you, *One-who-hears-horses*,' said Dr Birchall, immediately offering him his hand. The three men looked at one another as they stood in a tight circle at Shannon's head.

Then Shunka said quietly, 'It is good. He too has some of the earth ear.'

'Yes,' said Henry, 'He's like talking with horses. He understands before you have said it all. Things you cannot find the words for precisely.'

'Excellent, excellent,' said Dr Birchall, 'Shall I get in?'

He ducked under Liffey's leading rein at the back of the Hansom and opened the door. 'Good day to you Mr Smith,' he said to Kitty for the benefit of the curious starers.

Henry drove to within a short distance of the Earls Court show ground and there he took Shannon out of the shafts and Shunka unhitched Liffey.

He and Dr. Birchall watched Kitty and her Indian guide as they walked the two horses towards the side entrance, merging with trades people and other vehicles that were coming and going. Henry walked a little way after the pair on his own. After a few moments he lost sight of them. His eyes strained in vain to pick them out of the flow in and out of the gate and a sadness settled in his self. He wondered whether he would ever see her again and realised then it was the shape of Annie Lilley he had been looking for in the crowd.

Henry walked the short distance back to Dr Birchall. Now that there was no horse in the shafts, they both sat inside in the bow front to maintain the balance. Dr Birchall eased his lame leg out straight and rested it along one of the side cushions.

'Tell me about the leg then,' said Henry

'My own fault. Not looking where I was going at the diggings one day and walked straight into the path of one of the Arab workmen as he was coming down a wooden ramp fully laden. He couldn't stop and by the time I looked up at his shout it was too late. Hit me on the shin and cut me to the bone. The overseer started to give the poor fellow a dreadful beating. As if that would make it all better. So I was whisked off to the military hospital in Alexandria, but not fast enough to prevent the leg going septic. Touch and go for a while. I wrote to you, didn't I? Surgeon was sharpening up the old knife at one point. Excellent. Well not excellent then, of course, but excellent in the end.'

'So what happened to Sim Lilley? You wrote and said you'd seen him there in the hospital.'

'Poor fellow. He looked like Famine out of the Four Horsemen. I only saw him a couple of times before I was shipped out so I don't know what became of him….whether he…' Dr Birchall trailed off.

'I don't know why he was with the Essexes,' said Henry, ' Icingbury always join the Suffolks. I don't know why, but we do. But then if he hadn't have, he wouldn't have been in Egypt and you wouldn't have seen him.'

'No, it was an amazing coincidence. I just saw this face and thought I know you from somewhere, even though he was so gaunt. Then it came to me and I saw you and him racing across that flooded meadow when we found the skeleton. It was just that picture.'

It had been the same picture that had entered Henry's own head when he had read Dr. Birchall's postscript.

'It made you think about Reuben then, did it? When you saw him, I mean?'

'Well it did rather. I kept thinking about Robert Earl worrying away at the fact that we had left the skeleton in the church. I couldn't really understand why he was so edgy about the whole thing. Anyone would think we had wanted to carry out some satanic rights with it or some such.'

He became thoughtful. 'You know, it's odd Henry, but now you come to mention it, I have been thinking about him a lot. I was going to drop in at Icingbury and see him.

'Reuben?' said Henry, startled.

'Well maybe. But no, I meant Robert.'

Images of Icingbury began to fill Henry's mind like an urgent knocking on a door, the sound of the head baiter rousing late-sleeping horsemen. The new brick stuccoed villas of West Kensington and building sites where more were rising around them as they spoke, seemed insubstantial, paling to insignificance. That feeling that his time in London was done, now made him want to burst free as if he were harnessed to a great stone in the earth.

He shifted heavily, rocking the Hansom on its axle.

Dr Birchall gripped the upholstery. 'Steady old fellow.'

For an instant Henry's flying fancy was reined back abruptly as he recalled the rocking of the Major's pee and jay on those two earlier occasions. Cold fingers reached down deep into his guts and churned every dark remembrance he had ever hidden there, stirring them up like a nauseous smell.

'We have to go,' he said

'What about your friend? Shouldn't we wait?'

'No, I mean all three of us have to go to back to Icingbury. Reuben has called us. He sent Sim to fetch you back. It was as if he'd sent you a telegram in your head. He's found me a true warrior like himself. He's even bound Shunka and me together like brothers so that we shall not part. I think he's even made the Vicar jittery so that he keeps reminding us all. I'd lay money Mr Earl wrote to you about him and you to him.'

'Oh hello, steady on,' said Dr Birchall, 'All this is more than likely just the way things fall out. There doesn't have to be a connection at all. What if Reuben is just in your head?'

'Well if he is, he is. So that doesn't really alter anything does it?'

'But that's just the way witchcraft works, they say. You make someone believe something so strongly that they make it come true by themselves. Think about it Henry. Suppose, just suppose, you are right and that Reuben has some kind of existence. He's a pretty ruthless character, isn't he? He doesn't seem to mind how he uses people to get whatever it is he wants. He's left Sim at death's door in Egypt. He's presumably nearly lost me my leg. And what about poor Miss Shaughnessy? Is she part of this Minoan labyrinth he's letting you construct?'

'I don't know about Kitty. She's neither one thing nor the other.'

'Neither one what nor the other? Not Roman and not tribal either, is that what you're saying?'

'Well she is tribal, but in her head she's like a trapped animal. No, not trapped, more like a caged bird that belongs outside but has almost forgotten how to be free. She once told me she didn't mind the things the Major does to her. So although she's a prisoner, it's as though she will never be free even if she's let out.'

'My word Henry, that's a bit deep. So she doesn't fit into your Reuben theory then?'

'I can't see how at the moment. But sometimes my mind cannot see far enough without starting to blur with the effort. Perhaps she is playing a part in something further away than any of us can see.'

They sat in silence for a while.

Then Dr Birchall said, 'So how do you see me fitting into this grand design of Reuben's?'

'You already have,' said Henry, 'You found the rest of him when all we had was his skull and you persuaded Mr Earl to let them be together.'

'So what am I here for now?'

'Well I think you're probably meant to be a go-between. We have to leave the Major somehow without there being any fuss. At the moment he wants to be rid of us but at the same time he dare not let us out of his sight. He says he doesn't trust me. I think for two pins Mr Davies would cut my throat and Mrs Bullace's and blame it on Shunka. If we don't get Shunka away I think *he* will cut Mr Davies' throat sooner or later. I think you are here to get us out of Bayswater just like we were here to get Kitty out. Then when we go back to Icingbury you'll have to soft soap the Vicar about what happens to Reuben. He won't listen to me, he's a bit too lofty. He'll listen to you. You're allowed to be neither one thing nor the other like Kitty, but free at the same time. Mr Davies said something like that about you. Said you didn't know your place but it was all right because you are an acky something.'

'Academic.'

'Yes, academic.'

'Talking of words, our Indian warrior seems to have mastered the white man's tongue, doesn't he? Very impressive.'

'He's been to a school, he says. In Carlisle.'

'Good grief. That cannot be here. There must be one in America. Excellent. I must ask him about it. However, first things first. As it happens I already had a proposal to put to Gray Fitzgerald which might serve us all a good turn although from what I infer from you it sounds as though he ought to be charged with kidnap and assault, or worse.'

Henry looked taken aback. 'You wouldn't do that would you? I know he deserves it but somehow I don't think my word and Shunka's are going to be believed against his and we don't want to bring Kitty back from the dead. Then there's Mrs B and Sergeant Bullace to think about.'

'My thoughts exactly, Henry. And I'm hardly going to be any help to you resolving all that, because I've been out in Egypt, so I've only your word for anything as far as the authorities are concerned. Excellent. Well not exactly excellent, but you know what I mean, Henry, we are of one accord as usual.'

The door of the Hansom opened and there was Shunka.

'She is with the women,' he said gravely. 'It will be well enough.'

They put Shannon into the shafts and attached Liffey on a rein behind, Henry not being prepared to let the Indian ride her bareback through the London streets for fear he should be thought to have stolen the horse. Shunka said he would walk back to Bayswater but Roger Birchall was adamant he should ride with him in the Hansom.

'You can drop him off before we get to the front door, Henry, if you think friend Davies would take it amiss. I'm an academic and I need to talk to this man for the purposes of research. Excellent, excellent.'

'Well don't ask him too much when I'm stuck up here,' said Henry. 'Because I want to hear it too. Just ask him about the Wild West Exhibition because I know about that.'

So while Shunka and Dr Birchall settled down into the cushions of the Major's Pride and Joy, Henry perched above them, trying not to think too much about Kitty Shaughnessy as he drove them back to Bayswater. It was difficult for him not to begin to doubt the kindness and wisdom of what they had done to her. It would be better for her gradually to regain her health and strength in the Indian encampment, he kept telling himself; certainly better than coming to in a cellar cubby hole, helpless and despairing. Perhaps, he kept thinking, perhaps he should have found a way to take her to Icingbury after all and he felt a pang of guilt as he recalled how readily he had found excuses for dismissing such a notion. Had he done that before or after she had told him about the Major's baby? He couldn't remember now.

He searched around for some inner comfort with which to salve himself and found it inevitably in the guise of Reuben. 'She's meant to go to the Indians and in any case she probably won't stay with them long.' Henry made it sound like a man's voice in his head, a voice not his own. But it was not convincing and no matter how many times he took himself through the argument he kept being left with the irreducible conclusion that he had made a terrible mistake.

What he had done to Kitty was not part of that picture of Shunka's, of the mountain being one thing made of many stones. It was a stone left over, a stone that had no place in holding the earth together. An image of sadness and unutterable loss came into his head, bleak and cold, and for a moment it seemed to Henry as though it might be the image of a place.

It felt almost as though the Major had been waiting in the hall for the sound of the Hansom, although Henry could not suppose that he had. He came out onto the steps to greet his friend and guest which was not his usual controlled style. Henry, standing at Shannon's head in the street heard him say, 'Ah there you are Birchall. Everything all right? Turner been bringing you up to date?' He waited to hear what Dr Birchall would say to this, but was unable to catch his reply as the two men turned their backs and walked back through the front door.

Mr Davies, unusually too, did not close the door behind them, but came down to speak to Henry.

'Where's that savage? Bringing the traps on a handcart is he? You took your time. Train late or have you been gossiping to your old friend over a nice cup of tea somewhere?'

'His train *was* late and his baggage is coming later. It's still on the ship, I think.'

'So where's whatsisname, Shunka then?'

'Back in the stables.' Henry could see that Mr Davies was itching to ask him what they had done with Kitty's body and was equally desperate to know whether Henry or Shunka had let anything slip to Roger Birchall. Henry took the bull by the horns.

'It's all right, Mr Davies. She's gone for good and no-one will ever find her.'

Mr Davies looked up and down the street. It was empty. He thrust his face so close to Henry's that he was forced to retreat into Shannon's neck.

'You'd better have done this right, Turner, that's all I can say. I should have dealt with it myself and then seen to you too. If a whisper of anything comes back on the Major, then a whole tribe of fucking Indians won't keep you from what I'm going to do to you. I'll hang for you, Turner, if I have to, don't think I won't.' And he stalked off up the steps.

Somehow, though, Henry did not quite believe him. Shannon turned her head and nibbled his ear.

The presence of a guest in the house instantly reintroduced a feeling of normal order. Henry felt it as soon as he and Shunka walked into the kitchen that evening. Mrs Bullace had had a proper dinner to prepare for the Major and Roger Birchall and Mr Davies had served it. He had his mess uniform on for the first time for a long time and Mrs Bullace announced that it was a pleasure to have gentlemen dressing for dinner once again, Major Fitzgerald having taken most of his meals in his room or in the library while he had been recovering from his injuries. Now the arrival of Dr Birchall also signified the end of his invalidity.

Around the kitchen table, even when Ivy was out of the room, no-one referred to Kitty or the events of the last forty-eight hours and, indeed, Henry had difficulty in calculating how he and Shunka should behave towards one another in Mr Davies' company as a pair who were supposed to be only one step removed from Burke and Hare. So it was a relief that Mr Davies' deliberately exaggerated representations of the demands of the Major's house guest enabled Henry to avoid the task of maintaining the fiction.

He found it frustrating to know that Birchall, his friend and confidant, was now under the same roof as he and yet no more accessible than when he had been in Egypt. He wanted to sit down with the Major and him and listen to enthralling tales of desert lands and fabulous finds. But protocol dictated that their easy fellowship on the railway station bench and in the Hansom in a side street of West Kensington could not be perpetuated in Bayswater. Henry's impatience was all the greater knowing that the next steps in his life were once again in Roger Birchall's hands and there was nothing he could do but wait.

Try as he might, it was impossible to envisage Birchall and the Major closeted in the library after dinner and to imagine their conversation. Birchall had taken Henry's bald explanation of Kitty's distress and the vile behaviour of the Major that had led to it, totally in his stride, with little more than one or two 'Good griefs' and an occasional 'Oh I say'.

But inside himself Henry knew it was their shared image of Boudicca's miseries at the hands of the Romans that put the whole thing on a level with which Birchall, the practical historian, instantly sympathised. That and the fact that they were bound together by an Icenian warrior whose bones were lying in the crypt of St.Mary's, Icingbury.

Never for a moment did it even cross his mind Dr Birchall might find the situation a horse man from Cambridgeshire had created for him so alien and threatening that he would seek to distance himself from it all. Or that he might pull the protective cloak of social rank around himself and walk away.

Nevertheless Henry fidgeted and sighed anxiously as he tried not let his inability to lift a finger at this stage to assist or direct Dr Birchall interfere with the evening grooming.

True to form, Shunka Wicasa became more and more impassive as the tension grew, but when Henry said 'What do you think Dr Birchall is saying to the Major?' for the fifth or sixth time, he finally broke his silence and said, 'We can walk away into the night now. We are free men. Why wait any longer?'

But Henry saw it more clearly than ever.

They could not walk away into the night just like that, because they would be pursued, found and dragged down, wrenched away from their purpose. There had to be a closing to which all acceded, including the Major and Mr Davies. Especially them.

Permission had to be granted and received on both sides.

The following day was almost unbearable for Henry. He had to drive the Major and Roger Birchall to the club for luncheon. Apart from the brief circuit of the Park shortly after Shunka's arrival in Bayswater, Fitzgerald had not set foot in his bow-fronted Hansom and he had not been to the club since the night of his ambush by Kitty's brother and his compatriots.

For Henry, the old familiar route and its purpose presented a tired and aching resurrection of time he was desperate to leave behind him. He managed to catch Birchall's eye when he and the Major alighted and Fitzgerald was giving him his instructions for collecting them, but apart from a quick smile there was nothing to reassure him that this setting down and picking up was not to form the pattern of the rest of his days.

So when, the following evening, both the Major and Birchall entered the stable unannounced, they caught Henry entirely off guard. He was bent over cleaning Liffey's hoof and their figures suddenly darkening the doorway made him glance up. It was as if two emissaries had arrived and goose flesh made the downy hairs on his back stand up.

'I've come to make my peace with the quads after such a long absence,' said the Major. 'Mind if I take a hand?' He picked up the curry comb in his right hand. His left was still heavily strapped.

'You weren't thinking of using that on them, Major,' said Henry. 'We're rubbing them down, not giving them a good hiding. Your rules Major.'

Shunka Wicasa who was working on Shannon in the next standing, stopped what he was doing and stood up. There was just a whiff of menacing expectation in the air.

Dr Birchall stepped forward in what might have been taken as an unconscious gesture of conciliation. 'Major Fitzgerald has some excellent news. Well I think it's excellent at any rate. Oh I say, Gray, pardon me. Is it all right if I tell them? After all it affects them as much as anyone I suppose.'

It was all said in an engaging rush. The Major looked indignant and then just discomforted. Shunka resumed his rubbing down, hissing quietly as he had learned to do from his new mentor. Henry bent down and picked up Liffey's foot again.

Birchall continued unabashed and to all intents and purposes, oblivious of any atmosphere. 'Major Fitzgerald has agreed to take my place on the excavation. He's going out to Egypt just as soon as the Archaeological Society can make contact with Petrie. Excellent. Means I won't have to feel so bad about leaving them in the lurch.'

'Since Birchall has decided to discuss my affairs with the servants…'

'Oh come on, Gray!'

'…I shall be shutting up the house here. I may let it.'

Henry's heart soared. He nearly said 'Does that mean we are free to go?' But he waited expectantly. They all did.

Fitzgerald glanced at Roger Birchall, rather uncomfortably, Henry thought. For a moment there was no sound except from the mares moving and Shunka's quiet hissing.

'The Troop Sergeant-Major shall go to my estate in Ireland. My agent could do with some determined help.'

'And Mrs Bullace?' Henry ventured, wondering how the Major was proposing to dispose of the rest of the witnesses.

‘She can stay on here if I decide to let,’ said the Major, ‘If not…if not I suppose I can always lock her in the cellar,’ and he barked his short, mirthless, foxy laugh. ‘I thought you might want to come out to Egypt with me, Turner. See the world. Keep an eye out for one another.’

‘You’re to come back to Cambridgeshire with me, Henry,’ said Dr Birchall in an unusually businesslike tone, ‘Mrs Bullace, too, if she wishes. I’ll be needing a new place when we get back and a housekeeper, I dare say,’ he added, and Henry suddenly understood that all their dispositions had been ordered, not by the Major, but by Birchall.

It was Fitzgerald who was being sent a hostage into exile. It had already begun as he quit the stable like a battlefield, with a straight back, a hint of military swagger and never a backward glance at the victors.

‘And Shunka? He cannot go back to the Show. Not until it leaves for America and it’s going to Manchester first. Colonel Cody said he would send for Shunka after that.’

‘I will go with you,’ said Shunka Wicasa without looking up. ‘We are brothers in blood and there is a debt to be paid.’ There was no question in his voice. It was not a matter for discussion.

‘Excellent, excellent,’ said Roger Birchall. ‘Just what Icingbury needs. Are you a churchgoer by any chance, Shunka?’

‘He believes in the Great Spirit and has the Earth Ear,’ said Henry helpfully.

‘I cannot wait to tell Robert Earl that,’ said Birchall. ‘Excellent, truly excellent.’

‘And I shall write to Annie, now,’ thought Henry. It was time.

22

The late afternoon mistiness of autumn seemed to be waiting to meet the smoke and steam of the engine on the platform at Great Duster, at first standing apart, each indecisive, and then mingling like the descending passengers and their collectors.

Although she welcomed Henry with joy and Dr Birchall with the happiness of remembered affection, her eyes were only for Shunka Wicasa. They travelled slowly from his unlaced boots, the length of his body, up and up until she looked into his face and he into hers.

He did not need to have it explained to him. As he stood there, silent, while Dr Birchall fussed about his traps and bubbled inconsequentially about the coldness of the day and the lateness of the hour, Henry Turner beheld an Oglala Sioux from Pine Ridge somewhere out on the Great American Plains, and a young widowed country woman from Icingbury in Cambridgeshire, become as one, each consumed by the other.

As the engine gave a great sigh from its iron depths and a vaulting shriek on its whistle, Henry felt his own self leap, this way and that, uncertain whether to run free or stay bound.

'I've brought the tilt cart from the Veil House,' said Annie, still not looking at them, her eyes fixed on Shunka. 'Do you think we shall all fit in with the bags? I'm not sure now.'

'Take Roger to the Vicarage,' said Henry, 'Shunka and I will walk on. Is my father expecting us?'

'Your mother was sorry you didn't write to her to say you were coming, I think. But I made out the letter to me was for her.'

Henry wanted to spread his arms wide and cry out to the sky, 'The letters were always only for you. You know that, you know that.' And he was ashamed, not for the first time, that he had neglected his mother's needs, knowing that it would not be the last. But now there was no point. The time for explanations and agreeing understandings had already gone forever, a moment before. He might now never resolve what he had ever intended for Annie and him. It was passed.

Icingbury rushed in upon him as he and Shunka turned out of the station building and watched the trap disappearing up the road to the village ahead. He might never have been away, the months between simply imagined.

The Indian walked in silence beside him, a man who in the space of a few hours' train journey had been drawn out by Dr Birchall's inquisitive silences, like a faded painting revealed and restored to a greater brilliance than ever had been suspected.

As soon as they had settled themselves in the compartment it had become clear to Henry that Shunka was probably more experienced on trains than he was himself.

Dr Birchall had casually enquired whether the Indian was likely to need any comforting explanations about the 'railroad, as I believe it is termed in America, as indeed it is here in most countries of Europe, take for example *chemin de fer* and *ferrovia*,' his academic wandering designed, as Henry now knew, to disarm any possible tensions and disquiets amongst those of a nervous disposition.

For the time being at any rate, they had the carriage to themselves and Shunka had carefully removed his boots and placed them under the seat.

'I have been on many of these trains. The first time was two or three summers after the Greasy Grass fight.'

He'd stopped as he often did, when he spoke of something clearly of huge importance in his past, as if the evocation required a congregation's response in order for him to proceed.

Dr Birchall had one. 'Ah yes, the Little Big Horn massacre in, I think…'76. Well no, perhaps not. Perhaps I should say "battle" in the circumstances. My goodness, yes indeed. You were saying, Shunka, about the train.'

Henry had listened in amazement. He and Shunka related to one another within their selves. Little had passed between them by way of conversation about their pasts partly because the present had been so all consuming, but largely because they instinctively understood what the other was feeling. Henry, if he consciously thought about it at all, generally felt that he and Shunka were of a single mind, not in the sense of agreeing, necessarily, more like the dialogue of thought he might have with himself, alone on the wagon box driving to Cambridge.

But Dr Birchall had begun to wind open his sluice gate, at first just a fraction or two, but the possibility of a greater flood from Shunka was definitely there.

'After the Custer fight life became very bad for the Lakota. My father and brothers had won a great victory, but we had gained nothing by it. Before two springs had come and gone Crazy Horse himself was dead. Some chiefs wanted peace. Spotted Tail from the Brulé wanted peace. He came to speak to Red Cloud on the Pine Ridge and said he was sending his grandsons with Captain Pratt to a place in the sunrise. A long way. He said they would learn to talk the white men's talk and to draw the pictures of their talk. He meant learn to write. My father was at the talking in Red Cloud's lodge and told my mother, my brothers and me this to remember. It is our way. Red Cloud said he would not send any man's sons to be the soldiers' *wan'yah ka yuzape*. I do not know the word in your language; it is like a prisoner kept so that the others will not fight.'

'A hostage perhaps?' said Birchall.

Like Kitty, thought Henry, and a bit like Boudicca's husband.

'Perhaps,' said Shunka gravely. 'In the end Red Cloud saw that it would be good to talk your talk because then we would not have to have *e'ehskah* to tell us what was said and written.'

'Interpreters?' said Birchall, 'I say, just a guess.'

'So I went on the train with the others from Pine Ridge and Spotted Tail's grandsons from Rosebud, to Carlisle in Pennsylvania. This was my first time.'

'Were you afeard?' Henry asked.

'No. I had my brave name by then and my first *wechapaha*[*] in my bundle. But I did not take it with me. My father said it would not be wise. But I had it here in my head.'

'His first what?' said Dr. Birchall.

Henry had glanced up at the soft embroidered leather roll beside his own carpet bag in the luggage rack. He knew.

'I've no idea,' he said.

Roger Birchall warmed to the success of his interrogation. He rubbed his hands and hunched himself forward on the seat. 'So it was at this school that you learned to speak English…and to write too?'

'Yes, I have been given a medicine gift. I have the earth ear. I can listen and remember. I can hear the past and the future when the Great Spirit wishes it. It is all one. It sounds all the time. Our ancestors speak and our children's children not yet born speak. Another's tongue is not so difficult to hear. At first many could not at Carlisle, but we were punished for speaking our own tongues. So in the end Lakota and Cheyenne and Lakota and Apache all spoke with one tongue together for the first time. It gave us a new strength.'

'It would, it would. Excellent. Not what Captain Pratt had in mind, though, I don't suppose.'

---

[*] scalp

'He is not a bad man. He does not walk with death but even so he wishes us, the *wechash'tah*[*], dead just as Custer did and Crook does. But dead in here and here and not in battle.' Shunka had put his hand on his head and over his heart as he spoke.

'Excellent,' said Birchall, 'Well not excellent at all of course, but excellent the way you put it. The way you have learned that there are more ways of killing a man than by cutting his throat. It was the way of the Romans, wasn't it Henry old fellow? Often think that Caesar should have said "I came, I saw, I civilised" because that's what conquers them in the end. But at what cost, eh? And for what in the end? I've been digging up lost civilisation. The strong on top of the weaker and all on top of the weakest, and over it all, sand, nothing but sand.'

'So did you have to stay at the school? Were you a prisoner?' Henry had ventured to interrupt Dr Birchall's flow, anxious to return to extracting whatever could be extracted from Shunka, knowing that he would relapse into silence if Birchall let him off the hook.

'We had promised our fathers and our chief. We were free to walk in the town, in our blue soldier coats and our boots and our hair cut off. Everyone knew us. Then one day Spotted Tail and Red Cloud came and were angry that we were being turned into soldiers, being beaten for speaking our tongue and sometimes shut alone in the dark holes. Spotted Tail called everyone to a talking at the school and said chiefs' sons should not be made to work like farmers and he would take all the Lakota home with him. In the end Captain Pratt said he could only take his own blood family. I hid myself among them. So did some others and when the police searched the train they were taken back. But I hid beneath the seat where Red Cloud sat in his blanket and no-one dared to move him.'

Shunka had fallen silent. As Henry had waited to see if Dr Birchall would coax some more out of him or whether he should press on himself, not altogether sure what words of his would trigger a fresh narrative, the train had been briefly engulfed in a tunnel, its whistle shrieking as if in protest.

When it emerged into the light again, he could see that Shunka, for all his declared experience of trains, was not comfortable with sudden, dark enclosure.

'Yes, I have been on many trains since then, with Colonel Cody.'
But he had said it almost to the train itself rather than to his companions, as if to proclaim his refusal to be daunted by its tricks. It had had an air of finality about it.

---

[*] American Indians. Native Americans

Henry threw what he hoped was a meaningful look at Dr.Birchall. The doctor roused himself.

'So Little Big Horn...the Greasy Grass I think you said...you were there, then? You must have been a very young man. It's over ten years ago now.

Shunka assumed a dignified look. 'Yes. Before it I was a boy, and after I became a man. At Greasy Grass I counted first coup and earned my brave name. Before I went to Carlisle I had already made my sundance.'

Henry had let it all sink in. There were so many questions but he didn't know what they were. He had waited breathlessly for Dr Birchall to reveal another of his friend's layers

'Tell us, how did you get your brave name that day, One-who-hears-horses? Was that to do with the earth ear too?'

Henry wanted to lean over and shake Dr Birchall's hand.

Shunka looked hard at Dr. Birchall. 'What you ask me is not *unsiiciyapi*, to make me speak of my deeds in a proud way.'

'But if you do not speak of them, how is the history of your people to be remembered?' said Dr Birchall seriously.

'The council can ask me to do the *waktoglaka*, to talk of brave deeds so that the village may hear and the young men learn. But such deeds must be witnessed. It is not enough for me to tell them alone. That is not *unsiiciyapi*. What is this word in your tongue?'

'Humble, humility...something like that?' Dr Birchall suggested. 'What you are saying is not so different amongst our own soldiers. Their brave deeds have to be written down by an officer as a witness before they are worthy of reward. But I am an historian, Shunka. I am one who records the deeds of others, perhaps to write them down in a book for others to learn. May I not therefore ask you to speak for my benefit without you speaking for your own? Your language is not written down. Perhaps one day no-one will remember what was done and by whom. I know that even great cities decay and become buried so that people like me can only guess what happened once. How much more difficult for the people of the plains who do not even have cities to lie buried? How will we guess what really happened to you when the white man's civilisation presses you into the dust?'

Both Shunka Wicasa and Henry had stared at him. For Henry it was like a lesson from Miss Covington, sending him into a reverie so that he would be sitting there still, his thoughts racing further away than her words had designed, long after the class had been dismissed and his fellows had whooped off into the yard, none the worse for the drubbing she had failed to administer to their imaginations.

But for Henry it was a burst of simplicity, like a flash of sunlight on a shard of mineral turned over by the plough, instantly announcing its hidden existence within the jealous clay. Then when recalled and gently sent on his way, as like as not it would be Annie Lilley who would walk out with him fresh from her own dreaming.

Then for a while there had been no sound but the train's rub-a-dub-dub until Shunka spoke.

'Your words are like the talk of chiefs at council. I will tell you of my deeds. A witness to the truth shall have to come another time.' The warrior took a deep breath.

'There had been a great fight along the Rosebud River. Crazy Horse had beaten the soldiers led by their Chief, Crook, and many of us had come together for feasting and dancing by the Greasy Grass, the Little Big Horn, where it makes a big bend below the hills and there is good grazing for the ponies. I had never seen so many *wecash'tah* together in one place before. Cheyenne, Arapahoe as well as Lakota Sioux. The smoke from the lodge fires drifted like mist in the morning and the sound of the corralled ponies moving this way and that, as one animal, was like nothing I had heard until I came to the ocean and heard the water sighing beneath the ship.

'The chiefs had said there would be a week's dancing before the grazing and the small game were gone. There were so many of us to feed. But we had no fear, no need to hide in small groups as we usually did. Crook was beaten and had not followed us to the Little Big Horn and although my father said the blue horse soldiers would come again, it would not be yet.

'It was the middle of the moon when wild turnips bloom and the days are longest and hot. Before noon, I and my brother took one pony and our bows and went out after *zezecha*[*], the prairie birds. I ran and he rode and then we turned and turned about. We crossed the river and went up onto the first ridge above the valley. There we fastened the pony and scouted around for the game, lying on our bellies in the grass. My brother signed to me to move further round to the left in a circle to drive the game towards him. He was better with the bow than I then. As I lay on my belly and moved like *sintehda,* the rattle snake, through the grass and watched too in case I should come upon a real one, I was very close to the ground.

'Then, as before sometimes, but never so loud and strong, I felt the earth ear sound in my head and in my guts. It was a future time it spoke, but so loud it was not very far off. I could hear horses with shoes and metal jangling and rattling about them. I knelt up and looked above the

[*] turkeys

tall grass but there was nothing to see but our own pony quietly grazing below the ridge a long way back. Then the earth ear sounded inside me again so loud that I brought up my stomach contents onto the grass and I could see in my head horses and blue soldiers as if they were crossing the river and galloping into the lodge camp below. Then I ran, ran towards the ridge, past my brother and our pony and up the hill so that I could look down to the river. But there were no soldiers, no horses.

'My brother ran up and was angry that I had scared off the game too quickly by running. He yelled at me, what was I doing? I said to him, "There are blue soldiers coming". He looked all around and said "I see nothing" but I said "I hear horses coming It is the earth ear".

'My brother was still angry and did not want to believe me, but he knew that already the old men were listening to me sometimes and soon I would smoke the pipe with them. He asked me if I was sure and I said it was so strong I had brought up my stomach contents. So I rode and he ran after me down to river and across to my father's lodge where he was talking to He Dog, one of the Lakota chiefs. My father signed to me not to interrupt but the Chief could see that it was important. So I told him that blue soldier horses were coming in from the direction of the sunrise. He asked me how many, and I said I had not seen them but I had heard them.

'Then my mother came from the lodge and my brother came running up. He Dog asked if he had seen anything and my brother said no, he had not but that I had brought up my stomach contents and come back to the lodge.

My mother knew. She said, "He has the earth ear." He Dog asked if it was true and I said I had never felt it so strong before. Then he told my mother to tell the women to take down the tepees and prepare the lodge polls for travois. He called to his warriors to mount their ponies.

'When they had gone towards the river at the sunrise end of the village, my father looked at me with a black face and said in a harsh, mocking voice "Well, One-who-hears-horses, you had better be right. Because if you are right there will be a great victory for the Lakota people and you will be the spirit medicine that assures it and you will count your first coup. All this because you say you have the earth ear. But if you are wrong then you will have shamed your family. Tell me now, could you be wrong?" But I knew I was not wrong and as we stood there we heard firing coming from ground in front of the timber by the river.

'Because the earth ear had sounded in me the village had not been taken by surprise, the blue soldiers had not been able to ride in amongst the women and children and the old men. Our warriors forced them back and killed them in the river and wounded many who died in the night after the big fight.'

'Was this General Custer?' Dr Birchall had asked him.

'We did not know he was at the big fight later that day. Long Hair he was called but no-one saw him there. We thought it was General Crook. Afterwards I learned that the one I had stopped attacking the village was called Reno.

'Once when he had had too much whiskey, Colonel Cody told some cowboys in the Show that Reno had lost his men, his courage and his good name that day and that I had been the medicine that made it happen. Cody did not mean them to blame me. He had been told the story of my earth ear by another *wecash'tah* and thought that it was worthy of the telling, like a story for children. But afterwards it was told differently by the cowboys to one another. They said that I had led Custer into a trap. But the earth ear had sounded in me to save the women and the old men, I know. We did not know that Custer was on the hill.

'When the women went among their dead there was no Long Hair. Later I was told he had cut off his hair before the fight. An Arapaho must have killed him. They do not take short hair.'

Henry had sat like a child having a story told at bedtime. His father had never told stories as a matter of course, but occasionally had been persuaded to recount some piece of Icingbury folklore. More he remembered his grandfather's tales of fenland ghosts and horse fairies told at Christmas. Then Miss Covington had read them stories from books. But here in the carriage was a man barely older than he, if at all, who told a story about this magical gift he had. And it was true. And if this were true then so too was Reuben's story. It was there waiting to be listened to, waiting to be repeated.

'I'm bringing a man with this earth ear to listen for it or to waken it in me,' he thought, 'It is meant.'

When they had found Reuben's skeleton, his head too had been filled with pictures and he too had been sick.

'So the name stuck, I suppose, excellent,' said Birchall lightly, although the lengthy silence that had preceded the comment suggested rather more gravity.

'Yes. The name my father called me out of worry that I might have made it all up, was given to me by him as my brave name W*icasa Shunka'wakan Wanahan*, Man-who-hears-horses-coming.'

'But you're name is *Shunka Wicasa* I thought, not all that,' Henry had said.

'What is your whole name?' asked Shunka.

'Henry Charles George Turner,' said Henry.

'So you do not use it all either.'

'I suppose not, no.'
'I choose the words which mean only Horse Man,' Shunka had said.

Henry found it difficult to meet his mother's eye. Although he could see that she was overjoyed to see him walk back into the Veil House, her quiet told him there would have to be time for him to be forgiven his sudden departure and lately his neglect to write. But if she had decided to be rather reserved in her outward show of welcome towards her son, she made up for it tenfold by the effusive reception she gave Shunka Wicasa.

From the word go she called him Mr Wicasa, putting him somewhere on a par with their landlord's agent and it was not until some weeks later that she began to call him Shunka to his face. But she never quite overcame her first impression and would frequently relapse into that formal address, especially when referring to him in his absence to other ladies at church.

'Where's Pa?' said Henry after several minutes, beginning to become embarrassed by his mother's unaccustomed fussing round his friend.

'He's with the Head Baiter, I think. He knows you're coming,' she said, adding a little reproachfully, 'Annie told us.'

Henry and Shunka walked across the yard, their path across the cobbles lit by the oil lamps from the kitchen window behind them meeting the light being shed from the half opened doors of the stables in front of them. Before they reached them Henry stopped and laid his hand on Shunka's arm.

'My father is…my father is…well he's rather…'

'Fathers are fathers. I understand,' said Shunka helpfully, 'I would find it difficult too.' He bent down in the pool of yellow oil light and carefully tied his bootlaces.

Bailey Turner was standing at the far end of the stable facing the doors, talking to the Head Baiter. If he saw his son come in he made no acknowledgement of it and continued his conversation.

Henry barely noticed. The downy hair on his body was standing up with sudden warmth and joy and as if in response to it, Honeycomb the chesnut mare stamped her hooves and whinnied a greeting to him. Henry buried his face in her neck, letting her coat soak up the hot tears that had started in his eyes. Then, removing his groom's corduroy, he rolled up his sleeves and began the old familiar routine, hand raised, elbow turned out, fingers and the inside of his forearm working together down her shoulder.

'Well I suppose we might get a decent day's work out of her, now, seeing as you're back. You are back I take it, not just passing through with this romany you seem to have brought in.'

Henry straightened up at his father's voice, the words making him feel angry and sad. He turned to face him not knowing what he would say when he opened his own mouth.

His father must have seen the look on Henry's face because his own softened visibly. "Not that I'm not glad to see you, Henry, whether you're coming or going,' he added somewhat confusedly and he half stepped towards his son, making as if to offer both his hands to grip, but failing to reach quite far enough.

Henry, caught involuntarily by the movement raised both his arms too to receive the welcome that was intended but unconsummated.

Bailey Turner caught sight of Henry's misshapen fingers. 'Hands no better then?' he said, as if his gesture had been to enable him to examine them and Henry recalled their parting as if it had been that very morning.

'No better and no worse, Pa. They don't cause me too much bother now.'

The Head Baiter who had been hovering in the background clearly took this exchange as signifying that the homecoming had been successfully accomplished. He now stepped forward and shook Henry firmly by the hand, clasping him tightly round the shoulders with his other arm, making inconsequential welcoming noises and articulating those half-completed questions which bring absences to an end. But his eyes were firmly fixed on Shunka Wicasa, standing impassively in the shadow, his arms folded, taking in the scene being played out in front of him.

Henry saw the look. He was so familiar with it now.

'This is my very good friend, and Dr. Birchall's,' something made him add, 'Our good friend W*icasa Shunka'wakan Wanahan*, Man-who-hears-horses-coming.'

He had practised it over and over in his head on the train ever since he had heard the entire name, making it sound like the rhythm of the wheels on the rails to fix it.

'He is a Lakota Sioux from the Great Plains. Everyone calls him Shunka Wicasa, Shunka for short.'

'It is good to know the father of my brother,' said Shunka, 'And a brother horse man.' He inclined towards the Head Baiter as he said this.

Bailey Turner made an awkward throat-clearing sound, clearly searching around for something appropriate to say. After some hesitation he asked, 'So how come you're brothers, then? What does that make me, I wonder? Or is it just a manner of speaking, like chapel folk?'

In times to come when he recalled that first meeting of Shunka and the Bailey, Henry could never suppose that his father for one moment realised the seriousness of those questions, merely that he had been outfaced by the situation and latched onto the first thing that had come into his head.

Shunka had taken the questions entirely at face value. 'Henry turned the knife that would have ended my life and bloodied the hand of the man that would have taken it. That man will one day go into the spirit world with a hand more broken than Henry's when they meet there. He will pass his enemy by and will not need to look back. For this Henry is my brother in blood and soon perhaps we will make it truly so. For here when I was on the train I felt far from the cities and there was sometimes a look of the plains. Here perhaps there is a place of the spirit. Here it shall perhaps be done.'

The Bailey and the Head Baiter shuffled irresolutely like small boys whose innocent question to an elder about procreation had brought forth an unexpectedly elaborate and embarrassing response and who wanted nothing more than to be dismissed.

Henry felt like letting his father stew, but he could not.

'So there you are Pa,' he said, 'It is a bit like chapel folk isn't it,' and they all laughed gratefully with Shunka joining in rather half-heartedly. He asked Henry later what it had all meant.

'My father was worried that he would have to be your father too, I expect,' said Henry smiling again at the recollection.

'He shall, if it is his wish,' said Shunka gravely: 'And he shall always be welcomed as a *tahonse*[*] in my father's lodge and he will be as a grandfather to my children.'

Whatever it was Bailey Turner thought had passed between them all that evening certainly made him refrain from demanding to know what Henry's plans were, much to his immense relief. Events and Dr Birchall had swept them along at a run, closing doors behind them so that time and space seemed to cease to be with each slam; the journey itself a race whose purpose was to arrive, to breast the tape and not to ask 'what next?'

To the question 'will you be staying put now?' Henry could only say 'it all depends.' But he had no idea on what it depended, nor did his father ask him.

'Well I can let you have your keep,' he said, rather helpfully Henry thought. 'There should be some indoor threshing, but the harvest was poor again, very poor. It'll be some of the seed corn, like as not, but I have to pay the Baiter at least.'

---

[*] his father's cousin

Henry thought to ask about the other horse men, realising he had seen no-one else in the stable.

'Had to let them go for day men. That's why I cannot give you more than your feed and a roof over your head,' his father had said.

'What about Shunka,' Henry asked after supper, when his friend had taken himself off to a corner of the stable where he could make his bed and see the stars.

'What can he do? Is he a horse man or what is he?' the Bailey asked.

Henry searched around for something that Shunka was that his father might possibly find useful. He had been a good groom and had already learned a little from Henry to add to his Indian skills, but that was not enough on the farm. He was apparently a good hunter, but Henry thought he would not offer that thought.

'I think he must be a good gentler.' It was just a guess. Shunka must have been involved with breaking ponies.

The Bailey brightened slightly at this. 'Well I've been thinking of bringing on some mounts for the cavalry again. You might see what can be had at the sales. It's not a good time though. What about this Dr Birchall, what's he going to do for him?'

'What indeed?' thought Henry.

In the event the solution to the problem of what to do with a Sioux Indian in Icingbury, unused to farm labouring, came from an unexpected quarter. A short while after Henry's exchange with his father, the kitchen door opened and an 'it's only us' ushered in Aunt Elizabeth Lilley closely followed by Annie extinguishing the lamp that had lighted their way. For a while therefore the ritual of homecoming was reawakened. The kitchen became filled with laughter and questions, wonderment and interjections of old news and fresh gossip. Henry was in turn feted and mildly reproached by his Great Aunt while Annie sat exuding warmth and saying little beyond news of Miss Covington when asked.

Later the level of animation subsided, the Bailey started to nod in his chair by the range, Aunt Elizabeth and her niece began to confide in one another and by the natural process of elimination Annie and Henry stepped out into the yard to 'look in on the horses.'

'Where's your friend then?' said Annie as soon as they had closed the kitchen door behind them.

'Taken himself off to bed in the stable. I guess he can pick his own spot seeing as how Pa has stood off most of the horse men, but knowing Shunka, he'll sleep as close to the ground as he can and still see the stars.'

'What did you say his name was, I forgot to ask Dr Birchall.'

'Shunka Wicasa. Ma keeps calling him Mr Wicasa, but their names don't work like that. It means Man-who-hears-horses. Horsc man like me.'

'Lovely,' said Annie, 'What a lovely thing to be called. A whole picture of something. Not like our names. I suppose they meant things once, but now they're just sounds.'

Henry wanted to say, 'I saw the way you looked at him. I know what happened at the station today.' He wanted to say it was all right, but he was not sure whether it was all right, for him or for her. But if he did not say something that was true now, the world would drift and the truth would drift with it, changing its shape as it did. What was possible now might never be possible afterwards. He tried to think about what they had said to one another at the time of their parting.

'Do you remember when we saw the kingfisher?' he said

'Halcyon day you said. I asked Miss Covington about that after you'd gone. She was very pleased with you for remembering.'

'You said I should bring you my warrior when I'd found him or something like that, and that maybe you could have both of us.'

'Yes. Did I?'

'Well what I'm trying to say, Annie, is I think I have found him. Do you see?'

She took his hand.

'He says I saved his life and we are brothers. Brothers in blood, he calls it. We seem to be of one mind, so to speak. You know… like Reuben. He says the missionaries called him that. Reuben. It made my skin creep.'

They stood gazing up at the stars and holding hands for an age. Then Annie said simply, 'Thank you for him. He is the most wonderful thing I have ever seen. Wonderful. But impossible.'

'I know,' said Henry.

Then Aunt Elizabeth began to emerge, opening the door to let herself out, calling out to Annie to 'come along and light the lamp, we must be off', then remembering another piece of gossip to impart to Henry's mother and re-entering the kitchen.

Eventually she managed to bring herself entirely out into the yard. 'I'm sorry not to have met this friend of yours, the Indian man. Your mother says keeping him might be difficult, so if he can hold a paintbrush and a bucket of whitewash I'll keep him busy at the cottage.'

Henry did not know whether whitewashing cottages counted as the kind of manual labour that Shunka would consider unworthy of him. 'I'll put it to him,' he said, 'I expect it will be all right.'

He spoke to Shunka in the morning as they both naturally gravitated to the horses and set about the morning rituals and routines with the Head Baiter and the one other remaining horse man the Bailey had kept on. If Shunka had any doubts about whitewashing he kept them to himself, both before and after Henry revealed that his cousin Annie lived under the same roof as their Great Aunt.

His father came into the stable and stood watching Shunka at work rather warily. After a while he said, 'Henry says you're good at gentling.'

Shunka looked quizzically at Henry who did his best to explain and mime breaking a horse to bit and saddle. Shunka began to assume one of his grave looks and Henry realised that he was about to give Bailey Turner a lecture on the Indian way of dealing with unbroken ponies or something equally likely to leave his father entirely unimpressed with his skills.

'Yes, Pa, he is,' he put in hastily, catching Shunka's eye, frowning and shaking his head as imperceptibly as he could manage, 'He was in charge of the largest pony herd ever assembled on the Plains at a place called…' he struggled to recall it, 'Greasy Grass.'

'Well you can both go over to Bury and see if we can take an order for cavalry mounts from the barracks,' said the Bailey, 'Then I'll leave it to you to search out some yearlings to bring on. Do you have any of my money left?'

The question took Henry's breath away.

'As a matter of fact I have at least half of it,' he replied stiffly.

'What did you spend the other half on, or don't I want to know? That was a fair sum as I recall. Anyway seeing as you've had such a good time with half of it, you can spend the rest on yearlings. If you make a good job of it I'll give you some of the profit maybe.'

Henry nodded resignedly. He did not feel inclined to lie about the fact that he had given Kitty the better part of his nest egg.

'Shall I be able to paint?' said Shunka.

The Bailey stared at him in amazement. 'Paint what? Your…your face?' He had clearly heard something of the ways of the American Indian.

'The house of the woman Great Aunt,' Shunka replied unmoved by the misapprehension.

Henry roared. 'He's to whitewash Church Cottage for his keep, Pa, not go on the war path.'

The Bailey tried to maintain his dignity and then he too threw back his head and laughed, his weathered face assuming an even ruddier shade with embarrassment.

'May we be allowed to enjoy the joke?'

Roger Birchall and Mr Earl the vicar had entered the stables unannounced. Bailey Turner acknowledged them rather suspiciously.

'You remember Dr Birchall, Mr Turner,' said the Vicar.

'Indeed, he paid for draining the water meadow a year or so back.'

Roger Birchall seized Bailey Turner's hand and pumped it up and down enthusiastically.

'Do you want to pay for any more improvements to my land, Dr Birchall,' the Bailey said with a rare display of heavy humour.

The Vicar interrupted fussily. 'We have come for a little discussion with Henry and…and…er…'

'…Shunka Wicasa,' Roger Birchall finished for him.

'Well best look sharp,' said Bailey Turner ungraciously, 'Busy men, places to be, yearlings to buy, whitewashing to do. It's not Sunday yet,' and he took himself off into the yard with an air of injured satisfaction.

'I can never quite seem to say the right thing to your father,' Mr Earl said plaintively, 'I believe him to be a God-fearing man, but somehow he seems to resent my role as intermediary.'

'I expect he'd rather wait to haggle over his dues with the Almighty when he sees Him, rather than have to pay you on account every Sunday,' said Henry rather sourly, still recoiling at his father's earlier meanness and then instantly feeling mortified at allowing his feelings to break out. After all, he knew full well times were hard and his presence an added burden.

Mr Earl cast a glance round the stables. 'Are we alone Turner? I mean apart from…from…er…'

'Shunka Wicasa,' said Henry; 'Yes I think so. Why?' he added, knowing only too well, but feeling irritated by the Vicar's pusillanimous dithering. Mr Earl had not so much as acknowledged Shunka's presence yet.

'Fact is, it's the bones,' said Dr Birchall. 'Robert here wants me to cart them back to Cambridge, but I said that you had a say in the matter. Found on your land. Well not yours exactly, but you know what I mean.'

'Well,' said Henry wickedly turning the screw on the Vicar, 'In point of fact the land belongs to the estate so perhaps his Lordship…'

'Oh my goodness, no, no, no.' said the Vicar. 'The fewer the better. You have absolutely no idea how unsympathetic the diocese can be when it puts its mind to it.'

Roger Birchall was doing his best to look and sound solemn, but Henry could hear the suppressed giggle inside him.

'Apparently the Bishop will look unfavourably on Robert's, that is Mr Earl's keeping an Icenian warrior in the crypt. Inappropriate use of consecrated ground, not getting permission from higher authority *etcetera*

etcetera. Absolutely one hundred per cent, twenty-two carat excellent. Oh well no not really excellent.' Dr Birchall finally burst letting out a huge shout of laughter at the sight of the Vicar's pained and grieved expression at his friend's leg pulling.

'What warrior?' said a quiet, level voice from the shadows. 'Is it the spirit warrior who guides you, Henry?'

Suddenly the laughter had gone. The Vicar's aura of hurt pride evaporated. A silence fell over the four men. Even the horses were still.

23

Henry could never really fathom what, from that moment, had harnessed the Reverend Robert Earl to Shunka Wicasa. Henry himself, in no way felt that it rivalled or threatened his own bond with the Indian. That bond was a blending of equal minds, the creation of a comfortable singularity. But Mr Earl appeared bound tacitly by the threat of conquest. His bond was a yoke of fealty. It chafed him mightily, yet he could not throw it off, try as he might. His nascent fear that he had allowed himself to be drawn into a pagan conspiracy had suddenly come of age. He said as much to Henry, but when Roger Birchall sought to make light of his fears, Mr Earl blamed the archaeologist for allowing his excavations to contaminate his Christian duty.

But when Shunka Wicasa cut across the exchanges between the other three, insisting that he be taken to the place where the Icenian warrior was to be found, Mr Earl, staring at the Sioux like a mesmerised rabbit, seemed unable to find words to object.

So it was that the next morning Henry and Shunka slipped away from the farm on the pretext of going round to Great Aunt Elizabeth's and instead made their way to the side door to St Mary's vestry where Roger Birchall and the agitated vicar were waiting. As they descended into the sub-church Henry at first felt a tingle of excitement quickly growing into a choking plug of nervous anticipation as they approached the ancient tithe chest resting in the farthest alcove.

His tension communicated itself to Shunka who gripped Henry's arm above the elbow. 'This is not a good place for a spirit,' he said almost plaintively, 'This is like the place where the soldier Davies put the woman.'

'It's a church,' whispered Henry, 'It's a good place, full of spirits I shouldn't wonder.'

But the Indian was not to be placated. When Dr Birchall lifted the lid of the tithe chest revealing its contents in the lamplight, Shunka let out a groan. For an instant Henry was convinced that it was the skeleton in the chest that had spoken and he in turn involuntarily gripped Mr Earl by the arm. The vicar nearly jumped out of his skin, dropping the lamp, which although it did not break, rolled hither and yon extinguishing itself in the process.

'That wasn't at all amusing, Turner,' Mr Earl said in as brave a voice as he could muster while he hunted in his cassock for the means to relight the lamp.

When after a while the light was restored Dr Birchall raised the lid again. The skull and bones were, of course, lying as they had been left more than a year since, facing down on their hessian bed.

Henry felt a wave of relief come over him, as if he had expected to find them disturbed or rearranged. He felt relieved too to see the reality once more for what it was, where for so long there had been an insubstantial presence. When they had laid Reuben to rest there that Easter time, Henry had felt contentment. The right thing had been done. But he had sensed then that it would be only a temporary respite. Now there were still more things to be done, answers to be sought. But this time he had brought Shunka with him who understood, in the same way as he did, perhaps saw even more clearly or knew how. Henry's burden was not lifted, but it was shared.

Shunka had come forward to the edge of the chest. Unceremoniously he took hold of the Vicar's wrist, raising the hand that held the lamp higher so that he could see better. Mr Earl made no complaint at being so handled. He stood dumbly accepting Shunka's right to use him.

After a moment Shunka said, 'What did he make you do, Henry, when the spirit showed itself to you?'

'I put the skull back with the rest of him. They were separated. It had been chopped off by the Romans. Dr Birchall says that they just left him like that, unburied.

'So he has not gone headless into the spirit world. He still waits to be a whole man again amongst his friends and his enemies. This is what you have been chosen for and in return he has become great medicine for you.'

'So what are you saying, Shunka?' said Roger Birchall, 'That we should give him a proper funeral?'

'That may be it. We will know when it is time. But it is not now.'

'Oh I say, excellent. What should we do with him when the time comes?'

'Not the church, please not the church.' The Vicar had finally found his tongue. Shunka was still holding his arm with the lamp aloft.

'What is his tribal way?' said Shunka.

'The Iceni? Oh definitely burial,' said Dr Birchall. 'The Romans at this time went in for cremation but the Iceni preferred to bury their dead along with things they might need to have in the next life. This man was a warrior, perhaps even a chief. The Romans seem to have singled him out for some reason anyway. Interrogation, Henry always maintains, so they must have thought he had access to information. So if he had been a minor chief, a house carl perhaps, then he would have been buried with his weapons, perhaps even his horse and chariot.'

'Not in the churchyard, not a horse please.' Mr Earl, still standing as if hung limply from the end of Shunka's outstretched arm, appeared as one addressing his captor, a supplicant seeking a boon.

Shunka may or may not have understood Dr Birchall, but he showed no sign that he had not kept up. 'Then we must bury him, although it is not the true Lakota way. He must go in the way of his people.'

'So not in a Christian church then, would you say?' said the Vicar a little more hopefully.

Shunka finally released his arm. 'I must leave this place. It is like the dark holes at Carlisle.'

The four men climbed back up to the vestry and daylight. The Vicar spoke tentatively. 'So when can we say the bones will be gone then…soon?'

'We must wait for a sign. It will come.' Shunka appeared to be in no hurry and Mr Earl evidently was unable to press him.

Observing the two of them, Henry found their counterpoint amusing. He did not understand it but at least it was keeping the Vicar from nagging at him.

'What do we do then?' he asked Shunka when they had left the other two and were making their way towards Great Aunt Elizabeth's.

'A bird will come and then we must make a sweat lodge.'

Henry had learned by now that his questions would all be answered in good time, so he kept silent.

After a moment Shunka said, 'Is she taken, the woman Annie?'

'She's a widow. Her man died. There was an accident.'

'And now? Does her family give her to another man?'

'She doesn't really have any family, so to speak. Her Pa died a while ago and she doesn't live with her Ma any more. She really only has Great Aunt Elizabeth, and us of course, the Turner side. Anyway she's been a married woman. She can make her own decisions.'

'Has she finished her *waseh'da*…I do not know this word. Her time of sadness for her man?'

'Oh yes, I think so.'

'Does she have another man in her eyes?'

Henry said nothing for a moment or two. 'I believe there was a man she would have had, but he went away.'

The short walk from the church to Great Aunt Elizabeth's cottage took considerably longer than might normally have been expected. Henry's reappearance in the village was the signal for front doors to open coincidentally as they passed so that he could be welcomed and quizzed and Shunka stared at. A few steps from the Plough public house they ran across Josh Makepeace trying not to look as though that were his destination.

'Not working today then Josh?' Henry called out to him first in an attempt to circumvent the inevitable questions from him.

'Not if Gaffer Black can help it. You?

'Odds and ends, that's all. There's not much about is there? My friend here is doing some whitewashing for my Aunt Elizabeth.'

Josh had been looking curiously at Shunka Wicasa. 'Who might you be then?' he said, challengingly. 'Romany? There's precious little work round here for Romanies. Not now, not any time.'

'Lakota,' said Shunka meeting and holding his stare so that Josh could not immediately let it go.

'Why did Sim Lilley join the Essex's and not the Suffolks, then,' said Henry, feeling that a distraction might be in order.

'He was drunk wasn't he,' said Josh accepting the gesture with a slightly more conciliatory tone. 'Instead of taking the Bury road, he went wandering off towards Saffron. Just his luck he fell in with a recruiting sergeant at the first pub he came to and signed for the Essex's. Last we heard he was off to Colchester.'

'He's in Egypt. Dr Birchall who came here digging that time, he saw him there. In hospital.'

'Bugger me. Egypt? Egypt that we had at school?'

'Yes. But I never thought you were listening.'

Josh grinned. 'And you never stopped did you, Mr Know-it-all.'

Henry began to move on in the direction of his aunt's. The hurdle of the village men had been successfully negotiated for the time being. Josh would report to the other day men in the Plough that Henry Turner had a hard case in tow, but he didn't seem to be a gypsy, though he could be taken for one on a dark night and he didn't seem to be after day work.

'What did he say his name was?' Josh called after them.

'You can call me Chunky,' said Shunka over his shoulder, snorting his brief laugh as he caught Henry's look.

Both Aunt Elizabeth and Annie came to the door at their approach.

'I've brought you Shunka. Shunka Wicasa,' said Henry by way of introduction.

'You make him sound like a present,' said Aunt Elizabeth, ushering him in past Annie in the narrow passageway so that her great niece had to press herself against the wall to let him by.

Even so they brushed together heavily in the passing and Shunka paused to let her go first, holding her welcoming eyes with his as unerringly as he had held Josh Makepeace's challenging stare, so that Annie seemed to have to turn her head to keep hold of it as she led the way.

Their silent exchange entered Henry like a sound felt not heard, vibrating through him like the ring of the ploughshare cleaving flint. He felt hot and embarrassed as if he had opened a door and found them alone. But, he thought, not angry, not jealous, no feeling of loss. The uncertainty he had felt at Great Duster Station had been surpassed but not yet replaced by anything else. Another doorway had opened and the three of them had passed through together. The earth would not hold together unless everything was meant.

As the year moved towards its close and daylight seemed hardly to have come at all before it was being turned down like someone being thrifty with the lamp oil, life in Icingbury and at the Veil House seemed to catch its drift.

What wheat he had left to sow Bailey Turner had sown early, gloomily trapped between the fear of losing the opportunity if December proved hard and the fear of having wasted his chances if next spring was late again. So as Christmas approached Henry found less and less to occupy him usefully on the farm once the running chores had been performed and the pigs had been turned into the parts of their sum.

The Bailey made no further mention of Henry's hands, neither to ask whether he was able to drive a full team to plough, nor to suggest that he still could not.

Shunka Wicasa learned to make his own whitewash which he assiduously applied to every inside wall, nook and cranny that he could find in Aunt Elizabeth's cottage, as well as, weather permitting, the outside walls too. Far from practice making perfect however, each hour of each day he spent at his labours seemed to produce less and less progress.

Still, there were no complaints from either Aunt Elizabeth or Annie Lilley concerning his constant presence at the cottage. They became accustomed to having a man around the house and as time passed began to find him indispensable.

All the inhabitants of Icingbury managed to pass by the cottage when Shunka was working outside, to accustom themselves to the 'red Indian' in their midst, as word of his provenance began to circulate, at first fanciful and exaggerated and then as he became a more familiar fixture, more measured and informed. Henry would often find his friend apparently deep in conversation with one or other of the villagers over the cottage fence as the failing light and a soft drizzle put paid to any more work that day and ensured that most of it would have to be redone in the morning anyway.

'You'd best wait for better weather for the outside,' Henry would say him as they plodded back to the Veil House together. But Shunka seemed impervious to the advice and presented himself day after day at the cottage until Henry too ceased to remark on it and accepted the real reason for it.

Henry had little occasion therefore to be alone with Annie. If he dropped round to the cottage there would be Shunka and as like as not, Aunt Elizabeth busying herself all about like a blackbird turning over leaves. Not that he felt deprived of Annie. Somehow his feelings for her were in trust to Shunka now just as his duty to the Icenian warrior, still lying in the crypt, was. It was meant.

Only after church on Sunday did Henry and Annie walk alone together, followed at a distance by the mistakenly knowing eyes of the mothers of Icingbury. Shunka showed no interest in attending although Henry could never quite convince himself that he was any more heathen than a fair sprinkling of St Mary's usual congregation. It was a disappointment to Henry that he would not join them, however, as he would have vastly enjoyed viewing the discomfiture of Mr Earl he assumed it would cause.

'Did you go to church at the school in Carlisle?' he asked once. 'You talked about it as though you had to be a Christian there.'

'Captain Pratt had strong medicine. He talked long about his Lord and I listened. The Great Spirit comes in many different ways,' Shunka replied.

'So did you…do you believe?'

'Captain Pratt said the Great Spirit would walk the earth again as He had done before. This I too believe.'

So Henry used the walk after church to pump Annie about Shunka and she happily complied and demanded the same of him. They talked of little else, piece by piece forming the picture of him as if they had their heads bowed together over a jigsaw puzzle.

Annie made no attempt to conceal from Henry her love for Shunka. From that first evening of their return from London, she told him, she had felt as if Henry had turned into Shunka in her whole being.

'And it's still me isn't it,' said Henry, 'As though we've melted together and become somebody else, the three of us.'

'Have you noticed how he's beginning to speak like us. He's beginning to sound as though he's lived here all his life.'

'He says it's a gift...learning languages. He can do it just by listening. I suppose that's why.'

'He frightens me at times. He tells me things about fighting and hunting buffalo as though he had been there, in his land, only yesterday and will be there again tomorrow and he says it all in such a quiet normal way.'

'So has he told you what he's done himself then, in the way of fighting? Because he won't boast.'

'He says I must know that he is a good warrior and a good hunter, so that I will choose him. I tell him I've already chosen him, but I can't see what we can possibly do about it. I'm going through those doorways inside myself again. I'm trying to be strong but I keep looking and looking for one that will lead me out like yours do.'

'Has he told you about the battle?' said Henry after a while, wondering how much detail Shunka might have revealed to Annie

'About how he got his real name, do you mean?'

'Not just that. Afterwards. He must have done something afterwards. He has something he took in the battle. Has he told you?'

'No. What was it?'

Henry stopped and turned to face Annie, holding both her hands in both of his. 'I don't think I should say, because I don't properly know about it. But I think it's very important. Perhaps I'd better ask him, not you.'

Dr Birchall eventually limped back to Cambridge to live in College. He told Henry he felt he was in danger of outstaying his welcome at the vicarage. 'I think Robert is disappointed in me for not standing up to Shunka over the bones. He really wants them to be gone. To be honest I cannot understand why he feels so...so threatened by them.

'Perhaps he senses something about Reuben too. Perhaps they're not just bones to him like they're not just bones to me either.'

'Oh I say, excellent, Henry. I'd not thought of it that way. Still he doesn't go along with it like you've done.'

'No, but he doesn't argue with Shunka, does he? And Shunka is here because Reuben made me go and fetch him and made you come back from Egypt.'

'Oh come on Henry! We've been through all that. It's very fanciful.'

'Maybe, but you said that what people believe to be true probably comes true, didn't you?'

'Sensitive people like you, I suppose. Yes.'

'And like Shunka,' said Henry pouncing on Birchall's admission, 'So why not the Vicar as well?'

'Why not indeed? I have my own theory about Shunka and Robert and I suppose it might amount to the same thing. About believing things sufficiently to make them come true. You see, Robert is supposed to believe that all the time. It's called his faith and he has actually made it his calling. But I'm afraid I don't believe that educated men like Robert can actually believe it, deep down inside themselves. You believe in Reuben's purpose with passion even deep down in your self. Especially deep down. Deep down in Robert, I think there is fundamental doubt and it stops him. Or it did until Shunka Wicasa came along. Shunka is a heathen, the kind of man to whom Robert is supposed to feel so superior he must try to convert him. But that Indian has more spirituality in his little finger than Robert Earl has in his entire body. I think Robert is scared rigid that if he opens himself up it will be Shunka who shows him a vision of the universe so huge that it would threaten his sense of order and authority and control. And there Henry, there be dragons as they say. Don't look so pensive my friend, I'm probably wrong. Come and see me in Cambridge when I'm set. Come and buy a horse or something.'

Then he was gone in a flash and a whirl leaving behind, as usual, an air of unfinished business and a whiff of his return. Later Henry stopped by Great Aunt Elizabeth's cottage hoping to catch Shunka outside and unawares so that he might just look at him in the light of what Roger Birchall had said. He was not immediately to be seen but Annie was at the gate.

'Come through,' she said, 'He's out the back. That must be I-don't-know-how-many-times he's whitewashed that side.'

Henry followed her through into the kitchen scullery. There were five fresh rabbits hanging over the sink. 'Where'd you get those?' he said with mock severity. However, her response took him completely by surprise.

'Shunka brought them in early. I think he's been out with Josh Makepeace.'

Henry examined the illicit bag more closely. 'These haven't been snared, Annie. Looks to me as though they've been felled. Slingshot? My God, he is good. I couldn't hit a barn door. No more could Josh.'

'I don't think it's you or Josh he's trying to impress,' said Annie smiling quietly to herself.

It was as Shunka and he walked back to the Veil House in the dusk that Henry decided to tackle him about his grisly battle honour. To his surprise Shunka was prepared to be forthcoming.

'After we had driven the blue horse soldiers back across the river they went to the high ground. They had many wounded and moved slowly. My brothers rode amongst those who had lost their horses and could not cross the river. Then in the afternoon further along the valley the soldiers on the grey horses came down to river to attack the village. But we were many and they were few. Custer, the one we call "Long hair" stood them in a line to fight. I did not know he was there. I did not see his hair. When we ran towards them, some on foot some on ponies, we were like water running towards a fire and they saw they could not stand against us. They could not load their guns fast enough to stop us all. I heard the bullets hum like wild bees around me and each time I was five steps, six steps, seven long steps up the hill towards them. We all were.

'Then they mounted their horses again and began to move in front of us, up toward the ridge. I came upon one who was slower. He was pulling himself into his saddle and pointing his carbine at me. He was this close.' Shunka held his arms wide.

'What did you do?'

'I called out to his horse and it turned towards me with its head and shielded me for a moment.'

'What did you call?'

'It was the word, the old word. It is not even Lakota. We do not use it often.'

'I know,' said Henry, 'And so the horse turned to you.'

'His horse betrayed him because I asked it. The bullet missed me and I struck the blue soldier on the thigh with my war club and he fell on one knee. I struck him again in the throat and it burst in upon itself. I had not known it might do that. I was not trying, I just wanted to run up the hill with the other *wechash'tah*. I stopped and they all ran past me. But my father came on his pony and said "you have counted first coup, then, Man-who-hears-horses" but I just stared at what I had done.

'My father said "quick, quick you must take his hair" and I roused myself. "Show me, show me how". My father said, "I cannot touch him, he is your coup. Hold his hair with one hand and draw a circle to the bone with your knife. Pull as if you were skinning a fish" and he rode on up the hill. I did as he said and so took my first *wechapaha*.'

Henry said nothing. He wanted to ask if the man had been dead when this deed had been done. But he did not want to know. He had already asked and heard too much.

After a moment Shunka said, 'I have told you this because you asked me. It is not a brave deed and this is not *waktoglaka*[*]. Even in battle a

---

[*] To speak of one's victories at a formal occasion

man can feel sorrow the first time. Something is lost, there is a sadness after.'

'Have you taken any more of them since?' asked Henry and wished he hadn't. Shunka shrugged and did not reply.

'Shall we tell Annie?' said Henry.

'I know enough about your women to know that she will not think this makes me a better man. If I cannot share all the bad things I have seen done by soldiers and done to them then it is better not to share only a few. The mountain is one thing, but there are many stones, remember.'

24

Christmas came. Henry managed to find two colts coming up to three years old at occasional sales, and the barracks in Bury agreed to take them in another two years provided they developed well. Henry knew they would more than pass muster and looked forward to gentling them in the spring. They took another handful of his father's guineas, however, and Bailey Turner made no further reference to reimbursing his son.

'How do the Lakota gentle their ponies?' Henry asked Shunka as they were gazing speculatively over the additions in the indoor nursery they had prepared in one of the barns.

'It is not like this will be,' said Shunka. 'When I asked my father for my first pony he said when I could catch one and hold it, I could bring it to the herd. We do not ride the same horses all the time as the soldiers do. We do not shoe them as you do, so they tire and we change them. One family will have many ponies maybe. The winter is bitter on the plains and sometimes we must eat the ponies. But we eat the dogs first.

'So how did you catch your first wild pony?'

'When I found him I stood with my back to the sun and called "Come horse". Then I danced the horse calling dance. At first he ran further away. But then he stopped and turned and came back and then away again, and so and so for much of the day. Always I kept my back to the sun to make me seem like the air trembling over the hot grass.

'Then he became *wahs'dodyachin*[*] and like a man in a dream too and came to me to see if I was real. Then I held him by his…the hair on his neck and did not let him go. Sometimes I rode him and sometimes I ran beside him, but always I held his hair.'

'Is that what your father had shown you, then, the dance?' said Henry.

'No,' said Shunka simply. '*Wakan Tanka*[**] showed me the dance. All dances come from *Wakan Tanka*. It was the first time I knew I had the Earth Ear when I danced and the horse came to me.'

'What did you call him, your first pony?'

---

[*] curious

[**] The Creator, the grandfather spirit. Also Tunkashila.

'We do not give them names as you do. Men should not eat what they have called by name.'

'So that was it was it? You just wore him out before he could wear you out?'

'When he was tired, I rubbed him with my arms and hands and fingers. I found the places he liked. He was like a baby when his mother rubs his feet. He was like an old brave whose wife scratches his back scars when he can no longer reach them.'

'That's gentling. That's what I do too,' said Henry. 'Horses can't resist it either can they? They always come back for more.'

St Mary's was packed for morning service on Christmas Day. Halfway through his sermon Mr Earl stopped in mid-sentence. At first Henry and the rest of the congregation assumed he had lost his place for a moment and waited politely for him to resume. But gradually their heads began to turn, following the Vicar's fixed stare towards the back of the church.

Shunka Wicasa had taken a place right at the back of the nave just inside the door. He was wearing his doe skins and the blanket Henry had last seen wrapped around Kitty Shaughnessy in the stable in Bayswater. He had a magpie's feather in his hair.

There was a brief silence and then a low rustling hum from the congregation. Now that it was a reality Henry found he took no pleasure in the anguish visible on Mr Earl's face.

The vicar swallowed and visibly took several breaths.

'Welcome…welcome,' he stammered.

Someone snorted with suppressed laughter.

'Goodness,' Henry's mother whispered in his ear, 'It's Mr Wicasa.'

'I'll go back and sit with him,' said Henry. As he rose and walked down the aisle, Annie Lilley stood up and joined him.

'You two should be walking up it not down it,' said Great Aunt Elizabeth, her comment soaring above the low buzz in the church. The two cousins sat down either side of Shunka.

Mr Earl managed to get out some words about everyone and anyone being welcome in church especially at Christmas time.

'What made you come?' whispered Henry.

'Has the Great Spirit come again this time?' asked Shunka by way of reply.

'Not really, no,' said Annie sounding as though she knew what he was talking about, 'That's not what I meant about Christmas.'

'So we must wait again,' said Shunka in a matter-of-fact voice. 'He will come.'

The vicar stood at the church door to acknowledge the departing congregation. He had brought the proceedings to a rather swifter conclusion than he usually did, not that many minded that, particularly Bailey Turner.

Henry, Shunka and Annie hung back inside until everyone else had gone. Mr Earl stared at Shunka like a rabbit at a stoat, scarcely aware of the other two at all. His newest parishioner looked steadily at him, waiting. Then Mr Earl stammered, 'Soon, please make it soon,' and fled past them back into the empty church.

The three walked slowly back in the direction of the Veil House and a waiting Christmas dinner.

'What did he mean? Make what soon?' asked Annie.

'It is the Brave in the box beneath the spirit house,' said Shunka, 'Your *wakon wicasa** is troubled by him. The warrior calls to him, I think.'

'Who's in a box in the church?' said Annie.

'Reuben,' said Henry, 'He's in an old chest in the crypt.' No matter that he had broken his pledge of silence. Shunka was part of the secret and Annie was part of them both.

'Your clothes please me,' said Annie changing the subject to show that she had accepted and understood the explanation, 'So soft and strange. Your Sunday best for Christmas,' and she ran her hand down the supple skin of Shunka's jerkin. Henry felt included and gratified by the intimacy, as if Annie were expressing delight at some unlooked-for thoughtfulness he had shown her or a prettiness he had discovered by the wayside and brought to her in his cupped hands.

At the Veil House the Bailey, Mrs Turner, and Great Aunt Elizabeth were already ensconced in the kitchen. The Bailey was warming himself at the range and getting in the way of his wife's inspection of the bird that had been slowly and deliciously looking after itself since early that morning.

'Miss Covington was asking after you at church this morning. She missed you what with all the to-do about Shunka turning up. Where is he now?' he asked.

'I'll walk round and see her, perhaps tomorrow. I've been meaning to,' said Henry. 'Shunka's taken himself off to the stable.'

'Well fetch him in here,' said the Bailey, 'It's Christmas. Savage or not, if he can go to church, he can come and dine,' and he puffed his chest out looking very pleased with himself.

---

* Holy man

'He's not a savage,' said Mrs Turner unexpectedly. 'He's a real gentleman, isn't he Annie? You see him nearly every day. I expect he's a prince or something where he comes from, isn't he?'

'I dare say,' said Annie and she blushed to the roots of her hair, like a village maid.

On Boxing Day Henry took himself round to the cottage beside the schoolhouse to look in on his old teacher. As he drew near he felt a pang of guilt that he had not visited her sooner and when he thought about it realised that he had subconsciously been avoiding her.

True to form, Charlotte Covington went straight to the heart of things.

'I see you have brought an American Indian to Icingbury. That was him in church I take it,' she said using her best withering school ma'am tone, the kind that suggested he should have sought permission before producing in class something in a jar likely to cause a distraction.

Henry waited, still holding the outstretched hand she had proffered as she spoke.

'Is that wise, Henry? He must be a very long way from home in every sense of the word. What is to become of him? Perhaps more to the point, what are the good but simple folk of Icingbury to make of him? He caused quite a stir in church. I quite thought the Reverend Earl was going to produce a white flag from the pulpit. And somebody laughed, Henry, more than one I should think. Have you thought what you are doing Henry...bringing him here? Mark my words, he's too rich a morsel for Icingbury to swallow easily. Why have you brought him?'

Henry knew why he had been avoiding her. Sooner or later she would get round to asking all the questions he had been putting off himself. Shunka had a task to perform here, of that he felt certain. But was it just in his own imagination, that certainty? Was it, indeed, a kind of madness? And the task, when it was done, what then? He had no idea what to say to her. No idea where to begin, no idea whether to begin at all. He tried to summon up the feelings he had when he and Annie were with Shunka, when there did seem to be certainty and meaning and purpose.

'I saved his life. He will not let me go until the debt is paid,' he said hoping that heroic oratory would let him off the hook, but as he said it he knew he was guilty of that sin of pride Shunka would not have committed himself. It was for Shunka to say that, not for him.

'Fiddlesticks,' said Miss Covington. 'That might wash at the Little Big Horn, but not here. If that's the reason you've brought him to Icingbury, then it really won't do.

'You know about the Battle at the Little Big Horn too, do you?'

'Of course I do. Yes, and I know that America is busy building itself an empire inside itself, because it is big enough I suppose, just as we have been doing elsewhere in the world because we are small. I expect America wants your Indian's land so that they can sell wheat to us cheap enough to put men like your father on the parish. People like your *protégé* are casualties of that process. They are the ultimate losers and in a perverse way they are the scales in which the success of an empire is weighed. However, these are just my views and they are not fashionable so I tend to keep them to myself. Along with my views on the position of women in a civilised world,' she added tartly as if administering a rebuke to herself.

'So are the Americans Romans too, then?' said Henry.

'Still fascinates you doesn't it, Henry? Yes they are I suppose. They even have an eagle as a symbol now I come to think of it.'

'And should we rise up against it like the Indians and the...the Fenians, and the Iceni?'

'It's called progress, Henry. Where are the Iceni now? Where will your Indians be in two thousand years? Much changed but probably still here. There's probably Icenian in you Henry. I expect your people haven't moved very far in two thousand years. But you would not wish the clock to be put back, believe me. Oh yes, you can take sides over the Little Big Horn now. You can say these were right and those were wrong. But we are all trapped in our piece of time, we cannot see it all laid out forever, thank the Lord.'

'But some people do terrible things. Shouldn't we say those things were wrong? That they're always going to be wrong?'

'I hope so, Henry, I hope so. But it still doesn't stop progress. Perhaps it just nudges it in a different direction. What about your Indian? Do you think he will want to go back to a way of life in some wilderness preserved in aspic while everything else changes?'

'Well, he doesn't like boots,' said Henry.

Shunka had said a bird would come but Henry had decided not to question him then, knowing that these enigmatic statements had a habit of clarifying themselves in time.

When it did come it was a common or garden blackbird. What was strange was that it behaved as though it were already early summer rather than barely spring. It was nearly sunset and Henry was walking Honeycomb and one of the other chesnuts back to the Veil House from some early sowing. Shunka, who was still spending his days whitewashing, had met him on the way. The blackbird was perched high up on the weathervane on St. Mary's tower, fluting his complicated message to the world, his voice rising above the murmured conversation of the men below and the measured sound of the horses' hooves upon the roadway.

Mr Earl was standing at the lych-gate, his attention having been caught, too, by the blackbird's song. He looked around him at the approach of the two men and their horses as if seeking some avenue of escape.

'He's very early to be calling up the sunset,' said Henry, referring to the blackbird and apparently oblivious of the Vicar's anxiety to avoid Shunka. 'Blackbirds don't usually do that until after they've paired. April or May.'

'Well it has been a fine day,' said Mr Earl, 'Perhaps he's mistaken the time.'

Listening, they gazed up at the bird, who had not paused in his singing nor repeated a single line, for the sake of something to ease the awkwardness the Vicar clearly felt at their chance meeting.

Then Shunka said, 'He speaks to us and to the Brave in the box underneath this place. It is time to bury him according to the custom of his tribe.'

Mr Earl shot Shunka a look that was a mixture of fear and venom. 'Henry I cannot be doing with this. It is becoming very foolish.'

'Well,' said Henry, 'Are you saying that Shunka cannot understand the bird?'

'Of course he cannot.'

'Not even if he believes enough he can?'

'Not even then.'

'But isn't that called faith, Vicar? If we believe things hard enough then they become true for us, don't they?'

'I cannot stand here disputing theological principles of belief with you, Turner, over a damn blackbird on the church tower. I think I shall go mad.'

'Well he must be saying something to someone. He hasn't repeated himself once. It sounds like a whole conversation to me.'

Then Shunka did a strange thing. He reached out and gripped Mr Earl's forearms in both his hands, forcing him to meet his own eyes. The blood drained from the Vicar's face, but he did not try to pull away.

'Speak to the horses, Henry. Speak the word,' he said.

'No, Shunka,' Henry whispered, 'It is not to be said lightly, you know that.'

Mr Earl made a supreme effort to recover some of his dignity. He was like a dog shaking himself after emerging from the river.

'Don't say anything to the horses, or the birds. I don't want to know what you can do. I refuse to know. Just get rid of that thing in the crypt and stop it filling my head morning, noon and night when I should be thinking of other things.'

'I expect he's finished with you anyway,' said Henry. 'He made sure that you wouldn't let Roger Birchall or me forget where he was. This is not his resting place and he wouldn't just let himself be carted off to some old museum either. Well now we know, because the bird has spoken to Shunka. He is to be buried according to the custom of his tribe as he should have been two thousand years ago. I know I believe it, Vicar, and I'm willing to bet that right now you do too.'

Mr Earl looked at him bleakly. His silence said it all, expressing more vividly than words the jumble of confusion and pointless denial Henry could read in his eyes and around the corners of his dejected mouth.

'Please, just do it,' he said, 'I'm going for my tea.'

'Honeycomb, walk on' said Henry, interrupting the old mare's grazing on the verge by the lych-gate and when he turned to look back, Mr Earl was standing by the side door to the vicarage looking up at the weathervane from whence the blackbird had vanished.

'What now, then?' Henry said to Shunka.

The Sioux thought for a moment. 'Birchall-who-limps must come soon. He will know the custom. Perhaps there is a dance to be made. He must show us if he cannot do it with his leg.'

Henry chuckled. 'He's never mentioned dancing. I can't see it somehow can you? Not Roger Birchall. And one of my legs is a bit crooked now, too.'

Shunka paid him no attention. 'We must cleanse our spirits in the sweat lodge. This is my way, no matter what the other Brave wants. He must let me have my way in this. And Annie must help with the stones. This is work for a woman.'

Henry held his tongue. All would be revealed soon enough, he knew. Shunka paused on the roadway for a moment, bringing his chesnut up short on the leading rein. 'Soon we shall be brothers in blood, Henry. This is the time and the place.'

The next morning after Shunka had taken himself off to his eternal whitewashing at Aunt Elizabeth's, Henry walked to the station at Great Duster and bought himself a return ticket to Cambridge. He felt himself glowing inwardly as the little piece of pasteboard was pushed under the window towards him. It was a small rite of passage, a recognition that he was a travelled man of the world.

By dint of enquiry at the college he obtained grudging directions to Dr Birchall's new lodgings. He rang the bell and waited.

The door opened and there stood the familiar figure of Mrs Bullace, her round face wreathing in smiles at the unexpected sight of Henry.

'Why 'ere you are, 'enry Turner, my little pipin' bag. I recognised your ring, two shorts and a long.'

'Why Mrs B, nobody said. Have you been here long?' cried Henry.

'Just about a couple of weeks. Dr Birchall…'e is a good gentleman…'e sent my train fare as good as 'is word. So it was goodbye Paddin'ton and 'allo 'ere.'

Roger Birchall appeared in the hallway, summoned by the cheerful, raised voices.

'Henry, excellent, excellent. My dear fellow, excellent. I say, have you come to buy a horse?'

They all three ushered themselves by common unspoken consent along the hallway and into a little breakfast room at the back where Mrs Bullace hovered like a daring robin halfway in and halfway out of the kitchen beyond it, as if demonstrating her right to move from one status to the other on this occasion. Whether Roger Birchall noticed the challenge or not, he instantly resolved the matter.

'Let's all have some tea, shall we Mrs Bullace, or a Madeira and cake, what about that, Madeira and some of your cake? Excellent,' he chirruped, thereby elevating the cook by default.

When they were settled and served Henry explained that it was time to bury Reuben according to his tribal custom. When Dr Birchall heard that word had come to Shunka via a blackbird in the presence of the Vicar, he affected to become very solemn but his entire bearing was a huge suppressed giggle.

Henry became a little defensive, 'So do you think the bird spoke to Shunka or not, then?'

'Do the horses speak to you?'

'In a way yes. We have an understanding you might say.'

'Well then. Who am I, a mere mortal, to question the sons of Chiron?'

'Who's he?'

'Not important Henry. Just me showing off.'

'Well, Shunka says we are all to be cleansed before the ceremony or whatever we must do. He wants you to be there to tell us what to do about the burial.'

Mrs Bullace could contain herself no longer. 'I never did. Are you all to 'ave a bath together?'

'I don't think it's a bath as such,' said Henry doubtfully, 'Annie's to be there and there's something to do with sweat and stones.'

'Excellent,' said Dr Birchall, 'Like a Turkish bath of some kind. I had one in Alexandria. But I'm not sure about Mrs Westwood being there. Still I have every confidence in Shunka. So I'm to bone up on Celtic burial customs, am I? I'll tell you one thing though. Reuben will need some artefacts, come what may.'

'What are they?'

'Things made that might have some significance for him.'

'You said he might need a horse,' said Henry.

'Well his own horse has been dead these two thousand years. Anyway it would take the whole village to dig a barrow deep enough for a horse. Something to do with a horse would be a good idea, though. We want him to rest in peace don't we? We don't want any unfinished business.'

'There is something,' said Henry

25

Dr Birchall sent word by the Carter that the burial should be by water. Shunka grunted satisfaction when Henry told him this.

'The cleansing too must be beside water. Come, we will choose a place and build the sweat lodge and there too we will bury the Brave.' He handed Henry a billhook hanging on the barn wall.

Without a word Henry headed towards the water meadows. There could be no other place. Everything that had happened to him had begun with the Icing and the water meadows. It was fitting that the end should be there too. It was the centre of the world he had known all this while, the axle tree. He said something of the sort to Shunka as they approached the first gate, the scene of his beating at the hands of the unknown poachers.

'All that passes in life, how great or small, is a circle. The world and the star world are all circles turning together,' said Shunka.

'Like a clock, then,' said Henry, adding, 'Waiting to chime the hour. And what then? The end of the world?'

'And the beginning again. All is a circle. I have told you, the past and the future are always here. Even the sweat lodge is a circle. Come.' And the Indian vaulted the gate and ran towards the second and the river where it meandered away out of sight of the lane.

When Henry caught him up, Shunka had removed his boots, rolled up his corduroys and waded into the river. Feeling with his feet first and then his hands he fetched up smooth, round stones from the river bed. Some he rejected and the others he threw to Henry who, under his instruction, laid them carefully in a line on the bank, until there were twelve of a similar size and shape that met with Shunka's approval.

He did not seem to notice that his feet were puffed with the cold when he emerged from the water, but set off along the bank, examining the willows that grew along it. Every so often he would indicate a thick, pliable sapling sprouting from the pollard and Henry would sever it at the base with his billhook.

In a while they had sixteen, trimmed to an equal length. In a slight depression, well away from any curious passers-by on the lane which was a good quarter-of-a-mile back, Shunka marked out a circle using one of the willow saplings like a compass arm to describe the circumference while Henry held one end steady in the centre. As Shunka moved slowly and steadily round scraping the billhook through the soft meadow turf, sometimes pausing to realign the mark, he chanted softly as if the dark line he was drawing were a nervous foal to be coaxed into a strange place.

Henry had not heard him pray before. The flowing words seemed to blend with the murmuring flow of the Icing and to be taken with it to the distant point where it met faraway trees and the sky. It was evening and the setting sun, invisible in the clouded sky was nevertheless proclaiming its position by funnelling down great beams of golden light to the wide Cambridge earth below. Henry had a dreamlike feeling that Shunka's prayer song, carried by the water first, was now being drawn up their shafts and into heaven.

When the outer circle was complete, Shunka moved to the centre point where Henry had held the branch steady. There he described an inner, smaller circle occupying about a quarter of the larger one, chanting softly all the while. The setting sun suddenly fell below the cloud line and sat on the clear horizon in full, revealed splendour.

Shunka squatted on his haunches facing it and when it finally dipped below the curve of the earth, leaving only a painted sky to show where it had been, he marked the westerly arc of the outer circle and ceased his singing.

The two men made several journeys to bring up the stones that had been laid out on the bank. Then it was dark.

'This is all we can do now,' said Shunka. 'Tomorrow we will need three people to finish the lodge. Annie must come. We will need a skin for the covering. When there is a new moon, you, Birchall-who-limps, and I will sweat.'

It was five days to the new moon. Birchall had arranged to be at the vicarage before then so Henry had no need to get further word to him.

The next day they brought Annie to the lodge site in the water meadows. Henry and Shunka were carrying a canvas tarpaulin between them to make the skin of the structure. Even Shunka had accepted that buffalo hide was too tall an order for the Veil House. Annie looked curiously at the circles with the stones and saplings laid out around. Shunka was a little ahead of them.

'Is it witchcraft?' she said.

'Only like herbs and simples, I think,' said Henry. 'That kind of craft. He calls it medicine anyway.'

'Funny, you always said this place had a strange effect on you and now I feel that we are all somewhere else. As if we had walked through the gates from the lane and come into a different world.'

Annie looked round as she spoke. The two gates and the lane beyond were invisible from where they stood. There was nothing to indicate where the village lay at all.

'Does Shunka make you feel like that too?' she continued. 'When I am with him it is as if he carries a whole place with him, surrounding him. Wherever he is, is home to him and when he looks and speaks to you, you are in that place too, not your own. He...he wears the world like his shell.'

'He's said something of the kind to me, before,' said Henry. 'His people are wanderers, hunters not farmers. If they stay in one place too long they starve.'

'So do you think he won't stay here in Icingbury, then?' There was a sudden catch in Annie's voice.

'When the grass grows tall again and the game comes back, so do my people.' Shunka had rejoined them and heard Annie's last question.

Much later Henry found himself wondering what exactly Annie had meant when she had said 'when I am with him.'

Carefully setting them at spaced intervals, Shunka laid out the willow saplings around the outer circle, with two closer where he had marked the entrance facing west. Then driving in a thicker stem that he had roughly sharpened with the billhook he made a footing for each one and set about planting them upright. He started opposite the doorway placing one and then its fellow on the opposite side of the circle.

When he had two pairs facing he motioned to Henry and Annie to bend them down towards each other so that they met above the centre of the circles. Then seizing the ends, he wove them into a kind of cat's cradle. This process was repeated, not entirely without trial and error on the part of Henry and Annie, until all the saplings were evenly placed and held bowed over in the shape of an upturned bowl about five feet high at its apex. For good measure Shunka lashed the woven ends together with some old leading rein he had liberated from the harness room, although Annie said there was no need, so neatly and firmly spliced were they. At each stage of the creation Shunka softly chanted prayers.

Before covering over the framework he dug out the smaller central circle to make a shallow pit, first loosening the earth with the billhook and then lifting the soil with his hands.

'Take the earth in your hands,' he told Annie and Henry, barely pausing in his singing, 'And make a little hill. This is *Unci*, the grandmother of the world. She will bring the past and the future in our dreaming.' He pointed to a spot due west of the doorway where they should make the shape and his singing grew in intensity.

When the mound had been shaped to the Lakota's satisfaction, the three of them unfolded the tarpaulin and spread it double over the sapling frame, making sure that the two ends overlapped to form a heavy flap over the doorway.

Beyond the grandmother earth mound, still in a straight westerly line parallel to the course of the river Shunka dug out another pit, using the earth from that to weigh down the skirt of the tarpaulin to seal it to the ground. This second pit, he said, was for '*peta owihankeshni*', the endless fire.

'What happens if it rains before...before the sweating time?' asked Henry. 'Shouldn't we cover it over so it doesn't fill with water?'

'The bird came. I have sung *wochaykeyah**. It will not rain,' replied Shunka simply and turning to the west he spread his arms wide and threw out his prayer song to the sky so that Henry could not help but look and hearken for a reply.

Annie felt for his hand.

'What then?' whispered Henry feeling that he was in church.

'Do you feel it, Henry? Do you feel it, my Horse Man? This is an end and a beginning.'

'That's what Shunka said.'

'It's one of those doorways of yours,' said Annie.

'And one of yours too?'

She looked at him and there was sadness drawn over every inch of her face,

'One of mine too, Henry. I shall have to go looking for strength inside me now, I know.'

'Why? What's the matter?'

'We all feel it. An end and a beginning. This place. This thing we've made. But an end of what? A beginning of what? I'm going to lose him, I can feel it. The most beautiful thing I have ever known. And you will go too, his brother, his faithful dog.'

Annie dropped Henry's hand, turned and made her way alone towards the gate. He watched her go without attempting to follow.

Shunka sang on, his eyes closed, his face raised to the vast, white-gold sky.

On the eve of the new moon, Henry, Shunka and Annie made their separate ways to St Mary's and slipped into the vestry, the two men by

---

* prayers

the side door from the church yard and Annie a little later from inside the church, where she had been arranging flowers partly as a pretext. Roger Birchall was already there but of the Vicar there was no sign.

'He would not come,' said Dr Birchall. 'He's taking all this very badly. It was amusing to start with but this business has shaken him to the core just as I thought it had. I should take more notice of my own pronouncements or keep them to myself, one or the other. I don't know what he fears more, Shunka or the bones. He was talking about next Sunday's sermon over breakfast and the text. I said as a joke "What about the raising of Lazarus?" I thought for a moment he was going to strike me.'

Henry was not sorry that Mr Earl had failed to put in an appearance. He found the Vicar's attitude towards Reuben had changed from being merely irksome, to disturbing. He would not have put it past the Vicar to try to rid himself of the burden of the bones and to wrench himself free from Shunka's thrall with some desperate act of sabotage.

'When we brought Reuben here you said you would not put him back in the water meadows but Shunka and I think that is where he belongs now. You said it should be by water and that's where we have built the sweat lodge. Shunka says when we have purified ourselves we can bury him in the lodge. I suppose he means it will be like sacred ground when we have finished with it.'

'Water appears to be important,' said Dr Birchall, beginning to assume his lecturing attitude. 'Celtic sacred places were often associated with springs, rivers and lakes. The very name of our river here suggests that it had special significance for the tribe whose land it flowed through.'

'Won't he get wet if you dig too close to the river? The lodge is not far from the bank in the water meadows,' said Annie.

'They often seem actually to have buried people in well shafts, probably to propitiate the fertility gods. Water is always an essential,' Birchall replied.

'Anyhow, the graves in the church yard here always fill with water when they're newly dug,' said Henry. To him the water meadows felt more than right. They were an essential part of the plan, they always had been. Nothing should change.

The next question was the removal of the bones. The four of them went down into the crypt and lifted the lid of the coffer.

'He's still face down. Does that matter?' asked Henry. 'If we try to turn him, he'll end up all higgledy-piggledy.'

If this was a poser for Roger Birchall he did not allow it to show.

'Bones have been found in all manner of attitudes. I suggest we leave him alone. In fact I think we should bury him in this.' He laid his hand on the open lid of the coffer.

'Won't the Vicar mind?' said Henry.

'I should think after this he would be glad to see the back of it. Anyway, it's just mouldering away down here. It won't be long before it collapses altogether.'

'Then we'll need the tilt cart from the Veil House,' said Annie. 'We cannot carry it by ourselves.'

'The livestock cart would be better, it's got a tail board, so we won't have to lift the chest high.' said Henry. 'He's been in that before. At least some of him has.' He gave a short laugh, rather wishing he had not voiced the thought.

Shunka had said nothing all the while. He stood in his familiar way, arms folded and eyes ahead. 'We must take the brave from this hole. It is like Carlisle. Always white men make places like this, places of darkness and pain. And then when you die you put yourselves in other places like this. A brave should be nearer the sky when he makes his journey to *wakontonkate**. But if this is the way of his tribe...' he trailed off resignedly.

'He'll have to rest somewhere, then, while we dig,' said Henry. 'This old box will take some burying. Perhaps we could lay him up at the Veil House in the cart for a night or two. Somewhere where he can see the sky, eh Shunka?'

'Excellent, excellent,' said Dr Birchall, 'Like a progress to the grave, as befits a mighty warrior.'

Henry and Shunka hurried back to the Veil House to fetch the livestock cart.

Bailey Turner scowled at them as they came into the yard, 'At least you might make some pretence of doing some work around here,' he called. 'When are you going to make a start gentling those colts?'

'Sorry Pa. Just doing a job for the Vicar. Can I borrow the livestock cart? He wants a few things moving from the crypt.'

'I just hope he's giving you your dinner, then, that's all I can say,' the Bailey grumbled and Henry assumed permission had been given.

Shunka waited until Bailey Turner was out of sight and then let out a great guffaw. 'This is what I said to you in London about the white man's truth. This was a lie you told your father, and yet it was also the truth.'

'Can't fault it, can you?' said Henry smiling as they entered the stable. 'Come on then my lovely,' he said to Honeycomb, 'There's

---

* heaven

something important I'd like you to do for me even though it is only the old livestock cart.'

The chesnut turned her head at the sound of his voice and he felt her acquiescence as if she had spoken. 'So now we are five, then,' he said to himself. 'Is that a lucky number for such an undertaking I wonder?'

There was a double trap door in the churchyard that let down into the crypt. It was designed to allow coffins to be descended, since they could not negotiate the narrow stairway from the vestry. It was rare indeed, Henry supposed, for it to be used the other way round. Annie who from her flower arranging and share of the cleaning knew her way round the less public parts of the church had found the sexton's webbs and putlocks used for lowering coffins into graves at funerals. But when it came to lifting the dead weight of the tithe coffer once they had manoeuvred it into position below the trap, the task proved too much for Henry and Shunka alone.

'We need four men and both the webbs, or else a block and tackle over the trap which means taking the cart back to the Veil House. Blast!' said Henry.

'Wait,' said Shunka and he disappeared round to the front door of the church. He returned shortly. To Henry's immense surprise and a little annoyance, Mr Earl was trailing along behind him.

Dr Birchall looked a little dubious at the Vicar's appearance too. 'Come to lend a hand Robert? Excellent, excellent,' he said, nervously looking down at the coffer below as if it were a brace of pheasants and Mr Earl the keeper.

But the Vicar did not acknowledge him, waiting silently while the second webb was put in place and merely grunting a little when it came to taking the strain with Shunka on the other side. As the chest rose slowly up through the trap, the Indian began to chant softly.

A single tear trickled down the cleric's cheek and a lump came into Henry's throat as he witnessed this tiny outward sign of his total capitulation. He wanted to say 'how about a hymn and a few words, Vicar,' but he knew it would not help. It was not meant.

When the chest was safely in the back of the livestock cart and Mr Earl had gone as silently as he had come, Henry said to Shunka, 'Whatever did you say to him, then?'

'Just what I want to know, too,' said Dr Birchall.

'I said "Come and be strong. The warrior is going. He needs you one last time."'

'He was weeping, poor man,' said Annie quietly. 'Did you see?'

Henry said nothing. But he wondered after all, for whom the tear had been shed.

He half expected that Honeycomb might balk at the contents of her cartload. He had his hand on the lump of wax in his waistcoat pocket just in case. But she had no need of artifice and when Henry said, 'Honeycomb, walk on home,' every inch of her huge frame said that she was part of the conspiracy.

26

Early in the evening of the new moon Henry, Roger Birchall, Shunka and Annie made their way to the lodge in the water meadows. There had been another glorious sunset and, as Shunka had predicted, it had not rained since they had made their preparations.

Henry could take no joy in the magnificent sky, however. Its orange and yellow were flames of destruction like those from the blaze of a huge thatched store barn in which, as it might be, the hope and future of whole families were wrested from them in one massive, despairing conflagration. Its red the red of spilt blood, spreading and spreading, as if the sky had opened an artery and was pumping its life over the edge of the world.

There was a huge pile of wood by the lodge, some logs but mostly kindling and branches about the thickness of a man's wrist and a little longer than his forearm.

'Where's this come from?' said Henry. 'It's bone dry.'

'I have been gathering it,' said Shunka noncommittally.

'Out of someone's barn then.'

'It must burn all night. It is the *peta owihankeshni*[*].'

Inside the sweat lodge the trampled earth had been strewn with sweet smelling herbs, bundles of dried lavender mainly, but also sage and rosemary.

'I've been gathering too,' said Annie primly, 'Shunka wanted all sage, but we didn't have enough dried at the cottage. Some of the lavender is your mother's from the Veil House and the rest is from Josh Makepeace's mother.'

'And what do they think it's for?' said Henry.

'We just said Shunka needed it for his prayers and that. It was easy. Josh adores him. He's never caught so many rabbits and whatnot since Shunka showed him things.'

The Sioux was busy laying branches in a criss-cross pattern in the fire pit. When he had made a thick airy raft he placed the stones he had

[*] everlasting fire

chosen from the river on it and then covered them over with a similar criss-cross of branches.

'And how are you proposing to light it?' inquired Dr Birchall in a scholarly tone.

'With a lucifer and some turpentine. Some things are best done the white man's way,' said Shunka and he barked his short laugh.

The fire blazed up at the touch of the match and before very long had been reduced to a glowing bowl of charcoal in the pit. As they waited for the stones to become really hot, Shunka walked round it chanting. The others watched silently.

Henry felt his eyes being drawn deep into the embers. The sound of Shunka's singing seemed to be part of the fire, indistinguishable from its pulsing aurora and the stones themselves whose edges appeared to melt and waft in its heat.

Time passed. Henry could not say how long. Then Shunka said, 'It is ready and so must we be.' He began to remove his clothes, first his waistcoat and shirt, folding them carefully and handing them to Annie who took them without a word as a wife might do for her man as he prepared to step into a bath before the fire. She clearly knew what was expected of her. Henry wondered what had been said and when. 'Woman's work,' Shunka had called it.

With a deft movement Shunka stepped out of his corduroys. He was wearing no undergarments and stood naked by the light of the endless fire. Annie gathered up the trousers, unflustered and unabashed.

'She's seen me like that before,' thought Henry, trying to remember what he was wearing himself under his own corduroys, 'And by the looks, she's seen him like it too.'

He removed his own top clothes, folding them and handing them to Annie as part of the evident ritual until he too stood naked in the semi-dark.

As she took his trousers Annie smiled and said quietly, 'Well, you healed up well enough, didn't you? Still you had a good nurse I dare say.'

Dr Birchall had managed to take off his coat and jacket and his boots and hose.

'Are we going in now Shunka?' His voice quavered slightly and he cleared his throat, 'Ah, hmmm. Yes, well if it doesn't interfere too much with the… ah…proceedings, Shunka, old fellow, I'll hand my togs out to Mrs Westwood through the door. Different if you were a Lakota lady p'raps, if you know what I mean. No offence. Excellent,' and he got down on his hands and knees and disappeared through the flap into the lodge before anyone could reply.

Shunka seemed unperturbed by Birchall's heresy of having entered head first. He motioned Henry to go next through the flap, 'crouching as you came from your mother.' Then he followed stationing himself next to the doorway on the south west. Henry could dimly make out Roger Birchall in the dark on the north west and he himself squatted down just about due east, opposite the entrance.

The air inside the lodge was damp and still, but the scents of the dried herbs strewn on the floor beneath their bodies conveyed a semblance of warmth so that Henry did not feel particularly cold. He did not speak, nor did Dr Birchall. Henry had a deep sense of anticipation so that to have spoken without knowing what might be said would have been like finding a perfectly frosted field marred by a single footprint.

Shunka broke the silence calling out to Annie in his own Lakota tongue words that she must have been waiting to hear. The door flap opened and she thrust in the first of the stones from the fire gripped firmly in a pair of long handled farrier's tongs. Henry recognised them. They were from the Veil House stable. Shunka half-took, half-guided them so that he was able to place the stone in the place that had been prepared in the centre of the lodge. Annie withdrew the tongs and quickly returned with another stone until there were six of the dozen inside the lodge.

The temperature began to rise perceptibly with each heated stone that was laid in the central pit and Henry began to feel at first comfortably warm but soon hotter and hotter until, he thought, 'I hope this is as hot as it gets.' He felt perspiration spring out of his body as he had never before experienced without exertion, first from the hollow of his breast bone, then across his shoulders and back. The scent of the lavender, rosemary and sage began to mingle with the smell of the tarpaulin as it heated up.

Henry closed his eyes, partly because the heat was beginning to oppress them a little. He had a distinct impression that he was haymaking on a hot summer's day when the gaffer had just made the men and boys put the rick cover over the new stack for fear of a sudden thunder storm and they all stood panting and grumbling after the additional labour. It was the combination of senses. The heat, the feel and scent of the meadow flowers, the smothering tarpaulin and the smell of men's bodies. And all contained and magnified within the excluding universe of the lodge.

Shunka rocked forward on his crossed legs and ladled water on the hot stones from a pail. The milk ladle Henry recognised as one of his mother's from the farm dairy. He did not know the bucket. For a moment he thought it must all be over and Shunka was cooling the stones down. But when the steam enveloped him so that he could barely make out the forms of his companions and the searing heat struck him, first in the face, like opening the great oven on the kitchen range and peering in to see if the loaves were done, then swiftly smothering the entire surface of his body like hot lard, he knew with a mixture of anxiety and elation that the ordeal had barely begun.

As the steam began to clear leaving the atmosphere in the lodge invisibly shimmering to the touch, Shunka called again to Annie in Lakota. Once again the flap opened briefly letting in an icy draught, which Henry welcomed as a parched man a sip of water. Annie passed in another hot stone which Shunka placed in the pit, then removed one from the opposite side and passed it out with the tongs. As Annie took it away to be reheated, Shunka began to sing again.

Henry recognised that it was the same phrase over and over again and the thought came into his mind that Shunka was singing to give the stones strength in the fire to work ever harder.

Five more times Annie repeated the procedure by which time the first six stones had all been replaced and the heat in the lodge redoubled. From time to time Shunka ladled more water onto the stones and the heat would soar again. Each time Henry felt that he would faint away, his head began to swim and he made an effort to bring his thoughts to bear on things outside the lodge in the real world. But as frequently in dreams, reality had no sooner been seized hold of, than it would wriggle and slip away leaving a confused space to be filled with unfamiliar things and absurdity.

Henry lost track of time. Its passing was marked only by the changing of the stones and Annie's silent, unseen ministry beyond the heavy entrance flap served to accentuate the feeling that the interior of the lodge was the only world.

So it was afterwards, whenever he attempted to recall the things he felt and saw that night in the sweat lodge, Henry could only recollect them as one does a vivid dream. What had been real and what imagined became inseparable and sometimes he even wondered if he had never again truly wakened from that night.

He would see Shunka curiously bathed in light, so that he had to assume the heat had made him able to see in the dark. The Lakota would reach beneath the carpet of herbs and bring out his rolled doe-skin bundle and Henry would always ask himself how it had got there. Shunka would carefully unroll it, laying its contents reverently in a pattern of order, humming to himself as he did so. Henry never again saw the entire display of those objects in the doe-skin bundle. He would rack his brains to see and name them all, like a game of pelmanism at Christmas, but he never could.

Again and again there would be the knife. Perhaps not a metal blade, perhaps a stone one. He could not see. Always Roger Birchall would take it from Shunka with both hands as if he were performing a priestly act. Henry and Shunka would offer him the underside of their right arms touching side-by-side, each man's fist pointing towards the other's chest and Roger would make a shallow v-shaped cut on each of their arms, each cut about half an inch long, and raise the skin so that it bled freely, and ran from one arm to the other like one rivulet of rainwater meeting another on a pane of glass and becoming instantly one. When it was done the two would part and sit clutching their wounded arms with their left hands until the flow were staunched and their hands and arms caked with each other's dried gore.

And ever after whenever he recalled it being done in his head, Henry would become apart from himself, crouched again in the heat of the lodge whose walls would have ceased to be. And he would always look instinctively at the underside of his right arm, even if he were wearing a shirt and coat, and whisper to himself 'now we are *weh chinyeh*, now we are brothers in blood'.

Always the hollow pang would come to find his self. Always the icy fingers would reach down into his bowels as he remembered the feeling of what else happened.

Shunka would take up the red stone pipe from its place on the doe-skin and every time Henry would feel that it had not been there before. It would always be filled and alight, its wreathing smoke joining with the scalding steam from the stones Shunka had watered again.

Henry would take the pipe and always the memory of his yearning for the medicine that had been snatched away in the *tepe* at the Earl's Court ground would well up inside him as he did. He would draw the pipe smoke and the heat from the sweat lodge together down deep into his lungs and the pipe would pass from him. He would be by the Icing, perhaps close to the very spot where they had raised the sweat lodge. In his self he always knew it was the river, but it was very different. It was difficult to tell where the main stream ran, broader and shallower in places, but with many marshy pools and islets covered in sallows and blackthorn, sometimes joining sometimes dividing the stretches of grey water.

'A heavy horse might sink without trace there if she did not know the way,' Henry would repeat to himself each time he recreated the scene, knowing that such a horse would always come, always from behind him so that he would instinctively glance over his shoulder or turn upon his pillow, hearing it, smelling it first.

It would pass him close by, led by a dark figure of a man, his eyes fixed on the watery ground in front of him, picking a hidden path towards the main river. Then Troop Sergeant-Major Davies' words would come into Henry's head as if he too were standing beside him saying them over again, 'River slows them down you see. Wants to cross, wants to cross, but has to pick his spot. Let him come, let him come, gently gently.'

Henry would try to cry out 'Reuben, Reuben, Reuben' but always his voice would be wherever he was then, he could never throw it into the vision. And he would know that they were watching, hidden among the sallows and the blackthorn, a Roman scouting party waiting, Davies' troop waiting. Custer's blue horse soldiers with muffled harness waiting. All waiting for his Icenian warrior. All waiting to make him tell them things.

Then he would hear Shunka Wicasa's voice in his ear. 'Speak to the horse, Henry. Speak the word.' And Henry would try to say, 'If I say the word the horse will betray him for my sake, you know he will.' But he would always speak the word and this time it would sound in the vision in his head. He would see the horse rise up on her back legs and the Icenian taken unawares holding the leading rein would be thrown off the sunken path and struggling to keep his footing would sink to his knees in the treacherous ooze at his side.

Always Henry would try to leap forward to his aid, gasping with emotion, 'Yes, yes, yes, this time, quick, quick !' He must reach Reuben before the watchers in the trees sensed his helplessness. But his feet never moved. His body would sway and jar as if held in the coil of an invisible, malevolent serpent wreathing itself from the marsh to thwart him and uttering a groan of despair Henry would squeeze his eyes tight shut to make the vision pass, to save his Reuben from his inevitable, constant past.

Sometimes he could successfully wipe his mind clear. Sometimes, though, he would feel the craving for the pipe again and then it would be as it was in the sweat lodge when Shunka had passed it to him the second time. This time he would smell the smell of cold, turned clay and taste the iron taste of blood upon his lips. It was the last sense of ebbing life. He had felt it the day they had found the skull and Sim Lilley had nearly broken his nose for his trouble.

But now the smell of the clay was everywhere as if the land had been ploughed as far as a man might see in any direction no matter how far he roamed, and the taste of blood on his lips was not his own. It was in the air like a rank mist rising from the Icing meadows on a November nightfall. He would strain to see where he might be but this time sight was the least of the senses he felt.

Then, as if created from the smell and taste alone, a young man would come towards him, leading a Suffolk chesnut and he would look inquiringly at Henry as if Henry had already spoken to him and he had not understood. Henry would always feel that he knew the young man, his face had a familiar look to it, but before he could fix in his mind who it might be, the boy would be gone, leaving behind the same taste and the smell and this time a hideous din inside Henry's head like ceaseless thunder.

Shunka sang to the stones for the last time.

'It is finished,' he said and crawled out of the entrance flap as dawn was beginning to show in the eastern sky behind him. Annie had gone. She must have known somehow when the last change of stones had been made. Their clothes were lying neatly folded on the remains of the woodpile, thoughtfully close enough to the fire pit for its dwindling heat to keep the morning chill off them.

The three men dressed in silence, not catching one another's eyes either. When they were ready they walked away across the meadows towards the distant lane, following the track made by the swish of Annie's departed dress in the dewy grass before them. There was no question but that they would leave the place alone for now, leave it to deal by itself with whatever it had caused to happen.

It was Roger Birchall who first broke the spell.

'I've seen some excellent things in there, Shunka old fellow. Well not excellent at all, truth-to-tell, no not all excellent, not by a long chalk. But very clear if you get my drift, very clear.'

The other two did not reply.

'So did you fellows see anything, then?' Birchall said after an awkward moment or two.

Shunka halted abruptly. They had reached the gate to the lane.

'I have seen the past and the future as one. It is what happens. *Unci* brought it as I said.'

'And have you seen it too, Henry, the past and the future?' Birchall asked eagerly.

'I don't know,' Henry replied. 'I hope not.'

'It is enough to know that we are made clean together so that we can bury the Brave,' said Shunka, but the way he said it told Henry that he too was troubled by what he had seen. He made to open the gate but Dr Birchall put his hand on his arm to restrain him.

'Look here, old fellow, I cannot get any of this out of my blasted head and I cannot make sense of it either. Just listen. You must listen. I kept seeing you two and another fellow I didn't know, but he had that maid with the red hair with him.' He paused and thought a moment. 'Well no, she wasn't actually with him. She was there and I could see her but he could not. Then there would be the two of you and someone looking for you and I knew they shouldn't find you and I knew…I knew…that it would somehow be my fault if they did.'

Birchall looked pleadingly at them. 'Just a bit of a bad dream would you say? Shouldn't put any store by it. It was damn hot in there, wasn't it?'

'Perhaps,' said Shunka. 'But if you have medicine you will know the truth. I know it.'

Henry, too, wanted it all to have been a bad dream although in his self he already knew, like Shunka, he knew.

'Did you…dream anything else then? Something from the past maybe?' he asked.

'I did as a matter of fact. It's just come back to me with you asking like that. I kept seeing friend Reuben with that young fellow I met in Egypt that helped with the drains. Couldn't see Reuben's face, but I knew it was him. Odd that. Egypt. Shows it must have been a dream.'

Henry felt the hair rise on the back of his neck and on his arms. Reuben had sent Sim to Egypt, he had been certain, as a reminder to Birchall and to Henry of their unfinished business even though they were so far apart. He held his arms out in front of him at the feeling and noticed the dried blood on his hands.

Birchall followed his gaze, 'Yes we did that too, didn't we. Better not let Robert Earl see it, it'd probably put him in the insane asylum.'

That night at the Veil House, as he and Shunka were grooming the horses in the stable in adjacent standings, Henry had the first return visitation of his visions in the sweat lodge. All thoughts that it might after all been nothing more than a bad waking dream were banished from his head. As if exhausted he lent his head and arms on the side of Honeycomb's neck, unable to move. How long it lasted he could not tell. Perhaps only moments. When it was over he saw that the mare's ears were laid back along her head, her eyes were looking wild and she was shifting her feet fretfully on the standing.

Shunka had come round to his side, scraping the curry comb over the dandy brush in a deliberate way that implied he was waiting for the answer to an unasked question. Henry told him what he had seen in his head, blurted it out more like, as if he were bringing up something bad he had eaten, experiencing relief through the pain of it.

Frank, the Head Baiter, looked at them curiously from the far end of the stable. He did not approach them. He probably could not hear what they were saying across the standing divides and the huge dense bodies of their occupants. To him Henry was destined not to be part of the Veil House again. He had already gone away with his Red Indian, even if they had not yet physically left.

When Henry was done, Shunka gave a deep sigh as if he had forgotten to breathe. 'I must go back to my people,' he said, 'I have seen the Badlands of the Lakota and the plains in winter. I saw the sun die and I heard my mother and sisters calling in the darkness. I saw the blue horse soldiers we killed at the Greasy Grass rise up from the hillside and the deep ravine, mounted and armed again. I heard them playing their *Garryowen* again as they rode down to the Cheyenne River and on to Pine Ridge. It was an end and now it begins again. I must go and be with my people. See, Henry, my mother has made me a shirt,' Shunka spread his arms proudly displaying an invisible garment.

'I shall go with you then,' said Henry without hesitation, 'There is nothing here for me after Reuben is laid to rest. Perhaps I shall discover my fortune in America with you.'

Then he added, 'What about Annie?'

'She shall not come now,' said Shunka, 'When these things are done, then I shall ask her to come. I will not ask her to winter on the plains. One of us shall return to fetch her when the spring comes round again.'

He had not questioned Henry's decision to go with him. It was meant.

27

It took them three days to dig out a grave for Reuben, beneath the hollow where the stones had been inside the sweat lodge after they had dismantled it. Shunka cast the stones back into the river from whence they had come and burned the willow frame. Roger Birchall manfully took his turn at the digging but was soon defeated by his crippled leg which had not had as long to mend as Henry's injuries. Even so they were a sorry team of excavators, Henry and Roger both lame and Shunka unused to this kind of manual labour as well as being philosophically opposed to burial.

'At Carlisle we buried many children in these pits,' he said, disapprovingly. 'Separate pits for each child and a stone for each with the names Captain Pratt gave them. They died of the white man's ills and were given a white man's name and were buried in a white man's hole far from the plains.'

Eventually however, Dr Birchall declared himself satisfied with the result. The grave would be big enough to take the tithe chest with room to spare all round it.

'Ideally it should be lined with stones, flints for preference to create a chamber for the body, but we, I think, may be permitted to regard the tithe chest as the chamber,' he said, relapsing into his professorial role as though he were addressing his students.

'I shall however put some flints around the outside of the chest as a symbolic gesture. We must now carefully decide on the artefacts that are to be included for his journey. There is a school of thought that the dead man's goods and chattels, to say nothing of his livestock and even his thralls in some extreme cases, were all consigned to the barrow for sanitary reasons. Death might be considered catching, so to speak. In some cases, I believe food, and livestock have been found burnt around the perimeter of the barrow. But I choose to believe that the dead man was being prepared for an ethereal journey and that destruction by fire released the spirit of the food and animals heavenward in a gaseous form, as it were.'

Birchall caught himself sounding pompous and giggled nervously. 'I expect his relatives all came and had a thoroughly good blow out too. I think we should have a feast here when the deed is done. Excellent. Now, about the artefacts. As we don't have anything that actually belonged to our man we shall have to improvise symbolically.'

'Things to do with horses, you said before,' Henry put in just as Annie arrived carrying a basket containing their dinner.

'Certainly, certainly,' said Birchall. 'And with an element of sacrifice about it somehow. Something of his that those left behind could ill-afford to let go but would propitiate the gods and speed his journey better, that kind of thing. Good day Mrs Westwood.'

'What is his medicine, this warrior?' Shunka said when Birchall's mouth was sufficiently full of bread and cheese to shut him up for a moment.

Birchall swallowed most of it and said, 'By that I assume you mean what did he believe in. What did he hold holy? What, you might say, was his religion? That is a difficult one. He would have believed in qualities. Strength, courage in battle, fortitude in adversity, qualities he would have seen symbolised in nature and in the animal kingdom and then would have attributed to his different gods. Strength and courage in battle for instance was expressed through the cult of the severed head. The heads of enemies slain in combat would be taken and displayed as trophies.

'This I understand,' said Shunka nodding.

As they walked back to the lane Henry said to Annie, 'Roger wants to have a feast by the grave, but I can't very well ask my mother for anything can I?

'We'd better cook some of those rabbits Shunka keeps catching,' she said, saying his name as a wife would speak her man's. 'I could make a stew pot. Would that do?'

Henry wondered if now were the moment to tell her that they were leaving, but his courage failed him. She had already had a premonition that Shunka would leave. There would be time enough to put flesh on its bones, he thought guiltily.

They had left the livestock cart containing the tithe chest out of the way on the other side of the stables at the Veil House. If Bailey Turner had seen it he made no comment at any rate. He seemed rather to have washed his hands of both Henry and Shunka, having seen so little of them of late. By his sour remarks he clearly assumed that their absence for that entire night they had spent in the sweat lodge had more to do with illegal snares and traps. Henry asked him cautiously if he might take Honeycomb and the livestock cart out after supper.

'Please yourself. You usually do these days. I don't want to know about your goings-on after dark. You just watch you don't get set upon again like you were before.

Henry and Shunka, wearing his doe-skins and his blanket, walked the mare and cart round to St Mary's where Roger Birchall was waiting for them by the lych-gate clutching a canvas bag. He fell into step with them and they continued in the direction of Great Aunt Elizabeth's cottage.

'I've been thinking, Shunka, old fellow,' he said. 'Some form of prayers should be said, a service for the burial of the dead. Somehow "man that hath but a short time" and so on doesn't seem quite the thing in the circumstances. I was wondering if some of your singing mightn't be more appropriate. What do you think?'

'I will dance the death dance,' said Shunka without hesitation. Henry thought he detected relief in his voice, relief at being in control of the ceremonial again.

'What have you told Great Aunt Elizabeth?' Henry asked Annie when she appeared at the cottage door with her finger to her lips. She handed him a bundle wrapped in brown paper which he took without a word.

'The truth,' she whispered. 'Well, the truth after a fashion. I've said that you are helping Dr Birchall with his archaeology and it is something that cannot wait because he has to go back to Cambridge soon so it has to be done by moonlight otherwise it will spoil. So I am taking your supper up to you. I don't know whether she believes me or not but as Dr Birchall is such a friend of Mr Earl's she won't say anything.'

'What did she think you were doing the other night?' said Henry.

Annie placed a cooking pot under the box seat on the cart.

'I got home before she was stirring. Anyway, I expect she hopes I was with you. You know what she's like.'

The secret cortege met with no-one on its progress to the water meadows. To be honest Henry was past caring now. He relapsed into silence as his inner thoughts became louder and clearer to him than his companions' brief exchanges and the passing surroundings on either hand. It was nearly done. Soon Reuben would have no more demands to make on Henry.

'But shall I be free?' he thought. Indeed, would he want to be free? Would he have done enough to settle the Romans' hash once and for all? He thought about Shunka's view of the past and the future, how they were all one, indivisible from the present, just out of sight waiting to be revealed by some hot stones and a pipe. Would Reuben just be a thing of the past now or would he go on in Henry's head, being just out of sight?

Honeycomb turned off the lane through the first gate to the water meadows, unbidden. If Henry's hazy conviction that they had all been brought to this point in time and place by Reuben for this purpose was right, what would happen afterwards? Would he be able to see another purpose and another and another, or would he just be abandoned now? Shunka had said Henry had been chosen to set Reuben on the path to join his ancestors in the hereafter. But suppose Shunka was wrong. Even Dr Birchall did not claim he was always right, even about those things in which he was expert. As the horse and cart came to a halt beside the newly dug grave pit Henry could not prevent a sinking feeling seeping through him that this was to be no ending at all for him.

The three men manoeuvred the chest out of livestock cart and carefully set it beside the heap of freshly dug earth. Annie busied herself kindling a fire using the remains of the wood pile from before.

'Do we feast now or after?' she asked

'Oh after, after,' said Roger Birchall, 'So that we can put the remains around the chest as a burnt offering.'

'And what about the…things we've…?' said Henry

'The artefacts? Excellent. They have to go into the chest first. I suggest we lay out what we have brought and then Shunka, perhaps you would start the singing as we put them in,' said Birchall.

Then he reverently opened the canvas bag he had brought with him. Annie gasped and Henry gaped as he drew out the contents that glinted red and gold by the light of the blazing fire.

'Yes, oh yes!' Shunka hissed approvingly reaching forward both his hands as if to take it to himself as Birchall laid down an axe. But it was not just an axe, not one from the ironmonger for chopping kindling. It had two heads and a spike standing up proud between them set on a haft of oak more than two feet long. It might be held in one hand and tossed to the other or a man might wield it in both at once to cleave down through metal, flesh and bone in a single pass.

'A battle axe,' Birchall said gleefully, gazing down at it as if he were himself seeing it for the first time. 'I ordered it to be cast after we went down to the crypt with Shunka. Sent them a drawing. It only arrived last week. Mrs Bullace sent it by carrier and it just made it here yesterday. I was having kittens. It's bronze by the way. No expense spared. I should say not. What have you brought, Henry?'

Henry reached under the cart's box seat and retrieved the brown paper parcel Annie had handed him earlier.

'This is from me, Reuben,' he said. 'Annie has been keeping this for me for more than a year. And as a kind of Roman had it made it will serve to signify several things. Horsemen, blood and sacrifice.' He unfolded the brown paper and drew out the Melton coat Major Fitzgerald had given him.

'Oh I say, excellent,' said Roger Birchall. 'What about Man-who-hears-horses, Shunka? What has he brought?'

The Indian reached under his blanket and took out a little skin pouch of the same material as his leggings. At first Henry thought it might be his medicine tobacco, but soon realised it was an even greater sacrifice for Shunka than that.

'If I understand your meaning, my brother, this too came from a Roman of a kind,' and Shunka gently pulled out the scalp he had asked his father how to take that hot June morning above the Little Big Horn river.

Henry could see that, in the shadows cast by the blazing fire, Annie could not make out what it was. He wondered how Shunka would explain it to her now. Any thoughts of handling the matter delicately were, however, blown away by Roger Birchall's academic enthusiasm.

'It's a whatname, isn't it? Excellent. Oh how excellent. The cult of the severed head, you see.'

'My people stopped taking the whole head,' said Shunka gravely. 'Too many flies.' Henry could not see in the darkness whether he was in jest.

'What is it, then?' said Annie sounding interested but perplexed at the exchange.

Henry opened his mouth to say something, but shut it again, deciding to leave this explanation to his brother-in-blood.

Dr Birchall must have realised that he had gone too far, too soon.

'Ah... hmm...yes. Mrs West...Barbara. The fact is, it's a...it's a. What would you say it was, Shunka, old fellow?'

Henry was fascinated by Birchall's cowardice and his own. He could hardly wait to hear how Shunka would handle it now.

Shunka's voice became wooden, betraying no emotion. Henry recognised the tone, he had heard it before when the Lakkota Sioux was daring the world to intrude on his self at its peril. Henry knew that the world generally backed away.

'It is a blue horse soldier's hair. He would have killed me if I had not killed him first. I would be as this Brave now,' he gestured at the tithe chest. 'As would my mother and my sisters, the children. They came to kill us all that day and we stopped them. Now I have his hair.'

Shunka fell silent and when he spoke again his voice had changed. 'But I know it is not the way. I have seen the cities and crossed the ocean. I have ridden your trains. We will not stop you. You will eat us and we shall become a part of your strength even though we have died. Where is this Brave now, where are his people? Who? The Iceni? They are in you and you,' he prodded first Annie and then Henry. 'And even you Birchall-who-limps. I do not know. And where are these Roman *ahkecheta*[*] who killed him? They too are here, in you and you and you. Always a circle. Always it ends and begins again. The scalp says "once I was who I was and he was who he was".'

'Scalp?' said Annie, 'Is there skin on it then? Let me see.' She took it gently in her cupped hands, like a bird with a broken wing and peered at it in the fire's glow. 'Did you think I would be feared of it, then? I would hope that every man who is killed by another in a battle becomes special to him that lives and is remembered by him for better or for worse. We should be more to one another than we are to the beasts in the abattoir, shouldn't we, be we never so bad? I think your people do well to take something to remember them by.'

The three men stood silent. After what seemed a long time, Henry stepped forward and raising the lid of the tithe chest he gently laid his unfolded Melton over Reuben's bones. Then Birchall stepped up and placed the battle axe by the side. Then Annie who had not let it go, knelt down and placed the scalp on the other side, 'And a bunch of mistletoe, like you said, Dr Birchall,' she said.

'It's a pity we do not have anything of his, but we found nothing with him, did we Henry?' murmured Roger Birchall.

Henry untied the muffler he had round his neck and put it in. 'I have,' he said, 'I nearly forgot.'

Shunka shed his blanket and naked to the waist stepped forward into the firelight. He raised his arms and slowly began to step and sway to a rhythm only he could hear. Then he began to drone and hum in a way that seemed to counterpoint the dancing so that to Henry there seemed of a sudden to be more than one person singing and dancing. He glanced at the others to see if they had joined in, in the darkness beyond the light of the fire, but they too, were standing still, watching, each of them alone with themselves. The doubts Henry had been fostering in his mind about Reuben banished themselves and a fierce peace engulfed him as W*icasa Shunka'wakan Wanahan* called upon his ancestors to welcome a warrior whose time had at long last come, to that equal sky.

Once the pit was filled in, a task that took considerably less time to accomplish than had digging it out, the four fell on the rabbit stew as if they had not seen food for a week. Annie had brought a jug of home brew too, which Henry and Birchall soon saw off but both Shunka and she declined. The glow from the fire, food and drink began to thaw out the long silence that had lasted since Henry and Birchall had lowered the tithe

---

[*] soldiers

chest into the ground as the Lakota anthem for the dead had enveloped them and then faded away.

'Well,' said Dr Birchall.

There was an air of finality about the word. Henry waited with trepidation for the words he knew would follow.

'What happens now?'

The others digested the question. It did not refer to the coming day nor even the remainder of the week. Birchall was asking what they intended to do with the rest of their lives.

Henry searched inside himself for something, anything, which felt as though it were meant and in doing so triggered again the visions from the sweat lodge. They came into his head not as a sequence, more like a piece of music with one theme laid over another and another so that he experienced the entire thing in a single moment of emotion. But although the feeling shook him violently, he could not see that anything was meant as they had been in the past, except a sense of parting, of a journey and a search.

It was Shunka who responded first.

'I shall go back to my people. The Earth Ear sounded to me in the sweat lodge. I have told Henry. We shall go together.'

'To America?' said Annie quietly.

'Yes,' said Shunka.

'When?' said Annie

'Tomorrow, the next day, in a week, soon.'

'I cannot be ready to leave Aunt Elizabeth that quickly,' said Annie not quite succeeding in keeping a note of panic out of her voice. It was not a sound that Henry associated with Annie.

'I will not take a white woman to Pine Ridge in the snows,' said Shunka flatly.

'Not even one you love and who loves you?' said Annie

'Especially,' said Shunka.

Dr Birchall had moved himself a modest distance away during this exchange, but Henry was rooted to the same spot

'Shunka says he will send for you when everything has been resolved. I shall come back for you when the spring comes round again,' said Henry.

'If you go without me now, we shall never see one another again,' said Annie to Shunka. 'The world will turn and turn and part us.'

'Then Henry, my brother in blood shall stay with you so that he can bring you when the moon is right,' said Shunka.

Henry opened his mouth and shut it again, his mind in a turmoil.

'Like a hostage,' said Annie bleakly.

'No, no. Not like that at all.' Henry could not help himself as pictures of Kitty Shaughnessy sprang into his head. But he realised that the moment to refuse the role had been lost.

'I don't want him to stay. I must come with you now or it will be too late.' Annie was beginning to plead.

Despite his own seething emotions a little part of Henry remembered the only time he had heard that in her voice before, when she had asked him to forgive her for cutting his Melton from his broken body.

'It is decided,' said Shunka.

Annie went and stood, staring down at the mound of newly turned earth, clasping herself tightly under her grey cloak.

'What have you done to us? What have you done to us?' she sobbed. 'What's it all been for?' Then, still clutching herself she turned and ran blindly towards the gate. Henry waited for Shunka to run after her or call to her, wanting desperately to do so himself, but neither of them did.

'Oh I say,' said Dr Birchall from his little distance. 'Will Mrs Westwood be all right? It's very late.'

The sound of heavy rain on his window woke him sometime after dawn, otherwise Henry would doubtless have slept on well into the forenoon. Chiding himself under his breath he pulled on his clothes and boots as he stumbled down to the stable. Shunka was already ahead of him and busy with the first feed

'So when shall you go? Really tomorrow, or next week?' said Henry. 'How are you going to get to America? Do you know the way?'

'I shall find Colonel Cody. He plans to return in the month of Moon-to-plant-in.'

'When's that?'

Shunka counted on his fingers. 'Fifth moon,' he said.

'May,' said Henry.

'Yes, May.'

'Well it's April now, so you haven't got long. I wish you weren't making me stay. At least let me come and make sure you find the Exhibition all right and see you off.'

'Maybe,' said Shunka thoughtfully. 'Perhaps Birchall-who-limps has a *London Evening News*. That will say where the Colonel is.'

Henry laughed. 'Not in Cambridge,' he said. 'But there are other newspapers. It's a good idea.'

Later Henry walked round to the vicarage alone to find Dr Birchall, not wishing to bring about another confrontation between Mr Earl and Shunka. As he walked up the churchyard path to the side door, he met Annie coming away. She looked pale and grim and Henry's heart sank.

'I was coming to find you,' she said. 'Mrs Lilley's with the Vicar now. Sim's dead. She had a letter from the army and brought it round for me to read. Poor woman, they've buried him in Egypt.'

The door opened again and Sim's mother appeared being gently ushered out by Mr Earl while Roger Birchall hovered in the background.

'Six months ago, Cousin Henry, six months ago,' said the distraught woman. 'He's been in the ground that long and I never even knew he was ill.'

'I never thought to say. I thought she would already know,' Roger Birchall said. 'I'm mortified.'

'No,' said Henry, 'If anyone should have mentioned it, I should have done.'

He felt riddled with guilt. Guilt he bore for Reuben's sake. The Icenian had used Sim like an imaginary ball of twine to guide him back, having first planted thoughts of Icingbury and his bones in the archaeologist's head.

Now Sim was dead, thought Henry, already dying when Roger had run into him in the hospital at Alexandria. As good as murdered. But by whom? By a long-dead Icenian warrior? Or by Henry, for thinking it possible? He tried to distance himself from the burden, to grasp at that certainty he had come to know, that things were meant, that the jigsaw pieces were being turned over and sorted by a hand and mind other than his own. But he could not. Reuben, the Icenian warrior had departed to another place and left the rest of the pieces scattered and unresolved.

'And I have done this thing,' Henry's own voice kept saying. 'I brought them all together, not him. Shunka and Annie, Roger, Sim, and Kitty. What about Kitty?' His mind raced, a mess of disconnected memories.

Annie had led Sim's inconsolable mother off in the direction of Great Aunt Elizabeth's. The Vicar, after staring moodily in Henry's direction for a moment had shut the door leaving Dr Birchall and him alone together. They wandered through the lych-gate and into the lane.

'It's all going to go wrong now that we've buried him, isn't it?' said Henry.

'Uh-oh. So that's the way your mind's going is it?' said Birchall, slipping his arm through Henry's. 'I told you about feeling "chosen" a long time ago, didn't I?' Only you've taken it more to heart than you should have done. Robert Earl's just the same. I can't jolly him out of it. Keeps telling me that the skull and bones and Shunka were all brought here to shake his faith. Well, what's done is done and buried good and deep moreover. So I suggest you start feeling "unchosen" sharp-ish, old fellow.'

‘I think I have already. That’s the trouble,’ said Henry.

‘I’m going back to Cambridge later today,’ said Birchall, ‘I need to get away from hysterical clerics and back to some dull undergraduates. Want to come?’

‘I can’t,’ said Henry, ‘I have to stay here now for a while. That reminds me though. Will you find out when the Wild West Exhibition is going back to America and where it will be? Shunka says it’s next month some time. He wants to go home.’

‘I’ll send you a telegram.’

‘My mother will think somebody else has died,’ said Henry smiling grimly in spite of himself.

28

His mother's voice calling him from the kitchen door with, unusually for her, a note of urgency, immediately made Henry assume that his prophesy about the telegram had come true. He and Shunka were in what they called the 'back orchard' although the fruit trees that gave it its name were ancient and sparse. Henry was continuing the gentling of one of the colts he had purchased. By now accustomed to bridle and bit, he was trying him out first with just a small saddle before graduating to a dumb jockey he had made out of two crossed poles and an old hat and jacket. Shunka was looking on with some amusement.

'What are you laughing at then, *Mister* Wicasa?' said Henry annoyingly imitating his mother's voice. Shunka was beginning to say something about true warriors only needing a pony's back to sit on and not all this furniture, when the real Mrs Turner's summons interrupted them. Leaving Shunka to see to the colt, Henry hurried back to the farmhouse and entered the kitchen. A familiar figure was seated at the big table, puffing audibly as she removed her hat and saying 'No, I wouldn't say no' to Mrs Turner's offer of a cup of tea.

'Why Mrs B,' said Henry. 'Whatever brings you out here?'

'Why, 'enry Turner, if I'd 'ave knowed 'ow far it was to walk from the railway station I'd 'ave thought twice about it,' said Mrs Bullace.

'But something must be wrong,' said Henry. 'Is it Roger…Dr Birchall?'

Mrs Bullace rummaged in her capacious bag and pulled out an envelope and handed it to him. ''E asked me to bring this.'

'Is it about Buffalo Bill's Exhibition?' said Henry as he opened it. 'He was going to send a telegram. I know I made a joke about telegrams and bad news, but he didn't need to make you come all this way with it. Not that I'm not very pleased to see you,' he added hastily.

Mrs Bullace glanced at Henry's mother who was busy with kettle and teapot on the range and had her back to them. The cook reached out and grasped Henry's arm pulling him down towards her. 'It's not safe to use the post, the Doc says. Read the letter when your Ma's not around,' she whispered hoarsely.

The door opened and Shunka Wicasa stepped in.

'And there's my Chunky too,' said Mrs Bullace, returning to her normal self.

'*Hokohda*[*] She-misses-bee,' he greeted her. 'I knew it was you. You smell of *wahcha* ... flowers.'

'That'll be a little dab of Parma violets, you great sauce boat. Thinkin' you can smell me through the door.'

Henry took advantage of their renewed bantering and went to slip through the door into the parlour to study Birchall's letter.

'Not in those boots you don't,' said his mother, thereby acknowledging she had taken everything in but was not adding a blind eye to her deaf ear. He pulled them off and padded through into the next room with a perplexed sinking feeling.

Roger Birchall had written,

8 -------- Road
Cambridge
Monday 18th April 1888

My Dear Henry,

I am sending Mrs Bullace with this as I dare not commit it to the post. I only hope she is not followed. I told her to purchase a ticket to London in case they ask at the ticket office where she is going. I told her to ride in the Ladies Only compartment and only to alight at Great Duster as the train was about to leave so that she could see if anyone who looked as though they might be following her did the same. Oh goodness, I am beginning to prattle.

Yesterday, Sunday if you please, two policemen came to the house. I say policemen but they were not in uniform. Their warrants said that they were from the Irish Special Branch. I have heard of this organisation. It was formed about five years ago by the Home Office to root out the Irish Republican Brotherhood, the Fenians, as Fitzgerald still calls them. I did not like the look of them one bit, I can tell you, Henry and so I must urge you to take this very seriously and to take great care not to be discovered for I fear very much that telling the truth of the situation will be of little avail. I'm off the point again.

I do not think they can have known that I was involved in the matter of the red headed maid otherwise they would not have said as much to me as they did. Cambridge respectability will out, you see. They were looking for Mrs Bullace whom they had tracked from her friend in Paddington. But they are really after you and Shunka. They did not seem to know about Mrs Bullace's part in it all.

---

[*] Hello friend

It seems that they were trying to arrest Miss Shaughnessy's brother. There was shooting and he was fatally wounded. As he was breathing his last he either gloated about, or confessed to having killed Mr Davies whom he assumed had murdered his sister. It seems that Davies had not yet left Bayswater for Ireland when Shaughnessy caught up with him. The police found him in a kind of cubby hole in the cellar. He had managed to scrawl on the wall apparently in his own blood 'Turner and the Indian did it.'

I guessed at once that Davies must have been trying to implicate you in Kitty's disappearance. But it is clear that the police think it is Davies' murder for which you are responsible. Who knows what that man was trying to do by it at the last? My guess is he wanted to divert any inquiry away from Major Fitzgerald. He had served with him for a long time. Fitzgerald is out of it, I presume he is still en route to Egypt and in any case he is hardly going to be thought anything other than a target for the Irish Brotherhood.

Henry, my friend, this is a mess and no mistake. The Irish Special Branch think that you are hand in glove with Shaughnessy and carried out Davies' murder with him or on his behalf. They wanted to know how you both came to be in the house in the first place. They have you marked down as a Fenian spy and Shunka as an assassin. Thank goodness they have not yet worked out what kind of Indian he is. They think he is from the Punjab or worse still the North West Frontier. They actually think they might have stumbled on some form of conspiracy between the Irish and the Russians over India. Unbelievable. Fortunately Mrs Bullace had not divulged very much more to her friend in Paddington and I have to say she was discretion to the point of dumb idiocy when they came to ask her your whereabouts.

However, my dear fellow, I fear your trail has not yet gone cold. In Cambridge they are already too close for complacency. I am not a great optimist that the truth is always likely to be believed in the end by the police, especially when it happens to be as far-fetched as it is in this case. I think you should seriously consider making yourself scarce. Cody leaves Hull for America on May 5. Alexandra Dock. Mrs Bullace has some funds for you which are not a loan but a heartfelt gift from your companion and friend of the sweat lodge,

Roger

PS. Write to me from America so that I can keep you apprised of developments and let you have more funds should the necessity arise.

R

PPS I suppose you had better burn this.

R.

After he had read the letter about a dozen times Henry went back into the kitchen, his mind was already made up. If anything had ever been meant it was this. Shunka would not be able to stop him now. Mrs Bullace looked up at him as he came in and then quickly glanced in the direction of his mother as a warning to say nothing out of turn

'Will you have a bite to eat, Mrs Bullace?' Mrs Turner asked.

'Well thankin' you kindly, perhaps just a crumb of cheese or whatever you're 'avin' before I takes me leave.'

'Shunka and I will take you over to Duster in the tilt cart when you are ready Mrs B,' said Henry.

'I can't bear it,' said Mrs Turner suddenly bursting out of her reticence. 'It must have been something important, dreadful even, to bring you all this way unexpected. What has happened?'

Mrs Bullace threw an agonised look at Henry. An image of large menacing men appearing at the door of the Veil House, demanding to know 'the truth' from his mother, came into his head. She should know nothing, it would be better that way.

'Do you know what was in the letter, Mrs B?' he asked, playing for time.

'No. Well not as such. The Doc didn't actually show it to me. But 'e said it was important to get it to you quick, so I said I would fetch it myself 'cos I 'adn't seen that there Chunky since I don't know when.'

Henry sensed that there was a certain amount of truth in her explanation as far as it went, so he took up where she had left off.

'Dr Birchall wants me to do something for him. Shunka and I may be away for a little while, Ma. It's to do with some people we knew in London.'

He wondered whether to burden her with a request for secrecy, whether to ask her to deny that he and Birchall were acquainted if anyone asked. But there could be no point. The whole of Icingbury knew about Roger Birchall and Shunka. The Vicar knew, for goodness' sake. The Archaeologist must have said something more to the police than he had said in his letter. As he had said, it was a mess.

After their modest repast of cheese, cold meat and pickles, Henry put the gelding to the tilt cart and he and Shunka bore Mrs Bullace away towards the station. There were about twenty minutes to wait for the Cambridge train.

'What did Dr Birchall really tell the police, Mrs B?' said Henry as they stood on the platform, having first had a good look in the waiting room for any strange men. 'About our whereabouts, I mean? He doesn't say in the letter.'

''E said as far as 'e knew you were still in London somewhere. Then 'e got all 'oity toity with them and said "Really, 'e couldn't be expected to keep track of other gentlemen's servants and they should ask the Major. That's when they said they couldn't find the Major, 'im 'avin' gone off to foreign parts,' said Mrs Bullace.

'Oh dear,' said Henry. 'If they come looking in the village, they'll soon find it was a lie.'

'Yes, but they don't know where you live. I said I thought you came from up north. Maybe they won't find out. 'Enry Turner's a common enough name, I should think,' said Mrs Bullace.

It crossed Henry's mind that the wily old cook had had dealings with the peelers before.

'What about Shunka? What was said about him, then?'

'Well they asked me about an Indian. They obviously 'ad it fixed that 'e was the other kind of Indian, so I just said 'e was a swarthy gentleman and 'is name was something-or-other Chunky.'

Henry was not entirely convinced that the story would hold for long, but he was mightily relieved that he had not allowed Shunka Wicasa to reveal his origins to their neighbours in the mews. He tried desperately to think whether he, himself, had told any of them where he hailed from, but could not recall. He had not fraternised with them much, having no time for any of them as horsemen. So Shunka and he might get away with it.

He thought about jumping on the train with Mrs Bullace to go and confront Birchall with the holes in his story and see if they could do better, but his friend clearly thought he might be being watched.

The train appeared down the track in the distance.

''Ere, you're to 'ave this.' Mrs Bullace rummaged in her bag and drew out a manila envelope. Henry took it, wondering what to say next, but Mrs Bullace of a sudden pulled both men down to her own height and gave each of them a great kiss on the cheek.

'You take care, both of you, and don't go frettin' about the rozzers,' she said, tears in her eyes and enveloping them in a haze of Parma violets. Then she was gone

'What did She-misses-bee mean?' said Shunka. 'I did not understand. What has happened?'

As they trotted back to Icingbury Henry told him, sparing no embellishment that would not seem too extreme. He had made up his mind. They would both be on the boat for America, come what may, and Henry was not going to allow Shunka Wicasa to deny him. He peered into the manila envelope. It was full of bank notes. He did not count it then, but it looked like much more than a year's wages.

29

The human tide that had swept down to Hull's Alexandra Dock from the football ground after the final performance of the Wild West, removed any need for Henry and Shunka to ask directions. Henry's only concern was that the entire crowd would try to board the *Persian Monarch* as she cast off, sending her straight to the bottom, such was the level of ecstasy that had been achieved by the show's final encore.

As the two of them stood in the crush watching the animals and properties being loaded on board by the light of great phosphorous lamps, each recognisable creature or item being greeted with a roar from the spectators, Henry began to doubt that Shunka and he would ever get on board themselves.

He saw them having to creep back to Icingbury to face whatever risky future might await them, to say nothing of Annie Lilley's anger, sorrow and forgiveness. If the journey to Hull had been physically straightforward and uneventful, for Henry it had been a mental agony.

In the end they had left without a word other than they were undertaking an errand for Dr Birchall. Henry had almost managed to persuade himself that leaving Annie with this expectation of their early return, would be for the best if the police came looking for them. But he knew that hot irons would not have dragged their secret from her had she been entrusted with it.

No, once again she had been put to one side by a man she loved and one she loved more, with whom she would have crossed oceans and wilderness had they wished.

Shunka had said little more about the manner of leaving Annie. Henry tried to remain convinced that her warrior truly meant to send for her, one spring time not far off, but there was no comfort for him in that. He knew it would only ever be an intention.

From time to time on their journey he would try to coax out of Shunka his true reason for not bringing Annie with them and for not giving her another chance to understand it for herself. The Lakota would only say that he would not take a white woman to the plains in winter and after a while Henry began to understand that 'the plains in winter' was much more than a description of a physical place. So after a while Henry stopped asking and tried, too, to stop thinking about the miles they had put between Icingbury and them and the miles they still had to go. He tried to stop wondering how far they would have to go before Annie's hurt was too far away to be felt.

Henry had spent much of the day at the shipping office clutching Roger Birchall's five pound notes, trying to remain optimistic that someone would cancel a passage at the last minute. It was not likely. Most of the berths were taken by Cody's troupe and the Indians were occupying the steerage. When he reported his lack of success to Shunka, whom he had left minding his carpet bag in the far corner of some tuppenny dining rooms, with his hair braided and coiled under his large felt hat, the Indian was as usual unmoved.

'How do you say it, Henry? It is meant? This is meant. I have seen it. A bird will come.'

Henry tried to tell him that he was less confident about 'meant' things since the news of Sim Lilley's death, but Shunka remained unmoveable and said they must find the ship even if they did not have a ticket.

So here they stood at the water's edge at ten minutes to midnight, staring at the *Persian Monarch* only a few yards away with Henry wondering whether they would have to watch her slip away on the tide in three hours' time without them. He was just about to shout wryly in Shunka's ear that they would have great difficulty in hearing a bird above the din of the crowd, even if one did make an appearance, when he felt a tug at his sleeve.

'I knew that was you, even from behind, Henry Turner.'

He turned his head recognising the lilting Irish voice at once, but he had difficulty in recognising the looks of Kitty Shaughnessy. Her once fiery hair was deep black and Henry could see, as her hood slipped back, braided Indian-style like Shunka's.

'Have you come to see me off, then?' laughed Kitty. 'Isn't this a long way from home now? Or is it your man, here? Is he going home at last?'

'We both want to, but we cannot get a berth,' said Henry. 'The peelers are after us,' he added in her ear, knowing that the Irish maid would not require him to waste time with explanations just then. Nor did he ask them of her. Her appearance said instantly that she was still with Cody's Indians. Maybe a bird has come, he thought, hope beginning to well up inside him.

'Sure, and there's plenty of room with the *wehchash'tah*,' said Kitty. 'We've lost at least three along the way, not counting him,' she nodded at Shunka.

'Dead?' said Shunka. 'Three dead from my people?'

'Who knows? Maybe dead, maybe just lost somewheres. Chief Red Shirt's supposed to keep count but he's not very good at it. I don't think he's told Cody. There's a new baby though. Born in Salford. It was in the newspapers. Fancy that.'

She was leading them towards the back of the crowd, over towards some long, low buildings.

'Colonel Cody and the whites have all gone on board, but we...the *wehchash'tah* are camped for the time being in the emigration shed. We have to feed ourselves you see. So you can just slip on with us, easy.'

Henry was relieved to learn that the Indians and the cowboys did not share the same living space on board ship any more than they had done at Earl's Court. With no performances to put on until New York it might, he thought, just be possible that Shunka might not attract the attention of his old adversaries, nor Henry of the Colonel.

The Lakota women were inclined to make a fuss of Shunka at his sudden and unexpected return, but his kinsman, Mato Ska, displayed the same impassivity as Shunka did himself. The older man listened to his explanation of their predicament, or so Henry presumed, without comment. When Shunka had finished he spoke briefly to Henry in the Lakota tongue.

Before Shunka could translate, Kitty, who had been listening attentively, said. 'White Bear says he remembers you well. You are once again welcome to his lodge. Then he said something about something being unfinished. What was that?'

'It was the pipe,' said Shunka. 'You have the ear for tongues, too, then?'

'That's a strange way of saying what I think you mean,' laughed Kitty. 'Needs must here, otherwise I might have starved.'

Henry remembered his manners and said to Shunka, 'Say to White Bear that I am grateful for his hospitality and that his lodge is bigger than I remember.' He looked round the emigration hall and its temporary occupants huddled in little groups on blankets on the stone floor.

'Here,' said Kitty, who had been rummaging in a bundle by one of these groups. 'Put this on over your togs and borrow Shunka's hat. It's bigger than that old thing of yours.' She handed Henry an Indian blanket.

Shunka and Mato Ska had meanwhile been talking apart. Shunka came over to Henry. 'Mato Ska will speak with Red Shirt. All will be well. When he calls us I will tell him we are *wehchin yeh* and you must show him your arm.'

Mato Ska approached an imposing looking man in his own little group at the far end of the shed.

'That's Red shirt,' said Kitty. 'If he says a thing is to happen, then it happens.'

'Have you been with the Indians ever since London?' said Henry as they waited for their summons.

'The women took good care of me. I was very sick and hurt, you know, and then I lost the baby. He came in February but he was already dead. The Lakota woman, *Washteh Ptehahinsh'ma*, who had the baby…I told you there was a baby born…she had no milk of her own and I did, so…'

Henry did not know what he should say. He had put that wrong of the Major's so far to the back of his mind that he had forgotten it. He realised now that he had tried to put Kitty's fate out of his mind too. If he had thought of her it had been as an idea, not as a person and mostly it had been an intrusion. In all the business with Reuben he had never been able to see what Kitty's purpose had been. Yet here she was now, very much alive and about to return whatever favour he might have done her.

So is it still all going on after all, he thought? Or was there always something else other than Reuben's purpose going on, so big he couldn't see it?

'Have you been hiding all the time, or does Buffalo Bill know about you?' he asked Kitty

'Not so much hiding as keeping myself to myself,' she said. 'Chief Red Shirt's wife told the Colonel about the Major's baby, or rather his interpreter did, so he wasn't disposed to throw me out. I don't think he had formed a very high opinion of Major Fitzgerald anyway. And then when the babies came and mine was dead, poor wee thing, the Colonel had it put about that I had been taken on to help *Washteh* who was having a bad time of it. So as you can see, I dyed my lovely hair so as not to draw attention to myself. When we went north I felt able to move in and out of the camp more freely. Well, you saw tonight, I walked back from the show. I thought I'd take my last look at this country as a white woman, though I don't know why I should feel that, it's not my country, now is it? Outside poor Ireland one place is much like another to me, so I might as well try my luck in America I suppose. Why are the polis after you then?'

But before Henry could reply, they were beckoned over to the presence of Chief Red Shirt who addressed him in his Lakota tongue in a way that caused a silence to fall, as all in the shed felt compelled to give ear.

Not for the first time did Henry wonder to himself how these people could be uncomprehendingly dismissed as savages by the likes of Troop Sergeant-Major Davies. Henry felt himself being looked over closely by a man to whom he instinctively owed respect and awe, a man for whom it would be privilege to perform a service.

No matter, he thought, that he takes his enemy's scalp. Men like Mr. Davies would do the same and call themselves superior. The erstwhile Majordomo's ironic end had given rise to little emotion in Henry. He had read and re-read Birchall's letter so often now, having been reluctant to destroy it at once, keeping it instead with the other few that he had now received, all of them, it seemed, marking or pointing to one of his doorways.

He felt no exultation at the manner of Mr. Davies' death, still less any regret, only puzzlement and irritation. The dead man's last act of writing on the cubby hole wall surrounded by the military traps and memories of his dark past, a place where he had carried out one murder and sought to perpetrate another, struck Henry as something meant.

By its mistaken information it had nevertheless laid a true scent forcing Henry and Shunka to pin back their ears and race for sanctuary. But to what end Henry was mystified. The Icenian warrior no longer provided him with a point on which to focus his belief that there would come a time, a place, and a purpose. Now instead he was left with a feeling that, driven now by chance and error, he might next time miss all three.

Chief Red Shirt finished speaking and Shunka began to translate, almost to declaim his words in the first person, as if he were reinforcing their meaning by turning them into something to be remembered by all there and handed on to those less fortunate, who were not.

'I welcome you, Henry Turner, brother in blood to our tribe's Brave, One-who-hears-horses-coming. *Wakan Tanka* has put medicine in you to hear and understand what other men do not, as he has given the earth ear to this man, *Wica Shunka Wicasa Wanahan*. The grandfather spirit has chosen you to be brothers and grandmother earth's womb has given you a past and a future to share. You shall cross the great water with us and shall be known to us as *Keyuksha Heytahwah Nahpe,* Cuts-his-hand. It is your brave name, man of the Lakota. You sent the mother with milk to us. We shall keep you invisible, like the chick on the prairie, and none will speak of you to the *washichu*.'

Then Shunka bared his right forearm and indicated that Henry should do likewise and turning the undersides uppermost together, displayed the still livid three-cornered wounds to the company, from whom a low growl of approval went up.

'So you're a great man, so you are, Henry Turner. I always knew you would be,' said Kitty Shaughnessy, putting her arm through his and turning back his sleeve to take a closer look at his scar. 'I'd lay a shilling that brought tears to your eyes though,' she added softly, tracing round it with her middle fingers.

But as the beating of the *Persian Monarch's* two great paddle wheels steadily drummed them down the Humber, Henry had no recollection of having felt any pain. As they sat deep in the bowels of the ship's steerage, the last of England was not a sight but that sound. Nor did he smell the stink of the bilges, only the heavy scent of sage and dried lavender under a hot tarpaulin. Instead of the crowd of Lakota perched in what semblance of hierarchical dignity they could muster below decks, he only saw the image of Shunka's knife being lifted from its place among the other treasures on the doeskin roll.

Frantically, he tried to stop himself attempting to memorise them. Tried to put them away. But it was too late. A scrap of something else in a corner of his mind spread and spread so that it filled every nook of his head no matter where he tried to hide. When there was nowhere left to look for respite, and as he knew he would, a dark familiar figure leading a heavy horse came from behind him, slowly picking his way down to his death by the margins of the Icing River. Henry opened his throat to call to him, but his voice was drowned by the deep boom of the ship's siren as she crossed the bar and put her head to the open sea.

30

One Tuesday in the early spring of 1914 a man, well turned out in the American style, presented himself at the porter's lodge of one of Cambridge's newer Colleges. Its occupant stood up deferentially, bidding the visitor good day and enquiring how he might be of assistance. The man removed his grey Borcelino and flicked some imagined dust from it with the tan glove he was not wearing. When he spoke it was in a soft, assured accent that was difficult to place, although one would have been hard put not to describe it as American.

'Tell me,' he said, 'Is Dr Roger Birchall still here?'

'Sir Roger is, I believe, dining out of College today, sir. You may find him at home. And if I may make so bold, it's Professor Birchall.'

'And home is?' The American produced a leather pocket book from inside his overcoat and mentioned an address

'Bless you, no sir. That was a very long time ago. Sir Roger resides at…' The Porter mentioned a village on the outskirts of the city. 'Would you care to use the telephone sir?'

'No, I don't think so. If he's not there I can leave a note. Where can I find a cab?'

The Porter directed him to the nearest rank which was close to the market place and accepted the thanks and the florin the American proffered.

There were two cabs at the stand, one a motor taxi and the other a rather sorry-looking fiacre, its nag slumbering quietly in the shafts and its nosebag, while the driver was similarly nodding on the box. Glancing between the two options the American approached the horse-drawn vehicle

'You should find a slope to rest that horse on, or else you should walk him. He's about to go lame on you with too much standing on the level. Still, you can take me to the station to collect my bags and then out to…' He mentioned the village where he had been directed. 'That should ease his discomfort and make sure you get another day's work out him tomorrow.'

The cabman said nothing to the advice but looked his fare over, probably calculating the cost of his clothes and the likely size of the tip. 'And shall you be coming back?' he asked. 'You'll have to pay the return anyhow, that distance.'

'Maybe, maybe not,' said the American climbing into the carriage.

Slightly under an hour later he was ringing the bell of a handsome double-fronted house, dating probably from the first twenty years of the previous century.

Almost at once the door was opened by Roger Birchall himself. 'Maid's upstairs and I was in the hall,' he explained, peering somewhat at his visitor who was darkly framed against the sunlight.

'You always seem to answer your own door whenever I call,' his visitor said. At these words Birchall stepped out under the porch to get a better look at the speaker, who by this time had removed his hat. Birchall stared into his face, his own a picture of puzzlement and disbelief. For a long moment he just looked and then he said as if he was only addressing himself. 'My God! It's Henry Turner. It is. It's Henry Turner. My God!'

The two men stood looking at one another. Birchall was again speechless and in the end Henry laughed out loud at their mutual loss of words. 'Are you going to ask me in?' he said. 'If so I can pay off the cab.'

'My dear fellow. Of course, of course. Excellent, truly excellent.' Birchall recovered himself.

'I have my grip with me,' Henry said. 'I haven't fixed anywhere to stay yet, but I expect there's a pub in the village, isn't there?'

'Nonsense, wouldn't hear of it. More to the point, Mrs B wouldn't hear of it either. You shall stop here, of course you shall. Robert and I could do with some fresh company.'

Henry walked down the short drive to retrieve his valise and pay the cabman, saying as he did, 'The advice I gave you is worth a lot more than this fare. Stand him downhill when you're not working him.'

He returned to the house into which Birchall had retreated and stood and waited in the entrance hall. Very shortly Birchall reappeared with the familiar figure of Mrs Bullace bustling along behind him.

''Enry flamin' Turner!' she cried at the sight of him. 'My, but look at you! You've changed and no mistake.'

'Well you haven't, Mrs B, not a bit.'

''Ark at you. Fancy talker too. Well I 'ave changed. I'm turned seventy and I've the feet to prove it.'

'She won't stop,' Birchall said. 'I've offered her an honourable retirement, but she won't hear of it.'

'Yes and if I did, who's goin' to keep that girl at 'er chores and that good for nothin' boy? And who'd we 'ave cookin' in my kitchen, I'd like to know? If there were a *Lady* Birchall it might make a difference, *Sir* Roger. 'E's a blessed knight of the realm now you know,' she added to Henry.

'Yes, so I gather,' said Henry. 'Congratulations. How'd that come about?'

'Oh you know. Chaired one too many government commissions, published one too many reports. Stayed long enough in one Cambridge College to get myself noticed by the powers that be. But let's be hearing about you, more to the point. Almost back from the dead.'

Having divested him of his overcoat and Mrs Bullace having summoned the maid to dispose of Henry's valise, Dr Birchall ushered him into his library. 'Sherry?' he offered. 'It's a little early for whiskey and soda.'

Henry declined, but enquired if there was a cup of coffee to be had. 'I have acquired some of the better American habits,' he said apologetically.

Dr Birchall went to the door and called down the hallway to Mrs Bullace who met him halfway.

'Still reluctant to ring the bell, eh Roger?' Henry said, laughing. 'You never have quite been able to keep the lower orders in their place, have you?'

'Oh well, you know, "when Adam delved and Eve span" and all that,' said Birchall. 'Anyway, if my instincts are right and there's a war coming, we'll all have to learn to make our own coffee.'

'So who's Robert, who won't hear of my staying at the pub? The good-for-nothing boy I suppose?' said Henry.

'Goodness no! It's Robert Earl, you remember him. He lives with me, now he's retired. He left Icingbury some years ago, but could never settle anywhere. To be honest, Henry, he's not quite right in the head. Not exactly mad, but deeply sad inside himself, if you know what I mean. As if he's got something growing there which takes most of his attention most of the time. You'll see. He'll join us for dinner.'

'What of Icingbury, then?' said Henry quickly. 'How do folks go on there?' He fiddled with his watch chain in a preoccupied kind of manner, not meeting his host's eye. 'I have to say I've rather lost touch,' he paused. 'No that's a massive untruth. There has been no touch to lose and that's a fact.'

'I rather thought so, when I never heard from you. I thought you were dead, you know. Never wrote for money. Still you don't seem to lack for it now by the look of you,' said Birchall. 'Life seems to have dealt favourably with you in that respect, old fellow. What do you do?'

'I train race horses,' said Henry. 'In Kentucky. I'm rather good at it. That's why I'm here now. I've brought two fine prospects over for

Newmarket. First time I've ventured back to England and it's no distance from Newmarket to Cambridge, so I summoned up my courage.'

'And you haven't been out to Icingbury yet?'

'No. It pains me deeply to say that I don't know whether my parents are still living.' Henry fiddled with his watch chain again.

'Neither do I, Henry. I haven't set foot in Icingbury since...' Birchall looked at him squarely in the eye. 'Since we buried...'

'Reuben,' said Henry. 'Sometimes that only seems like yesterday. I still get the visions from the sweat lodge, you know.'

'So do I, so do I,' said Birchall quickly and then. 'So what has become of One-who-hears-horses-coming? Is he training them to race now, too?'

Mrs Bullace came into the room, bearing a coffee pot and cups on a tray so much on cue that Henry guessed she had been biding her time outside the door

'What's that?' she said as she put the tray down between them. 'That Chunky? 'Ow is 'e?'

Henry waited silently while she poured his coffee and handed it to him. 'And Annie Lilley? Do we know how she does?' he said.

Sir Roger shook his head as he peered fixedly into his own cup. 'As I say, haven't set foot in the place. Robert left for the first of his other failed parishes shortly after we...shortly after. And so I never had the occasion to...'

'But what about Chunky whatsisname?' persisted Mrs Bullace, not making any move to leave the room.

'Perhaps Mr Earl has heard something, though,' said Henry.

Birchall shot him that quick glance of his that was more like a shaft of light than a look. Henry had forgotten it until then. It said. 'I expect you want to keep some of this for another time, another place, other people first.' Henry looked at him gratefully, silently thanking him for the like mind, for understanding the inexplicable.

'Now then, Mrs B.' Birchall turned his attention to the cook, 'All in good time, eh? Excellent. What have you planned for dinner? Some fatted calf would seem appropriate.'

'Well, it was to 'ave been just some liver and onions, bein' a Tuesday. But I can send that good-for-nothin'-boy to the butcher's again if it's not too late for a decent cut of veal. No p'raps in the circs I'd better go myself.' Mrs Bullace had once again been distracted from her purpose and allowed the lid to be quietly replaced.

'Look who's here, Robert,' Sir Roger said, a little over-enthusiastically, as the former Vicar joined them in the library before dinner. 'It's Henry Turner. You remember Henry Turner, from Icingbury days. Sherry or whiskey and soda? Excellent.'

'Can't say I do. Haven't set foot in Icingbury for many years. Turner was a common enough name in Icingbury, but,' he studied Henry for a moment without apparent curiosity or recognition, 'They weren't gentlefolk. Farmer labourers mostly.'

Henry shook his hand and was about to say. 'It's because you wouldn't expect to see me dressed for dinner and in a stiff collar,' but something made him hold back and he merely said, 'How do you do?'

Sir Roger caught his eye and gave him a significant look. A tacit understanding passed between them that, in the presence of Robert Earl at any rate, the events of late April 1888 would not be spoken of since they were clearly banished from the Cleric's mind either by conscious or unconscious choice.

Robert Earl chattered about the garden and Birchall responded to Henry's inquiries about his various advisory positions in Government circles, where his reputation as a modern historian had made his opinions on the Balkan States and the Ottoman Empire much sought after, 'Not that they seem to pay a great deal of attention.'

'So, you train race horses now,' Birchall said as they sat at dinner, neatly eliding that enormous piece of Henry's history he had accepted, for the time being, he should leave undisturbed.

'Yes, my wife and I came out of Pine Ridge in the Dakota Territory in the spring of 1891 and began to work our way back East.'

'Your wife?' said Birchall, a fork full of veal held motionless halfway to his open mouth.

'Well, Kitty and I didn't actually make it legal until we eventually arrived in Louisville about a year or so later.' Henry glanced instinctively at Robert Earl for a reaction to this.

'Don't look to me for approval or disapproval, sir,' said the Vicar. 'I no longer have the ability to feel strongly about anything other than my own immediate comfort.'

The other two waited, looking questioningly at each other.

Mr Earl finished his mouthful. 'I destroyed my soul you see, if indeed that's what it was.'

'Robert, you must not keep tormenting yourself with these ridiculous fancies,' Birchall said, not unkindly.

Mr Earl continued as though no-one else was there. 'They kept him in a box in the crypt and he kept calling for my soul. I tried to believe he was a devil, but I didn't believe it could be true. I used to pray for him to be gone, as if that would make a hap'orth of difference. But he came for me anyway. We all looked into the box and he was just bones but he was standing beside me all the time. A tall, dark, young man. He had suddenly appeared, but it was as if I had been waiting all my life for him to come. I thought to myself, "He is the Angel of the Lord". It was as if he opened a doorway and I could see his soul. My own cried out in me to go through, go through the doorway. But I could not. That moment was the only time I have ever truly believed in my own immortal soul and now it has gone.'

He folded his napkin and pushed his chair back from his half-finished plate. 'I'll bid you good night, I think. So nice to have met you, Mr Turner. Give my felicitations to your wife.'

Birchall did not attempt to stop him going. He waited until the door had closed behind him. 'Not quite right in the head, you see. But it's all his fancy. I try to jolly him out of it, tell him I've never believed in the immortal soul either and I seem to rub along pretty well without it, but it doesn't do any good, poor fellow. His trouble is that he had something astounding in his grasp, just for a moment, and then it was gone and he can't get it back. It's a dreadful curse. I feel responsible in a way, although, as you can see, he's put the reality of it out of his mind. I used to try and talk him through it step by step, how it was just an archaeological discovery. But I doubt that he even tries to remember that now. Mostly he's good company. Not nearly so pompous as he used to be.'

They finished their own dinner and adjourned to the library. As the evening gradually retrieved some equilibrium, Sir Roger encouraged Henry to pick up the thread of his story where he had left it. 'You were telling me about your wife. Kitty? Not by any chance…?'

'Indeed,' said Henry. 'Catherine Shaughnessy.'

It had been a hard journey to begin with, coming off the Pine Ridge reservation. A question of finding what work they could along the way to tide them from township to farmstead and farmstead to township. Henry's hands were not good for much manual labour and they had not been improved by the privations of winter. He would work with horses when the opportunity arose and his gentling skills had stood them in good stead.

'It was Kitty mostly kept us on the road East. She was a wonderful card player. As she would say, "I may not be much for the reading but, by God, I've learned to count." Poker mostly. Not a proper occupation for a lady here, but somehow country Americans don't seem to mind.'

Henry glossed over the subterfuges and moonlight flits they had had to employ to avoid Kitty having to deliver the implied promises she had given in the event of her losing more than she had at her disposal.

Then they had had a stroke of real luck when Kitty had won several Indian ponies from an Irish fellow countryman. He had been on his way to try to sell them to a Kentucky breeder, also an Irishman to whom he had provided trotting ponies in the past. Instead of selling their winnings on then and there, Henry and Kitty had gone into partnership with their grateful owner and headed more south than east to clinch the deal. By the time they arrived in Kentucky, Henry had the ponies responding to every slight gesture and click of his tongue. For him they would have raced for days on end and never broken the trot.

'That was more than twenty years ago,' said Henry. 'I've trained a lot of winners since then, flat racing, steeple chases, but my first love will always be the trotting. Trotting made me my first thousand bucks.'

'And where is Mrs Turner? Did she stay behind in Kentucky on this occasion?' Birchall asked.

'Kitty always stays behind,' said Henry. 'She passed away more than fifteen years ago trying to have our daughter. They both did.'

'My dear fellow,' said Birchall, and he sat glumly staring at his brandy glass.

After a moment Henry said. 'That sonofabitch finally did for her, you know. And do you know? What makes me long for the day I meet him face to face again, is that he used me to do it in the end, even though I was two thousand miles away. He reached out and used me. Like it was always meant. Almost the last thing her brother ever said to me was, "Sure and doesn't he make my sister bleed?" Well he did. She bled to death.'

'You mean Fitzgerald, don't you?' Birchall said.

Henry grunted assent.

'Well, you won't see him face to face this side of the grave,' said Birchall.

'That's a great pity,' said Henry. 'I hope he died with his boots on.'

'If that means what I think it means, then I suspect he did not,' said Birchall ruefully. 'After he left England, he joined Petrie for a while and then went off and made quite a reputation for himself in Turkey. Recovered his fortune I believe with some of the stuff he found. But he never came back. Didn't dare, I always supposed. Apart from anything else, there were some questions beginning to be asked quietly inside Government, I discovered, when I started getting involved, about the conduct of some of those old special service officers. I even heard it suggested that Fitzgerald was giving the benefit of his dubious experiences to the Khedive. He certainly settled in Cairo. Became rather fat, someone at the British Archaeological Society told me. He died a couple of years ago. There was a short obituary in the Morning Post, I saw, and then a little while later a solicitor wrote saying that he had left Mrs Bullace two hundred pounds in his will. Thing is, they wrote to me at the College. So Fitzgerald must have put that in his will after…you know…after we got rid of him, so to speak. I have puzzled and puzzled over it and I can only assume he wanted to buy her silence even after he was dead and could no longer threaten her about her husband.'

'Well he managed to keep control of Mr Davies, even when death was staring him in the face, didn't he?' said Henry.

'I never did hear any more from the Irish Special Branch you know. I have often wondered since if they were who they said they were,' said Sir Roger and then he added. 'Oh I say, Henry old fellow, I hope you didn't go all that way for nothing. Nothing seemed to go quite right after we buried that warrior, did it?'

'Well, we've both become Romans, haven't we?' said Henry.

As the smoke from the departing train left him standing alone on the platform of Great Duster station, that feeling of being a stranger lost amid familiar surroundings gripped Henry, a mixture of foreboding and elation, fear of what he might find that was unchanged or what he would discover was lost forever.

'You can telephone for a taxi from the office, if you want,' said the Station Master helpfully, looking at Henry's fine boots. 'Just ask the exchange for Makepeace's.'

'Thanks all the same, but I'll walk,' said Henry.

'Do you want to leave your bag then?' said the Station Master. It was a small Gladstone belonging to Roger Birchall.

Again Henry declined. 'There's something I need in it,' he said, and slipping through the gate he set off along the road to Icingbury, buttoning his overcoat against the breeze which had a hint of rain in it.

Before he had covered half the couple or so miles to the village it was drizzling steadily and Henry began to wish for the sake of his Borcelino he had taken the taxi, although for himself he just wanted to enter Icingbury unremarked and quietly take his bearings.

He realised he had little or no plan but every step he took he wanted to be bringing him nearer to Annie Lilley and with each of those steps another fragment of his courage deserted him. His visit to Roger Birchall, he had assumed, would have forearmed him with information on what might await him in Icingbury, and it only served him right that it had not. So he had punished himself by declining Birchall's offer to accompany him.

It was raining quite smartly as he drew level with St Mary's, but the wet morning had at least kept the village indoors. He had seen a team of Suffolk chesnuts working in one of the Veil House fields on the horizon and had strained his eyes through the rain to make out a familiar shape, before recalling with a start that even at that distance the man was too young to be known to him and the horses too.

He took shelter for a minute under the lych-gate, then on an impulse strode up the churchyard path and into the church itself. Removing his hat and wiping it carefully on his sleeve, he sat himself in a pew at the back and waited in the half light of the church for the patter of the rain to give over.

It was the pew where Annie and he had last sat to support Shunka Wicasa on Christmas Day 1887. He put the Gladstone bag on the floor underneath it.

For a while Henry sat, quietly lost in the gloom, putting off the moment when he would have to decide where to go next, whom to seek out from among the living or the dead. He remembered for the first time in a long, long time how he had yearned for the miles he and Shunka had put between them and Icingbury eventually to break the thread of pain and guilt at their abandoning of Annie. But as he sat in the church he knew that time and distance had only spun it out finer and finer, knew that now he had returned, so had his shame, made stronger by the stretching of the years, made greater now that he had, at last, shrunk the miles.

He became aware that he was not alone. A woman was seated in one of the pews nearest to the choir stalls. She had not apparently heeded Henry's presence. He rose and softly stole round to one of the side aisles so that he could approach her unobserved.

As he did so a voice he knew well, although slightly tremulous with age said, 'Still playing grandmother's footsteps at your age, Henry Turner?'

It was Charlotte Covington. She turned rather painfully with her whole head and shoulders to look at him as she spoke.

'You took your time,' she continued. 'I'm stiff with waiting here in the cold, but now you're here you can walk me back.' She held out her arm towards Henry and he moved across her pew to help her up.

'Good day, Miss Covington,' he said. 'And how have you been keeping this long while?'

She shot him a curious glance from under her bonnet, as if she were not so sure of herself as she had been at first.

'Have your poor mother and your father gone? He'll be wanting you up at the farm, not walking me home, Sunday or no Sunday.'

Henry's heart had taken a bound at the mention of his parents, but then he could tell that all was not as it seemed.

'It's not Sunday, it's Thursday, Miss Covington,' he said gently.

They emerged into the church porch. The rain had given over.

'Thursday? Is it? Oh dear,' she said. 'I thought you were going to walk me home after church. You wanted to ask me something. What was it now?'

'About my Ma and Pa, perhaps,' said Henry sensing a need to jog her into the present.

'I thought it was about Boudicca, the Queen of the Iceni, wasn't it? Your poor mother's over there.'

Henry looked up quickly, expecting to see his mother by the lychgate or in the lane. A heavy stone sat in the pit of his stomach as his mind raced over all the things he would need to say to her, trying to decide what should come first. But Miss Covington was not looking towards the gate. He followed her eye to the middle of the churchyard across the graves of the Turners and the Lilleys that stretched back from the edge of the path. He walked between them until he came to his mother's.

For a long time he stood looking at the inscription turning his hat over and over in his hands as if he were screwing down a sluice gate with an iron wheel against a mounting flood.

Here lies Adelaide Turner
Born May 1840. Died July 1901
Beloved wife of
William Henry Turner
Born August 1839.
Died

The rest had been left blank and then further down the stone another inscription said,

Also the mortal remains of their Aunt
Elizabeth Lilley
Died July 1901

Henry wanted the tears to come, but a voice told him that it would be himself for whom he would be weeping, that his grieving would be for the deaths of friends.

As he made his way back to Miss Covington, sitting patiently in the porch, he found himself almost laughing aloud at the thought of his father's indomitable thrift even in the public face of bereavement, and at the realisation that he, at any rate, must still be alive.

'Have you been away Henry Turner?' Miss Covington asked as he helped her to her feet.

Henry was uncertain what period the question was referring to, but took a chance and replied. 'I've been in America, Miss Covington, making my fortune.'

'Did you go with that Red Indian who came to church?'

'Yes I did.' He changed the subject. 'Do you remember how my mother died and Mrs Elizabeth Lilley, my great aunt?'

'Are they dead? I'm sure I've just seen your mother,' said Miss Covington. She looked at him quizzically for an instant and then pulled one corner of her mouth down in a wry grimace. 'I'm doing it again aren't I? Let me think a moment.' She tapped on his arm with her fingers as if beating out the rhythm of her memory. 'Getting old you see. Don't do it Henry, take my advice. Scarlet fever, that was it. We had a bad go of it in the village about the time the Queen died, I remember now, thinking how we were all in mourning for her and for our own.'

Henry hesitated, not wanting to overload the old lady, but it was important. 'And Annie? What of Annie Lilley?'

'She used to help at the school with me,' said Miss Covington. 'But I've been retired a long time now. There's a Miss Milner there now. I'm not keen on her.'

'Annie Lilley?' Henry ventured again.

'No, she doesn't help there any more. Miss Milner does not share my views about the position of women in the late nineteenth century, let alone the twentieth,' said Miss Covington.

Henry did not know whether this remark concerned Annie or not. He tried again. 'So where is she? Still at my great aunt's?'

'No, she's dead.'

'Dead?'

'Yes, it was scarlet fever, I think. About the time the Queen died.'

Henry stopped in his tracks not knowing whether he was on the brink of a precipice or not. 'Annie's dead too?'

'Is she? I get so confused sometimes. Take my advice Henry Turner, don't go getting old.'

A thought occurred to Henry. 'Where do you live now Miss Covington? I suppose this Miss…Miss Milner has the School House.'

'Ah, you can't catch me on that one. That's the one the Doctor always asks me. I live at Rose Cottage, Number Three, The Green, Icingbury. It's just over there, look'

Henry did not know whether to laugh or cry. It was his Great Aunt Elizabeth's cottage. But where then was Annie Lilley to be found? He knew he should just go into the pub or the Post Office and ask, but a part of him held back, ashamed to be a stranger in his own country, not to know the whereabouts of those who had been dear to him, not to know whether to enquire for them in this world or the next.

Perhaps he should not have been so hard on himself. Once he had seen Miss Covington to her door and left her in the parlour where he had sojourned for the long weeks of his recovery from the poachers' beating, the faces he began to pass in the lane outside, though some were vaguely familiar to him, stared back at him, an unknown gentleman. But the more he became aware of this, the more he knew it would not do for Annie Lilley, to have him asking after her.

His footsteps led him inexorably in the direction of the Veil House farm. Thoughts of his mother jostled in his head, how he had forgotten to run her errands that day in Cambridge, how she had called Shunka 'Mr Wicasa' to her gossips in the village, how he had neglected to understand her need of him as a son, how he had left her unmourned. A blackness settled over him, unrelieved by the sunlight suddenly bursting through the cloud and lighting up his old home.

He approached the front door and tentatively rapped on it with his knuckles. There was no reply. He tried the handle and the door opened, as he knew it would. Stepping inside he tried to call out 'hello', but it came as a reedy croak. He walked through to the kitchen. The range was alight and a pot and a kettle simmering gently on the top but there was no-one there.

Then Henry heard the sound of the jug being emptied in the privy outside in the yard, followed by the slight groan he remembered, from the hinge, as someone came out. He waited for the kitchen door to open. It was his father.

'Is that you Annie?' the old man said, peering into the kitchen and feeling round the edge of the door frame in a way that immediately told Henry he was having trouble seeing.

'No Pa,' he said. 'It's me. It's Henry.'

'Henry?' Bailey Turner manoeuvred his way carefully into the kitchen, avoiding a chair. He placed the jug carefully in its place under the stone sink. Winding himself upright again slowly, he turned towards Henry. 'Henry?' he said again.

'Yes, Pa, Henry.'

'I can't see too well. Come out in the yard where the light's better.'

When the two men were standing outside the kitchen door in a patch of sunshine, Bailey Turner looked him over closely in a way Henry remembered him examining the colts he had been entrusted to buy. He half expected him to look in his mouth.

'Gentleman,' his father said. 'Done well then. Where have you been?' He made it sound as though Henry was late back from a horse sale.

'America,' said Henry beginning to feel back home already as the years dropped away like a blown dandelion clock.

'America? If I were a younger man I'd give you a damn good hiding. In fact I still might. Your mother's passed on, do you know that?'

Henry felt his confidence returning with every word his father uttered. He had not changed.

'I know Pa, I know. I've been to the grave.'

'Well, so I should hope. That stone cost me a pretty penny. Not that I begrudged it. I've never begrudged my own, you know that.'

'Yes Pa, I know that,' said Henry, smiling to himself.

'I furnished you handsomely when you went to London, now didn't I? How are those hands of yours?'

'Still serving me well enough,' said Henry, I'm prone to a bit of rheumatism when it's cold.'

His mind fled back to winters bleak as death in the Badlands of the Dakotas, when he thought his hands had seized forever into unmoveable claws of pain. The recollection brought a moment of silence. Bailey Turner, too, seemed somewhere faraway in thought. Then he suddenly reached out clumsily and took both Henry's hands in his, turning them over one way and then back again, running his own horny thumbs over the knuckles, whose slight enlargement and lack of symmetry still hinted at the damage they had once suffered. For a long time, they stood like this, Henry waiting, patiently at first, then with a growing sense of incomprehension, for his father to release him.

At last, still grasping Henry's hands the old man said. 'Do you forgive me, son? Can you ever forgive me?'

'There's nothing to forgive Pa,' Henry whispered. 'I'm the one should be asking for forgiveness.'

'I did what I could after you'd gone. For Annie and him. And I've needed a good man here lately, since my eyes started going. He'll make Bailiff here when I'm gone.'

Henry did not at first take in what his father was saying. He was still trying to deal with the still-glowing, unfettled lump of emotion that his father's request for forgiveness had caused.

Then it began to sink in. Annie had married after all. His homecoming would perhaps be less poignant than he had selfishly assumed. Perhaps his task less cutting.

'Where will I find her, then, Pa?' he asked.

Letting go his hands finally, Bailey Turner said, 'I expect she's taken him his dinner, he's sowing in the Long Acre, above the water meadows.'

'I think I saw him from the other side when I walked from the station,' said Henry.

'Likely. The others and a couple of day men are with second baiter harrowing in the Five Furlong.'

'I'll walk down and meet her, then. Annie,' said Henry.

'You'd best take some boots. Those fancy ones of yours won't do off the road. Got them from America, I expect, along with that twang. You'll find your boots somewhere. I've not thrown them out. Too much wear in them still. ' Bailey Turner was beginning to return to his natural state of testiness.

He saw her from the second gate. She had her back to him so he did not call to her, being still so far off. Henry had expected to find her walking back to the Veil House and when he did not, had begun to become nervous at the thought of meeting her unannounced, still with her man at the lower end of the Long Acre where, he remembered, the teams would rest for dinner. Unsure what to do for the best and needing time to think, he had turned down the lane towards the water meadows and climbed over the first five bar gate. Quickening memory made him press on to the second, anxious for a sight of the Icing.

She had spread her shawl on the grass beside the low mound and was sitting hugging her legs, her chin resting on her knees gazing across the river. Henry's approach had been so silent across the damp meadow grass and she so wrapped in thought, that he found himself standing only a few feet behind her and she still unaware of his presence.

He took off his hat. The soft movement made her glance down to her right, aware of his shadow-fall. He held his breath, not daring to move, fearing that something would break the moment before it came, change it before they could know how it might have been.

She did not turn her head to look at him but instead gazed at his shadow beside her on the grass.

'I was thinking of you Henry. Wishing for you,' she murmured. 'And now I see your shadow-fall beside me on the ground. I know your shape so well. I've traced around it in my head so often, as you lay broken on the bed, or nodded in the chair beside Aunt's cottage door, mending your bones in the sun. Am I doing that now, just putting your shape there in my head? If I turn will you truly be there? If you are truly there, will you reach and touch me before I turn?'

He dropped to his knees behind her, putting his arms around hers, his chin on her shoulder. She sank her chin to her chest and looked down at his arms, her tears falling on his clasped and crooked hands, his in the hollow of her neck.

Nothing more was said for a long time and Annie did not try to turn her head to look at him. Eventually she spoke again.

'If he's not here, he's dead isn't he? I've known that for a long time now. Known that I have been given everything he had to give me in life. Known that I should not long to be with a man who went home to die.'

Henry gently disengaged himself from her and stood up. She too rose, her head still lowered, and smoothed down the front of her dress and apron. Then they looked into one another's eyes for the first time and he saw what he had not seen for a long time, those essences of her self, those reinforcements drawn up, waiting to be joined.

'But you have another man now, Annie,' he said, wishing to seal the wound of the past with a balm from the present. 'My father told me. You brought him his dinner.' His trite words trailed off. He felt hot and foolish. He wanted to go back in time and start afresh.

Annie smiled and put her hand on his sleeve. 'I like your clothes Henry Turner, she said. 'Even if you have got grass stains on your knees. Old men. The things they say. I have no husband, Henry. He means Shunka's son. His name's Reuben. Reuben Turner. Your father gave him his name and brought him up as if he were his own grandson. Why, Henry what is it?

He looked at the river and then at the low mound beside them, and then back at the river again, chuckling by.

'Reuben? Reuben Turner?' he cried fierce and proud. 'It was always going to be, wasn't it? Always meant to be. It's all been meant.' He stepped up and stood atop the mound, his feet planted firmly apart. 'What next? What next? I'm ready,' he roared and he laughed with angry joy at the sky above them and the Icenian warrior's grave beneath his feet.

The afternoon sun was high enough in the spring sky for it to be pleasantly warm. Henry took off his overcoat and despite Annie's protestations laid it out under her shawl.

'I've been a long way and taken a long time about it,' he said. 'And if I am to make my peace with you, here would be just about the only place in the wide world I should think of doing it.'

He lay back, but propped up slightly by the grave mound. Annie lay against his shoulder and they shared an apple she had kept back from Reuben's dinner for herself, bite for bite.

'So you and Shunka went to America after you left here, like you said you would.' There was no reproach in Annie's voice. She was a child prompting a story at the end of the day. Henry told her of their meeting with Kitty on the dockside in Hull and what had happened then. Annie knew something about Kitty from Shunka's conversations with her over the whitewashing. But Henry did not tell her then that he and Kitty had married, nor yet that she was dead.

Nor did she tell of the passion she and Shunka must have shared during those months, so long ago. There would come a time, a moment in the story, he knew.

'We crossed on the *Persian Monarch*,' said Henry. 'A real tub of a boat compared with the *Lusitania* I came back on this time. It took best part of three weeks, most of which Shunka and I spent confined in the steerage for fear of discovery, he by the cowboys and I by the captain. The last thing I wanted was to be handed over to the police as soon as we docked in New York. The Indians were sick and so was I. But they were sick at heart, too, fearing to cross the mighty ocean, believing still that their spirits would pine and fade the further from land they were, even though they had already crossed once.

'Then, when we were about twelve days out of Hull, a buzz went round the steerage that Colonel Cody's horse, Old Charley, had taken sick to dying. Shunka had been close to that horse and he was all for revealing himself so that he could see if anything could be done. I persuaded him to lie low and instead I went and made a clean breast of it to Cody in his cabin. Then I went and spoke to his horse in my own way. Yes, you may laugh Annie Lilley, but we both knew he was too far gone. Still I calmed him, so that his self inside, his soul or whatever it is horses have, left of its own free will and Colonel Cody didn't have to put a gun to his head. He was mighty thankful for that. He offered to square everything with the Captain, but I said "No, I would stay with the Indians now". I showed him my arm and he understood.'

Henry pulled back his sleeve and turned the underside of his arm to the sun. The three-cornered scar was white now, and flat, as if it had been painted with two strokes of a brush.

'And then, after the crossing?' said Annie, taking the last bite of the apple.

'When we arrived in New York, the show was all set for a long summer season on Staten Island, which is just off Manhattan. People would go out in ferry boats to see it every day, and sometimes twice. Colonel Cody could see that it would not do for Shunka to stay out there and Kitty and I did not have any passport papers, so he decided to smuggle us all into the Waldorf Astoria Hotel where he was staying. He took Shunka as his body servant and no-one questioned that. Buffalo Bill was far too important for anyone to question his having his own personal Indian, in fact they expected it. But Kitty and I had to slip ashore from the *Persian Monarch* when the hullabaloo of the show's arrival had died down, hoping that we would be taken for local visitors going ashore.

'So did you all stay at this hotel? What did you do?' said Annie.

‘Kitty and I stayed in the rooms they have there for guests’ servants. But the management were none too happy about Shunka. Cody said he could sleep in his dressing room. He had a whole suite of rooms and an office as well. But Shunka hated that. Said it was like the dark places at the Carlisle barracks. So mainly he slept out on the roof somewhere. You could see that he was getting his mind and body ready to go back to his people’s lands.

‘Kitty kept us afloat. It was always Kitty who did that, then and later. Cody would have enormous poker parties at the Waldorf, and invite so many people that there wouldn’t be room for them all at one table. So Kitty put on East Coast clothes again and would run a blackjack table on the side. And would get tipped real handsome on occasions, while Shunka would go round with the whiskey tray wearing his full war paint. But he never got tipped, not once.’

‘And what about you, did you play cards?’ asked Annie, nestling further into his shoulder.

‘Nope, I never did. Never play cards and never back horses neither. Just train ‘em to win,’ said Henry. ‘I guess if we’d have stayed there the whole season, we’d have become real comfortable on what Kitty made. But Shunka had gotten deeply unhappy, not just with being cooped up in the Waldorf and being hissed and booed when he went round with the whiskey, like he was the villain in the playhouse, just like the folks used to do to the Indians at the show. No, it was more than that.’ He paused as if the memory had suddenly dimmed for a moment.

‘What was it then?’ said Annie.

Henry held her shoulders and sat himself up.

‘It was here, Annie, that night in the sweat lodge. We all saw things, things we’ve never spoken of to anyone else. Shunka said less about what he had seen to us. I used to see mine again from time to time. But I can’t remember when the last time was now. But with Shunka it was different. Instead of fading away with time, I think his visions became stronger. I know they were why he left you behind. He wanted me to leave Kitty behind in New York, but by then I could not and he was so consumed with wanting to go that he was past caring about her. But he never wanted to leave me behind. I had become his medicine, like a talisman, the night I stopped Kitty’s brother from cutting his throat. And then, here that night we became as men reborn from the same mother. I felt it too. We became one another.

He leaned forward and picked a lone crocus that had been bruised and bent where he had laid his coat half over it. He hadn’t noticed it before. He touched the stamen gently with his thumb and forefinger and then rubbed the saffron on Annie’s brow.

'We just walked away one morning, almost without saying a word to one another. We somehow knew it was time. Kitty and I didn't even know where we supposed to be going. When we tried to ask Shunka he would only talk about following the sun. At Grand Central Kitty bought tickets for a place called Cold Springs, some ways up the Hudson River. It was not so far that we couldn't have changed our minds and come back later and no-one any the wiser. Not that I guess anyone in New York cared. When I think about it now, I've always started those long journeys in my life, like that, as if I were only going maybe for a day.'

'You did, didn't you? And do you still, I wonder? Go on.'

'At Cold Springs the railroad to the West carried on too. A pretty place with woods and steep hills falling down to the river. It already felt a thousand miles from the city streets and all. You could see that Shunka was already shaking the dust and noise of it from out of his memory. We wouldn't be going back.'

'It sounds lovely,' said Annie wistfully. 'Did Shunka ever talk about me as if I might really be there one day?'

Henry did not reply.

'I suppose he just wanted to be back with his own people,' she said, as much to herself as to Henry.

'I think Shunka knew from that night in the sweat lodge that he was going to die,' said he said. 'Do you remember when he appeared at St Mary's that Christmas morning?'

'He asked us if Jesus had come yet,' said Annie. 'The Great Spirit, I think he said. I thought he'd just not understood that Christmas is every year. He thought it was something special just that year.'

'He kept looking and waiting. I realise that now. Then he said that he had seen the past and the future that night here on the banks of the river. It had something to do with a Messiah. Perhaps the idea was planted that Christmas, for him. I've often tried to make sense of what I saw myself, trying to figure out whether I'd just planted the ideas there on my own, all of it, the Icenian, those doorways we used to speak about. Perhaps it doesn't matter. Where is an idea? It can be in your head and mine at the same time, so perhaps it can be somewhere, anywhere else, as well, searching for a head to get inside.'

'Perhaps we just breathe them in, you mean?'

'Maybe. We found out later that this Indian Messiah vision was something that had been cropping up all over the Dakota Territory and Nebraska. Montana too. Shunka had it, I'm sure, but the difference was that he happened to be across the ocean when he did. But it reeled him in all the same, slow and sure, slow and sure. Just like this warrior behind me, picking his way through the marshland to this river. I used to wonder where he was going, so intent. Still do.'

Annie slipped her arm back through Henry's and drew him nearer to her again. The sun had sunk in the sky a little and cloud was beginning build again. She shivered a mock shiver.

'Shall we go?' asked Henry, but she shook her head. He moved so that he was sitting behind her with his legs either side of her and wrapping his arms around her pulled her back close to his body for warmth.

'Don't stop,' she said.

'It seemed like every hour we passed on the train heading west, Shunka shed some more of his coil, like a rattler in the spring. Only, he started emerging again as a Brave. Soon he had put his doeskins on and his blanket and his moccasin slippers. Not like when he was serving shots of whiskey at the Waldorf. This was real. He even began to smell different. But I guess we all did, on that train for days. Kitty would take a bath at the railroad hotels when we stopped long enough. Being a woman she had a private place to sleep on the train, but Shunka and I used the sleeping boards between the carriage seats at night. One morning, I remember, I saw that Shunka must have thrown his boots off the train in the night and I knew that he could scent his homeland.'

'How he hated those boots!'

'He sure did. Anyhow, the looks he'd been getting from our fellow passengers, at first just curious, began to get downright hostile the further west we went. In the first place people didn't cotton to the idea of a full-blown Lakota Sioux travelling with a white couple, added to which the Indians were supposed to be holed up on their reservations living on government rations that never turned up, not riding round the country on the railroad.'

'Why not?'

'Shunka wasn't supposed to be out of the Pine Ridge reservation without a permit from the army, now that he was no longer under Cody's jurisdiction. So we had a council and decided the best thing would be to leave the train, buy a horse and rig and take the back trails to Pine Ridge, which was where Shunka was headed whether we liked it or not. Either that or find ourselves put in jail somewhere just for being the wrong people in the wrong place. Shunka couldn't abide the thought of that. So we quietly left the train at a little place just outside Omaha, Shunka rightly reckoning that we'd be in trouble if we took it as far as Fort Kearney in Nebraska on account of the army being there in numbers.

'The rig and horse took a sizeable hunk of what money we had left from Kitty's tips. I'd never thought to get the money Roger Birchall had given me changed into dollars and the country banks were not interested in Bank of England paper. We only had a hazy idea of where we were and how far we still had to go, but we knew it was several hundred miles. There was little point in asking the way. It was like asking folk round here how to get to get anywhere further than Cambridge or Bury, they'd just point vaguely in the wrong direction. Added to which you could never be sure what kind of a reaction Shunka might provoke.'

'What was the horse like?'

'He was not one I would have looked twice at an occasional sale, although the price I had to pay for him would have brought tears to my father's eyes. Still, with Shunka and me speaking to him in a way he could understand, he began to recover an honest eye in place of his watchful one and get his mind straightened out even if we could never do the same for the rest of his anatomy. Of course he went lame, and the wheel came off the rig a time or two when there wasn't a blacksmith nearer than fifty miles and we had to make do and mend as best we could, storing up a heap of trouble for the next time it would happen.

'Winter came early. One day it was a fine, warm day in the late fall, only there weren't nothing to fall on the plains excepting snow, because the next day the rig was up to its axles in it and the clothes were freezing to our backs. We had to go back several miles from where we'd camped so that we could hole up in an abandoned cabin we'd seen by a creek the previous day.

'We planned to let the snow harden up for a day or two and then move on again. But the horse wasn't up to it. I remember Shunka saying to me in that way of his, when you couldn't tell if he was laughing inside or not, "it is as well you did not ask the horse's name when you bought him, we may have to eat him soon". I remember I told him he had been too hasty in throwing his boots away. If he didn't want to wear them in that weather, at least we could have made a stew with them.

'In the end we were in that cabin for most of the winter. I walked back to a homestead back down the trail to see if could get some supplies and physic for the horse, but I was gone nearly three days and came back with almost less than I started with, having eaten it on the way. I'm afraid I have never learned how to be a good backwoodsman. Unlike Shunka of course, who was at last in his element. We all got mighty thin that winter, but we would surely have starved to death if it hadn't been for him. We ate some peculiar creatures that he trapped or brought down with a sling shot, after we ran out of ammunition for the Springfield. I even refused some of the things he managed to dredge out of the creek through a hole in the ice.'

'It sounds dreadful,' said Annie.

‘Thing is,’ said Henry. ‘I’ve known worse since. The next winter, the winter of 1889 was bitter, so cold your spit would freeze in your mouth if you left it open an inch. But first things first. I have to tell you most of this in the order it happened. I have been keeping this thing, this history, inside my craw like a piece of black cud for a quarter of a century. I put it there when Kitty and I came out of the Badlands and said it could stay there until I saw you again.’

‘I’m sorry,’ said Annie. ‘This is hard for both of us, I know. But you have come back from the dead and taken me in your arms after all this time. It is as if you have brought him back with you. He was always the other side of you and now I know for sure he has gone, it seems he walks with you, out of sight, but there. Like you were when you walked up behind me and I saw your shadow-fall. I find a strange comfort in it, Henry, a strange comfort where I always thought I would find grief and despair.’

She patted the mound. ‘My warriors three,’ she murmured. ‘Or were you all only ever one? Go on then.’

‘We finally made it to the Pine Ridge Indian Agency in the late spring of 1889, more dead than alive, but we were in no worse shape than Shunka’s family. His father and mother, brother and sisters were all there. His father welcomed me as a son because Shunka and I were brothers in blood. But it was difficult for them and for Kitty and me on the reservation. The Agent and the whites at the Agency post had no time for “Indian lovers” excepting we had been missionaries and they didn’t have much time for them neither. No more did I. Roger Birchall once said something like Shunka having more spirituality in his little finger than people like them did in their entire bodies, and it being a threat to them, when it should have been a wonder.

‘So there was no question of us living with the Indians. Not at first. Kitty and I hung around the Agency, feeding on the Agent’s scraps of work. I got to know his horses pretty well. They were better shod and had a better gloss on their coats by the time I had been with them a month, than they had ever known before, or since, I should imagine. Kitty helped out at the mission school as best she could, but there wasn’t much call for teaching Indian *shechecha*[*] how to play poker and blackjack and her reading and writing never was up to much.

‘When I could, I would see Shunka. I’d borrow a horse with or without say-so when they needed exercising and ride out to the camp or he’d come into the Agency in the hopes of picking up the government’s rations. Then all of a sudden he didn’t show up when I expected. I rode

[*] children

out to the camp to see if he was sick. They were all pretty much stick thin and things like measles and whooping cough would pick them off, soon as look at you.

'I managed to make out from his father that Shunka and some of the other braves had gone deep into the reservation for some kind of religious ceremony. I knew what it was. The whole Agency was buzzing with rumours by then. It was a ghost dance. It was all to do with the coming of their Messiah, how he would bring back the buffalo and the game to the plains. The dance would last five days and the braves and women too would get so worked up they would see their ancestors in the spirit world in the sky. I didn't disbelieve it, not after that night here in the sweat lodge.

'Something Shunka said to me about what he had seen that night came back to me too. He said his mother had made him a shirt and he held it up for me to see. There was nothing there, of course, but he could see it as plain as day. If it had just been the dancing maybe the army would have let it go. But I think it was these shirts that made them so nervous and jumpy. The braves wore them during the dance and they were supposed to take on magical powers that would turn away bullets and make the man who wore one, invincible. I guess the army thought that if an Indian felt he had need of a shirt like that, he must be planning a war.

'The dancing continued on and off through the summer. I went looking for Shunka, even though I wasn't supposed to ride out into the reservation without the Agent's permission. But I was beginning to feel safer among the Sioux than I did with the blue soldiers who were getting more and more in evidence with each passing week, it seemed.

'When I eventually tracked him down, the ghost dance was breaking up but all the Sioux including Shunka were in a pretty wild state, cold sweat and hollow eyes darting everywhere, just like frightened horses, ready to lash out at anything that made a sudden movement. They had been somewhere, I couldn't tell you where, but in their heads or out of them, it was nowhere on this earth.

'Shunka didn't see me waiting in the long grass, which was unreal in itself. This was a man who could smell the difference between a live body and dead one through walls in the dark. I thought to myself then, whatever this dancing is doing, it's taking away your sense of self-preservation. I grabbed hold of him as he went past me. That was a foolhardy thing to do, even to my own brother in blood, because I was on my back with his knee in my chest faster than the earth could spin. It was providential that he was not armed, not even a knife. It seems that weapons were forbidden on the dancing place.

‘I called out to him and he began to come to. He recognised me and sat back on his haunches. He was wearing the ghost shirt his mother had made for him, painted red with blue at the neck. It was fantastically embroidered with blackbirds and stars and painted quills hung in a fringe below each arm. I remember thinking I, too, would want to believe in a shirt like this. I couldn’t take my eyes off it.

‘In the end I said, “Will it stop bullets then, Shunka? Is that what you believe? That you will be unharmed and victorious in battle? Because I have to tell you, that’s what the army thinks you are all up to and frankly I wouldn’t bet my shirt against one of their new Hotchkiss guns.” He laughed then, you know Annie, that short barking laugh of his, and said, “No, neither would I, Keyuksha, but it is not the bodies of the Lakota that will need to be victorious and unharmed in the battle, it is their spirits. It will be our last battle under the equal sky. The shirt is an idea, I know that. I wear it on my body because I cannot wear it in my head.’

Henry paused, recalling that moment so many years ago, smelling the crushed long grass and the scent of sage mingled with the dust where the dancers had beaten the earth bare with their feet for days. Hearing Shunka’s words again.

‘It’s true,’ he said. ‘More spirituality in his little finger…Perhaps we should begin to get back Annie. I’m nearly done and I can talk as we go. You’ll be getting cold.’

They picked themselves up and slowly walked arm-in-arm towards the first of the two gates, their gigantic shadows pacing beside them across the water meadow.

After a minute Henry resumed.

‘I’d been away best part of three days by the time I got back to the Agency. Kitty was very edgy when I walked in and said that I had been missed. There had been a lot of talk and accusations flying around. The upshot was that I was thought to be some kind of a spy. I suppose I was in a way. I knew where my loyalties lay and they weren’t with those Romans from the Seventh Cavalry.

‘Shunka had told me that because they were fearful of what the blue soldiers might be planning to do to suppress the ghost dancing, many of his people were heading off into the Badlands, a strange place of rocky hills and canyons carved out, they say, by a huge ocean that used to cover them. I knew that this would, strictly speaking, make them outlaws because the Badlands were forbidden to the Lakota by the government.

‘So the next morning just before first light, Kitty and I packed a few provisions, borrowed an army horse without asking, which in those parts could be considered a hanging offence and headed north up the trail to the Badlands. I think Kitty was positively relieved to get away from the missionaries and be back among the Lakota again. The women dyed her hair for her, braided it with quills and she was back in doeskin before you could whistle a dog.

'Over the next couple of months more and more Lakota joined us in the Badlands. The game began to run very short added to which, by being there they were denying themselves the government rations. By November it was beginning to become cold and there was a promise of another bitter winter in the air. Some parleying went on with the army and the chiefs decided to take the people in to "surrender", at least that's how the army put it, but it was either that or starve to death.

'Once again Kitty and I found ourselves out on a limb. Not that we weren't being made welcome in the lodges. We were. But these people had nothing and we were making it less. We were white folk and could take our chances in the world. Whatever happened, they had to be better than the Lakota's.

'I decided to follow the Indians back into the reservation and wire Roger Birchall for money. They were headed for the settlement at Wounded Knee. Shunka said there was a Post Office there. I just hoped that the army would be too busy feeding several hundred Indians to notice Kitty and me, especially if she kept that red hair black. As it turned out the army had a deal more on its mind at Wounded Knee to bother about the two of us.

'You could tell that something was wrong. The army had two of its new Hotchkiss guns unlimbered on a hill overlooking the Indian encampment and about four troops of cavalry strategically placed all around them, including on the other bank of a dry ravine that formed a kind of moat on the opposite side of the lodges to the guns. In addition there were a good few men from the press, obviously waiting for something to happen, although I don't believe they were expecting what did.

'At about eight o'clock in the morning I made my way to the Post Office to send my wire to Roger Birchall. Inside there was a crowd of reporters waiting to send dispatches to their papers and I could see I was in for a long wait. One of them asked me which newspaper I was from and I told him *The London Evening News*. It was the only one I could think of. I felt very uneasy.

'As I stood there waiting, I heard the Seventh Cavalry band outside practising. They were playing *Garryowen* and it came into my head what Shunka had told me about what he had seen in the sweat lodge. Something made me turn to Kitty and tell her to find a civilian rig that was heading back up the road to Pine Ridge and beg a lift. With all these reporters around, I said, you could get into a poker game and make us some money. I thought she would object, but I was mighty relieved when she agreed it was worth a try. I think we were down to our last twenty dollars. I kept three for the wire and gave her the rest and Roger Birchall's Bank of England bills on the offchance she might find an Englishman to part with his money.

'It was about twenty minutes later, perhaps less, when the firing began. Small arms first, the double *tictac tictac* of Winchesters and the single *crack crack* of Springfields. The reporters and I all ran out of the Post Office to see what was happening, but it was impossible to tell at first. I began to make out the screams of the women coming mainly from the lodges. I knew they were mostly women with children there, and old men, waiting to be fed. Only a relatively few braves had come in to surrender. I knew that Shunka was with them, too. But I knew surrender was the last thing on his mind.'

They had reached the second gate that gave onto the lane, and stood looking towards the setting sun to their left. Annie gripped Henry's arm tight and waited in resigned silence.

'I ran towards the council circle, which was where I thought Shunka would be, because of his English. There was to have been a parley that morning with the army officers, but they had not got that far. I learned afterwards that the soldiers had been searching the lodges for weapons when the first firing broke out. That was what we had heard inside the Post Office.

'I turned left and ran towards the lodges, shouting for Shunka. Miraculously, I heard him answer and ran towards his voice. The firing became more intense and as I reached the outer lodges, the Hotchkiss guns on the hill opened up, starting to set fire to them.

'Then I saw Shunka standing in his ghost shirt, but without a weapon in his hand. He was waving at me to go back, but I wanted to pull him out of there. He came towards me and as we reached one another I could see the dismounted cavalry further to my left preparing to turn their fire towards us.

'It had snowed in the night and then frozen hard. I remember thinking that I had never seen grasshoppers in winter before and wondering why not, because there were clouds of them jumping out of the frozen snow. But they were not insects, they were bullets. Shunka put his arms around me and covered me with his body, clad in the ghost shirt his mother had made for him. We fell together and the snow was red with blood like that sky across the river. It was all his. There wasn't a scratch on me where he had lain over me in his shirt. Then the firing seemed to move away and it almost became quiet.

'Shunka's mouth was near my ear and I heard him say something.'

A single tear trickled down Henry's face. Turning towards him at his sudden silence, Annie saw it and traced its progress down his face with her finger.

'What did he say, Henry? What was it?' she whispered.

'He said, "It is meant. I have repaid." They were the last words he said.'

'I've left something in the church,' said Henry, as they reached the lych-gate. 'I'll catch you up.'

'Don't you be long, Henry Turner, I've only just found you again. But I'd better hurry on. Your father will be fretting,' Annie said over her shoulder.

He watched her disappearing up the lane in the direction of the Veil House and then made his own way up the churchyard path. Pausing in the porch he looked down at his boots and decided they were in no state to be worn inside the church. He cleaned them a little on the scraper at the entrance and then wrestled with the wet laces to remove them entirely. Padding into the darkened nave in his stockinged feet, he went to the pew where he had sat that morning and cast about underneath it for the Gladstone bag. It was not there.

With a sense of mounting urgency he moved forward up the aisle to where he thought he recalled Miss Covington had been sitting, thinking he might have misremembered where he had left it. It was not there either.

In his anxious haste he stumbled over the end of a pew with a loud thud. The door to the vestry opened and a man in clerical garb looked through it at Henry.

'May I help you?' he asked.

'I do hope so, Vicar. I left a small grip here this morning,' said Henry.

'Grip?' The Vicar looked puzzled.

'Sorry, a bag, a small leather bag.'

'Ah. I have it here in the vestry, Mrs Lilley found it this afternoon when she came in to do the flowers. So it's yours Mr…Mr.'

'Turner, Henry Turner. Is that Mrs Lilley, Simon Lilley's mother?'

'The young man who died in Egypt? I never knew him. Before my time, I'm afraid. But that is she.' The Vicar disappeared from view for a second and then reappeared holding out the Gladstone bag.

'You are from hereabouts, then, Mr Turner? There are a few Turners in this locality,' he said.

Henry took the bag. 'I'm an American now,' he said. 'From Kentucky, and late of Pine Ridge, South Dakota. But as a friend of mine used to say, we all live under an equal sky.'

‘Very true, Mr Turner, very true. I might use that thought in a sermon, if I may.’ The Vicar walked with him to the church door and stood awkwardly while Henry sat and pulled his boots on.

‘Are you staying for long in Icingbury?’ he said, making conversation.

‘I have to see some men about some horses in Newmarket. After that, I don’t know. I might come back here for a while. Icingbury is never very far from my thoughts,’ said Henry, and donning his hat, he raised it slightly to the Vicar and set off down the path.

‘Here’s a Turner coming now,’ the Vicar called after him. ‘He’s very good with horses, too, I believe. A horse man as they say round here.’

Henry had reached the lych-gate. A young man leading a Suffolk chesnut was coming along the lane from the direction of the water meadows and the Long Acre. Henry waited. The young man watched him too as he approached.

‘Honeycomb, whoa, gee back lass,’ the young man said, bringing the heavy horse to a halt when they were level with Henry

‘That’ll be a The Veil House mare then,’ Henry said. ‘By her name.’

The young man looked at him curiously as though he thought he was not sure he had understood Henry’s words through the unexpected accent.

‘There’s always a Honeycomb at the Veil House, sir,’ he said after a moment.

‘Yes, there was in my day too,’ said Henry.

Then he added, half musing to himself. ‘You have the look of your father about you. Enough, but not so much that it would cause your mother a sadness. But one day when you are older, you will pass for your grandfather and no mistake.’

‘Bailey Turner’s not my true grandfather,’ said Reuben.

‘I know, but I knew your father and your true grandfather both,’ said Henry. ‘Let’s walk on. Your mother will be waiting. I have something of your father’s in here.’

‘Of my father’s? What is it?’

For the first time in a long, long time Henry felt the moment of his visions by the Icing. Not drawn out. All together like a momentary burst of sound and taste and smell.

‘What is it?’ the young man repeated eagerly.

‘I pray you never have need of it,’ said Henry. ‘It’s the shirt he wore.’

Acknowledgements

∞∞

To those of my friends, colleagues and chance acquaintances who have given me so much support and, at times, tough advice, and have thereby contributed so much to the outcome of this first book, I give my grateful thanks.

I would like to mention in particular, Charlotte Landreth Melville, of Bristol Pa, whom I met outside the former United Services Club in Pall Mall and whose grandfather was part of the 1887 American Trade Exhibition at Earls Court, of which Buffalo Bill Cody's Wild West Exhibition was a sideshow, for sharing her family's unpublished documents with me and her generous hospitality in the US; John Slonaker, US Army, retired, who gave me access to the former Indian School at Carlisle Pa and the benefit of his considerable knowledge of its history; Jerilyn Elk of the Wounded Knee Information Centre, Pine Ridge SD, for being there; the Lakota Sioux volunteers at the Crazy Horse Memorial, South Dakota for their help with names; my good friends Ian Herbert, Chairman of the Society for Theatre Research, and David Hughes, Chief Leader Writer, *The Daily Telegraph,* for their literary, stylistic and editing advice, although none of this is their fault; John Kenworthy of Cambridge University and a former Secretary to the Navy Board, for his suggestions concerning Victorian army and Irish Home Rule politics; and David at the Working Horse Trust in Kent, for letting me get to know a Suffolk chesnut *(sic)* and teaching me the rudiments of long lining and horse commands.

I have read widely but should especially mention the late Paul WarCloud's *Dakotah Sioux Indian Dictionary*, published by Tekakwitha Fine Arts Center, Sisseton SD; Leonard Crow Dog and Richard Erdoes, *Crow Dog. Four Generations of Sioux Medicine Men,* Harper Perennial; William S.E.Coleman, *Voices of Wounded Knee,* University of Nebraska Press; Richard G. Hardorff, *Hokahey! A Good Day to Die!* University of Nebraska Press; Gregory F. Michno, *Lakota Noon. The Indian Narrative of Custer's Defeat,* Mountain Press Publishing; Joseph M. Marshall III, *The Lakota Way,* Viking Compass; and from the London Library, George E. Evans, *The Horse in the Furrow;* Alan Gallop, *Buffalo Bill's British Wild West;* E. Mayhew, *Illustrated Horse Management.*

Stephen Reardon
February 2007

The Author

Stephen Reardon was born in Barnet, England, in 1947. He spent thirty years working in Government in London's Whitehall until the incoming Blair administration in 1997 decided to dispense with his services as a senior ministerial Press Secretary and to provide him with the opportunity to concentrate on writing full-time on his own account. He lives in South West London and in the Pas de Calais, with his wife, Jane. They have two grown-up children.

On one side the Reardon family forebears were from County Cork in Ireland, who settled in London in about 1830. On the other side, generations of the family were farm workers from that part of Eastern England where the borders of Suffolk, Essex and Cambridgeshire meet. Among them were several gifted horse men. This first novel is respectfully dedicated to them and, in particular, to Private Reuben (Ben) Turner of the Ninth Battalion, the Suffolk Regiment, who died at Mailly Maillet Wood, on the Somme, on August 23, 1916, aged just 21.

Next for 2008...

Stephen Reardon's second novel

The Middle Room

Florence Draper is newly married to a young English corporal who has been posted as a clerk to the offices of the recently arrived Free French in wartime London. In the terrifying claustrophobia of the 1940 blitz, she finds herself vividly recalling her French grandmother's tall stories of her life in the siege of Paris more than a generation earlier. But it appears her tales may have contained more than a grain of truth when Florence's husband is threatened by a Vichy agent in De Gaulle's headquarters to make her reveal her Grandmother's secret.